Ticking the Boxes

John Huggins

Published by New Generation Publishing in 2021

Copyright © John Huggins 2021

First Edition

ISBN   978-1-80369-005-6

www.newgeneration-publishing.com

New Generation Publishing

Main Characters

Law & Government

Jerome Whitcott. Chairman PLAD committee.

Susan Smallstone. Home Secretary.

Barrymore. Personal Assistant to Home Secretary.

Nigel Woodberry. Middle ranking officer with MI5.

Arthur Rochester. Junior officer with MI5.

D.I. James Leeming. Head of Organised Crime Squad.

'Belushi'. An undercover operative working for Leeming.

D.I. Calvin Mortley. Head of Gang Related Crime Squad.

D.C.I. Edward Sangster. Chief Constable with Metropolitan Police.

D.I. Christine Ho. Sangster's No2.

D.S. Harold Bonnet. Detective Sergeant in Metropolitan Police.

Gangs

'Snapper' Cosgrove. Head of main gang operating out of Bermondsey.

Shaun 'Squid' Simons. Holborn gang, second in command.

'Brooksy'. Head of Holborn gang

'Goose'. Woolwich gang member.

Furtado. Head of Battersea gang.

Others

Jeremiah Jones. Facilitator with connections.

Harold 'Harry' Sebastian Litmus. Enquiry Agent.

Elizabeth 'Beth' Newall. Computer Hacker.

Wilfred & Emily Litmus. Harry's parents.

Bob Travis. Jobbing actor.

Marian Lambert. Dinner Lady.

Tomas Korczak. Builder.

Debbie. Nurse.

Emma Beaton. Staff Nurse.

Magnificent Max Higginbottom. Retired Boxer, now Sports Personality.

John. Aged football supporter.

Sharon. Waitress.

Barry Oates. Property Developer.

Sam. Bar worker.

Pat. Sam's sister.

"Before you embark on a journey of revenge, dig two graves."

Sara Shepard

John Huggins was born in North London, but relocated to South Yorkshire in the early 1970's. He worked in the steel industry for the best part of forty years before taking early retirement in 2009. He is married with three children and claims all his books end up as black comedies by design or accident.

Huggins' first novel **Mothballed** was released in 2010 and greeted with universal indifference. Undeterred, **Angel Smith Returns Home** (2015)**, A Dip in the Gene Pool** (2016), **Consequences** (2017) and **Wrong Person Singular** (2019) made their way off the production line in subsequent years.

Unrepentant, and predominantly un-vaccinated, the black comedy **Ticking the Boxes** was fashioned from the meagre resources at the author's disposal during the various lockdowns of 2020-2021.

Many thanks to Nick Garrett for his IT wizardry and technical support, and to my wife Anne for her editorial skills and limitless patience.

Synopsis

In an uncaring world Harry Litmus represented many people's only chance of getting a fair deal. That was Litmus' take on the situation, anyway, and it is necessary to have a positive mindset a good degree of self-belief if you ever intend to realise your full potential.

Tragically, it seemed that things had rarely panned-out the way they should have for a man who had chosen to base his entire life strategy on being selfless and putting other people's interests first. Currently, his career had stalled, his finances were bleak, his love life non-existent, and he had successfully frittered away the money that would have represented his best hope of a fresh start on an ill-advised foreign vacation to discover his long-lost roots.

It wasn't as if things had been any better in the days when Litmus had enjoyed regular employment. As if the gods of misfortune were conducting a personal vendetta, people standing a little too close to Harry's side had developed a tendency to die. Nothing to do with Litmus of course, but it's easy to get a reputation when that sort of thing becomes a frequent occurrence, even if your innocence was never in question ....in Harry's case, a presumption that was possibly open to debate.

Still, it wasn't all misery for Litmus. After years of teetering uncertainty on the edge, life had finally taken a turn for the better. He had acquired a new lodger who was downright gorgeous and following her arrival a lucrative job offer had materialised from out of the blue. A somewhat unusual focus with the employment opportunity he was forced to admit. Conducting an evaluation of a Government backed commission to evaluate a stalled Police investigation into the deaths of fifty people caused by an unexplained explosion. Not good people either; not by any stretch of the imagination; the dregs of society if you weren't too well mannered to speak ill of the dead.

But even taking that into consideration the question still remained, who in their right mind would be capable of sanctioning a death sentence like that? An interesting situation for Litmus to get his teeth into, wouldn't you say?

CHAPTER ONE

North London, Saturday June 29th 2025

Snapper Cargrove walked slowly into the room maintaining a look of marked disinterest in anything that crossed his eyeline. It was amazing how much suppressed energy it took to sustain a demeanour suggesting total indifference whilst making sure you missed nothing that was going on, but in this capacity he had the dress shirt, the bow tie and the pair of shiny shoes. He stepped past the platform with his nose in the air, before walking slowly up the makeshift aisle and seating himself at the very back of the hall.

He had caught a small buzz of whispers as he made this short journey, showing that the presence of a man worthy of respect had been noted. He would have expected no less. According to the word on the street every gang with ambitions would have representation at the meeting, but that would still amount to a lot of people who wanted to get to the top of the greasy pole, and very few who were cut out to make the climb. Even while he sat there assessing his surroundings it was impossible not to notice members of the next generation puffing out their chests and trying to stare each other down. What a set of space-wasters all dressed up in their best suits and designer shirts trying to give the impression they were somebody special, which in Snapper's view only served to make them look like a gaggle of second class rent boys out on the make. If they lived long enough, experience would someday teach them that overdressing was the badge that would always mark the wearer out as a mongrel street dog trying to con its way into Crufts.

Furtado had a seat on the adjacent aisle and looked like he had come to much the same conclusion. Furtado ran a large chunk of Battersea, but it was far enough away from Bermondsey that it had never been necessary for them to come to blows over border disputes or customers for drugs. Not that Battersea was a territory to get overly excited about these days. Fast being overrun by middle class white families with small dogs and bawling brats; but Furtado had a hard-won reputation for holding thing together, and with this new wave of second-class space wasters entering the mix, wise heads would be sorely needed in the years to come. Respect where respect was due, that was Snapper's motto. Furtado had paid his dues and earned his seat at the top table. Snapper turned a little to his left and gave the slightest nod in his rival's direction. It was immediately returned by a raised eyebrow cast in the direction of the bit part players strutting around at the front of the hall. Snapper shrugged and rolled his eyes in agreement, then they both gave a small smile before returning to studiously ignoring each other's presence, in case a bromance could come into being with a person whose throat you might find it necessary to introduce to the sharp edge of a knife in the weeks ahead.

Scanning slowly around the hall Snapper counted to thirty-eight before losing interest. He only recognised five or six faces but that was only to be expected because he knew virtually nobody from north of the river, barring Elvis from Chelsea and a pie-eater from Stepney with a shaved skull whose name he could no longer recall. Both qualified as fully paid-up members of the idiot brigade in his opinion, and that wasn't a view he saw himself changing anytime soon.

A quick up and down confirmed that a lot of those that had already arrived were obviously several years younger than him, but maybe eight or nine would be men of approximately his own age and they were the people who were avoiding getting drawn into the chest puffing contest that was now taking place. He tried to associate faces with gang names but, apart from neighbours from Southwark and Deptford with whom he had regular run ins, it was proving a difficult task. The East End spreading north to Tottenham and Wood Green would be the money bet for most of them, but who fitted in exactly where was likely to remain the sort of mystery that he didn't intend to lose a lot of sleep over not solving.

Snapper cast his mind to how this had all come about and had to admit he was somewhat in awe. Whichever way you looked at it, this Jeremiah character had to have serious balls. He had somehow gathered up representation from all parts of the capital and talked them into putting tribal rivalries to one side while they listened to his proposals. If there was any justice in the world, he should have been awarded a blue rosette to pin on his chest for achieving that part alone.

How many of the people in attendance had actually met this dude face to face, Snapper wondered? He had no idea. He only knew that he hadn't, and that he found more than a little bit annoying because he was used to being the man who was the first to be consulted before any new deals went down. When you were floating a proposal in the capital there were certain prerogatives that it was wise to follow, and the one that it was smart to have at the top of the list was that you ran any new ideas past Snapper Cargrove. It was polite, and having manners cost you nothing at the check-out, whereas offensive behaviour could very easily come back and bite you on the bum. Snapper had wielded the most power in this neighbourhood for a lot of years now, and it was the way things were handled if you had ambitions to stay healthy and come out on top.

But despite his feelings on the matter, Snapper wasn't stupid. Sometimes it was necessary to turn the other cheek, even when doing so affected your pride. Once you were aware that certain other people had an invite to a party, you needed to make sure that you were in line for a share of that action as well. That was the way it had to be, and nobody with anything between their ears pretended something different. It would only be an idiot who got swallowed up by their pride and found themselves out in the cold when a serious business proposal was being laid out on the table. Live in the moment, was Snapper's attitude to life. Play along for the time that it was necessary but keep a running tally in your head. Sorting out a lack of respect could easily be taken care of further down the line once the heat had died down.

Snapper glanced around the hall again and took in the faces. From what he could see, there was no great fear that this set of dorks would have the brain power to manoeuvre themselves into a position where there was any possibility that they could get the jump on him. Nevertheless, it was still important that the man from Jamaica learned how thing were done in this city. Particularly if he intended to live a long and happy life. There was a certain way that things were handled, and he would make it his business to point exactly how the system worked. Propositions like those that he had heard might be bandied about were distributed on a priority scale, and when you looked at the number on the reader Bermondsey always came up number one. So, if the offer was judged to be kosher, after the talking was over, then out of politeness it would need to be run past him first; and if there was any danger of a queue forming, Bermondsey had to be right at the front.

Snapper scanned again, just keeping tabs on everything that was going on. Knowledge was power in this game, and you could never know when a little vigilance might pay off further down the line. Maybe this Jeremiah was following the lead of Jesus and gathering his disciples from all walks of life, because this crew didn't lack in variety. That didn't seem likely though, because it was a fair bet the earlier contingent hadn't carried machetes, knives or dusters as standard accessories, and that they didn't have criminal records that ran to several pages before they were old enough to vote. They were a mixed bunch alright, weighted heavily towards immigrant stock from one continent or another, but with no marked bias in any direction except for the colour of their skin. The common denominator wasn't how they looked or dressed, but that same show of hunger in their eyes. Scumbags to man, drawn together by a single common interest, if Snapper's instincts were telling him

4

right. A real rainbow nation, up and running and ready for action. Mister Mandela would have tipped his hat in their direction back in the day, except for the fact one of these bastards was likely to have stolen it before he got the chance.

Snapper's next thought was to question what the new man might be trading. Friend Jeremiah would need to be hitting treble twenties with every dart or he would lose goodwill from this bunch of wasters pretty damn quick. That wasn't likely to be his only problem either; not by a very long chalk, if Snapper knew his stuff. If Mr Jones suggested cutting the cake into equal chunks the big boys were bound to feel they were being shown a lack of respect, but if he offered the minor outfits too small a share of the goods on offer, they would consider they were being disrespected and edged to one side. Snapper didn't envy the man his pitch. It would be a delicate balancing act, with a very long fall if you lost your footing. Even with golden tonsils, he would need to be extremely careful, or matters could very quickly get out of hand.

Still, this Jeremiah must be a high wire artist with the instincts of a cat, or he would never have had the smarts to get things going as far as he already had. Anyway, the man would have heavy advantages if he knew how to use them. Word had it, his Columbian connections were solid, and if you combined that with a sure-fire shipping route through Eastern Europe then you were talking a slam dunk with points on the board for those hungry faces down at the front, because in their eyes it would look like easy money just waiting to be grabbed. Girls on the block didn't cut it these days with the home-grown sisters getting slowly edged out by imported talent that cost less to dress and feed; but nobody turned their noses up at a good dope connection if they wanted to grow their share of the number one trade.

The bit that Snapper found hard to understand was the logic behind the way Jeremiah was fronting this operation. Word had it that he owned this building but to Snapper's way of thinking that didn't make any sense. It wasn't the right way to set up this sort of operation. As a hub it was in a bad location and was much too full in your face to have any chance of passing under the radar. Granted it wasn't the Ritz, but the building had enough sleeping accommodation to house the motley bunch of shitheads that were busy comparing dicks down on the front row, and that still left plenty of rooms to spare; and if his information was correct, this wasn't the cheap end of town, so how did owning a place like this make any sense?

Snapper scanned up and down to further his appraisal. The building had clearly been redecorated from top to bottom, and there was a faint smell of white spirit in the air which indicated the painters hadn't been out of the door for very long. The pool tables in the bar weren't pitted with scuff marks. A fair indicator they were probably fresh out of their packing cases, unless friend Jeremiah had managed to secure them on a hire contract, which bearing in mind the way they tended to get treated by shitheads like those currently in attendance wasn't very likely. The bar seemed to be well stocked with all the right sort of bottles, and although the carpet in the reception area was clearly of very poor quality it definitely hadn't seen a lot of footfall, so that would have set the man from over the waters back a bob or two. It was dead money to Snapper's eyes but perhaps the main man knew something that he didn't, and Snapper would be the first to admit, you were never too old to learn.

A chair scraped sharply against an area of newly polished flooring and Snapper's thoughts changed direction. A glance at the car park showed it was almost completely empty. The boys in the shiny suits and gelled back hair had at least managed to follow instructions and get dropped off at the front of the building so no vehicles were visible in the car park from the open road. The meeting was for gang leaders and their second in command only, but he assumed that most of the larger territories would demonstrate their confidence by sending in their main man only. If you were a big enough noise, it was the way it was done. Snapper had been out of bed early and instructed his driver to scoot him round the M25 in double quick time so he could witness the arrival of the shakers and movers from the half-arse gangs who were holding their own private dick measuring competition to see who could arrive in the biggest car with the widest wheels and the most gleaming set of chrome accessories. These were the same masterminds who posted pictures of themselves on Facebook waving wads of bank notes and pointing handguns at the ceiling, so Snapper hadn't been expecting an awful lot. The same set of halfwits who would still manage to look vaguely surprised when they were banged up on the basis of evidence that they had up-loaded to the internet themselves.

Over to his left Snapper's attention was caught by the tall bloke in the smart dinner suit who had overseen the preparation and serving of breakfast. He looked hazy round the eyes and didn't seem to fit in with this operation at all, so he was probably on hire. The food had been good enough though. Nothing fancy, just bacon, eggs, sausage, mushrooms, hash browns and tomatoes, cooked to perfection and delivered in large silver dishes that rested neatly on an extended sideboard so you could serve yourself with whatever you required. Nice and simple with no frills so people would not get distracted and keep their minds on the fact this was business, not pleasure. Neat and professional, the way Snapper always admired.

The Dinner Suit coughed in a meaningful way, so it looked like things were starting to move along in the right direction. Snapper stretched his leg out into the aisle and glanced at his timepiece. It looked like it was running to schedule for the ten thirty start they had been warned to expect.

The Suit walked to the front of the dais, fiddled around with his tie for no good reason and then got round to thanking everybody for their kind attention, and pointing out that luncheon would be served at approximately one to one-thirty depending on how the morning session progressed. He made a big thing about special dietary requirements being catered for, though as far as Snapper could see there was only one Rasta in the room. He then announced that the key speaker would be making his entrance in the next couple of minutes so people who were still standing should find themselves a seat and make themselves comfortable; and that at the request of the management no alcohol would be served until the lunchtime break. He changed feet a couple of times like he was checking that he hadn't forgotten anything important, then appeared to give up on whatever that might have been. He checked his watch, faced his audience, and wished everybody an interesting and rewarding seminar, before excusing himself and walking through the assembled masses and out by the door at the end of the hall.

Muttering quickly petered out as people settled down and prepared to get serious. Nobody clapped the Suit's departure and only one meathead put his fingers in his mouth and whistled as he disappeared out of the door. Apart from feet shuffling the room had now descended into complete silence as everybody waited for the mysterious Jeremiah to put in his appearance and tell them how he proposed this set-up was going work.

Snapper glanced out of the window and saw the Suit heading across the carpark towards a waiting car that had its nose pointing directly at the front gate. The vehicle was roomy and appeared to contain the rest of the kitchen staff in the back seats, so possibly they had another booking before they returned to serve the midday meal. He noted the departing supervisor must be in a rush because he hadn't even stopped to change out of his classy work-suit which would most certainly get creased when he sat in the car. Seconds later the engine fired up and the vehicle shot through the front exit and onto the main road where it disappeared from view. Several seconds ticked by before there was a very loud bang.

CHAPTER TWO

Central London, Monday July 8th 2025

Squid Simons found himself in a difficult position. Barely a week had elapsed since the explosion and already his world was beginning to crumble around him. From what he could gather, other gangs were experiencing a similar dilemma. Trying all they knew to get past the loss of their leading men, while battling hard to hold on to hard-fought territorial rights, with chaos staring them right in the face everywhere they looked. Things were falling apart in front of his eyes and Squid knew he needed to do something about it. The trouble was any sense of order had vanished overnight and, without people knowing their place within the hierarchy of the system, discipline was very quickly falling apart.

Brooksy had run Holborn for a lot of years and Squid had never had a problem with working as his number two. But as the erstwhile leader was now out of the picture on a permanent basis his time had come to step up and take control, and so far, the transition hadn't gone at all well.

Only a few days had elapsed, and already he could hear whispers from the troops that maybe he wasn't cut out for the job, and that it might be better to do something about that situation before everything turned sour. The trouble was he shared their doubts. He was only too aware of his limitations. As a number two he was right up there with the best of them, but leading the pack was a skill he had never pretended to possess. Brooksy had always been certain about everything, and if there was any remaining doubt after he had thrown his weight behind a proposal, he could always carry the decision by force of personality alone. Squid just wasn't that man. It took him longer to come up with answers and sometimes when they eventually arrived, they didn't sound overly convincing, even while he was laying them down. What a bloody mess this had so quickly become, and he couldn't see it getting better anytime soon.

The trouble was, if he didn't grasp this opportunity while it was on offer it was difficult to see where else he could fit into any revised chain of command. Going back to being a foot soldier would never work out. He had his pride, and, if he were being honest, it was painfully apparent that he was now carrying a lot too much weight and a few too many years to slot back into working the streets. Besides, if he were removed from his current position and booted back downstairs there would be the humiliation of everybody taking the piss and whispering behind his back, and that would be the worst of it all. Whatever else happened that shame had to be avoided whatever the cost.

The main problem was, once you lost the leadership, even if you had only held it for a matter of days, there was no real place where you could slot back into the pack. It was like in the animal kingdom. The unwritten rules said you were meant to just bugger-off into a quiet bit of wilderness where you could curl up and die.

He and Brooksy had come up through the ranks together and despite having quite different characters they had always been tight. But despite their close friendship there was never any doubt who was the organ grinder and who was the monkey. That situation had never represented a problem for Squid. Brooksy had a better head on his shoulders for thinking things out and that was just the way it was. Why would you feel jealous of someone who had been born better equipped to handle the main man's job? The reason that they had worked well as a team was because they were comfortable in their respective roles; and as they were solid and there was never any friction, they found no difficulty in stamping on anyone who started mouthing off and, as a direct consequence, bust-ups in the ranks never really got out of hand.

A couple of months back their prospects had never looked brighter. That Jeremiah character had flown in from Jamaica, tapped them up with a smile on his lips and laid down the ideas for his plan; and you didn't need to be Einstein to see there was big time profit written right through the middle of that particular stick of rock. What he was proposing was a small revolution and would set this town on fire.

Why Jeremiah had banged on Holborn's door first off was a bit of a mystery. Admittedly, the Holborn gang had been running for a very long time, but it had never been a big outfit compared with those from the East End or the south side of the river. Yet the man had come all the way from Jamaica, and Holborn had been at the top of his call sheet, so bragging rights were there for the taking, and respect for their little gang had sailed right through the roof. From that minute on the clock Holborn's status had gone into orbit and soon the other gangs were clamouring to be in on the deal, including a number of the big boys who had been a bit sniffy about having anything to do with Holborn when they had dealings in the past. So, the whole crew had sat back, puffed out their chests and felt pretty good about themselves; because no matter who else got an invite to the party, Holborn had still been the first name on the big man's invitation list, and in this neck of the woods that fact alone stood for quite a lot.

Once they had talked it through and agreed it was a winner, Brooksy had used his personality to sell the plan for the grand get-together as if he had had a major big role in putting it together. Only Squid knew that Brooksy didn't really have a clue what was going on. But that was Brooksy for you. You had to love him for the way his mouth kept moving up and down, even when it should have been clear to a blind man that he was making it up as he went along. He could sell fridges to the Eskimos, could Brooksy, and do it without breaking sweat. Mr Personality, at the peak of his game, and nobody could get a word in edgeways to knock him out of his stride. So, it was a tragedy for Squid that he now stood alone, because unless resurrection came back into fashion pretty damn quick there was no way that Brooksy was ever coming back.

Squid had been due to go to the meeting along with Brooksy but had been pulled over by some dumb arsed traffic cop over the tax on his car, which as it later transpired had run out three years back. Then after a frank exchange of views on the subject he had ended up spending the morning in a pokey cell in the arse end of Camden. Ironically, that copper had probably been responsible for saving his life, but Squid wouldn't be writing him a thank you letter with kisses on the bottom anytime soon. By putting him behind bars the dipstick had dropped him in the deep pile of shit that he was currently trying to negotiate his way out with such little success. If Squid were being honest, he would rather have been blown up with the rest of the boys, than have to navigate his way through the minefield that he had finished up inheriting.......... and despite all the stuff in the papers, he still had no real idea what the hell had happened, let alone why.

That wasn't the only reason he was now in an embarrassing position. Holborn had been the big noise when it came to setting up the meeting and Brooksy had handed out invites to the other gang leaders like he was a person who was very much in the know about what was going on. Total bullshit of course. Brooksy didn't know his arse from his elbow, but with his old mate being unavailable for comment it left Squid in a very delicate position. In a lot of ways, it was lucky that Brooksy had been taken out along with the rest of the big hitters or he would have been strung up from a lamppost long before now. Tempers were definitely getting frayed and with his old mucker out of the frame he had been the one who had been left holding the parcel at the exact moment the music had stopped. He had already been made fully aware, in not very subtle terms, that he would be ill advised to enter any popularity contests in the foreseeable future; and it had now reached the stage where he had started to think twice about leaving the house after dark, even if it was only to walk the dog.

Damn the lot of them! Squid decided he might as well drag his body up the road and get himself a drink. Something, anything to help take away the feeling of total isolation that he had been experiencing for the past nine days. The pub on the corner was miserable, the toilets stank, and the bits of carpet that hadn't already worn away stuck to the soles of your shoes; but at least it served alcohol, and Jesus he was in need of something to lift his spirits right now. Nobody would know him in a place like that because under ordinary circumstances he wouldn't have crossed the threshold if they had paid him to do it in gold. What the hell. It would do the job as well as anywhere else in this area, and at least it wasn't much of a distance to walk.

He was still pulling on his jacket, having gone less than twenty-five yards, when a figure came out of nowhere and crossed in front of him to walk on the same side of the road. Jeremiah Jones: buggered, if the bloke walking directly in front of him didn't look the spitting image of Jeremiah fucking Jones. Squid had assumed the Jamaican had been blown up along with the rest of the boys, but either his eyes were deceiving him, or his fucked-up state of health was causing him to start hallucinating. He called out at the top of his voice, but the retreating figure didn't seem to hear him and just kept on walking at the same steady pace. What was this bloke's problem? Was he deaf or something? Regardless of whether or not it was Jones, the fucker couldn't have failed to hear him shouting at the top of his voice. There was nobody else on the street.

Squid was carrying too much weight to break into a sprint, but he did lengthen his stride in an effort to close the gap; but regardless of his exertions the margin between them always seemed to remain stubbornly the same. Squid was sure that it was Jones, but not quite sure enough. Then, Jeremiah's back disappeared round a corner and Squid started to breathe a little more easily. He knew it round here like the back of his hand and the turning friend Jeremiah had just cut into was most definitely a dead-end street.

He couldn't be wrong about the identification, could he? Well yes, he had to admit that was a possibility. His powers of recognition were legendary in the Holborn gang, and for all the wrong reasons. But he was pretty damned certain this time. That was Jeremiah fucking Jones alright. He would put money on it. The cut of his hair and the way he carried himself was distinctive, even when you were viewing him from the rear.

Squid felt happy for the first time in days as an immense sense of relief washed over him. Now at last, he would be able to get some proper answers. Maybe even learn enough to bring this bloody nightmare to the sort of conclusion that didn't result in him finishing up dead.

Squid hit the corner with adrenaline pumping in his veins. At last, some sort of resolution was in prospect, and whatever it turned out to be he would be ready to grab it with both hands. For his own peace of mind, he desperately needed the Jamaican to furnish some sort of explanation for what had gone on.

He took a first step into the side-street and immediately stopped dead. He stood completely motionless and let his eyes drift up and down both sides of the cul-de-sac. Nothing; not the slightest sign of a single living soul. The road was as dead as a tomb. Christ almighty, the man he had been following had only been thirty yards in front of him when he turned the corner. The bastard didn't have wings and there was no way he could have sublimated into thin air.

The nervous excitement and the unwanted exercise were causing Squid to sweat profusely. He made a spot decision to go on a diet once this whole thing was over and had been soundly put to bed. He wasn't going to end up croaking with a heart attack like his old man.

He moved to the centre of the road and checked in all directions while assessing his options. He took a couple of deep breaths and mopped at his face and balding scalp with a disintegrating paper tissue that he dragged from the pocket of his jacket. Not a solitary sign. Where the hell had the bastard got to? One thing was sure, he couldn't have got far.

Squid set off slowly up the road, methodically checking behind dustbins and at the back of every parked car. Nothing; absolutely bloody nothing. This was doing his head in. Didn't he have enough to worry about without playing hide and seek with this Jamaican tosser. It was demeaning to a man of his standing, scrambling about in the middle of the road.

He caught his breath and bent to tie a shoelace which had come undone as he had scrambled his way up the road. With the weight he was currently carrying it seemed a very long way down. He grunted in discomfort while struggling to form a knot with sweating fingers that worked no better than sausages fresh out of the pan, but at the third attempt his mission was complete. He even let out a small gasp of satisfaction to confirm he had completed the task to his personal satisfaction. Stupid bloody design. He was definitely getting Velcro next time. He was slowly dragging himself to his feet when something hard hit him from behind and knocked him off balance. Momentarily he was stunned; what the fuck. He spun round to better assess the source of the provocation, thoughts of retribution instantly barging their way to the front of his mind. But the world went out of focus before he could properly react, and in that precise instant he felt shards of glass rip into his throat.

Suddenly there was an awful lot of blood covering the front of Squid's shirt and he didn't need a medical degree to figure out where it had come from. He grabbed ineffectually at his neck and covered the wound with the palm of his hand, but it was an automatic reaction because he knew from bitter experience that he would almost certainly be wasting his time. He tried to yell out but no sound came from his lips. His throat hurt a bit, but more than that he just felt ridiculously tired. He thought about what he should do next, but it was a problem that was too difficult to contemplate until he had more energy. He knew he would need to retrace his steps to get back onto a main thoroughfare if he were to stand any chance of being discovered, but quickly came to the conclusion that in his current condition even a short walk like that would be beyond his physical capabilities. Any strength he had previously possessed seemed to be leaking away. Everything was so difficult to figure out that he began to wonder if it was really worth the effort. He needed to formulate some sort of plan if he wanted to survive, but he couldn't summon up the mental concentration necessary. He stood entirely still for a moment, looked up to the heavens, then allowed himself to slowly crumple until his bulk was settled on a convenient kerb stone. That was better, now at least he could properly relax and that would help him to get his brain working again. It occurred to him that he still didn't know for certain if the person he had been following was Jeremiah Jones, and he was relieved to realise that the answer to that question didn't seem of so much importance anymore. Sleep beckoned, so Squid allowed his eyes to close as he toppled slowly backwards to rest comfortably in the gutter; and he felt quite contented as he visualised his worries breaking into tiny, little pieces of brightly coloured paper which rose in the air to be carried away on a gentle breeze.

On a Monday in July, Holborn's main roads would expect to experience plenty of footfall as streams of office workers bustled back and forth attending to their business affairs; but in some of the back streets it could remain very quiet until the commuters turned out from their offices to make their way home at the end of the day. People from London have a reputation for minding their own business, so it was no great surprise that Squid Simon's corpse had begun to stiffen before the authorities got round to manoeuvring it into a body bag and taking it away.

CHAPTER THREE

Sheffield, Monday September 22nd 2025

Harry Litmus stared across his desk and contemplated how a very ordinary day could suddenly have gone so fast downhill. Jerome Whitcott sat opposite looking contented with life, clearly feeling he was doing Litmus' second-best visitor's chair a favour by condescending to park his bottom on it. The kettle could be heard whistling plaintively in the background. Dust motes danced freely in the air. The sharp blast of a car horn sounded from the main road outside. A dog could be heard barking from a long way away. Nobody said a word.

The rain beating against the building's newly fitted double glazing made a musical accompaniment to the groan of the floorboards as Beth's feet neared Litmus' office. The door flew open with a kick. Beth was carrying two cups of coffee and didn't look pleased. In the ordinary course of events Beth wouldn't have contemplated making coffee unless she had a sworn affidavit testifying to the fact that the Costa outlet across the road had been firebombed and razed to the ground. The fact that she had condescended to do so demonstrated that the severity of the situation must have been telepathically communicated. Litmus wondered how that could have come about; were his thought processes so horribly transparent? And if that were the case, might it be a good time to consider knocking the on-line poker sessions on the head for a time.

Beth departed and the door slammed shut. Litmus sighed. Time for thinking had now run out. Nothing for it but to pull himself together and give it another go.

'Mr Whitcott, I can only repeat myself. I'm completely overburdened with work at the moment and won't be looking to take on any new clients for the foreseeable future.'

Whitcott uncrossed his legs, leaned forward, and picked up the coffee cup. He examined the contents quite carefully, smelled it, then returned it to the tray untasted. Smart move, thought Litmus.

'You still don't seem to have quite grasped the situation, Litmus,' said Whitcott, stirring to life. 'This isn't so much a request for your services, as a Governmental appointment........an opportunity to express a hitherto unrecognised patriotic zeal......and hence the only excuse for not taking it would be if you were dead. A circumstance, which as you are well aware, could quite easily befall the unwary and, in chosen specific instances, the uncooperative as well.'

Whitcott looked at his coffee again and appeared to shudder. Litmus could easily relate to this reaction, and it wasn't as if the tea would have been any better. Beth had a bad relationship with beverages, and you just had to accept it. It was just the way things were.

'Perhaps it would help if I put your mind at rest,' Whitcott continued. 'Word might not yet have filtered through to this god forsaken corner of the universe but in simple terms, I'm no longer a spook.'

He paused, as if waiting for a clap of thunder to underscore the announcement. When that failed to happen, he immediately continued.

'Some months back I took charge of PLAD, the Pre-emptive Logistical Augmentation Directorate. I now sit between all branches of the security services and Whitehall, and report directly to Cabinet.'

Litmus considered knocking over his coffee mug to cause a temporary diversion while he assessed the implications, but as there was every chance the liquid would burn through the small square of carpet that was protecting his feet from the infestation of woodworm below, he thought it wiser to give that a miss.

'Sorry Mr Whitcott, even if you were reporting direct to the Archangel Gabriel, I'm afraid the answer would still be no.'

Whitcott shook his head sorrowfully, then reached for a black attaché case which had until now been stored underneath his chair. He withdrew a file, rested it on his knee and started to read out loud.

'Harold Sebastian Litmus, age thirty-one....'

'Thirty-two,' interrupted Litmus.'

'.......only son of Wilfred and Emily Litmus, unexceptional childhood, educated at a middle ranking comprehensive, academically gifted, progressed to a red brick Midland's university, graduated with a two-one, blah, blah, blah.........currently residing in Sheffield where he advertises his services as a Private Enquiry Agent, but displays little evidence of doing any sort of work. Runs business from a dilapidated house situated on the main southwest thoroughfare into the city which he inherited, along with a legacy, from an uncle on his mother's side. Supplements income by taking in lodgers (which he doesn't declare on his tax return) who currently include a male jobbing actor of dubious pedigree and a female who operates as his secretary/receptionist, and with whom he could possibly be conducting a clandestine relationship.'

Whitcott scowled, scribbled an amendment to his notes and continued.

'Previous history. Talent spotted at university (see subfile JX3) and referred to the appropriate authorities. Worked for three years.......'

'Four,' said Litmus in anticipation of the next item on the agenda.

'...............four years,' continued Whitcott, before dropping the notes in his lap, looking Litmus in the eye, and changing to a more informal tone, 'under my direct supervision at a place the Official Secrets Act would encourage us not to discuss in loud voices, until the strange incident with Arthur Rochester...... after which you inexplicably terminated your employment.'

'Rochester fell down a flight of stairs and broke his neck. He tripped. I wasn't anywhere near him when he fell. His death was nothing to do with me as the subsequent investigation clearly established.'

'If you say so, Litmus, I'm sure that's correct,' said Whitcott in a neutral tone. 'Although in my recollection of events the tribunal returned an open verdict.'

A further pause as he cleared his throat and turned a page.

'Then lo and behold, you upped and joined the Police Force; where after four years defending the British public from the untold horrors of graffiti artists and litterbugs you attained the dizzy heights of Detective Sergeant.'

'Three years actually, but who's counting?' said Litmus.

'And then a further career change and the move north. Was that anything to do with the death of your Police colleague Detective Constable.......err......??'

'Detective Sergeant Bonnet,' said Litmus. 'Harold Bonnet. He walked into traffic and was hit by a taxi.'

'Fell under a coach, according to my version, but I bow to superior knowledge,' said Whitcott. 'After all, you were the man standing directly behind him when it happened.'

'This is getting rather tedious, Mr Whitcott. If you think you are going to pressure me into taking on this bloody job by taunting me with a heap of unsubstantiated allegations, then you are very wrong. Oh, and you missed one. When I was eight a friend of mine fell out of an apple tree and broke his leg. Want to add that to the file?'

'Yes, Terry Willcox,' said Whitcott. 'We've got young Terry already. Family were totally distraught by all accounts.'

'Look, I've got work to do,' said Litmus. 'I don't want your job under any circumstances so perhaps you would be kind enough to show yourself out.'

'What, not even if it served to keep Miss Tappy Boots, the queen of the baristas, out of prison? *Possible relationship* I believe it says on the file. You surprise me, Litmus, I thought that, given the circumstances, you would be a bit more gallant than that.'

CHAPTER FOUR

Sheffield, Monday September 22nd 2025

Whitcott's smile lit up the office like a beacon. He looked like he could hug himself.

'She's a hacker, Litmus, you bloody idiot. Surely, even someone as incurious as you couldn't have failed to notice. Quite a good one as well, from what my technical staff tell me. Want to know how the lady weaves her wiles?'

'Rubbish,' Litmus said with all the conviction he could muster. He suddenly felt very ill at ease. A lot of things were beginning to fall uncomfortably into place.

Whitcott chose to continue as if there had been no interruption.

'Quite clever really. One of those situations where you come across a scam and wonder why you never thought of it yourself. I'll give you the under eights' version, Litmus, because the truth of it can get a bit heady for the untrained mind; and despite my ministrations over the years your mind has remained nothing if not totally untrained.'

Whitcott paused briefly to smile at his own joke.

'Madam settles on a large corporation she wishes to target, then utilising that box of tricks on her desk along with a bit of undefined know-how, she finds a way to hack into their computer network. Having done that, she makes contact with the Company's Chief Executive, explains what she has accomplished and offers to demonstrate the most efficient method of blocking her point of entry. No threats or anything unpleasant. Nothing in any way untoward. Just an everyday business transaction conducted by civilised individuals. Harmless, you might say. An aid that could only serve to improve the company's data security, and by doing so enhance its corporate efficiency. Damned pity it is totally illegal.'

Whitcott hesitated just long enough to enable him to adopt a worried expression.

'The only reason your lady isn't currently sharing a cell in Holloway with an overweight dyke is that so far we haven't been able to verify the method she uses to receive payment. I mean, she's not doing it out of the goodness of her heart, is she? She's got to be getting paid somehow; it's just that we haven't yet figured out how. And the truth of the matter is until we can nail down how the money transfer takes place there would be no hope of a successful prosecution under current UK law.'

Whitcott duly adopted a look of sadness on UK law's behalf.

'The beauty of the scheme centres around the fact the companies she targets are hardly going to admit that anything is amiss and draw attention to their own shortcomings. The publicity would be truly appalling, and you could lay money that they would be crucified by their shareholders at the next AGM. No, they all fall back on the standard option; sack the IT department en masse, employ a fresh set of nurds with greasy hair and halitosis and hope that the next time the rollercoaster comes off the rails they are taking their annual vacation in Porta de la Cruz. Sadly, I suppose that these days we have to accept that it's the world in which we live.'

Litmus shifted uncomfortably.

'Even if what you tell me has a shred of truth, which I very much doubt, you've admitted yourself that you can't touch Beth without proof she received some form of payment,' said Litmus, grasping at a nettle that he was pretty sure would soon be responsible for causing an unpleasant rash.

'Moot point that, Litmus. Worth mentioning to show that whilst you might not be very bright, at least you've been following the argument.'

Whitcott seemed to increase in size. This was the moment he had been waiting for and he was going to enjoy it to its full.

'As it stands, we could probably still make a case for the hacking alone, but who is ever happy settling for a bacon sandwich when there's the prospect of securing a whole pig which would feed the entire village for a week? It's U.S. law that concerns us here, Litmus. The software she uses goes through a server in America and Tony Blair's Government were kind enough to write the Yanks an open cheque for extraditions in cases of this type. A word to the cousins and little missy nimble fingers will be on the first plane to the US of A before you could get your lips puckered up sufficiently to whistle the first notes of Yankee Doodle Dandy. They've got some very nasty prisons that side of the water, Litmus. I could show you some pictures if you think that I'm making it up.'

Whitcott hesitated, as if an idea had just occurred to him.

'But of course, I am talking hypothetically here, because to date there are no aggrieved parties resulting from the transaction; and as currently no one seems to be busting a gut to get involved in any sort of legal tomfoolery, there is always the possibility that no action would be deemed necessary. In which case, of course, the whole matter could just be allowed to fade into the ether.'

'And who exactly would make that sort of decision?' queried Litmus.

'Me,' said Whitcott, without the trace of a smile.

Litmus hesitated, but there was really nowhere to go.

'Just supposing I agreed to ....'

Whitcott immediately interrupted.

'Right, let's stop playing silly buggers, Litmus, and just get down to it. I'm requisitioning your services for a period of one month to undertake an investigation and write a report. Time constraints mean there isn't the opportunity to approach the matter in any great depth. I just require an oversight from a new perspective and a concise statement to the effect that you consider the pertinent authorities are approaching their enquiries diligently and professionally and........basically that they are taking the course of action that you would consider as appropriate given the evidence that is currently in their possession. This will obviously involve you in a little detective work but nothing too arduous. As to the subject matter, it's something that you can't fail to know a little about already because it still puts in the odd cameo performance in the newspapers and broadcast media three months after the event.'

Absurd though it sounded there was only one thing Jerome Whitcott could be talking about. A quarter of the year had elapsed, and the north London bombing still attracted column inches and the odd in-depth interview whenever the media were experiencing a quiet day. Logic demanded that Litmus should show some reaction. In consequence he sat very still and attempted to display no emotion whatever. Annoyingly, Whitcott didn't seem to notice and ploughed on in the same steady monotone.

'I can't at this stage go into greater detail, but you will doubtless find that action and words will at some stage collide. In a short time, forces will be mobilised against the suspected perpetrators of this outrage and at that juncture you will be consulted for your opinion; always assuming you have by then had the opportunity to formulate one. If you are two hundred percent sure that the proposed action is....err.... shall we say, totally unwise, then use the opportunity to make your feelings known and offer evidence to support an alternative stratagem....... or even, dare I say it, no action at all. If you are anything less than two hundred percent sure of your facts, then smile politely and get the hell out of the way. I have no wish to influence your decision in this matter but if word reaches me you have got under the feet of a Police Operation that could have brought those responsible for this dastardly and cowardly act to justice, then don't waste money topping up your pension pot and tell your little friend outside fiddling with the keyboard to develop a strong tolerance for poor hygiene and confined spaces; because I can reliably assure you, she will most definitely be seeing a good deal of both.'

There was a short silence, followed by a crashing sound from the front office which they both chose to ignore.

'I suppose you realise this is utterly ridiculous. I am totally unsuitable for taking on an enquiry of this type, with or without the time constraints involved. Police and Forensics will have gone over every millimetre of the bomb site and questioned everybody who had the slightest possibility of having seen anything that might have been considered even vaguely relevant to the case. You must have access to several hundred people who would make a better job of this than I am likely to do, and if you use your own people there is the added advantage that you could make absolutely certain that any report arriving on your desk will contain the exact wording that you're looking for. Mr Whitcott, it must be blatantly obvious we will just be wasting each other's time.'

Whitcott brushed these comments aside with a sweep of his hand.

'Litmus, now that we've covered all the main bases, let us enjoy a brief conversation off the record. I see in front of me a young man from a stable working-class background who has strived hard and obtained a university education. A man who has devoted several years to working for agencies responsible for the defence of this great nation and several more safeguarding the wellbeing of its illustrious citizens. Granted, this person has probably gone slightly off the rails in the last year or so, but he is still of tender years and has his whole life stretching out before him. Even this recent slide into delinquency might not necessarily be viewed as a total waste of time. Doubtless there are addled minds that might regard the pursuit of errant husbands and the retrieving of stray cats from up trees to be a worthwhile use of a man's time. Take a step back, Litmus. Examine matters from a wider viewpoint. Can you afford to turn your back on a substantial cheque for a mere four week's work.......or for that matter a chance to save a damsel from what I can absolutely guarantee will be copper bottomed distress? Would it not be wise to consider the financial burdens that I sense are even now weighing heavily on your slender shoulders; or to put it in painfully frank terms, embrace the chance to get this shit-hole looking like something other than the backdrop to a sixteenth century leper colony.'

The expenditure of emotion appeared to have exhausted Whitcott, who stretched his legs, placed a hand over his mouth and yawned. Duly refreshed, he gathered together his paperwork and unceremoniously crammed everything into his briefcase.

'Probably best to keep your little friend with the mouse fixation out of the loop on this one for the time being, don't you think?'

Litmus nodded. 'We haven't talked about money.'

'Ah, I was wondering when the wheels of avarice would point once more to the open road! Twenty thousand, five up front, the balance on delivery of a report compiled to my satisfaction; expenses reimbursed on production of suitable receipts, but try not to get too carried away. The country's got Brexit, the further rerouting of HS2 and the aftermath of Covid already tugging at the purse strings.'

Litmus thought quickly. 'Thirty with fifteen paid now.'

'Young man, you are hardly in a position to negotiate. Give it another punt when Lady Luck has taken it upon herself to deal you a better hand of cards.'

Litmus shrugged. 'OK, but despite all you've said I still don't see what will be achieved; why me? As far as I can see what you are asking me to do serves no purpose whatever.'

Whitcott chose to ignore this comment and quickly rose from his seat.

'My secretary will be in touch with travel warrants, and an identity card to confirm that you are pursuing your enquiries on the Government's behalf. I'll designate a driver to pick you up from the station. He will be available to you for the duration of your tour of duty. This man will have full clearance so you can talk to him freely if you consider it appropriate. There is no time limit for this operation. Kill it off and you can book yourself a ticket on the next available transport heading north.........depending, of course, on you having come up with satisfactory results.'

Litmus remained seated, but reluctantly offered his hand which Whitcott shook without any great enthusiasm. He walked halfway to the door then turned.

'For an educated man, Litmus, you really are surprisingly dim. Exercise your brain a little. Ponder the question, why would I choose you above anybody else? Treat it as an academic exercise with marks out of ten.'

Whitcott took a further stride, but still failed to reach the door. He gave it one last try before his resolve could be seen to melt.

'I thought you were meant to be good at thinking outside the box. The answer's pretty much staring you in the face. Our current government, Litmus, is a coalition of Lefties and Losties. Every time I see ten people sitting round a Westminster table, I know there will be five paper shufflers and five bleeding-heart liberals and that my first job will be to define precisely who falls which side of the fence. Think of the people this involves. How do you think this sort of setup makes the security services feel? Bring a man in off the street who has committed a double murder and there is more chance the arresting officer will be disciplined for rumpling the felon's suit than that the perpetrator will receive his just desserts in a Court of Law. I don't need a man from the inside looking out, Litmus, because he will be compromised before he even sets foot outside the door. I need a maverick on the outside looking in, and like it or not my friend you are the best I've been able to secure at very short notice. You are young, educated, experienced, reasonably presentable, and best of all the colour of your skin is brown. In consequence, there is every chance your findings will be viewed sympathetically based on the final observation alone. Not by me, Litmus. I don't give a hoot what colour you are. By the faceless wonders to whom I might at some stage be obliged to present your findings. They are the sort of cretins who could choose to take it into account. Pity you aren't gay as well, Litmus, but that would have been a bonus and I'm fully aware that you can't go into battle with everything on your side. You are far from ideal, my friend, but in the limited time I have available you were the best I could come up with by a country mile.'

CHAPTER FIVE

Train to London, Tuesday September 23rd 2025

The nine twenty-nine was scheduled to complete the journey from Sheffield to London St Pancras in two hours and seven minutes and would arrive in the capital at eleven thirty-six precisely, allowing that essential maintenance work to the track south of Derby didn't cause an unwarranted delay. Harry Litmus liked train journeys and would have been happy for this one to be routed via Aberdeen if only he could have been provided with a set of earmuffs. His booked ticket was in the corner of carriage A, away from the shared tables and close to the toilet, all of which was good. Three rows up were a crowd of students who were travelling to a midweek football match in the capital and were very excited by the fact, which wasn't. Litmus produced a crumpled tissue from his jacket pocket and with considerable difficulty stuffed half of it into each ear.

There was no point in blaming Beth, he reflected. If it hadn't been her, Whitcott would have found some other means to hang him out to dry. Litmus had known Whitcott for a very long time and it was what the son of a bitch did for a living. He was a past master. Had the T-shirt and a certified accreditation embossed in gold italics on specially commissioned parchment with painted serpents running down the side. He was a bastard that even the Union of Master Bastards acknowledged as one of the very best.

Litmus had waved Beth off that morning with as brief an explanation as possible. She had looked so cute with her white towelling dressing gown and sleepy eyes that he had wanted to fold her neatly into his travel bag and take her with him. Sadly, for the moment at least, that wasn't a realistic option. Despite Whitcott's allusions to the contrary, he was no nearer to persuading her that he was the man she had been waiting for all her life than he had been on the first day they met. As he ripped open the packet of dry roasted nuts that were designated as the opening salvo in his personal battle to consume five a day, he recollected the scene. Six weeks ago! Six bloody weeks was all it had been. It seemed more like six months!!

Beth had wandered in off the road having spotted his advert for a lodger in the window of the downstairs front room, which at the time had been masquerading as his office. Five feet six in snakeskin boots and black trousers that you could only have removed with a shoehorn. White T-shirt with something written on it that he had quickly lost interest in when noticing the curve of her breasts. Black shoulder- length hair that looked like it had failed to make peace with a tornado. Small, flat nose, cautious smile showing teeth that were just far enough out of skew to be interesting, but not enough to look unsightly, and eyes that you could swim in forever without ever hoping to touch the sides. This woman was beautiful beyond compere. She personified everything he had always wanted, but invariably failed to get, so he resolved to make a major effort not to bugger things up.

He had boldly stepped forward, shaken her hand formally and prepared to take charge of the situation.

'As you can see the downstairs area is currently office accommodation and.....'

'Right,' she interrupted, 'let's take a look at the room you are advertising straight away, shall we? Then if I don't like the look of it, I won't be wasting your time. You lead the way. I was going to ask if I should take my shoes off, but obviously not.' She ran her finger along the dust on the lower section of the banister rail as they ascended to the first floor before wrinkling her nose.

He thought it was probably the nose wrinkle that finally pushed him over the edge. Two minutes in and already he was hooked.

'Shall we check out the bathroom first? What sort of shower........... electric......good water pressure?'

'Just been installed,' he had stammered. 'As you can see this place is a bit of a work in progress, but I managed to get the roof, the windows, the bathroom and the central heating sorted out before I realised that I was the sole owner of the country's largest black hole.'

'OK, let's go straight to the room, shall we?'

'Well, there's two actually,' said Litmus proudly. 'One at the front overlooking the park and the middle room that I'm currently using as a ......as a.....as a sort of storage area. It offers a view onto the back garden, which is what you might call another development project for further down the line. There's a fox I call Rufus who visits every night and does his level best to vandalise anything new that I put out there, so it's very slow progress. I ought to put poison down, but I haven't got the heart. I look on the animal as a representative of the conservation lobby. It's also a good excuse not to get carried away and try to accomplish too much too quickly. Not that there's any great fear of that. By the way, there's an actor renting the attic room but he's something of a travelling player, so he only puts in an appearance once every blue moon. I can guarantee he won't get under your feet. I'm starting to babble, aren't I?'

Then, after the briefest of surveys she made her decision.

'I'll take the one at the front. I'm sure that Rufus will understand that it's all about me and not about him; and that it will be better for both of us, given time. Do you mind if I reserve the bathroom for 8 o'clock each morning? I like to operate to a fixed schedule. Any chance you can get this junk shifted out of the room by tomorrow? I'd like to make a start on cleaning out some of the muck and then get onto redecorating as soon as possible. I'll also need to get some furniture it appears. I must apologise. Stupid, I know. I thought the room was advertised as furnished.'

Junk! Junk! The bed and mattress were both genuine antiques and he had been reliably informed that Victorian brown was coming back into fashion at such an alarming pace that only a fool would consider burning it off.

And before he could fully come to terms with the latest flurry of developments,

'I couldn't help noticing that in the window there was another note advertising for a Receptionist.'

Take that, Employment Bureau! The power of the written word, affixed with two strips of Sellotape and a small lump of Blue-tack, had proved more than capable of doing the job. Classified advertisements in the local paper, job vacancies on-line! Who needs them? Read 'em and weep, suckers.......except they wouldn't have the opportunity now, because I didn't put it in.

Casual now, Litmus: don't get over eager. There's nothing more pathetic than a man on his knees.

'Why yes, I am indeed looking for a Receptionist. Would you be interested at all? The pay's rubbish but the hours are rather good.'

'I've got a proposal, Mr Litmus. I work at the University teaching History of Art to mature students in the evenings but I'm completely free during the daytime. You need a Receptionist, I need a room, perhaps we could reach an accommodation?'

Way to go, Litmus. Accommodation. I'd have paid her to take the job and thrown in the room for free.

'I could start from next Monday if that would be convenient.'

It certainly was. It was hard to think of anything that had ever been more convenient. She worked out the terms in a matter of seconds; and, as she exited with a waft of perfume that would have caused any man's head to spin, spoke those immortal words which now hung like a scimitar over his head.

'Can you shift that old PC and the monitor if it's no trouble. I've got a whole heap of modern kit that I use for my work, and it would be a pity not to put it to good use.'

A week later her room had been redecorated, refurnished, recarpeted and re anything else you might care to think of, all at her own expense ....and on the large desk nearest the door, which he had now been obliged to vacate, stood a mountain of black boxes with different coloured flashing lights that appeared to hiss with displeasure and cackle with scorn every time he came in through the door.

Litmus' reverie was interrupted by a loud cheer from the student melee further up the carriage. One so loud it successfully penetrated his hastily constructed auditory barricade. Either the, *Who can balance the plastic cup on their head while drinking a pint can of lager in one go?* competition had finally reached a satisfactory conclusion, or the train had successfully passed the Derby rail maintenance site without being flagged to a halt.

Litmus' withdrew the tissue from his ears, fingered it into a slightly better shape, and hastily stuffed it back in. Having wasted a quarter of his journey pondering something that currently served little or no purpose, he now felt morally obliged to do a bit of work. He pinged open the catches of the pigskin briefcase his mother had bought him as a Christmas present somewhere between ten and fifteen years previously, which was currently enjoying its third excursion into the bright lights of the outside world, and withdrew the clutch of papers he had received by courier the previous evening and had since been doing his level best to ignore.

He weighed the content in his hand and flicked haphazardly from page to page. Considering the amount of time the Metropolitan Constabulary had been working on the case the content appeared meagre in the extreme. If these were the results you got when unlimited resources were thrown at a case, then heaven help your cause if you were flagged up as a lesser priority. He yanked out a pen, gritted his teeth and steeled himself to address the detail.

A property developer by the name of Barry Oates had been contacted by a film company and asked if he would be interested in renting out a site he owned on the outskirts of north London for a period of two months in May and June of this year. Phoenix Films wanted the dilapidated 1950's hotel, which was the central feature of the location, as a backdrop for a horror movie they were in the process of shooting. As the site on which the hotel was situated had for the last five years been mothballed by the Oates Construction and Development company while its unlovely chief executive waited for a surge in the property market, Mr Oates' ears immediately pricked up. Phoenix would of course need to make a few alterations to the structure of the building, as the script had need for the hotel to be situated in the Florida everglades, he had been advised. Something to do with a previous producer having hired the writer of the book on which the film was based as a consultant, and her turning out to be a total pedant about sticking to the precise narrative she had massaged onto every individual page of the rather weighty tome which she now regarded as sacrosanct. A complete pain in the arse, but that was women for you. Give them the slightest authority and they turn into a female version of Hitler overnight. Things had run a lot smoother in the days when they stayed at home, looked after the kids and baked cakes, in the procurement executive's opinion; but now the genie was out of the bottle it would be a hell of a job to get it back in again what with the *Me Too* lobby and all this equal rights garbage they were constantly banging on about or trying to peddle in the press.

A large company like Phoenix films was of course vastly experienced at the sort of short-term acquisition that this transaction would involve, and fully understood how difficult and time-consuming rental agreements could prove, what with the draconian legal requirements and all the unnecessary paperwork that would be entailed. So, if Mr Oates agreed, why didn't Phoenix just pay the whole deal off in cash so they could keep the deal between the two of them, and kill that particular turkey with a single shot? They would of course guarantee to leave the site exactly as they found it, not to disturb the neighbours and make absolutely certain that every vestige of their very existence had totally disappeared by end of June.

It took Mr Oates somewhat less than three seconds of hard thinking to figure out that this was a case where he couldn't possibly lose. This was literally money for old rope, and he was doubly delighted when the promised payment was delivered by courier first thing the following day. As far as Oates was concerned the film company could do what they liked to the hotel building because he intended to demolish it and level the land as soon as the market warmed up. The bricks and mortar just represented hardcore stacked neatly in a vertical position, as far as he was concerned.

When I said do as they like, I obviously didn't mean blow the fucking place up, a disgruntled Mr Oates insisted on having recorded in his statement, on the off chance there might be a misinterpretation of his standpoint on the agreed Terms of Contract.

Despite exhaustive investigation no record of a company called Phoenix Films, or a similar derivative, had been located in business registration records in either Britain or America, and no courier would admit to having delivered a sealed package to the offices of Oates Construction on or about the specified date. Reference to the company in any context whatever appeared to have gone up in flames. When Mr Oates was advised he could possibly have left himself open to prosecution on a variety of charges for hiring out the site without the requisite authorisation, he commented, *'How the fuck was I supposed to know I was dealing with criminals? The bloke on the phone sounded alright to me.'*

Litmus moved on to the pages covering the building work which had been undertaken at the location, and quickly reached the conclusion that the section in question could just as easily have been sub-headed *NO REAL IDEA*.

Construction workers had been observed arriving at the site entrance in a large, unmarked van (registration unknown, colour probably white) from the first day of May, but sizeable wooden hoardings had immediately been erected to block any direct line of visual access. However, neighbours with an elevated vantage point could still see a small section of the upper building and roof over the top of the plywood construction and they confirmed that work appeared to be undertaken in a diligent and professional manner. In addition, a dog walker called Cyril Creasy admitted that he knew a way in *over the back* and claimed to have checked progress on the renovation project most nights of the week after the builders had left without ever noticing anything he regarded as unusual or irregular. Mr Creasy said, *He carried a torch for that specific purpose and used to shine it in through the windows because he liked to know what was going on.* (Mr Creasy was found to have been bound over to Keep the Peace by Peterborough magistrates in 1996 when he was apprehended in the grounds of a girls' boarding school with a torch. Mr Creasy claimed to have been looking for his dog which had slipped its lead.)

Builders' merchants, which were numerous in the area, failed to locate any history of site deliveries, but as a lot of their sales were cash and collect transactions it was entirely possible that materials had still been sourced in the local vicinity without it necessarily being apparent that this was the case.

Any number of residents from the local community claimed to be extremely interested in what was going on at the building site but not, it appeared, interested enough to make enquiries with the builders direct or for that matter the local council, who would presumably have had to at least rubber stamp the project. This part of the borough could be termed as decidedly middle class and according to whoever had compiled the report that was enough of a reason to explain why *people tended to mind their own business.* What supposition there was by the local residents took the line that a renovation of the derelict building was a good thing providing it was re-established as a proper hotel rather than something disagreeable like a late-night bar that might attract car door slamming in the small hours of the morning by an undesirable element. The site workers were suspected to be East European, probably Polish, based entirely on the fact they appeared to be industrious and were prepared to work long hours; sometimes not being picked up by the returning van until as late as seven o'clock in the evening. Men were occasionally seen congregating at the site entrance smoking cigarettes at around lunch time, but nobody chose to engage them in conversation, and nobody had any idea what language they spoke, or indeed if they spoke at all. A lady who lived diagonally opposite and only agreed to comment if her submission to the report was classified as anonymous said: *They are a snotty lot round here. Fur coat and no knickers, a lot of them. Full of airs and graces. You wouldn't catch them talking to builders if their very lives depended on it.*

One of the few things that had been positively established was that the explosive used to blow up the hotel building was called Semtex and that it had been installed under the flooring of large sections of the refurbished structure. The underside of the floorboards also appeared to have been painted with a solution of the highly combustible brush cleaner and thinner methylated spirits for good measure, though what contributory factor that provided remained unquantified. The specific quantity of the explosive used was difficult to positively ascertain due to the large area over which it had been deployed, but it was suggested that the severity of the damage to the structure and surrounding grounds raised the possibility that the basic product might have been enhanced by something referred to as BCHMX. There was no question that the explosive could have been manufactured pre-1991 as it carried something called a detection taggant which was only introduced at that date. As a basic standard of explosive intensity, it was broadly recognised that 100 grams of Semtex plasticine would be capable of destroying a large car; and taking that as a reliable starting point it was estimated that five times that amount would have been more than adequate to completely demolish a comparatively flimsy structure like the dilapidated hotel. However, the total devastation of the site area tended to suggest that as much as three or even four times the required quantity of explosive had been utilised in the actual operation, suggesting that possibly the person laying the charge was not totally familiar with the devastating power of the explosive they were handling. The Semtex material could apparently be detonated by either shockwaves or heat, and if there was a firm conclusion on which method of triggering the combustion had been selected, Litmus failed to spot it. No speculation was forthcoming in relation to the sourcing of the explosive, and it appeared that neighbours living close to the building only become actively engaged with what was happening on their doorstep when a number of properties adjacent to the site had their windows blown in. Fortunately, this resulted in only a few very minor injuries and several cases of shock, but no loss of life.

Litmus skimmed over some more technical blurb that he didn't fully understand before arriving at the header of an even more weedy section of the report marked *Victims*. If details were scant on the pages covering other aspects of the disaster, they were a regular thesaurus compared with this section of the abject compilation.

On 29th June, expensive cars had been observed arriving at the newly refurbished hotel in the hours leading up to the tragedy. Neighbours speculated that it was probably a grand opening ceremony and the fact that a large percentage of the men arriving seemed to be black*/coloured*/persons of colour* (in case of publication in amended format seek ethnicity guidance and strike in accordance with latest directive*) made several suspect that the old hotel building had undergone a complete redesignation and was either going to be used as some sort of sports facility or had possibly been consecrated as a non-sectarian church.

Due to the magnitude of the explosion, it proved impossible to positively identify the number of people who had been killed by the blast, but it was estimated to be in excess of forty and probably less than sixty-five. A ferocious fire had followed the explosion which, aided by the accelerant (see previous detail) {*presume they are referring to the meths*} reduced any meagre remains of the building to charcoal. Quite naturally, there were no survivors. Attempts made to secure DNA samples from the scanty remains had proved largely unproductive. {*Attempts to find fingerprint evidence drew a total blank.*} The little DNA that was obtained suggested that a high percentage of the victims had been of mixed race. {*Whatever the fuck that meant!*} The arrival of the tail end of hurricane Rupert in the early hours 30th June resulted in a month's worth of rain being deposited onto what was already a scene of utter devastation, and the fact the rutted ground was composed largely of London clay reduced accurate scientific analysis to little more than intelligent guesswork.

Over subsequent weeks a number of enquiries were received by the Police in relation to missing persons (see appendix e4) {*there was no trace of a photocopy of appendix e4 in the report*!!}. The enquiries were not localised and usually not at all specific in nature, following the line of, *I've not seen ****** for several weeks. How can I find out if he's been banged up or if he's in hospital because he's been missing for a long time now and I'm starting to feel concerned?* The common thread with the enquiries was that the missing person was often, though not invariably, of Afro Caribbean heritage and in every case had a history of gang related activity and usually an extensive criminal record. Investigations in this area were detailed as ongoing, but surprisingly had been met with a wall of resistance. It seemed that regardless of the severity of the carnage, word had quickly been circulated to family and friends of the victims that nobody was to talk to the Police.

A final addendum which it appeared had originally been compiled in the days immediately following the explosion, was entitled *Resultant Casualties*. It detailed the names of forty-four men and carried the reassuring rider that at this stage of the investigation the list should be treated as a work in progress, because more names would be added in the coming weeks as further detail was forthcoming. This had seemingly proved an accurate prediction because the header, text and first thirty-two names of the deceased were neatly typed, while the next twelve entries had been made by hand and appeared to show a variety of different styles of writing. {*Presumably, this was a copy of the original in-house listing of those confirmed as deceased which originally comprised 32 names, and the 12 new names had been added to the sheet as they were reported in by whoever was on duty at that time.*} One typed name had been crossed through and then re-entered in pen on the same line, for no apparent reason. The original document was undoubtedly the in-house update sheet, but why someone hadn't taken the trouble to tidy it up and get it properly typed up before it was couriered north reflected badly on the way the administrative side of the investigation was being handled.

Closer scrutiny revealed the listing to comprise a mixture of proper and street names and in most cases a reference to both. There was a number logged after each entry, which related to the dead man's seniority in the specific crew to which he was attached. In a couple of cases the number was followed by a question mark. The area the gang controlled was also detailed, so you could begin to build up something of a thumbnail sketch, an example being:

Edward 'Heady Eddie' Brewster, (1), Senior Cutting Crew, Marylebone. Data in this section had been provided by the head of Gang Related Crime, a certain D.I. Calvin Mortley, of whom Litmus had a vague memory which at this stage he wasn't able to pin down.

Litmus looked up in time to see the train pulling out of a station that he thought he had successfully identified as Wellingborough. He sighed and tucked the report back inside his briefcase. It was apparent the account that he had just laboured through was a hotchpotch of assorted records that had been hastily photocopied and put together in order to give a semblance of a full and comprehensive report, but in reality, was nothing of the sort. What the hell; at least it gave him some facts to chew over. He leaned his head out into the aisle in time to see the students' *Who can balance the polystyrene cup full of lager on their head for the longest period of time while standing on one leg* competition reach a disastrous conclusion before closing his eyes so he could concentrate his thoughts on the course of action that would prove most productive when the bloody train eventually reached its destination.

CHAPTER SIX

London, Tuesday September 23rd 2025

The train slid comfortably into its designated berth in St Pancras railway station pretty much on time and the one-man welcoming committee provided by Jerome Whitcott was easily identifiable, lolling against a stanchion next to the exit barrier brandishing a copy of Private Eye magazine. In consequence, Litmus had little trouble in avoiding him. He put his head down, barged through the barrier, and struck out for the lower concourse which led to Kings Cross, before taking a further flight of stairs which led to the underground station. Fifteen minutes later he had arrived at Liverpool Street where he purchased a limp pasty and a luke-warm cup of something that was posing as tea but making a poor effort at the subterfuge. The train to Enfield Town was a little delayed but still got him to his destination inside an hour and by two o'clock Litmus had booked into a small but comfortable hotel, twenty minutes brisk walk from the scene of the explosion, using the name of Dunstable.

Upon arrival, Litmus deposited his bag in a suitable corner and made a brief attempt to get some of his shirts onto hangers. He then headed up the road and collected the hire car he had pre-booked, which he drove to the Edmonton, Tottenham boundary where he dumped the vehicle in a quiet street at the side of Pymmes Park. That done, he immediately headed back to the main road, crossed the line of congested traffic and by three o'clock had settled into a booth in a bar that had never been called Grouty's, but was always termed as such by the locals in honour of a long-deceased landlord who the vast majority of them would never have known. Five minutes later he was joined by Nigel Woodberry.

Woodberry was tall, thin and sallow and appeared painfully malnourished. He was extremely well dressed in a slightly old-fashioned pin striped suit, matched with a tie that blended so well with the colour of his shirt that there had been little point in tying it around his neck in the first place. Woodberry bore a look shared exclusively by the persecuted and put-upon. He didn't fit in with the ambience of the bar and seemed immediately aware of the fact. Grouty's exuded the knock about air of a casual liaison where there would be no recriminations from either party if it didn't work out. Woodberry came across as the sort of person who would only have crossed the threshold once he had double checked that the glass cleaning machine had received its annual service and none of the bar staff had ever been hospitalised with an unpleasant infectious disease. The pub and Woodberry seemed unlikely to become happy bedfellows. A divorce, citing irreconcilable differences, should have been entered into immediately the two parties first came into contact, and certainly not delayed until there was the remotest chance that they might become better acquainted. Out of kindness, things of this sort should be nipped in the bud at the earliest opportunity, because in the great scheme of things they were destined never to be.

Litmus decided to leave Woodberry to order his own drink which proved to be a mistake as it led to a heated exchange with the barmaid over whether his large gin had been requested with a bitter lemon or a bit of lemon. Woodberry lost an eight-round bout on points and settled in opposite Litmus looking like a man with a score to settle.

'Typical of you, Litmus. Why we couldn't have met somewhere where the bar staff were vaguely familiar with the Queen's English, I have no idea.'

'There's a nice ambience in here,' said Litmus. 'Anyway, this far from the river we're not likely to bump into any unwelcome faces, are we?'

'So, what can I do for you?' said Woodberry tasting his drink and grimacing. 'It's not a social visit, I presume. Eight years if it's a day and not so much as a solitary post card. Rumour had it you were out of the game altogether these days. Joined the Police Force or had gone insane and moved north, or something of the sort. Tell me, Litmus, strictly off the record, was it anything to do with Arthur Rochester falling down that flight of stairs? Did they bring pressure to bear? You can tell me, you know. You'll remember, I was always able to keep a secret.'

'A small favour', said Litmus ignoring the Woodberry entreaty as if he hadn't spoken. 'Just looking for the inside track on the explosion up the road that's got everybody chasing their tails.'

Woodberry didn't hesitate.

'Nothing to give on that one I'm afraid. Exclusively a police operation once we established to our satisfaction that the Ivans and the Towel Heads weren't in anyway involved.'

'Come on Nigel, don't tell me head office isn't overseeing every development in case there's collateral in it for future exploitation? Just think of the Brownie points if it came to a happy conclusion because they had indicated the pathway that led out of the enchanted forest without the need for a trail of breadcrumbs. Pats on the head all round if that happened, I would have thought.'

Woodberry looked vaguely uncomfortable.

'No can do, Litmus. I've moved upstairs since your rather abrupt departure, but only as far as the third floor so they still keep me on a pretty tight leash.' He paused, but only for a second. 'Seen anything of Whitcott lately? You were quite the blue-eyed boy at one time, weren't you? He took it badly when you took your ball home. As far as he was concerned, you'd committed a personal slight. I hear he's hobnobbing with the mandarins these days. Were you aware? I hope they count their fingers after he shakes hands with them. I know I always did.'

'Don't change the subject, Nigel. Look, all I'm seeking is a guiding light. A small piece of tallow to help an old friend see his way home on a darkened night.'

'Sorry, Litmus, more than my life's worth. You know how it is. I was never Mr Popularity to start with and everybody hates a snitch.'

Litmus shrugged. 'No matter, I can pick the word up from another source. Just offering you first bite at the cherry. No big deal.'

'Thanks for taking it so well, old boy. You know I would if it were at all possible. It's just with the never-ending stream of redundances you have to be so careful these days. It only takes the slightest blot on your copybook, and you find yourself top of the list when they conduct the next review. We're all nervous, I can tell you. Everybody's got an exercise book down the back of their trousers just in case.'

'It's really not important, Nigel. Don't give it another thought. Confidentially, and please keep this under your hat, I'm doing a bit of undercover investigation for one of the big beasts down at Westminster. He was fully intent on going straight to the higher echelons, but I advised him to hold his horses because I had a contact who had been around the block a few times and could possibly circumvent the need for any bawling down the phone and all that sort of unpleasantness. You know how it is with the high and mighty. Westminster hates to have to ask, and the top floor at Five despises the fact they can never say no, because it wasn't really a question. Don't be concerned, Woody old chap, I made certain not to mention you by name so there will be no repercussions.'

Woodberry suddenly seemed a lot more interested. 'This big beast, Litmus, roughly how large are we talking?'

'A hunting trophy if he ever got bagged, Nigel. Enjoys a regular seat at God's right hand. Word has it he might come to inherit the kingdom and all the principalities in the fullness of time. That's if the meek don't get in there first, but as we both know, with the way politics is today, there's bugger all chance of that happening.'

Woodberry extended his hand, but instead of shaking with Litmus, he seemed to reconsider and instead pulled gently at the cuff of Litmus's sleeve in an odd and slightly creepy gesture of supplication.

'It has been such a long time since we got together, old chap. A lot of water under a lot of bridges since we were raw recruits sharing a desk. Bright eyed and bushy tailed back in the day, weren't we? What the fuck happened to that? I hope you aren't in a rush to get somewhere. I reckon we deserve at least a couple for the road.'

Woodberry pursed his lips in thought and appeared to struggle to find the words he was looking for.

'If by chance I were to pass on a smidgin or two on the subject you mentioned earlier, I suppose you could see to it that I was mentioned in despatches....... on a confidential basis, naturally?'

He checked carefully around the room, then bundled Litmus back into his seat and set off for the bar where he seemed to reach an immediate accommodation with the barmaid, because he quickly re-emerged from the small crowd that were watching the horse racing on the television, burdened by drink refills, an assortment of nuts and several packets of crisps, all carefully balanced on a very battered tin tray. Woodberry regained his seat, breathed out theatrically and puffed out his slender chest.

'So, Litmus, how specifically can I be of help?'

Litmus feigned disinterest, but felt it wasn't his most convincing performance.

'General SP really.' Then feeling obliged to retain the analogy. 'The runners and riders, who's got form, and who looks good for the course and distance. Anything by the way of tips that you picked up from the stable but considered it wise to keep to yourself would also prove a big help, I'm certain.'

Woodberry pulled a face.

'No need to be obscure, old boy. We're old friends round this table so let us talk plainly. I'll just read off the hymn sheet the way Five views the situation and you let me know where a little clarification might come in handy. I realise you will be a little rusty on the protocol these days having been out of the game for a while.'

He paused to compose himself.

'Well....the Investigation is officially being headed up by a D.C.I. called Sangster, a man of considerable experience but precious little acumen; and he's making such heavy weather of getting his arse into gear that he should be cannon fodder if matters remain unresolved for very much longer. Not that that will trouble Sangster unduly. He's only six months short of pensionable age and from what we hear can't get out of the door fast enough. Sangster's number two is a woman called Christine Ho, Anglo-Chinese, new school and a lot brighter than Sangster, which begs the question, why is she being kept out of the firing line? A strange woman by all accounts but certainly not short on ability, so why she is being kept away from the day-to-day stuff is anyone's guess. The important peripheral players are Organised Crime and Gang Related Incidents both of which fancy their chances of emerging into the limelight wearing the victor's laurel wreath despite the fact the case is actually nothing to do with either of them............but more of that in a minute.'

Woodbury stopped to take a sip of his drink and make an unsuccessful attempt to open a packet of salted nuts.

'Now, this is where it begins to get interesting. It has been positively determined that the deceased were approximately fifty in number and nefarious by intent. I presume you've seen the list of probable cast-members? Thugs to a man, it has been positively confirmed. The sort of people it's an absolute joy to see taken out of the loop by any means possible.'

'On the face of it, it seems extremely probable that the explosion of that bomb deprived the world of a large part of the elite echelons from street gangs north and south of the river. Targeted hit in anybody's book. Not the slightest doubt about it. There is even speculation that there might have been participation from further afield but that is yet to be confirmed, and personally I find it unlikely in the extreme. London gangs look down on the provinces as you are no doubt aware, and they wouldn't spit on anyone from outside the M25 corridor if they caught them on fire. How the hell this number of reprobates managed to organise themselves into a mass meeting when they share so little love that they regularly fight to the death over ten yards of neglected turf on a derelict housing estate is open to debate....... but, once again, we'll get more into that a little later.'

Woodberry stopped to fish a small chunk of lemon out of his glass and give it a delicate squeeze. Litmus reached for the nearest packet of nuts and opened it with an aplomb that spoke of countless hours spent pondering the meaning of life when he should have been doing something more constructive.

'Organised Crime is headed by an Inspector called James Leeming, the walking definition of a hard-arsed old bastard, and he has a strong fancy that the bomb was planted by the Albanian brotherhood that currently enjoy exclusive rights to the supply of class A into the Square Mile. They are well organised, very well-armed and extremely vicious, so there is no saying that Leeming is wrong on that score. Leeming's deduction is based on the fact that there had been a series of minor scuffles between the Albanians and local gangs in the months leading up to the explosion. The fact that none of these confrontations could be described as anything meaningful doesn't signify much. These days it's all about showing respect and saving face in the dark little world these cretins inhabit, so you can easily get utter carnage resulting from someone tripping over an outstretched foot. And the final piece of the jigsaw as far as Leeming is concerned, is that the explosive used in the massacre was Semtex, which as you are fully aware is manufactured behind the old Iron Curtain and in consequence is more easily sourced by an outfit with good connections in that part of the world. Like I say, he could be right. It certainly isn't beyond the realms of possibility; except to my mind Leeming's developed a bit of a fixation with the Albanians and that could be warping his thinking. He's experienced and crafty, but you wouldn't describe him as the sharpest chisel in the box.'

A quick slurp and a swallow of three or four skilfully accessed peanuts and Woodberry was once again ready to rumble. He was really enjoying himself now, Litmus could tell. He had a captive audience of one, but that was probably one more than he had been used to in recent times.

'Gang Related are also showing a big interest in this one. They are headed up by one of the bright young things that have been fast tracked through the ranks to help with the ethnicity quotas. Calvin Mortley is barely out of short trousers and is several shades browner than you. He also boasts a black belt in karate, which probably came in handy because he was raised on the rough end of an estate that bordered London Fields. One of the major strengths he brings to the table at Gang Related is that he not only speaks the language and understands the motivations of the current set of street thugs, but for reasons that I don't pretend to understand, they still regard him as one of their own. Good old Calvin might have gone over to the dark side but, deep down, they reckon, he is still a brother under the skin. His other big plus is that he hears things. If there's word on the street, then Calvin Mortley gets to know what's being said before a lot of the gang leaders become aware of it themselves. His networking facility is second to none, which is mind boggling when you consider which side of the fence he's on.'

A furrow crossed Woodberry's brow and he broke off.

'You're being straight about this, aren't you Litmus? To put no finer point on the subject, I could really use a leg up with my career right now. Things have been tough for the last couple of years, but I've invested too much in the job to consider getting out.'

Litmus smiled. 'Have faith and you shall be rewarded, Woodberry. When did I ever let you down?'

Woodberry returned the smile as if to say, *frequently,* but none the less appeared satisfied with the response. He even condescended to loosen his tie and undo the top button of his shirt, something which Litmus could not remember ever having witnessed in all the years he and Woodberry went back. He picked up his monologue without the need for a prompt.

'The Mortley take on the situation is rather different from Leeming's. He's picked up word........ that's all you ever get with Mortley, no names, so there's never any chance of getting back to the source........ that the gathering of the clans was put together by an important visitor from over the water. Someone with bucket loads of kudos flew in from the West Indies, snapped his fingers and the locals immediately stood to attention and saluted. Sounds preposterous I know; and if it were anyone other than Mortley who was telling the tale I would dismiss it out of hand, but that fellow didn't manage to clamber this high up the treacherous mountain slopes at his tender age by being wrong very often.'

'Did you get a name?'

'Jeremiah; biblical prophet, wasn't he? Christian or surname unspecified initially but now thought to be followed by the moniker Jones. Spook central checked out the last six months' incomings from Jamaica and registered a blank, so it might be that for once brother Mortley has been bowled a googly. I wouldn't place a great deal of money on it though. Mortley's a bright cookie and doesn't have a history of making silly mistakes.'

Woodberry sat back in his seat and took a good bite at his drink. He looked a lot happier than when he had walked in the door and Litmus reckoned that wasn't entirely attributable to the booze. The pink flush his cheeks had acquired rather suited him. The man now looked three parts human, which was two and a half up on when he had come through the door. Working for the Security Services could take a lot out of anybody, something Litmus could confirm from bitter experience.

'Want a tip on the outsider I wouldn't entirely rule out?'

Litmus blinked in surprise and made an effort to immediately refocus. He had thought Woodberry was finished his narration, but it looked like there was more to come.

'The way I see it, the answer to this conundrum is best solved by figuring out who had most to gain. Who exactly would be occupying the comfy chairs when the music came to a stop? Let's run it through and see where it gets us.'

A small pause while he conjured a knowing look, then straightway he was off.

'The smaller gangs probably benefitted very slightly but can you imagine any of them being able to organise an operation on this scale? Trust me, not a snowball's chance in hell. The Albanians? They already have The City stitched up tight and have always been operating with limited numbers which aren't as easy to supplement as once was the case. Try though I might, I can't imagine them wandering all over suburbia where they could easily get picked off by the locals a few at a time. Outsiders? Who exactly? The mafia are more interested in property speculation and laundering money through the London banks. The last thing they want is a spotlight being shone in their direction when they are busting a gut to appear legit. A terrorist's main aim is to undermine stability and order. They might try to infiltrate an established network if it offered a base for future operations, but they certainly wouldn't want to put out of action one that was already functioning efficiently. So, who benefits, Litmus? You're a clever fellow, you tell me.'

Litmus decided that actually he wasn't, so he kept his mouth shut. He shrugged his shoulders and waited to be informed of the answer.

Woodberry seemed pleased by the lack of response.

'The question wasn't entirely rhetorical, Litmus. I have a hypothesis, but I'm reluctant to share it because it scares the shit out of me. When you think about it, the greatest beneficiary from that explosion up the road was the state itself. The citizens of this country are those who served to gain the most. Want me to go a little further or do you think I'm starting to sound paranoid?'

This was getting interesting. What exactly was Woodbury trying to say. Before Litmus could begin to speculate Woodberry had pushed ahead without any need for encouragement.

'The logistics involved in an operation of such colossal ambition would in themselves be a deterrent to anybody with limited resources and even a small degree of sense. It's not even as if the perpetrators showed any inclination to cut corners. They didn't make up explosives from weed killer using a formula concocted by some nutcase on the internet. They acquired Semtex, and that stuff isn't something you score from your friendly local dope dealer after the pubs have closed on a Friday night. The rebuilding programme, probably a bodge-job, granted; nonetheless someone had to have the knowledge to purchase the materials, obtain tools, organise the workers and give directions as to how things were supposed to proceed............and don't forget they had already needed to be smart enough to blindside that man Oates, the owner of the site. In other words, they needed finance and a fair degree of technical knowledge in a number of spheres. The undertaking would in my opinion be totally impossible unless you had money, resources, a high degree of training and a fair amount of logistical brain power. So, we can automatically limit the outside possibilities to the Mafia, al Qaeda, a Columbian drug baron sensing the chance to forge an opening in a fast-expanding market, or at a pinch the Chinese Triads, were they not already totally absorbed with their own set of problems in Hong Kong. Can you see any of them dipping their toes in this particular pond, because in my opinion there's more chance of meeting a hedgehog carrying a handbag.'

Woodbury paused and stared meaningfully across the table.

'However, if you move the telescope round by 180 degrees and look inside the castle rather than out over the moat, then the possibilities increase considerably. There are the various Security Services, the upper strata of the Policing network with open access to a disaffected member of the bomb squad, the more sophisticated army units, a fixated arm of the establishment with their own agenda utilising hired labour and money from abroad.......and so it goes on. In short, an operation like this would be very much easier to organise from within some arm of the state machine or even a militant offshoot, than from the outside.'

'So, are you proposing state sponsored terrorism or something?' Litmus ventured.

'No. I have to admit that would be too ridiculous to seriously contemplate, though now that you've mentioned it, it does give you cause to stop and think. It's no less plausible, than trying to pin it on some evil genius from the mythical unknown. What I'm trying to say, Litmus, is it's one of those situations where it's virtually impossible to find a premise that is even vaguely believable because absolutely nothing fits neatly into place the way that we might hope; and on that basis alone I'm finding it impossible to rule anything out.'

CHAPTER SEVEN

London, Wednesday September 24th 2025

Litmus rose early and ate a hearty breakfast before setting out to climb the hill that led to the scene of the crime. He had slept surprisingly well and felt better than he had any right to after drinking far too much the previous day.

He pocketed a bottle of water to avoid being poisoned by the vile liquid coming out of the north London taps, and hit the road the minute he was able to extract himself from an in-depth conversation with his landlady about the best time to plant spring bulbs; a subject he knew less than nothing about.

The hill in front of him was steep from a Londoner's perspective but barely qualified as a bump in the road by Sheffield standards, where the nature of the terrain suggested local inhabitants would benefit greatly from cloven hoofs and a wooly coat. He ascended at a good pace and had very nearly reached his destination, when the smell on the wind stopped him dead in his tracks. God, it was awful. Like an airborne eruption of rampant decay. How the residents of a respectable neighbourhood like this were putting up with such an assault on their nasal passages was beyond him. It was like living in the middle of a stagnant swamp.

He forced himself to press on, and it was only when he was standing with his forehead pressed up against the plywood structure that marked the periphery of the cordoned off area that he appreciated just how powerful the explosion must have been. It would have come as one hell of a shock to the orderly lives of the nearby residents, and doubtless would be dined out on for many years to come.

He yanked apart a length of red and white tape that was impeding his progress, choosing to ignore the warning notice hanging from the remains of what once would have been a good-sized tree. He squeezed carefully through a gap that wasn't really large enough to accommodate a man of his girth and came to an abrupt halt. In front of him, he was confronted by what could only be described as a waterlogged morass. Nothing stood more than inches above ground level and the foul stench coming from combustible material that had been saturated in water still hung in the air three months after the explosion had taken place. If this were the impression it gave on a bright day in late summer, he dreaded to think how it would appear in the teeth of a winter's gale. It was positively other worldly. A direct attack on the senses. No wonder the area remained still cordoned off after all this time.

He instantly withdrew the derision he had heaped on the report he had studied on the train coming down. There had been nothing to use as building blocks to construct a more reasoned explanation because there was nothing of the slightest consequence that hadn't been totally devastated. It looked to him like a clip from one of the old News reels depicting the horrors of no-man's land in the First World War. Add to this scene the barbed wire and rotting corpses and an accurate depiction would have materialised right before your eyes.

No matter how grizzly, the original setting at least offered some sort of barbaric context. Here he saw only utter devastation. A place where human frailties weren't a lesson to be learned from, so much as a morbid obituary to an opportunity that had already been lost. An apocalyptic vision of a future that nobody would have the desire to live long enough to witness. Feeling like a traitor to a cause that had already ventured some distance past possible redemption, he turned and struggled back through the hoarding and was very much relieved when he once more felt solid tarmac materialise underneath his feet.

'Mr Litmus I presume........or are we sticking with Mr Dunstable for the time being?' enquired an authorative female voice. 'You're not meant to go in there, by the way, not even with your newly acquired green pass. It's strictly off limits in case further analysis is required, unlikely though that might sound.'

'Hi Ho', said Litmus, a reflex action that immediately had him cringing in horror. 'Hello, Ms Ho ......Inspector. Sorry, you caught me completely by surprise.'

'How do you know my name and rank, Mr Litmus. I can't remember us ever having met?'

'How many Chinese lady detectives do you think there are in the Metropolitan Police, Inspector?' You are very easy to spot and already held as something of a legend, I'm led to believe.'

'Don't believe everything you are told, Mr Litmus, and for the record this Chinese lady detective was born in Hammersmith, yet despite that fact has yet to acquire an English sense of humour. Two things you might find it worth your while remembering for future reference. And while we're on the subject of locations, how did my team fail to make contact with you yesterday? I had someone on the station at St Pancras, someone at Enfield Chase and someone up the road at Oakwood. Your friend, Mr Whitcott, wasn't at all happy. Deeply concerned for your welfare, was the way he put it. It's not always easy to judge if Mr Whitcott is being sarcastic or sincere.'

Which was precisely why I decided on the alternative route, thought Litmus, edging a little further away from the Detective Inspector who didn't look in the best of moods. A minder was the last thing he needed. If he was going to screw-up, he was more than capable of accomplishing that without help from anybody else.

'I'd suggest you opt for sarcasm, Inspector Ho. It works for me every time. As for us failing to make contact, I'm like a phantom in the night. A regular chameleon. I have an ability to blend in with the pavement,' Litmus ventured amiably.

Ho didn't look impressed. She clearly hadn't exaggerated about her lack of a sense of humour.

'To make it plain, Mr Litmus, I've already reached the conclusion that you are not a person I feel I can altogether trust. There's something about you, I'm not sure what it is. I have an instinct for these things. I've worked hard to get where I am and anybody who does anything to jeopardise further advancement in my career gets their name written into my little black book. And you are not only in there, Mr Litmus, but already you've earned a star against your name. Something of a record for a person I hadn't until two minutes ago met in the flesh.'

Litmus shifted uncomfortably. He unthinkingly kicked at a loose pebble which bounced off the hoarding and veered in the direction of Ho's car. All in all, this wasn't going as well as he might have hoped.

Ho hadn't finished. As it turned out, she was only warming up.

'I was told you worked in policing for several years, so I pulled your file and found it fascinating reading up to a point. You always had a reputation for pushing things a little bit too far, didn't you, Mr Litmus? Pushing perhaps being the operative word. Never quite knowing when enough was enough. The point at which it was wise to leave well enough alone. Not an ideal mindset for policing in the modern era. These days we are more drawn to team players. Prima donnas are a little high maintenance for our current budget and in my experience rarely provide value for money.'

'Oh, and I was really interested to read the accident report relating to the death of your partner. I think I would have gained a real insight into your personality by speaking to him, but of course that will never be possible because he's long dead and buried. Partners get to know every tiny detail about their counterparts, as I'm sure you will agree. They have to, because the reliability of the man standing closest to them in a moment of crisis could prove the difference between life and death. Weren't you the person standing next to D.S. Bonnet when he died, Mr Litmus? Rather demonstrates my point, don't you think? I did manage to find out that Harold Bonnet was reported to be unhappy and distracted in the weeks leading up to his death, and I wonder what might have caused him to feel that way. If I ever get to find the answer to that puzzle, I'll be sure to share it with you. You can certainly trust me on that.'

Litmus backed further away, but he wasn't escaping so easily.

'If by chance you happen to be in conversation with your friend Mr Whitcott before I get a chance to phone him with my report, you might mention that he'll be receiving a bill for yesterday's fiasco. And one further thing Mr Litmus; mess me about like you did yesterday on one further occasion and I will make it my business to see that your body is discovered under a paving slab, not blended in with one. And assuming that is entirely clear, I think that satisfactorily concludes our discussion for today; unless of course, you have anything you would like to add?'

Without another word Inspector Christine Ho stalked off and got into her car, before viciously dropping the clutch and accelerating away at considerable speed.

Litmus watched Ho's departure with some trepidation. He had wanted his enforced assignment to be completed with the minimum of stress. He certainly didn't want to be making waves, and Ms Ho looked like a bad person to rub up the wrong way. Oh well, you couldn't please all the people. At least she hadn't asked why he had failed to answer his mobile which as far as he could remember was still buried at the bottom of his travel bag. Presumably, that was how D.I. Ho had managed to track him down. He had been told that it was possible to get a pinpoint location of a person's whereabouts even when the bloody things were turned off.

Litmus checked he wasn't being observed by anyone else, then quickly gathered himself and walked half a mile in the direction of the town centre. He then turned about face and returned to the site before setting off in the opposite direction.

There it was. He knew there had to be one not too far away on a busy A road like this. The Ridgeway

Rendezvous, a roadside diner in the modern idiom, or a cafe with pretentions if you were talking to anyone over the age of thirty-five who didn't listen to loud rap music with the windows wound down when they were driving a car. Nothing special, just somewhere you could grab a coffee, a bite to eat and possibly even a beer providing you had shoes without holes and looked like you knew how to behave yourself. No tablecloths of course, but the Formica tabletops gave the impression they had experienced the recent ministrations of a sponge cleaner, and the plastic sauce bottles weren't gummed shut by a glutinous mass. Whoever ran this place should be given a pat on the back. A brave attempt was being made to offer a smiley face to the outside world.

It was early in the day by the standards of this sort of establishment which generally stayed open late into the night to accommodate the needs of long-distance lorry drivers and random insomniacs. Custom-wise they would presumably be setting out to attract a little bit of anything that was going in these decidedly uncertain times. Passing traffic heading for the motorway, the odd local who wanted to get out to stretch their legs but didn't fancy straying too far from home, young courting couples conducting their liaisons on a tight budget, white van men delivering parcels, people who trimmed your privet or manicured your lawn until it looked like a bowling green. It was probable all branches of society would be treated with the same welcome or indifference regardless of their wealth or status. When you were doing your bit to get an increase in custom, one person's money was very much as good as the next.

Litmus turned back to face the road and observed a large, shabby looking building a couple of hundred yards further on that might possibly be a hospital; he wasn't sure and would need to check his map to confirm if that were the case. If he was correct the diner would also do a good trade in take-out sandwiches and burgers as well as offering a refuge for stressed doctors, nurses and ancillary staff at the end of an arduous shift. This place was perfect. If anything, it fitted the image he had conjured up in his head just a little too well.

Early in the day was perhaps a good time to ask a few questions in the hope of a civilised response; with breakfast a distant memory and lunch still some way off, this was probably his best chance of getting a few answers without being pointed to the door. He headed through the entrance, grabbed a window seat that offered a first-class view across a virtually empty car park and was quickly engaged by a waitress called Sharon.

He knew she was Sharon because it said so on the plastic badge that was pinned to her green uniform just above a formidable left breast. Excellent. So far, his luck was holding. The place seemed entirely empty, and the waitress looked pleased to have someone to serve to fill in the time.

Litmus engaged his best smile. 'Just a black coffee and a scone with butter, please. Has it been quiet like this all morning, or did I just fall lucky?'

'Dead all morning', said Sharon, with what seemed like genuine regret. 'It's the weather. Everybody's taking advantage of the sunshine. I hate it when it's like this. It really makes the morning drag. A good downpour and they'd be fighting for seats, but not much chance of that today.'

Good; a talker, thought Litmus.

'Must admit I've been hitting the outdoors myself. You never know how long it's going to last, do you? Walked up from town. That hill's a bit of a killer isn't it.'

'Tell me about it. Try doing it with two shopping bags when you're pushing a pram. Taken years off my life that hill has.'

'Just walked past the bomb site and had a look through a gap in the woodwork. One hell of a mess and the smell's really shocking. Have you heard when they're going to get round to sorting it out? Never seen anything quite like it, and I've seen a few demolition sites in my time.'

'You haven't seen the half of it. There was rubble all over the place before the storm arrived and it sunk into the mud. God alone knows what they'll find when they excavate the ground properly. I reckon there's rotting bodies down there that will never be found. I go cold whenever I think of it. It's a bloody disgrace and God knows when they'll ever get round to sorting it out. I hope it isn't down to the council because they're bloody useless at the best of times. We're still putting plastic sacks out for the dustmen round here, when everywhere else had wheelie bins fifteen years ago. I reported my gutters six months back and still haven't seen any sign of a workman. They couldn't run a whelk stall that lot down at the town hall.'

'Bet they were all in here after the explosion, weren't they?' said Litmus trying to steer the conversation onto more fertile ground. 'Did you get to see anyone off the telly? They say that Fiona Bruce can be a bit of a madam when things aren't going her way, but I liked her on Antiques Roadshow.'

'Nearly took the front off the building, that explosion did. See the crack in that window over there; we're still waiting for a glazier to sort that out and he's been promising to come for three months or more. No, we only got the gawpers. Plenty of those, mind you. All the big knobs would have finished up somewhere a lot posher than this. They'd be on expenses, wouldn't they? That sort always are.'

'What about the blokes who were doing the actual building work. I bet a few of them came in for their breakfast. Only natural with you being so close at hand.'

'Never saw hide nor hair except for a couple that sometimes slipped in for a quick beer when they were on their lunchbreak. Only in for about half an hour but they could shift three bottles each in that time without breaking sweat. One of them used to pack a couple of cans of Guinness in his lunch box to take out as well. Men and their beer. My fella's just the same, bloody waste of space that he is.'

'Were they Polish like they said in the newspapers?'

'Probably. They definitely didn't talk like they came from round here.

Oy John, those builders from the site up the road; were they Polish? They used to talk to John a bit, the builders,' she added in less strident tones.

'They used to talk to you about football, didn't they John?', she yelled at the top of her voice.

'John's a bit deaf', she mouthed confidentially in Litmus' direction, screwing up her face so she could overemphasise each word with her lips, without making more than the slightest sound.'

Litmus hadn't seen John lurking in the shadows nursing a cup of tea. He was probably in his late seventies, wore glasses with thick frames and looked like one of those South American tree frogs that had evolved to blend in with their natural surroundings. His old jacket melted in with the décor of the cafe to absolute perfection.

'Alright if I join you, John?' Litmus enquired before moving over to his table quickly before he had a chance to reply.

'Sharon, can you fix John up with another mug of tea?'

John eyed the new arrival with lip curling scepticism.

'Not a copper, are you. I don't talk to coppers. Only, you ask a lot of questions if you're not a copper. I'm not half as deaf as she thinks,' he said nodding towards the other side of the counter where Sharon had turned on the radio and was busy knocking out a moving rendition of *Girls just want to have fun*'.

'Market Researcher,' said Litmus, 'but one day when I'm retired, I'm going to write a book about my experiences on the road. Sorry, I'm afraid you're one hundred percent right. I do ask too many questions and I'm afraid I always have. My teacher at school said I was born with an enquiring mind and one day it was going to get me into big trouble because it was only a matter of time before I poked my nose in where it wasn't wanted, and someone took offence.'

Seemingly satisfied by the explanation, John fished out a battered tin and started to tailor a roll-up as thin as a bootlace.

'Can't smoke indoors anymore, fucking Government,' he added as if this was news straight off the presses. 'One of the great pleasures in life was a cup of tea and a fag, and now you have to go out in the carpark if you fancy a quick drag. Smoking outdoors was regarded as uncouth when I was a lad and now we're forced to do it if we don't want locking up. The country's going to the dogs.'

John coughed to emphasise the level of life's injustices.

'Where you from, anyway? That accent don't nearly match the colour of your skin.'

'Sheffield,' said Litmus.

'Wednesday or United?' John enquired, quick as a flash.

'Neither,' said Litmus, 'though I've watched both teams over the years. I'm not often at home at the weekend so I've completely given up on football except for catching it on the box; especially since they ruined the game by introducing VAR, offsides when any fool can see that they're level and the bloody stupid hand ball rules that change every five minutes and nobody understands. I still follow the results every week just like the rest of us mugs, but I really don't know why I bother.'

'Hillsborough, Sheffield' said John, settling into a narrative he obviously enjoyed. 'I was up there for the semi in '67. Got pissed as a rat celebrating us winning and was sick out of the train window on the journey home,' he added with unmistaken relish. 'Couldn't get a ticket for the final though. Crap game that was, but at least we won.'

'Bit before my time', said Litmus, managing to summon up a note of sincere regret.

'Not Polish, not all of them anyway,' said John out of the blue. 'East European for sure, but not Polish; not the ones who came in here. My sister married a Pole. Drank like a fish, he did; used to keep vodka in the fridge and drink it neat with his morning breakfast if the weather was cold. Bloody uncivilised if you ask me, but I had to admire his spirit. Colour of piss and it tasted like petrol, but Jesus it was strong; two shots of that and you could forget about getting to work. You'd do well to find your way out of the front door. Scared to strike a match in case the whole kitchen went up in flames; couldn't let him get within a yard and a half of the cooker, just in case. Dead now, God rest him, but he used to mumble away in Polish when he'd put away a few and it didn't sound the same. Don't speak a word of the language mind, but it didn't sound right, the way I remember it.'

The order arrived and Sharon wiped down the table and called John a dirty old git with a distinct note of affection. The discussion broadened into politics, the fallout from Brexit, the raft of pub closures in the local area, and how football on the television was being strangled to death by the intervention of BT and Sky Sport; but Litmus made no further progress on the subject that interested him most until he had shaken hands and was ready to go.

'The builders; Albanian. I'd put money on it,' said John as if he was replying to a question that had just been asked, and not something they had been discussing half an hour previously.

'Why Albanian?', Litmus asked, trying to keep his level of interest as muted as possible.

John sighed as if Litmus was an errant child missing the most obvious of answers to a straightforward question.

'They supported Tirana, didn't they? Tirana. They were in the UEFA a couple of years back, surely you remember. Albanian team, Tirana, aren't they? An educated man like you, I'm surprised that you didn't know a thing like that.'

CHAPTER EIGHT

London, Thursday September 25th 2025

Litmus awoke to find the sunshine of the previous day had turned to light rain. He showered, ate a hurried breakfast in order not to get further engaged on the subject of spring bulbs, and prepared for the road. He had no real idea why he had received the summons from Calvin Mortley, but regardless of the reason it would be interesting to meet up with Gang Related Crime's head man face to face. Mortley said he would be travelling from his home in Walthamstow, so he had picked out somewhere that was about midway between the two locations for them to meet up. Litmus wasn't that familiar with the area and so was in no position to contradict a man who was on his home turf. He didn't have any clear idea where Waltham Abbey was situated but the satellite navigation system seemed confident, so he relaxed a bit and followed the directives laid down by the lady with the authoritative voice.

After leaving the cafe yesterday, he had followed a downward trajectory until he located a nice area of wooded parkland, bisected by a river that seemed in no great hurry to reach anywhere at all. It couldn't have been far from the town centre, if his sense of direction was right, but you would never have guessed it by the tranquillity of the setting. If it hadn't been for the faecal deposits provided by the flock of Canada geese that appeared to have taken over the area, the situation would have been almost idyllic.

Upon arrival, he had located an unoccupied park bench and sat mulling over recent events, in an attempt to put them into some sort of context. Everything seemed to be falling easily into place, possibly a little too easily. Maybe he had hit a lucky streak for once in his life: long may it last. At the rate he was going he would be in a position to write up his findings in a matter of days, never mind a month, and that would suit him admirably.   Whitcott had hardly indicated he wanted anything too deep and meaningful. Just something that indicated the current line of enquiry wasn't entirely bizarre; and as it seemed the investigation was going in several directions at the same time, or more specifically making no progress whatever, he could probably get away without being overly precise.

On an impulse he had returned to the hotel, dug in his bag, retrieved his phone and powered it into life. Then, ignoring a host of incoming texts and missed calls, he phoned Beth; only to check in and hear what he hoped would be a friendly voice, he told himself. She picked up straight away and gave him a precis of what had been happening, all of which sounded fairly uninteresting if he took it at face value.

The woman he had been working for when his orderly life had been interrupted by Jerome Whitcott's unscheduled visit was threatening to sue him for leaving her in the lurch. Beth said she had calmed her down as best she could and apologised profusely for the fact that he had experienced so little success in tracking down her missing husband, but the lady said she would probably sue him anyway. One of the hoses at the back of the bathroom sink had mysteriously become disconnected and caused a small flood, but the man from the nearby second-hand book shop had known a neighbour who used to be a plumber and he had fixed it in no time at all. (She had paid him out of her own purse because the key to the top drawer of his desk was missing and there had only been a woodlouse and a bit of fluff in the box marked Petty Cash.) No new clients had yet materialised, but she had been talking to the woman who ran the dry cleaners across the road, and she said at this time of the year it was always a bit slow for everybody, no matter what type of business you were in. As instructed, she had opened the post and there were several more final notices and one solicitor's letter, but she suspected that it might not be genuine because the wording was different from the others that had recently been received. There was still no sign of the actor who was renting the attic room, so she had been unable to talk to him about the back rent that was owing. She had forgotten to put food out for Rufus the fox last night and the animal had taken umbridge *and knocked over all the flowerpots in the garden and chewed some of the flowers. She was of the opinion that Rufus didn't seem to like her very much. It could be that it regarded her as an interloper on its territory or was maybe jealous. Oh, and his cannabis plant had died. She thought she might have over watered it because it had turned a peculiar shade of brown and all the leaves had fallen off. So, all in all everything was fine, and she hoped he was relaxing and getting to see a few shows in the West End while the opportunity presented itself.*

The sat-nav woman bought him back to the present with a firm instruction to take a right at the monument in the centre of the road and continue on for half a mile after crossing a railway bridge. A little further down the road he was advised he had arrived at his destination. Litmus promptly dumped the car, paid an extortionate parking fee, and pottered off into a pedestrian precinct that probably hadn't changed drastically for the last thousand or so years. A picturesque church, that he later found out was the abbey that earned the town its title, loomed majestically over a courtyard that boasted a couple of decent looking pubs and the increasingly rare vision of a proper old-fashioned pie and mash shop. Litmus walked on and located the café that had been specified for the meeting without undue difficulty. Only one table was occupied by a brown face, so he took it for granted Calvin Mortley had been successfully located. He took off his jacket, pulled out a chair and stuck out his hand.

Mr Mortley was indeed on the young side for a fully-fledged Detective Inspector; little more than thirty by Litmus' reckoning with hair only marginally short of full-blown dreadlocks and a six o'clock shadow that even at this early hour of the day was closing in on eight-forty-five. He looked very fit, but street fit; exhibiting no evidence of the showy but ineffectual muscle obtained by the use of steroids or wasted hours doing weight training in the gym. He was obviously keen to maintain his street image because he was immaculately dressed in an outfit of clothes that marked him out as the man you hoped you spotted early enough, so you had adequate time to cross to the other side of the road without making it look obvious. So much so, that he was already attracting sideways glances from a group of middle-aged ladies seated at a large table in the centre of the room; but whether that was because of his film star profile or the fact he looked like he might at any second pull out a knife and hold it to someone's throat, was open to speculation.

Mortley sized Litmus up with one penetrating glance, then cut immediately to the chase.

'Thanks for coming over at such short notice. I am having trouble figuring out how you fit into the bombing investigation, Mr Litmus, so I thought there was no harm in us meeting up so I could ask you face to face. It's the only way I'll know if you are telling me the truth.'

Litmus bristled at the opening salvo but when he spoke, he was careful to keep his voice soft and calm.

'Firstly, I don't fit *anywhere* into this inquiry, well not in any conventional sense; secondly, nobody is supposed to be aware that I'm down here, let alone *why* I'm down here, so maybe you would like to tell me who tipped you off; and thirdly, if my understanding of the situation is correct the investigation you are referring to has nothing whatever to do with you, so what's your interest? Lastly, call me Litmus without the mister; the front end always makes me feel slightly uncomfortable when it's coming from somebody who I'm beginning to very much dislike.'

Mortley completely ignored the questions, but none the less smiled and even seemed to relax a little.

'Touché, Mr L, spoken like a true Tyke. No offence intended. I'm feeling a little raw this morning, that's all. Any chance I can encourage you to expand a bit on the reason for your visit or are you Yorkshiremen tight with your words as well as your money?'

Litmus maintained eye contact but nodded his assent.

'Alright.........I'm here to write a short report on the direction the bombing investigation is taking. The reason I got chosen appears to be primarily because I'm the same colour as you. The person appointing me being under the clear impression that as far as his superiors are concerned brown is very much this year's black.'

Again, the answer appeared to satisfy Mortley, who didn't even look a little surprised. The waitress arrived and Litmus ordered coffee and a pastry to get rid of her before he lost the opportunity to pose a question of his own.

'Now one for you Mr Detective Inspector. Why are you showing so much interest in a case that, if I understand correctly, doesn't fall under your jurisdiction.'

Mortley, stared across the table for the best part of half a minute apparently in deep thought. He then ran his fingers through his hair as if he were attempting to brush crumbs from a dinner table.

'You really can't be that dumb, Litmus. Are you putting on an act or is this the real reason they gave you the job in the first place?'

'Sorry to be a disappointment. It's no act; I am most definitely that dumb. Any chance you could enlighten me.'

Mortley gave another one of his meaningful looks but didn't waste too much time blending it with malice this time around.

'OK, try this for size. Doesn't anything strike you as peculiar about the way this investigation is being conducted?'

'Like what?', Litmus countered. 'Bear in mind I'm the new boy from the sticks and I've been down here for less than twenty-four hours.'

Morley sighed. *Like*, it's being led by a DCI who knows as much about the supposed victims in this case as the hole in my back passage. *Like*, his Assistant Detective Inspector, who is a grade A bitch but can at least walk and chew gum at the same time, appears to be spending all her time straightening paperclips while the investigating officers that should be following her directives run round in ever decreasing circles. *Like*, the fact I'm recognised as the card-carrying authority on the various gangs operating in the London area, and to date nobody has so much as knocked on my door and enquired where these people can be located. *Like*, the general feeling of apathy that's exuded like exhaust fumes from anyone connected to this case, which is starting to feel like an epidemic of sleeping sickness. *Like*, the general sense that getting to the bottom of what happened to the victims that got blown through the roof doesn't seem to be any sort of priority. *Like*, the fact everyone directly connected to this case gives the impression they are more concerned with tidying up the living room after the party's over, instead of investigating who might have committed the crime. Want some more *likes* Litmus because I've got a bucket load of them to spare?'

Mortley hesitated for a second to take a breath, but immediately was back on the bus.

'Have you ever walked into a room full of stoners when you were totally straight? After a couple of minutes, you experience role reversal, and it begins to feel like you're the one who's out with the fairies. That summed up the feel of this investigation right from the word go. Nothing about it feels in any way right. Surely, it was obvious to even those of the most meagre intelligence that I should have been given the lead. OK, if they wanted a D.C.I. in charge for appearances sake, then put me in the number two seat and tell the ranking officer to keep the hell out of my way. It doesn't matter to me who gets the credit once the case has been solved as long as I get to call the shots while the investigation is ongoing. All I'm interested in is getting some results.'

Mortley's phone rang just as he seemed to be getting into his stride. He checked the number, snorted with derision and immediately directed the call to voice mail.

'Listen, Litmus, I knew a lot of those homicidal fuckers that were blown up on an intimate basis. I played in the street with them, went to school with them, grew up with them, even in some cases hung out with them. Then one day they turned to the left at the same time I took the decision to turn to the right; but that didn't mean I suddenly stopped understanding every thought that went through their twisted little minds. Believe me when I say, I can still read them like a book. Half the time I know what the dumb arsed fuckers are thinking before they know it themselves.'

Keen to prove his point, Mortley immediately changed tack.

'Listen, a few weeks back I spoke to a girl I keep in touch with from the old days; pretty little thing but seriously crazy in the head. Until recently she lived with a meathead called Mouse who ran a good-sized firm on the other side of Poplar. Mouse didn't block out a lot of daylight, but nobody jumped the queue to get on the wrong side of the man because he was a vicious little mother; but he and the girl had been an item for a lot of years, and their relationship was solid as it comes. I speak in the past tense because the girl hasn't clapped eyes on her man since he walked out of the door on 29th June, so it's pretty much certain that he is one of the dumb arsed bastards who is currently pleading mitigating circumstances in front of the pearly gates.'

Mortley leaned in closer scanned the room and lowered his voice by a couple of octaves.

'The lady couldn't tell me much about what went down because Mouse wasn't a big talker. All she knew was that word had been put out to the top dogs all over London to get their arses hauled over to a meeting that was going to be addressed by someone called Jeremiah who was over from the Indies and looking to set up a new type of deal. She said she could tell Mouse had been lit up by the prospect, but all he would say on the subject was that he thought it was going to be the start of something big.'

'Any chance I could talk to the girl? Perhaps just for a couple of minutes?'

'Over my dead body, Litmus. Don't you know anything at all about what is going on out there in the big wide world?

Word has been put about that anybody seen talking to representatives of officialdom should hold back payments on their retirement policy. The idiot fringe might be getting themselves banged up all over this fair town of ours even while we speak, but that doesn't mean the old laws aren't still enforced when the need comes about. No matter what the circumstances, you never talk to the Police.'

Litmus thought quickly. 'I'm not law enforcement in case you hadn't noticed. If not the girl, someone else perhaps? Anybody who was even vaguely connected would probably be a help.'

'What part of no don't you understand, Litmus. No! Do you want that answer written up in braille?'

'OK, OK. Don't get excited. What do you know about this Jeremiah character?'

'Not much unfortunately; a lot less than I would if I were calling the shots, and the little that has come through appears to be more rumour than fact. Jeremiah Jones comes across as a mixture of crime guru and urban myth. Someone who doesn't fit very neatly into any damn box. As far as I've been able to make out, he's what you might call a facilitator. A sort of make-it-happen man who has the confidence of the Yardie fraternity in Jamaica, connections to the drug lords in Columbia and knows the people that count in Eastern Europe. What he was intending to put together this side of the water is anybody's guess but he sure as hell must have sold it well because gangland cooperation was never high on the agenda of any of the weasels I've got into discussions with in the last few years.'

'Why don't you try meeting up with Sangster and running this past him. It can't do any harm, and if things are going as badly as you think with the investigation, he'd probably be delighted to welcome you on board.'

'Don't you think I gave that a go already? All I got was a straight order to get back on my bike and start pedalling; and the bastard outranks me, so I've got to at least appear to be towing the line.'

Mortley seemed to be getting more and more agitated so Litmus decided he might do worse than appear the voice of reason.

'The trouble with you, Mortley, is you've got an outraged sense of injustice over something that happens in the Police Force every day of the week. It's not about you personally or any sort of prejudice. It's about total incompetence. They are happier having the investigation in a safe pair of hands, no matter how ineffectual, rather than someone like you who is quite likely to end up rocking the boat.'

'Not in this case, Litmus. The stakes are too high for the top brass to let a deaf man conduct the orchestra this time around. Well, not unless there's a specific reason for them doing so. The more I've thought about it the less sense it makes. There's nobody else equipped to be running this show. If I weren't so well adjusted, it would be easy to end up with a complex because it's obvious I'm being blind-sided for no good reason at all. What's the matter, am I black or something?'

For a minute they looked at each other, before bursting out laughing. The party of ladies at the centre table gave inquisitive glances and clearly wanted to be included in the merriment.

Litmus tried to kick Mortley under the table.

'Shut up you bloody idiot or you'll get us both chucked out.'

Then, feeling more relaxed than he had since he had walked through the door Litmus pressed on.

'Think about it, D.I. Mortley. It's not hard when you sit back and add up the numbers. They know it's going badly so the arse covering exercise is fully underway and gathering speed by the minute. In fact, if you look across the table, it's staring you right in the face. I'm being employed to say that despite difficult circumstances this investigation is being carried out to the highest possible standards and the public need be in no fear because, despite all evidence to the contrary, everything that is currently happening is absolutely fine; and they know I can be trusted when delivering this verdict because I'm from outside the fold and have the same colour skin as you and a lot of the headcases that got themselves blown up, so why would I report back anything other than the truth?'

Mortley gave another one of his penetrating stares.

'And that's the complete limit of your ambition, Litmus? It doesn't worry you in the least that mass murder has been committed and nobody seems overly interested in finding out why it happened?'

'No, Mr Mortley, it really doesn't. I can safely say, it doesn't trouble me one little bit. Sometimes you have to bow to the inevitable when it's very clear that nobody is looking for answers. Personally, all I want to do is get this whole mess catalogued and shoved in a neat little file so I can pack my bags and head off home.'

CHAPTER NINE

London, Friday September 26th 2025

Much to his surprise yesterday morning's meeting had extended into yesterday afternoon. He and Mortley had ended up eating pie and mash on a very damp bench outside the abbey before retreating to a handy pub to wash it down with several too many beers. They had discussed the case in greater depth, then veered off into careers, bugbears, annoyances and very much more. Mortley had proved interesting company once he had loosened up a little and Litmus had been more than happy to listen and learn. In no time at all he had gone from petulant adversary to brotherly confidant. A little too quickly, possibly. It was difficult to tell.

There was little doubt Mortley was a highly driven individual, but if you scratched below the surface there was more to him than that. He was a man who spent each day walking a precarious tightrope, aware that the slightest slip could prove disastrous. He was obliged to inhabit two distinctly different worlds, doubtless conscious that his success in one was largely dependent upon his access to the other. For Mortley, each day must seem a little like being a spy masquerading as a diplomat in a foreign country. Everybody in the business would know his true vocation and yet, when it suited them, people might still choose to whisper the odd word into his ear. He would be freely used by anybody who judged he might best serve their purpose. The failure of an enemy equated to a home team success when you tallied up the points at the end of the season.

In this respect Mortley made a unique contribution to the Metropolitan Police Force. If you frequented the Badlands, you didn't under any circumstances cooperate with the law; and yet if the circumstances were right, you might feel free to pass the odd tip on to Mortley, because by some warped social distinction he wasn't seen as the enemy. You could use Mortley in the same way he would most certainly use you. They must be extremely strange circumstances for the Policeman to cope with on a daily basis.

Litmus wondered, how much Mortley remained a man of the street, and how much it had now become an act? Only the Detective Inspector with his big ambitions for the future knew the answer to that. It struck Litmus that the role Mortley was playing must have a limited shelf life, and that its sell by date might not be too far in the future. Nothing stayed the same for ever, and how long would it be before another generation took over the running of the street firms, relegating Mortley's relevance to that of a redundant fossil whose usefulness had come to an end. Mortley was by no means dumb. There was little doubt he would recognise how this situation was bound to develop, but what exactly could he do about it? Without a change of career path, the quick rise through the ranks could be followed by an equally rapid decline. The force was no different to anywhere else in that respect. Friends and allies could prove extremely short on the ground once your usefulness had effectively come to an end.

The day had run on convivially, but Litmus didn't learn as much as he had hoped because Mortley never seemed fully able to relax. Even when the detective did make an assertion it was difficult to decide if he was speaking from the heart or just presenting a viewpoint in order to try to gauge the reaction it might solicit. Mortley seemed like an actor on stage who was permanently trying to measure the mood of his audience, never at rest, constantly probing; but when you considered the nature of Mortley's job, that perfectly represented the situation he would find himself in on a day-to-day basis.

The weather had eventually brightened a little and the local ale had proved very decent so there was nothing for him to complain about. If he escaped this trip without being breathalysed it was going to be a minor miracle, and he didn't have the slightest excuse to offer to a court in mitigation against any charge that might be coming his way.

Yesterday seemed a very long time ago as Litmus prepared to once again hit the long and winding road. If any new information were going to be forthcoming it would probably be found in the immediate locality, and he had been tasked by Whitcott to undertake *a little detective work* so that was precisely what he now felt obliged to do. The weather had once more brightened. It wasn't exactly sunny, but the clouds looked like they were only going through the motions rather than seriously threatening rain. The area that would have the greatest chance of yielding results would be that between the bomb site and the railway station at the top of the town. It would probably be a waste of time enquiring if shop assistants had come into contact with men who might have worked on the building renovation, but it was better than sitting in his hotel doing mental gymnastics or staring at the wall.

Earlier in the day he had made repeated phone calls to D.C.I. Sangster who was leading the investigation into the bombing, but pleas for him to grant a short interview had made little progress. *Sangster was unavailable and there was no point in repeatedly phoning this number with the same request*, he had been informed by a subordinate officer who didn't seem in the least sorry about the fact; and no, D.I. Ho wouldn't be available any time in the immediate future to assist Litmus' enquiries by filling in a few blanks. If they were so damn busy, how was it the investigation had made so little progress? Three months had elapsed since Sangster had been appointed to head up the team and in that time it was difficult to see that any significant advancement had taken place.

Oh well, it could be worse. At least it wasn't raining. He would start with residences close to the site and work on to food shops, garages and pubs. It was reported that the site workers arrived and were collected in a large white van, but there must have been occasions when that didn't exactly go to plan. They had been working at the site for the best part of two months in all weathers, after all.

It occurred to Litmus that it might be worth checking with staff at the local train station as well; not that train stations appeared to be overburdened with staff working in any capacity these days. Gone were the good old days when porters were on hand to carry old ladies' bags and solicit for a tip. Still, there was always a chance that an alert ticket collector might remember something unusual that had come to his attention; but if such an individual actually existed, you would have thought Sangster's team would have tracked him down by now.

By lunchtime, Litmus' enquiries had made little progress, and by six o'clock with commuters from the city already confronting the last leg of their journey home, he decided it was time to put away his notebook and cut his losses for the day. As a reward for having walked for nine hours solid, while achieving nothing but two aching feet, he decided he had earned a pint of best bitter, and as the thought came to his mind a suitable hostelry hove into view.

The pub looked presentable from the outside. A proper dispensary of vintage ale. Not somewhere that gave the impression it suffered from the tables being over polished or boasted hi-tech hand dryers in the gentlemen's toilets. More the sort of place that had been standing where it was for a few hundred years getting on with life and interfering with no one; a place that wouldn't take kindly to being turned into a kebab shop or a pizza bar the moment it dropped its guard.

Litmus placed his order, gathered his drink along with a packet of crisps and quickly headed for a bench in the open air. There had been nobody in the smaller of the two rooms that he could annoy with his enquiries and the couple of bodies he could detect slouching in hard backed chairs in the off-shot vestibule to the main bar had been playing dominoes and didn't look like they would welcome an interruption to their game. At least the weather was still holding up and the lure of breathing in more carbon monoxide fumes from the passing traffic was hard to turn down. He could also enjoy the sight of ravaged commuters returning home to their loved ones. A spectacle that always made him feel grateful for his bachelor status when he had a pint in his hand.

He settled at a convenient bench to ruminate. Taking the positives from his day of enquiries would not take up too much of his time, so he might as well get it over with as quickly as possible: a woman from a block of low-rise flats on the top road said she was fairly sure she had seen small gangs of builders heading in the direction of the town centre in the late afternoon on more than one occasion. However, she had no idea whether the workers had been working at the hotel renovation project or elsewhere and couldn't be sure exactly when the sightings had taken place. A baker who also traded in sandwiches and hot pies said he had sold lunches to people wearing paint splattered overalls and speaking with a foreign accent on a number of occasions, but couldn't specify precisely when those encounters may have taken place. The downside didn't really bear much thinking about if you weren't a connoisseur of salivating dogs with large teeth and short tempers, or people who weren't overly delighted at having been interrupted from their viewing of daytime television programmes that were holding their interest. In consequence, Litmus brushed these horrors from his mind and focussed his attention on two small boys kicking a ball around on a surprisingly well-kept area of grass just across the road.

After a couple of minutes, the overweight bloke who had served him at the bar came out for a cigarette and they exchanged meaningful nods. He followed Litmus' eye line and shuffled nearer the road so he could get a better angle to view the spectacle that was attracting his customer's avid attention.

'Wish I had done more of that and less of this when I was their age', he said, simultaneously indicating the kids kicking the ball and the cigarette burning away between his fingers. 'I was halfway useful as a young 'un but these days I can barely raise a gallop to run for a bus.'

'I never had the talent', Litmus admitted. 'Fine on the physical side: I could get up and down with the best of them, but I never had the touch. Terrible shame, but the difference in earnings between playing that game at a decent level and what I do now only ever amounted to a few million quid a year, so don't get the impression that I'm bitter about it.'

The bartender chuckled softly and eased onto the bench next to Litmus.

'Only Duane and Arthur in there at the moment and they've got full glasses which if I know those two will last half an hour, so there's no real point in me rushing back.' He nodded his head casually towards the pub, took a long drag at his cigarette and blew a perfect circle of smoke that drifted off on the breeze.

'I've got talking to more people since you have to go outside for a fag than I ever did when all I had to do was nip to the other side of the bar. When I read all that stuff in the papers about people being lonely and finding it impossible to get a social life, I always feel tempted to write back and advise they take up smoking. Granted, it will probably kill them in the long run, but I can guarantee they would never be short of someone to talk to while they were still alive. Added to which, it would guarantee a decent turnout for the funeral, and some people hold a lot of store by that.'

Ah, a philosopher, Litmus thought.

'I sometimes wonder if we encourage it', Litmus responded in kind. 'Not smoking. Being lonely. I think people can be very impressionable when it comes to emotions like loneliness. There they are, perfectly happy to be sitting down watching the television or reading a book and then somebody tells them they must be lonely because they're doing it by themselves. Then in no time at all that message begins to play on their minds and they start to worry about something that didn't bother them one little bit until it was pointed out. A sort of insecurity inflicted by people who should be minding their own business and keeping their thoughts to themselves. We never had this problem before we started training up thousands of psychiatrists every year. I can honestly say that some of the happiest moments in my life have occurred when I was completely by myself. Nice to meet you by the way, my name's Litmus.'

'Gordon. A pleasure to make your acquaintance,' they broke off briefly to shake hands. Gordon took the opportunity to light another cigarette.

'I sometimes wonder if they should issue different colour mood badges. That way you could wear green if you were feeling sociable, red if you wanted to be left alone and amber if you were still trying to make your mind up. It would be very useful for young people going to a dance, wouldn't it? Especially the ladies.'

'Sound idea, Gordon. You've obviously given this sort of problem deep thought. You been in this place for long?'

Gordon considered. 'Forever, seems like. Six years this Christmas but it seems like forever. It was this or working as a delivery driver for one of the supermarkets and my back's not what it used to be since I fell off a ladder about a decade ago.'

Litmus turned so he could gauge the reaction.

'A stupid question, Gordon. Hope you don't mind me asking. Did you ever get foreign builders dropping in lunchtime or early evening May, June time?'

Gordon viewed Litmus speculatively. 'You a copper?'

Litmus shook his head.

Gordon looked him up and down and nodded to indicate that was the right answer. That was the second time he'd got the same reaction when posing a question. Was it his face? Perhaps he should consider gelling back his hair or growing a beard.

'Nothing lunchtime that comes readily to mind. Under normal circumstances I don't come downstairs until nine on a weekday so I can't be sure about early evening. Today is what you might call an unusual situation. My teatime cover is taking a cat to the vets, so I got landed with filling in. It always comes back on the Landlord in the end. If you call back later, you could maybe ask the question of Sam. We have happy hour from five to seven thirty on weekdays in the summer and it usually gets a few through the door. No point after August Bank Holiday. Nobody would be tempted across the threshold early evening if we were giving it out for free.'

'Makes sense; what time is Sam expected?'

'Tonight? Working half eight 'til closing as payback for me doing the early turn. Always assuming that the cat stages a recovery, that is. Tricky operation that one. You can't stitch them back on once the decisions been taken, you know.'

'Right, I'll drop back later, maybe,' said Litmus, not feeling entirely sure that it would actually be worth the bother.

'I'll let Sam know to expect you,' said the landlord with a smile.

CHAPTER TEN

London, Friday September 26th 2025

He knew in his heart it would turn out to be a total waste of time. A waste of time that Litmus deeply begrudged because it would involve him in a further walk that he really didn't fancy after pounding the pavements all day. However, on the basis that it was Friday, and only really sad people went to bed early on a Friday night when they could be experiencing the unfettered debauchery on offer from a strange town, he went back to the hotel, had a shower and changed his shirt, before setting off back down the road. If he were being honest his decision had little to do with the prospect of meeting up with Sam the barman and a lot more to do with imbibing a couple of pints of ale, which by the standards of the southern muck usually on offer down this way wasn't quite as bad as he had been expecting. Later, he would treat himself to an Indian or a Chinese, because since breakfast he had only eaten a meat pie, half a Kit-Kat and a packet of cheese and onion crisps.

First viewing of the night-time activities at the local hostelry proved something of a disappointment. Alright, he hadn't been expecting Sodom and Gomorrah, but this was a bit underwhelming no matter how low you had set the bar. In fact, compared with the activity in the rest of the pub the game of darts in the public bar looked like an eruption of unabandoned hedonism. Only half of the tables were occupied, and he struggled to see anyone under pensionable age seated at any of them. Even the two dogs asleep under their owners' benches looked like chasing a ball would have put them at the front of the queue at the vets the following morning, and the juke box in the corner was playing something that American servicemen had boogied up the gangplank to when they were intent on liberating Europe in 1944.

Litmus sidled to the bar; was it his imagination or had everything suddenly gone ominously quiet? He looked for a friendly face that he could address loudly in warm tones to confirm that this particular brown man came in peace, but Gordon the licensee was nowhere to be seen. OK, Sam would do. At least it was a name he could throw around with a small degree of confidence; so where the fuck was Sam?

A girl who had been crouched down shelf stacking beer bottles beyond his range of vision suddenly materialised in his eyeline. Litmus jumped back startled.

'I know I didn't have much time to do my makeup tonight but that was a bit uncalled for!'

Under ninety-six and with a sense of humour. There clearly was a god.

'Sorry, bad week. Bad lifetime, to be honest. Please take it from an expert, you look extremely lovely. Pint of bitter and could you tell me where I can find Sam?'

'Four pounds fifty and you just did.'

There was a long pause while Litmus tried to think of something intelligent to say. When the silence had reached the stage of embarrassment, he gave up.

'Sorry again, I wasn't expecting.......'

'Don't worry. Nobody ever is. My Dad set his heart on having a son so don't call me Samantha if you value your life. I'm still trying to live down not making the school's first fifteen at rugby. The look of hurt in his eyes will stay with me to my dying day.'

Sam brushed the hair back out of her eyes and smiled to indicate she was joking. She seemed to be stalling in order to gain time to form an opinion.

'Gordon told me to expect you. Sorry, can't talk now, but if you want to park yourself over by the door, I'll be finished up here by about eleven thirty; but I can't hang around for long because I need to get home to Pat and Eric. If you need to get off before then, I'll be down here tomorrow from five. There's no happy hour, but if you play your cards right, they'll probably let you join in in the arguments over the football. Gordon tells me you're a fan.'

'Thank you. I'll hang around if that's alright by you.' Litmus looked back over his shoulder. 'In the meantime, I'll stand over by the door and try to avoid being hustled into a game of dominoes. They'd take me to the cleaners by the look of them.'

Litmus retreated to the corner to bide his time. Sam seemed warm and friendly, but possibly his assessment was affected by the fact she was the only person in the pub who didn't produce an ear trumpet when you started a conversation.

He turned his attention to his pint and peeped furtively over the top. Nope, his eyes hadn't deceived him, she was gorgeous alright. He located a seat in the corner and exchanged smiles with a couple of geriatrics who were probably exchanging tips on models of Zimmer frame currently of special offer. Smashing looking girl. He was beginning to begrudge being already in love.

Four and a half pints and two and a quarter hours later Sam arrived with her handbag clasped to her chest and a look of apprehension on her face. She glanced nervously at her watch which encouraged Litmus to voice an idea.

'If you live locally, could I perhaps walk you home? That way you won't be losing any time and your husband won't be worried because you're late back. We could maybe talk on the way. I've only got a couple of questions.'

'That's the first time I've had an offer like that since I was thirteen. Are you going to offer to carry my schoolbooks as well? Allowing that you aren't a sex offender that's a very sweet of you. It's only about half a mile but I need to stop off at the fish and chip shop on the way because I'm in the bad books at the moment. Pat's my sister and Eric's my cat, by the way. It's Eric who isn't talking to me at the moment, but a bit of fried cod might earn his forgiveness. We went to the vets this evening and more of him went in the door than came out the other way if you follow my meaning.'

They walked. Litmus asked both his questions. Sam responded with strangely noncommittal replies. Litmus bought three portions of fish and chips which they decided to eat back at Sam's flat. Litmus made up several more questions but didn't get a clear reply to any of them either. It was nice feeling walking at night with a pretty girl by his side, so Litmus had no cause for complaint. Sam texted while she was walking and continued to say nothing of value, and in no time they had arrived at their destination.

The sisters rented the bottom floor of an old house that looked extremely decrepit but would doubtless display lots of character when a firm of estate agents got their opportunity to advertise it for sale. They had been lucky to get it, Sam informed him. Living accommodation cost a small fortune on this side of the town.

Litmus was introduced to Pat who bustled round gathering plates and forks while smiling a lot. She seemed really nice and friendly, as opposed to Eric the cat who swished his tail looking sullen and resentful. They drank tea, ate fish and chips and talked about everything other than the subject he should have been pursuing; but for some reason Litmus really didn't care.

Sam's phone burbled and Litmus lost the thread of what he was saying. Everybody laughed. Pat yawned and collected the dirty plates. She retreated to the kitchen. Sam looked pensive.

'I've texted someone Pat and I know who might be able to help you but.......well it's complicated. He says he'll think about it and get back. I can't say any more than that because.........'

'Because it's complicated?' said Litmus.

She nodded and they both smiled.

'If you give me your mobile number, I'll give you a ring when I hear from him, assuming that I do. I think he'll get back. He's a good person. A very special friend.'

'Best offer I've had today', said Litmus. 'Well, to be honest, the only offer I've had today.'

They walked to the door. Sam opened it ushered him through and pecked him on the cheek.

'Thanks for supper and walking me home. It was very gallant, especially for this day and age. You are under sixty, aren't you?'

Litmus planted a farewell kiss that accidentally on purpose landed on the side of her mouth. Thankfully, she didn't take offence. They stood there for several seconds looking at each another, with neither saying a word.

'Push him out of the door or pull him in,' shouted Pat cheerfully. 'Either way, shut the bloody door. It's freezing in here.'

'Why are you helping me?' Litmus asked.

'I don't know' Sam replied. 'I can honestly say I haven't got a clue.'

CHAPTER ELEVEN

London, Saturday September 27th

Yesterday had been decidedly weird, but weird in a nice sort of way.

At least the ending had been good. Today had every prospect of being a different matter entirely. Today he needed to shine up his shoes and put on his big boy trousers, for at last he had secured an appointment to meet up with the all-important D.C.I. Sangster, who was nominally overseeing all branches of the investigation. Sangster, the old fox with years under his belt and retirement beckoning. Sangster, about whom he had yet to hear anything approaching a positive word.

Without access to the interviews Sangster's team would have already conducted, Litmus had little prospect of making further progress with his enquiry. At best, all he could claim to have so far assembled was a scrawny carcass with very little meat on the bones. There was more to be had but Sangster held the keys to the larder door. This was his big opportunity to get a better picture of what was really going on. No room for cockups. He really needed for today to go right.

He employed the train and the underground to reach New Scotland Yard so he would be able to have a beer with his lunchtime sandwich without being accused of endangering the lives of the lycra clad yobs that comprised the extensive cycling community which plagued the inner London roads like a swarm of locusts. Mind you, as most of the bastards including the silly-boy brigade reliving their childhood on electric scooters insisted on driving on the pavements, probably there was little to fear in that respect.

The current New Scotland Yard building was said to be neoclassical in design. Litmus decided that it was a distinct improvement on its predecessor, which had struck out strongly in the direction of neo-naff. He was forced to admit the structure looked very impressive from the outside, whilst at the same time appearing vaguely apologetic about its real purpose in life. Twenty first century policing, to Litmus' way of thinking, appeared to be less about arresting criminals and malcontents than ensuring you didn't offend their civil liberties while banging them up. No wonder the British public were getting increasingly disillusioned with being promised that a firm hand would be applied to encourage an adherence to the rule of law, when in reality the firm hand rather more resembled a soothing velvet glove clasping a mug of hot cocoa and a high fibre nutrition bar. It was blatantly obvious what the public expected of their Police Force and it was equally plain that in the current political climate they had very little chance of getting it. It was with some relief that he remembered it wasn't actually his problem anymore.

Litmus entered the building and approached the reception desk. He noted the aroma was more of floor polish and air freshener than sweat and urine and that there was no marked evidence of blood on the walls. Sad, but pretty much as he had expected.

'Litmus for C.D.I. Sangster', he proclaimed to the Receptionist. 'His eleven o'clock,' he added with a smile.

The lady behind the desk (was she an officer or a civilian? It was the sort of thing he felt he should have known but didn't) abandoned her sudoku puzzle and gave him her full attention.

'Chief Inspector Sangster has been unexpectedly called away on urgent business, Mr Litmus. He sends his apologies and suggests you make another appointment, but he asked me to point out that his diary is full to overflowing until well into next month.'

Litmus contemplated saying something rude but decided it would serve no purpose.

'Any chance that D.I. Ho is available?'

The Receptionist looked mildly scornful and shook her head. They had clearly anticipated a counterattack from that direction and taken the necessary steps to render it futile.

'Someone working on the same enquiry who could give me an update and access to the files?'

'Not possible, I'm afraid. Not without D.C.I Sangster's personal authorisation.'

'How about D.I. Leeming from Organised Crime?', Litmus ventured, more in hope than expectation.

The Receptionist was temporarily wrong footed with that one and forced to examine a chart that was laid flat on a shelf behind where she was seated. Litmus decided she was probably civilian because those legs didn't look like they had spent a lot of time pounding the pavements on a cold winter's night.

'Logged out on operations', she said with some satisfaction.

'Locally?' asked Litmus. Surely it had to be locally. This was the MET. They hadn't ventured outside a ten-mile radius of the Tower of London since the miners' strike.

'Really couldn't say', replied the receptionist, with evident annoyance that she had been saddled with one of those annoying people who didn't understand the meaning of the word *no*.

'Any chance you could give me his mobile number? No, don't tell me. More than your job's worth. Right, alternative plan of action; can you summon someone who can check out my credentials and then phone D.I. Leeming on my behalf and see if he could find the time to talk to me?'

'I could do that', she said with a fixed smile. 'It would be a pleasure to be of assistance. No need to be sarky; you only needed to ask.'

Just under an hour later Litmus found himself in Stoke Newington Police Station. The building had initially seemed eerily quiet when he had entered through the front doors, but this was an impression that was quickly dispelled. The bowels of the edifice, to which he was promptly conducted by a wizened Desk Sergeant who looked like he had just got out of bed, resembled nothing so much as the dressing room of a non-league football team minutes prior to them embarking on a third round FA Cup tie against Premier League opposition. Without warning he was confronted by several dozen hulking males in various stages of undress, a good number of whom were screaming some form of unintelligible gibberish at the wall in front of them. Having seemingly become involved in a mass escape from a lunatic asylum, Litmus endeavoured to pick up his pace, only to be unceremoniously deposited in a private area at the very back of the building that could conceivably have been utilised as a broom cupboard in a former life if it had been slightly larger and considerably better decorated.

'You took your time', said a voice that made its way into the room through a small opaque window with wire strips embedded in the glass that was open about a quarter of an inch. 'Be right with you. Just having a piss.'

D.I. James Leeming was a hulk of a man. He resembled a retired heavyweight boxer who had gone slightly to seed. His face was one that only a mother could love, but after assessing the body on which it was indelicately positioned it was unlikely anybody who retained a vestige of sanity would have been unwise enough to draw that conclusion to the Detective Inspector's attention. Leeming was currently stripped to a pair of sagging underpants and a sweat stained vest and appeared to be labouring under the impression that Litmus knew something that had by some means succeeded in passing him by.

'What do you think of it then?' snarled Leeming. 'Are you up for it or not?'

'Umm'

'Listen, let's get things straight right from the start: it doesn't matter to me one way or the other because it's happening regardless of what you think.'

'OK.'

'I've covered my arse as well, so you've got no need to be concerned about that. I've got papers as far back as

March and beyond that testify to the fact, so it doesn't really matter to me what your views are on the subject.'

'Right.'

'In point of fact, I don't give a flying fart whether you're with me or not, except it will help to keep the paperwork straight and that fellow up the road satisfied that I've complied with procedural etiquette. Procedural etiquette, Litmus! Don't make me laugh. I can't fucking spell it let alone abide by it. Who is this tosser with the fancy line in words anyway? Fucked if I know!'

'Sorry D.I. Leeming, you've lost me. In fact, to be perfectly honest you lost me right at the start.'

'Mr Litmus, straight question, are you signing up for it, or aren't you? Just let me know then I can decide whether to talk to you like a rational human being or chuck you through that window.'

'For what?'

Leeming took the one stride necessary to cross the room which now seemed even smaller than it had a moment ago.

'Are you telling me you haven't read it?'

'Yes, I've got a feeling I probably am.'

'When's the last time you looked at your text messages?'

'Look, I've been chasing across London all day. I haven't read anything except the adverts on the tube.'

Leeming let out a deep breath of exasperation which he punctuated with a loud fart.

'Right. Let's start from scratch. Don't be frightened to take notes. My name is James Leeming and I'm the Detective Inspector currently running the Organised Crime squad. Organised crime is....'

'Miss that bit out; I know what organised crime is. I used to be a copper back in the day.'

'Tonight, or more specifically this evening, fourteen of my officers led by me personally will be entering premises in the north London area currently occupied by a large contingent of gentlemen of Albanian extraction. We will be looking for illegal drugs, money that can't be accounted for, evidence of prostitution and/or modern-day slavery, illicit firearms and anything else that we happen to trip over in the course of our search. To paraphrase the above more concisely, in language you can't fail to understand: we are going to kick our way into a building inhabited by bunch of neanderthal lowlifes and rip the place apart in search of material evidence that will put that gang of Albanian bastards behind bars, or at the very worst on the first plane out of this country heading in the direction of the God forsaken shit-hole of a country from which they originated.........and heaven help anybody who tries to impede us in the course of our duty to Queen and country, because I can assure you we will be going in heavily tooled up and with a little bit to spare.'

Litmus reminded himself that earlier in the day he had been bemoaning milksop policing. He now seemed to have encountered a working example of the power of law enforcement when fuelled by utter determination infused with a strong dose of neat testosterone. He had to admit it was impressive even if it did scare him to death.

Leeming soldiered on.

'The way you figure in this is pretty basic, so no need to get out a notebook and pen. I have been instructed by some faggot called Jerome Whitcott, who has something to do with a Liaison Committee set up between the Security Services and Whitehall that until five days ago I had never heard of, that before I proceed to kick shit out of that bunch of Albanian cocksuckers, I need you to sign off on the operation. Yes Litmus, you did hear right. You are to sign off on my operation!!'

The horror of this situation appeared to render D.I. Leeming totally speechless.......but sadly, not for very long.

'The sign off is in relation to you being satisfied that the Albanian contingent in question were in your opinion partly or wholly responsible for the massacre of your people in the explosion of June this year; and, taking those facts into account, I was merely taking the opportunity to point out that whether or not you choose to put pen to paper is largely irrelevant to me because if you decide not to, I'll be going ahead anyway because I have a logged paper-trail that shows I had the Albanians under investigation for several months before that fucking explosion even took place. This might come as a surprise to you, Litmus, but because I can verify the timing of the initiation of the Albanian surveillance, I have indisputable grounds to proceed as I see fit because I am conducting an independent manoeuvre over which you have no jurisdiction whatever. So, like it or lump it, there's no way you will be stopping me from marching my men into that den of thieving bastards and in consequence you can make your own decision whether to sign off on it or not. Now, is that plain enough for you or do you need me to repeat any of the big words?'

'Hang on a minute, Leeming, let's get one thing straight from the beginning, they aren't *my people* as you so delicately put it. I'm not a representative of anybody in this. I've just been hired to write an independent report on the direction the investigation is taking and possibly make recommendations as to how it could be more effectively pursued. You know how it works, the sort of thing that's useful to have in your bottom drawer in case anything goes wrong, but which in ninety-nine percent of cases never finds its way into the light of day.'

Leeming was obviously taken slightly aback, and equally obviously didn't want to show that was the case. He mopped sweat from his brow with a red and green rugby shirt that appeared to have been abandoned by a previous occupant, while he figured out the best way forward.

'Alright, sorry, perhaps I might have got the wrong end of the stick on that bit. I thought you were some sort of legal creep representing the interests of that bunch of black bastards that got blown up, or some shit like that.'

'I think you are meant to refer to them as victims, D.I. Leeming, especially if there are representatives of the press in the room. Also, it's people of colour, these days, if you want to hang on to your job and you might be better to leave references to their parentage out the equation altogether. Listen, what the hell gave you the idea I was representing the deceased? Let's get it entirely straight. I am most definitely not representing anybody. In fact, my enquiries have so far turned up nothing to contradict your assessment that there was possible involvement by the Albanian faction, and I can see no good reason why you shouldn't bring them in for interrogation so you can confirm that fact one way or the other.'

Leeming caught his breath and looked slightly aghast.

'Bring them in? Well yes, if no other alternative presented itself then I suppose that could be regarded as a legitimate fall-back option.'

Leeming stretched along the bench on which they were sitting and retrieved a water-stained piece of paper from beneath a pile of discarded clothing.

'As you are broadly in agreement with my strategy, Mr Litmus, perhaps you would be kind enough to append your signature to this docket so I can push on with my preparations for tonight.'

Litmus signed while D.I. Leeming looked thoughtful.

'Listen, Litmus, as it seems we are seeing eye to eye on this one I might be able to do you a bit of a favour. The reason I'm so confident nothing can go wrong with tonight's operation is that the Neanderthals took possession of a drug consignment last night that we've been tracking halfway across Europe for the last three months. And we know for sure it hasn't yet been passed out to the pushers because for the last month I've had a man under cover on the inside. So, as we're batting for the same team on this one, I can perhaps see my way to giving you access to him for twenty minutes or so tomorrow morning if you want to come over. Would that be useful at all?'

'That, D.I. Leeming, would be extremely useful; and is it safe to presume that now you want me to make myself scarce?'

Leeming pulled a face.

'Afraid not. Please don't take this the wrong way, Litmus, but as of now you are on unofficial lockdown until such a time as me and my boys get to our target. Sorry, but we've had too many of these things blow up in our faces at the last minute to take any chances. You can head off home as soon as it is confirmed we are inside the building but not a moment before. And in the meantime, would you mind if one of my lads takes possession of your phone?'

CHAPTER TWELVE

London, Sunday September 28th 2025

It had made the ten o'clock news in an abbreviated version, and the Sunday papers were all over it, despite the fact it must have caused them to rejig their planned exposés at the eleventh hour. Litmus flicked through The Sunday Express while waiting for D.I. Leeming to complete his umpteenth statement to the press. This would run for days, and the weeklies were already chafing at the bit, doubtless feeling a tad peeved to have lost first dibs on one of the top stories of the year to their weekend rivals. Litmus could picture the pandemonium now taking place at the Northern & Shell complex a few miles off in the Docklands area of the city, as the retrospective on Princess Diana and the latest photographs of Amanda Holden or Elizabeth Hurley with not many clothes on were hastily shunted to one side in favour of the images of the blood strewn corpses that the previous evening had littered one of suburban London's main thoroughfares.

Litmus was not best pleased, having arrived at Stoke Newington late despite there being little traffic on the streets and the train departing precisely on time. He had overslept because that pock marked idiot of a Desk Sergeant had gone off shift without returning his mobile phone the previous evening, and for the last couple of nights he had got used to relying on it to serve as an alarm. Worse, when travelling home the previous evening he had been advised by a British Rail employee (who he sincerely hoped would burn for all eternity in the pits of hell, in the odd moments when he was dragged away from having little devils with pointed tails sticking pitchforks in his arse) that a train to a station obliquely referenced as Southbury Road was very nearly as good as catching one to Enfield Town. This hadn't proved to be the case and had involved him in a one hour walk in the rain after he had passed through the unmanned ticket barrier at the other end.

Still, at least things were now looking up a little. He was reunited with his phone, the initial press reports had proved broadly supportive of the previous night's Police action and, if his luck held firm, he had every confidence that in a few days' time he would be safely ensconced on a train destined for Sheffield with enough information to bodge up a masterly overview of the Police investigation and its obvious shortcomings.

After a further thirty-minute delay, Leeming emerged from the press scrum and gathered him up from his temporary refuge in the hallway which led to the back of the Police Station. The Detective Inspector exuded joyousness that knew no bounds and gave the impression that the smile on his face would at some stage need to be surgically removed. They exchanged pleasantries and quickly retired to the broom cupboard they had haunted the previous afternoon.

'Bloody triumph, Litmus. I've got those press bastards eating out of my hand. Nailed four of the twats, four of them; and two out of the four we have every reason to believe were higher ups! Eleven more taken into custody but three of those were women who were on the game and they will walk as soon as their Brief convinces them to say they were forced into service with threats of violence. Still, another eight that we can have meaningful discussions with until the Legal Aid Johnnies come stomping in with their size tens. That's one of the beauties of dealing with East Europeans, Litmus. They can't get their heads around the fact that something like Legal Aid can possibly exist because it is so alien to anything they had experienced in their own lands. In consequence, they very often refuse to engage with their legal team altogether, because they can't comprehend that someone has been appointed to represent their interests and is actually on their side. I tell you, Litmus, I couldn't be happier........well not unless we had shot the other eleven godless cock-suckers as well.'

Litmus cringed. 'Have you given an interview to The Guardian yet, Detective Inspector? Because it might be wise to............'

'Don't worry about me, Litmus. I'm a master at tailoring my speech to the audience. I'll be ready to tone it down for that set of tree-hugging, mealy mouthed, Trotskyite bastards, don't worry about that.'

Leeming paused to ponder a memory that was obviously rankling. Something that was bothering him, but which seemed too horrifying for him to share. After further contemplation he decided to get it off his chest.

'You know, Litmus, last night I was cornered by a bunch of those bleeding-heart liberals who wanted to know why we hadn't used tasers when we conducted the raid? This is the type of crass stupidity I'm now obliged to deal with on almost a daily basis, and it terrifies me to think of the direction in which we might be going. Can you guarantee to take someone down at five metres with a taser, Litmus? Of course, you can't. Besides, have you ever read of anybody being killed when they were hit by one of those stupid contraptions, because I know that I haven't.'

'No, I can appreciate that a weapon of that sort would be ineffective for the type of operation you were conducting, Inspector, and I will be certain to mention that in my report', said Litmus warily.

Leeming looked meaningfully at the door and lowered his voice by a couple of decibels.

'And did you notice that the initial report confirmed that every last one of those miscreant reprobates was shot in the chest, so when matters get referred to the Police Complaints Commission, as will inevitably be the case, my boys will come out of it smelling of roses.'

'Well, that's excellent,' said Litmus. 'Really fortunate as well, bearing in mind the way these things can so easily get misconstrued.'

Leeming moved nearer, winked meaningfully, then cupped a large hand near Litmus' ear.

'Luck didn't come into it my friend. It was down to planning.'

Litmus resisted an overwhelming desire to put his fingers in his ears.

Leeming smiled menacingly, tapped the side of his nose several times with his index finger and continued.

'We had someone on the inside, remember?'

Litmus did, and he had a horrible feeling he knew which direction this conversation might be taking.

'Our man came back with names and descriptions of everybody who crossed his path; sometimes he even managed to back them up with photos that he took on his phone. By the time we entered their premises yesterday evening we had an accurate idea of what everybody in the building looked like and even what they would probably be wearing.'

Litmus frowned. 'And in respect of them being shot in the front, this helped how?'

'We knew their names, Litmus. If somebody yells your name in a stress situation you turn round to face them. It's not a thought process, just an automatic reflex. Trust me on this.'

Leeming formed a gun with his index and middle fingers extending straight out from a clenched fist. He supported his wrist with his other hand and took an imaginary pot shot out of the back window.

'I think you might have heard my boys practising when you got here yesterday. Scream a person's name good and loud and you can bet that week's wages that they will be facing in your direction when you come to pull the trigger. Like I say, not luck, Litmus my friend, it was down to meticulous planning; and there were handguns that had been recently fired by the side of each body as well.'

Litmus shuddered, but decided it was best to let Leeming bask in the glory of the moment for a good ten seconds before moving the conversation on. This man was truly something else.

'Is it still ok for me to meet with your spy who was operating on the inside?'

Leeming pondered for several seconds, then appeared to remember his promise of the previous day.

'No reason why not. He's waiting in the front office up the hall even while we speak. Just two things before you start. You can talk with him, but you can't see him. You speak from in here; he answers your questions from out there.'

Leeming waved a giant fist in the general direction of the door leading to the large changing room which had been in full use when he had arrived yesterday afternoon.

'The door is opened just a crack and it doesn't get any wider if you want to have the equipment to sire little Litmuses at some stage in the future. Second thing, we are talking ten minutes here; ok, twelve minutes tops. I'm loading up now and I want my man out of this place and in the back seat of my car as soon as I'm ready to go. Capiche? Give me a second to fill him in with the rules and regulations I'm applying to your discussion, and I'll tell him to bang on the door when he's tanked up and ready to roll.'

The Policeman pulled himself to his feet, shook hands quite formally and immediately disappeared from view. Litmus heard a muffled exchange echoing off the walls at the other side of the door. This was followed by total silence. Two minutes later there was the sound of knuckles rapping on wood.

'What do I call you?' asked Litmus.

A hesitation. 'Anything, I don't care.......no, call me Belushi like the actor, a hero to many, but also a bloody mad man.'

'OK, Belushi it is. Tell me about your part in the operation.'

An extended pause. This chore had obviously been foisted on him at the last minute leaving no opportunity to prepare.

'D.I. Leeming told me to work under cover. No contact unless I had something important to report. No routine. We call it going blank. Unless we report in it is accepted that we don't even exist.'

Another pause.

'I was on the streets for weeks. Living in doss houses. Getting my face seen in pubs, arcades and snooker halls near to the target. I drank a lot. Told anyone I met that I was looking for work and wasn't fussy what that work involved. Got myself into a few fights which I made sure I won. Eventually I was contacted, interrogated about my background, and when that checked-out I was employed.'

'You must have been nervous.'

'I was, but my cover had been worked on with care so I knew if I kept my nerve and didn't say anything stupid there would be no problem.'

'I presume you are Albanian, Belushi.'

'No, English, but my parents were from the old country and Albanian was spoken in the house, so I am fluent in the language. Street Albanian you understand. Not like they would teach you in school. All the right curses in the right place.' Belushi laughed.

'The gang; did they put you on deliveries?'

'Sometimes; anything small and unimportant. I was pushing a broom, a lot of the time. Loading, unloading. I was the very bottom of the food chain......but gradually I became more accepted, and people began to talk to me.......a little at least.'

'And you built up a picture of the people involved in the operation. Took photos I understand.'

'Yes, it was easy to see who was important and who wasn't by how quickly people jumped when a command was given. Fetch me a bottle; yes, sir. Get me cigarettes; yes, sir. Not that shit tobacco, the good ones at the back of the cupboard; yes, sir. You learned very quickly how it was best to react. It wasn't hard to learn.'

'And you knew from D.I. Leeming a consignment of drugs would be delivered to the cartel very soon?'

'No, I knew nothing. Detective Inspector Leeming is a very careful man, and he trusts no one. I admire him for that even if he is also a lunatic like John Belushi.'

'Why do you say he is a lunatic?'

'Ha! Leeming, he hates Albanians. Sometimes even me, I think. But today he loves me because the operation was a big success, and tonight he will buy me many drinks and light my cigarettes. But tomorrow; tomorrow, who knows what will happen? Perhaps a very different day.'

'Leeming told me you are a very brave man, Belushi, and I know he thinks highly of you. He is obviously anxious to protect your identity, or we wouldn't be holding this conversation from two different sides of a wooden door.'

'That is because he hates Albanians and if he keeps me fresh like a daisy, he can maybe use me again in the future. One day things will go badly, and he will read a speech in my name and maybe cry a tear into a big handkerchief. But the next day he will think, huh. Why am I sad. He was useful for a while, but there is no point in crying real tears. After all, he was only an Albanian. Because no matter what I do I will never be English enough for Detective Inspector Leeming to completely accept.'

'Why the hatred?'

'I don't know. Perhaps he will tell me tonight when we are drunk, but somehow I don't think so.'

'This is probably a stupid question, but did you ever see anything that connected the Albanian operation with the big explosion that took place in June?'

'No, nothing. Such a thought to me is stupid.'

'Why do you say that?'

'Because the people who were killed were not dangerous; not important as rivals, in the trade.'

'But surely, that's exactly what they were, Belushi? Business rivals.'

'No, not rivals. Rivals fight over the same thing. This is two different things. It is like two countries selling the same shit to different places. No conflict unless you want the trade that the other person has. The blacks blow up the

Albanians; not likely, but maybe. The Albanians blow up the blacks; no sense.'

'I'm black.'

'Are you from one of the gangs? I don't think so, because if you were, you would maybe understand better that what I say is true.'

'I'm not sure about that.'

'Well, what about the trading?'

Litmus paused, was he losing the track of this conversation.

'What exactly do you mean.......trade........cooperation?'

'Yes, supplies.......the coke they sell on the street. If the Albanian gang had drugs to trade and someone from outside wanted to buy at the right price, then there was no problem, it was business.'

'Are you saying the Albanians bought drugs from the gangs?'

'No, never.'

'Then, are you saying the gangs bought drugs from the Albanians?'

'Of course, but only if they had more dope than they needed to supply their own customers in the City. Like I say, it's business.'

'I think I'm beginning to understand. You are saying it wasn't in the interest of the Albanians to get into conflict with people who could be their customers; and as customers provided a route to a market to which they had no direct access. Am I reading that right?'

'Of course, and that is why I don't think they would ever have a reason to cause the explosion. Who kills their own customers? Only a mad man. It would make no sense.'

'Why didn't you tell this to Leeming?'

'I did.'

Litmus wasted a full fifteen second feeling stunned. Had he really heard that right?

'Belushi, can you tell me a little more about the set up inside the Albanian organisation; the hierarchy, the way things worked?'

No reply.

'Belushi.'

No reply.

'Belushi.'

No reply.

It appeared the window of opportunity had just been firmly slammed shut.

CHAPTER THIRTEEN

London Sunday September 28th 2025

Litmus' return journey to the outskirts of North London involved a lot less drama than the previous evening. He grabbed a seat in a nearly empty carriage, closed his eyes and ran back through the previous twenty-four hours. The more he considered it, the more it became apparent he had been duped. D.I. Leeming was clearly a man with his own agenda, and he had become involved simply because he had arrived at Stoke Newington at precisely the wrong time. This had all been caused by that bastard Sangster ducking their prearranged interview. It was a fair bet that hadn't come about by accident, but there wasn't much he could do about it except fume.

Going anywhere near Leeming had been a poor judgement call but he couldn't rewrite history. He had walked into the deal with his eyes open and if there were repercussions, he would just have to take what was coming. You never knew how these things might pan out; there was always the possibility that his unlovely mentor, Mr Whitcott, might prove completely supportive of his chosen course of action, but on that score he certainly wouldn't be holding his breath.

Despite the seismic fall-out from the events of the past twenty-four hours his mind kept wandering back to the previous Friday evening. The possibility of making contact with somebody with first-hand information to pass on still offered far and away the best chance of him gaining a greater understanding of what had actually happened at the building site. Since regaining possession of his mobile, he had checked every five minutes in case a text had snuck in without him noticing. He fervently hoped he hadn't missed a communication from Sam while his phone had been out of commission the previous evening, but nothing was showing in the log of missed calls. Besides, it would be nice to talk to her again no matter how things had worked out with this possible contact. She and her sister had seemed really nice, genuine people and that commodity had been in short supply in his life for a very long time. To hell with the investigation. He was forced to admit that he wanted a reason to meet up with Sam again and any excuse would do.

At that exact moment, his mobile let out a dull grumble of complaint. If this were another offer of a penis extension or contact from the daughter of a Nigerian general who wanted to share her fortune with him, he thought there was every chance he would lose the will to live.

Incoming text. *Thought I had better text rather than phone. Heard from our friend and he's prepared to help (within limits.) I'll be in from eight if you want to drop round. Sam*
Outgoing reply. *Brilliant. L x*
Incoming text. *Don't eat. Pat making lasagne. Eight sharp. Trust me, it's good. S x*
Outgoing reply. *Ask her if I'm the sort of bloke she would consider leaving home for? L xx*
Incoming text. *She said to enquire if you are the owner of a vineyard or live in a castle?*

Litmus arrived promptly at eight, carrying two bottles of wine because he didn't know whether his hosts would be happier with white or red. As it happened, they didn't prove overly discriminatory in that regard, and with comparatively little assistance proved outstandingly successful in finishing off both. The food was indeed up to expectations and Eric the cat seemed to have regained his good humour following his recent trip to the vets, rubbing his body against Litmus' legs and even occasionally condescending to let out an affectionate purr. Lasagne was apparently a big favourite with Eric, which might have explained why one large portion was missing from the baking tray when it rested on the table prior to being served: but then again, possibly not.

After the plates were cleared and the last of the wine divided between glasses the girls got straight down to business. It seemed Sam had been designated to take on the speaking part, while Pat's role was to provide supportive nods at points that she considered appropriate, and interrupt if she thought Sam's monologue had in any way veered off course.

Sam sat up straight in her chair and slipped on a pair of black framed glasses. She pushed them down her nose and looked directly at Litmus over the top of the frames.

'Before I start can I just have your agreement that none of this will go any further. That you'll make do with what we tell you today and make no further efforts to track these men down. They've stuck their necks out because we think we can trust you and if they end up getting themselves into trouble for trying to do the right thing, we will never forgive ourselves.'

Litmus nodded, then thought he had better put action into words.

'No problem. You ladies set the rules on this one. Believe me, I'm just grateful that you're offering to help me at all.'

The sisters exchanged glances which appeared to indicate they were satisfied with the response.

'OK, let's get started. Jimmy, we'll call him Jimmy though that obviously isn't his real name, did site work up on the top road in May and June of this year.' Sam inclined her head in the vague direction of the building site in case Litmus was in any doubts about the location to which she was referring.

'We......that is Pat, met Jimmy at a pub in early May and they got talking. He is a nice man and proved very good company. He has an infectious sense of humour and his English was already really good considering that at that time he hadn't been in the country for very long.

Jimmy and a few of his mates used to go for a drink on the odd occasion that they weren't transported out of the area after they had completed their shift. They weren't meant to. One of the rules that had been laid down from the very start was that they were never to linger anywhere near the building site once their working day was over. Looking back, it isn't difficult to figure out why that was the case, but at the time the site workers just thought it was some sort of stupid bureaucratic rule that made no sense, so on occasions they chose to ignore it. Obviously, after what happened they are as nervous as hell in case they are traced and ended up getting involved in something which they are still struggling to understand.'

Sam looked at Pat who nodded her approval and passed over a large sheet of paper with spidery writing on both sides.

'In a manner of speaking Jimmy has been elected spokesman for his group of mates, so It's probably best if I clarify their joint position before we get in too deep. He and his co-workers are mortified at what happened but none of them want to be involved with anyone who is conducting any sort of investigation, not even you. What follows is a sort of joint statement from the ones that To....Jimmy was able to track down which they hope will prove of assistance; but regardless of whether it does or it doesn't, this is as far as they want to go. Not all of them have great English and obviously none of them have been in this sort of situation before so Pat and I have tried to prompt for the sort of thing that we thought you might find useful. I'm afraid you'll probably find it less than perfect, but we did the best that we could under the circumstances.'

Sam paused and gathered herself. Litmus smiled encouragingly.

'Please bear in mind these men are builders and a lot of them don't have the paperwork required to be working in this country. In consequence, they are only employed on a week-to-week basis and receive their wages in cash. They haven't got a Union or any form of representation, so they are totally out there on their own, and whilst they genuinely want to be of as much assistance as they can, it has obviously been necessary that they set some limits for their own protection. I'm sure you'll understand why that is without me going into any further detail.'

Litmus nodded and the sisters again exchanged glances that seemed to confirm that so far all was well.

'Site work when your employment is semi-illegal: I don't know if you are aware how this thing works?'

Pat interrupted. 'Better to just tell it the way it happened. He's not stupid. If he doesn't know now, he'll pick it up as we go along. Start with the numbers and countries they came from. He'll be interested in that, if half that stuff they've been putting in the morning papers is to be believed.'

Sam looked slightly confused but checked with the sheet of paper and quickly resumed. Regardless of Pat's intervention she attempted to take things gently. Something for which Litmus was more than grateful.

'Builders........East European builders have what we would call staging posts where they stand on a morning if they are looking for work. An employer pulls up, shouts, three brickies, a chippy and a plasterer and lets them know what he is prepared to pay. The workers then jump into the van and seconds later they are whisked off to where they will be working. It doesn't actually work anything like that, but at least you've now got a picture in your head.'

'Jimmy was in on the hotel job right from the very start. The number of men working there was never more than twenty at any one time and when the job was nearing completion, there were as few as seven or eight. They were a mixed crew, all Eastern European and mainly comprising Poles, Serbians, Latvians, Romanians, Albanians, Bulgarians and probably one or two other nationalities that failed to register. From time-to-time people were added to the work team or disappeared from it, never to be seen again. It's normal in the building trade; pretty much the nature of the job. Nobody expected it to be different on this contract from any other.'

'Nine of the regulars were Poles like Jimmy, so that meant there were only one or two of each of the other nationalities. Are you following this alright? You are beginning to look a bit lost.'

Litmus stirred. 'Yes Sam, I'm following. You're doing great. Keep going. This is just what I was hoping for.'

Sam went slightly pink but appeared to be suitably reassured.

'They were brought in by van, and always from the same pick-up point, but Jimmy won't say where that was because although he's no longer using it himself, he's fairly certain it is still seeing a certain amount of action. The site workers received their instructions from a tall bloke who was also the driver of the van. I've jotted down a description that Jimmy passed on, but I don't think it will be a lot of help; nondescript pretty much covers it apart from his height. The van was fairly new, white in colour and had no company name or other insignia on the side; naturally nobody noticed the registration plates, assuming that it had one, which presumably it did. The driver was English, or at least spoke like he was English, and acted as a sort of Foreman figure, while at the same time remaining extremely aloof. He didn't stay on site during the day. Just told the gang of workers what was required and left them to get on with it. Jimmy said they quickly learned that he didn't have any idea what he was talking about, so very soon they stopped asking him questions because he clearly didn't know how to reply.'

Litmus interrupted. 'Sorry, are you saying this driver bloke, the Foreman, wasn't a builder?'

Pat put her hand on Sam's arm and answered in her stead.

'Not going by the condition of his hands. Jimmy said it looked like he had never picked up anything heavier than a pen in his life. His knowledge of building practice was also scanty to say the least. Jimmy said it was like he only ever knew as much as he could have picked up by going on the internet the night before. If you asked him a question, he just said something vague that was no help at all, so after a bit they stopped asking questions and took to figuring out problems for themselves. Whatever they did was never queried. Nobody seemed very interested in standards of workmanship as long as it looked alright from a surface inspection. As long as they just got on with their work and kept the costs down everything was fine. Jimmy said, they cut corners all over the place. Half the down pipes just spewed water out onto the ground and there wasn't even any insulation in the roof ducts, but apparently nobody batted an eyelid.'

'What about the sourcing of supplies?' Litmus added.

Sam scrutinised her piece of paper and looked pleased when she located the answer.

'Everything they needed was already in the hotel building when they arrived on the first day, or was stored at the rear of the building in a sort of outhouse building if it was bulk supply stuff like sand and cement or if it was non...non....can't make out the word....'

Pat leaned across. 'Noncorrosive. If they wanted anything extra, they either bought it themselves and claimed the money back by providing a receipt or wrote a note for the driver and he would collect it, and in most cases they would have it by the following day. The storeroom building also acted as somewhere they could retreat to for lunchbreaks. It had electricity so they could boil a kettle and have hot drinks. A few of the men went for a walk if it was a nice day but most were only too happy to take the weight of their feet and settle down with a brew'.

'When were the final lot of builders last on site?' Litmus asked.

Sam scrutinised the sheet of paper. 'It doesn't say but it would have been midway through the last week in June, I think.'

'Yes, that sounds about right', Pat confirmed.

'And they only got a lift home sometimes?'

'Not home', Sam said. 'Back to the place where they were picked up in the mornings unless they found it more convenient to jump out on the way. The driver didn't seem particularly bothered one way or the other. He always seemed in a hurry and just wanted to get them dumped off as quickly as possible.'

She hesitated and looked meaningfully at Pat.

'Jimmy said it was as if the driver had another job to go on to after he had dropped them off in the mornings, and the same sort of thing applied when he picked them up at night. Like, sometimes it was convenient to collect them and sometimes it wasn't, but even when he did pick them up, he was always in a hurry to be somewhere else. They thought initially he was working on another site that was operating twenty-four hour shifts and that was the reason he disappeared each day after he had run them into work, and why he couldn't guarantee he would pick them up in the evening; but after they figured out that he didn't have a clue what he was talking about they didn't know what to think. Basically, they just gave up on him, apart from getting a lift in and out, and when they needed him to pick up extra supplies. Even then, half the time he would come back with the wrong stuff, which was why they resorted to writing everything down and presenting him with a list instead of just telling him what they needed. By the time the job was coming to an end he was being treated as a bit of a joke. His contribution to the project was minimal. He was obviously a long way out of his depth.'

Sam stopped to check her sheet of paper. Immediately Pat added a bit of clarification.

'The way Jimmy told It, most of the men he was working with were experienced professionals, and as it was pretty obvious what needed doing next, and as nobody was going to be on their backs if they used their initiative, they just got on with it to the best of their ability.'

Litmus smiled reassuringly at them both.

'When were they paid?'

113

Sam checked without success, then turning over the sheet of paper without any better luck.

'Doesn't say, but it would definitely have been cash in the hand because I don't think the majority of them would have had a bank account.'

'How did they know when he would collect them and when he wouldn't?'

'He phoned some of the time, but quite often he just didn't show up. He wasn't what you would call Mr Reliable. That was one of the reasons why after a day's work they sometimes strayed down the road and into the pub. Even when he did arrive on time, which wasn't often, he'd usually get one of the site workers to do the driving. A horrible man, and bone idle as well.'

Litmus decided the time had arrived for him to move onto more controversial ground. He needed to be careful though. The girls had been so kind and what they had told him so far was dynamite. However, it was obvious they had divided loyalties, so he needed to proceed with care.

'As you've probably gathered from the newspapers and television, somebody planted explosives under the floorboards. Anything that might be of help on that direction?'

'Jimmy said he was absolutely certain it wasn't any of the crew he was working with. He acknowledged some of them were a bit dodgy, but he is a hundred percent sure none of them would have been involved in anything like that. Jimmy's been around a bit. If anything were going on, I think he would have sniffed it out. He's a seasoned hand in the building game and very far from stupid.'

'Does he say who worked on the flooring?'

Sam consulted. 'Only that it wasn't in bad condition to start with because although the hotel looked a bit of a mess from the outside it had remained watertight during the time it was unoccupied. The odd bits of floorboard that were added were cut to size, slotted into position and just left to be nailed down at a later date. If I've read this right, there weren't any specialist floor layers on site, because they weren't really necessary. The builders would have assumed that the reason they had been told not to finish off the new floorboards was in case extra wiring needed to be installed, that's assuming any of them gave it any thought at all.'

'So, the boards definitely weren't nailed or screwed?'

'No, they were told just to leave them, and it would get sorted out before the final clean-up took place.'

'Anything else you can find on your list that might be of help?'

'Nope, that's about all we've got', said Sam with evident relief.

She and Pat smiled at each other like they were pleased to get a weight off their chests.

'Sorry it all sounds a bit confusing but from the information passed back from the men working on site, that was just the way it was.'

CHAPTER FOURTEEN

Train north, Monday September 29th 2025

Litmus was safely closeted on the mid-afternoon train heading Sheffield. He had to admit he was experiencing a feeling of mild exhilaration to be returning home, having survived the horrors of the writhing metropolis relatively unscathed; not that the metropolis had done a great deal of writhing, or that he had been in mortal danger of being unduly scathed, if he were being honest with himself. It was more about a general feeling of unease that he experienced in the capital that was strangely unquantifiable. London always seemed too big for him to feel entirely comfortable. Sheffield was a city of more manageable proportions and in consequence it was a location he coped with a good deal better. Having been born there probably had something to do with it as well.

It was too early in the day for this train to be an attractive proposition for heavy-duty business commuters, so he was enjoying an oasis of comparative peace. Two women returning from a long weekend's shopping extravaganza were busy concocting the story they would tell their husbands when the credit card bills turned up on the mat. A teenager dressed in a green school uniform with a very short skirt was prodding the screen of her phone as if her very life depended on it. A sunburned elderly couple, returning from a holiday abroad, were looking tired but relatively contented. They only needed to hold on for a little longer and they would have survived the rigours of language, travel, strange food and dubious plumbing. Just another couple of hours and they would be happily seated in front of the television watching Countdown with the crossword puzzle and a nice cup of tea. Pure bliss to be home; not entirely sure why they had bothered in the first place, but at least it was all behind them for another year.

Litmus abandoned his seat, pushed through the semi-automatic doors that always chose to close at exactly the wrong moment and slumped in a spot opposite a toilet that offered baby changing facilities of which he currently had little requirement. He tapped in a stream of numbers and considered crossing his fingers for luck.

'What the fuck........Leeming here. Litmus, you bastard, what the hell do you want at this time in the morning?'

'It's the afternoon, Detective Inspector. Just a call to say thank you for taking care of me yesterday. How did last night's celebration go? Take it from your tone that you finished quite late.'

'It finished at ten this morning, Litmus, and I was just catching up on the sleep I would now be enjoying if you hadn't dragged me out of bed. What the hell do you want? You didn't phone just to massage my ego, did you? Christ, it was a night well spent though. Those boys can certainly put it away. I've got a mouth like the bottom of a parrot's cage.'

'Well, there was one small thing. A suggestion that might be of benefit to both of us.'

'Spit it out Litmus and make it short. If I don't get my head down in the next few minutes I'm going to keel over. Not drunk that much in quite a few years.'

'Your man. When we were exchanging pleasantries through the door, he happened to mention that when they had surplus dope on their hands the Albanians weren't averse to trading with the local gangs, in order to oil their channels of distribution.'

Leeming didn't answer straight away, and Litmus wondered if he was calculating whether a well told lie might serve better than the truth. After several seconds had elapsed, he seemed to arrive at a decision that a middle course was the best way to go.

'You don't want to take too much notice of that man, Litmus. His family are Albanian so he will have inherited some very suspect genes. Anyway, hypothetically, just supposing that they did?'

Steady now, Litmus.   Tread very carefully with Leeming, especially in his present condition. Let's get the next bit nailed down tight, because for both of their sakes it was important that they reached a firm understanding and stuck with it, no matter what evidence later came to light.

'Well, it occurred to me that that sort of talk could easily be misinterpreted by a bunch of pen pushers with too much time on their hands. It could possibly give the mistaken impression that the two factions were banded together in some sort of liaison. And whilst we both know that isn't in the least bit true, it might be a smart move not to open any doors that are better left locked and bolted, if you get my drift. But if it were the case that your man's report made no mention of any form of collusion between the two factions, then you could never have had any knowledge that anything of the sort might have occurred and if that were the case...............'

'Litmus, I'm beginning to think you aren't quite as stupid as you look, even if it is a pretty close thing. You have my assurance that the written report I receive from my Field Agent will contain no reference to any form of inter-trading, nor will my man have ever seen any evidence that any took place.'

'In which case, as neither of us have any knowledge that any form of liaison between the separate factions took place, there is no way I can legitimately record it in my report because.........'

'Goodnight Litmus. If you think of anything else you want to talk about then save it for tomorrow......... or better still, the day after. Now fuck off back to wherever you came from and let me get some sleep.'

'Sleep well, Detective Inspector. Litmus, over and out.'

That didn't go too badly, considering. Hangover or not, Leeming still knew what was in his best interest. One down, one to go. Litmus prodded the device in his hand back into life. Jerome Whitcott invariably let his phone go to his messaging service but there was always a chance.

'Yes, Litmus.'

'Just reporting in, Mr Whitcott. I'm on the train back to Sheffield and I've just finished sketching out the basis of my report. I'll buff it up tonight and it will be sent by registered post no later than midday tomorrow.'

'So kind of you to interrupt a very important meeting in order to appraise me of that, Litmus. What were you hoping for, some sort of medal?'

'I just thought you would want to know I had left the capital and was on my way back home.'

'Well Litmus, now you are fully aware that I didn't.'

A pause of ten seconds and a sound of glass clinking against glass.

'Are you sure you've got enough material? You've haven't been down there for more than five minutes.'

'It's more a case of feeling I wasn't going to obtain any more information than I've already got. The natives were pretty hostile when they thought I might be interfering on their patch. In my opinion any more time spent in London would just have been a waste of the taxpayers' hard-earned cash. And, if you remember, you warned me to be careful in that regard.'

'Your decision entirely, Litmus. I look forward to reading your words of wisdom.'

'And about my expenses, Mr Whitcott, where should I......?'

The line immediately went dead.

Litmus decided his arrival back in God's country should be celebrated by a taxi ride to his door. The cab was big enough to seat a full orchestra including a double bass, but the Sikh driver didn't seem to mind a single fare; perhaps aware that owt was better than nowt in these extremely trying times. There were no lights on in the house when he arrived so obviously Beth was out or had opted for an early night. He dragged his travel bag across the threshold and clicked on the central heating which was unaccountably not in operation. Christ it was cold. The first thing you noticed when returning from the south was always the drop in temperature, but that was meant to be outdoors not inside your home. He tiptoed up the stairs, did some brief unpacking and fired up his laptop ready for an assault on Whitcott's accursed report.

It was then that he noticed it, tucked neatly between the pillows on his aged double bed. The envelope read *Litmus*, nothing more, but it was enough to forewarn him not to expect anything that would raise his spirits. These weren't going to be glad tidings; he would put money on that.

Putting off the inevitable, Litmus opened the door and walked up the hall. He tapped gently on Beth's door, knowing before he turned the handle that he was wasting his time. The room came as no surprise. Neat, pristine even, but very, very empty. He closed the door quietly, returned to his bedroom and tore open the envelope.

Litmus,

This is not going to be my best composition because at the moment my head is all over the place. First off you are a bloody idiot, and that extends to second and third off as well! If you haven't already figured it out my arrival at your doorstep wasn't entirely accidental. It was caused by me getting caught with my hand in the till, or more specifically with the cursor of my computer's mouse in the website of places where you most definitely aren't encouraged to go. In short, I was invited to do a bit of spying for the good Mr Whitcott, and if I chose not to play ball, I took a fall. So, there you have it. You stuck your neck out to bail me out of trouble and I reported on what you did so as to drop you in it. Facts unassailable. Cow of the year award presented and accepted to a chorus of boos.

You are an idiot.......did I mention that already? I don't know why I was designated to hold your hand. You presumably have a history of taking to your heart unstable women with no moral compass. That's how Whitcott saw it anyway and as usual he was one hundred percent correct. If it's any consolation I told him virtually nothing and now I see he was clever again, because what I reported back didn't actually matter one little bit. He only wanted me here so I would provide something he could use to blackmail you; and didn't that work out a treat? Why didn't you tell me what was happening before you packed your case and disappeared off to save my soul because I could have saved you a lot of unnecessary trouble? Whitcott gave me all the gory details once you were gone, but why didn't I hear it from you? You must have had your reasons, but from where I'm sitting it doesn't seem to make any sort of sense. Why was saving me from a fate worse than death so damned important? You didn't owe me anything and Jesus H Christ I must have proved to you by now that I certainly wasn't worth the effort.

There are any number of things I don't understand about this whole charade but the main one is, what the hell did you do to make them, ('them' ....I don't even know who 'them' are,) so intent on getting you involved, because that's what it's about, my dear, whether you choose to acknowledge the fact or not. If it weren't that you hardly know how to plug a computer into the wall socket, I would have thought you were in the hacking game as well; but it isn't that, is it? It's something completely different and on female intuition I think that it's very much worse......and in consequence I'm quite desperate to know the detail.

This morning I examined my trading balance and I have in excess of twenty thousand English pounds, a slightly smaller amount of Euros and just over 2.7 million American dollars. Hacking into the core programs of the computers that run multinational corporations is a very lucrative business providing you don't let yourself get caught. You would not believe the money they will pay out so they can quickly plug the system leak and avoid looking silly; and if the leak plugging is regarded as very important, it is dwarfed by their anxiety that no word of their misfortune finds its way into the outside world.

Today I have deposited into your bank account five hundred thousand pounds sterling. If anyone asks, you sold me the house at a suitably inflated price and are very pleased with yourself for having done a shrewd bit of business. It's not charity, Litmus. I would willingly have paid that figure and more in order to retain my freedom and that's effectively what you accomplished without telling me a word.

I'm going underground for a while because I don't know what's going on, and not knowing is the most frightening thing in my nefarious little world. I'm good at hiding under rocks as you might well imagine. Also, it occurs to me that if I'm not around it makes you less vulnerable to our friend Mr Whitcott, and that can only be a good thing.

Use some of the money to finish doing this place up the way anybody with a modicum of common sense would have done in the first place. Don't let anybody take my bedroom for the time being in case I decide to come back. I love that view across the park, and I've left some clothes in the wardrobe which is like the Germans putting towels on a sun-lounger, or in my case a very strong version of the scent marking undertaken by that god awful fox.

Obviously, I don't know when you will be arriving back so I can't tell when you will be reading this. Whenever it is, I'm one hundred percent sure they will be coming for you very soon so either get out of the house and run very fast or be well prepared when you hear the knock on the door.

I must see you again because I desperately want to know what this is all about. However, be totally assured it is for no reason other than that. So, in a few months, a year, a decade, who knows when, our paths will cross once again............allowing that you aren't dead by then my dear Litmus, which, if my reading of the situation is correct, might be a bit of a stretch.

With gratitude and friendship because that is all I've got to offer.

Litmus, you are an idiot!
Beth X

Litmus read the letter three times and then put it a long way out of reach so he wouldn't read it again. He contemplated for several minutes, then picked up his laptop, made himself comfortable and proceeded to type.

CHAPTER FIFTEEN

Sheffield, Tuesday October 14th 2025

Nothing. More than two weeks had elapsed with not a solitary word. His calls went to messaging or the recipient was always otherwise engaged. The postman ignored any Samaritan instincts and chose to pass by on the other side of the road. The doorbell remained resoundingly unrung. Litmus lived the life of a hermit priest awaiting a higher calling that seemed never destined to materialise. Then, rather than a mighty clap of thunder, there was instead a small squeal from brakes being forcefully applied, and Litmus sensed the waiting had finally come to an end.

The same car as last time, he observed while standing back some distance from the front window in the hope of remaining unseen. Even the same driver; but a passenger as well this time. God almighty, surely not her! Where the hell could she possibly fit into any of this?

The front door swung open with the velocity of a bolt from a crossbow and across his threshold strode Jerome Whitcott, accompanied closely by Litmus least favourite Policewoman of all time, Detective Inspector Ho.

'Coffee, Litmus, strong as you like. Perhaps you wouldn't mind making it yourself this time.' A surreptitious glance at Beth's unoccupied workstation which perhaps indicated Whitcott hadn't yet been made aware of her departure. 'Oh, would I be right in saying that kitchen duties are no longer a matter of choice?'

Whitcott divested himself of a scarf and appeared to consider following it with his rather smart raincoat. However, after a quick appraisal of the redecorating project, which despite Litmus best intentions had made little progress, he seemed to reconsider and made do with loosening a couple of buttons.

'You know D.I. Ho of course. I've managed to enlist her services on secondment, and she has kindly agreed to act as our stenographer while we get the detail of your report put to bed.'

For no apparent reason Whitcott and Litmus formally shook hands. Ho and Litmus aimed a noncommittal nod in the general direction of each other, in place of something more meaningful like an exchange of snarls.

Litmus produced coffee and they quickly took their places. Litmus, at his desk, Whitcott facing him and Ho tucked away in the far corner of the room, in an apparent effort to divorce herself as far as possible from whatever proceedings were about to unfold.

'Where shall we start?' said Whitcott with unnecessarily levity. 'With your report of course Litmus, where else?' he continued, effectively answering his own question. Looking the epitome of corporate efficiency, he delicately extracted a thin file from his case as if he were examining it for the very first time, before frowning at the dearth of papers it contained.

'There's a fine line Litmus, between being concise and leaving yourself open to accusations of scribbling your findings on the back of a cigarette packet. That boundary, you have not only crossed but pretty much obliterated for the benefit of all future generations. Remind me, you were down in London for how long?'

'About a week.'

'And did you not think that devoting a little more time to the project might conceivably have aided you in delivering something a tad more meaningful than this meagre offering?' Whitcott thumbed through the sheets with a look of disdain.

'As I explained in our brief telephone conversation, I thought this was as much as I was likely to get from my London visit. Neither D.C.I. Sangster nor D.I. Ho seemed over keen to welcome me into the bosom of their investigation, nor indeed, to meet face to face with me under any circumstances at all.'

Whitcott made a minor adjustment to the position of his chair.

'Let's not enter into pointless bickering, Litmus. You were charged with preparing a reasoned report and what I've got before me can only be described as underwhelming in the extreme.' He paused. 'Anyway, I suppose there isn't much we can do about that situation now, so let's press on with the little you have provided and not waste time on something that is beyond our powers to correct.'

He opened the file and skimmed the front page.

'You travelled down on the twenty third of last month blah, blah, blah. How did you come to miss the reception committee D.I. Ho had laid on for you, at my request?'

'You indicated that you wanted my personal perspective on the investigation, Mr Whitcott, so I thought it would be wise to avoid any form of outside influence.'

Whitcott's mouth formed the shape of a perfect O.

'And you construed being welcomed at St Pancras railway station and being conveyed to your hotel by members of D.I. Ho's team as an attempt to influence your report on the investigation? Since escaping my sphere of influence, you appear to have become totally deluded, young man.'

He read more, then looking across the top of his glasses he glared in Litmus' direction.

'I'm not even going to ask you why you chose to book into your chosen accommodation using an assumed name. Let's move on to day two, shall we? I'm already finding this interview rather depressing.'

Litmus coughed and Whitcott glanced up at him expectantly for a brief moment, before registering a look of further disappointment when the throat clearing wasn't followed by anything of more substance.

'The dust from the building work', Litmus explained.

Whitcott looked pityingly. Ho ignored him.

'On the twenty fourth you visited the scene of the outrage, and finally made a brief contact with D.I. Ho. Then, doubtless wearied by this colossal output of energy, you retired to a nearby café to recharge your batteries, at which point......'

'I visited a café called the Ridgeway Rendezvous because it was the food and drink outlet nearest to where the explosion occurred. It seemed logical to check if it had been used by the site workmen to buy whatever they needed to get them through the day; and it just so happened, I struck lucky.'

'Indeed, you did, Litmus. Indeed, you did. You made friends with a mixed gender version of The Chuckle Brothers who were only too pleased to clasp you to their bosom and confirm what you appear to have already decided upon, based, so it would seem, on little or no evidence at all; namely, that miscreant Albanian site workers in their multitude had regularly flocked to their premises in search of nutrition and sustenance.'

Whitcott again paused, removed his spectacles, and scratched at his forehead with his index finger.

'You hadn't at this point spoken to Detective Inspector Leeming, had you, Litmus? So, the question I'm obliged to ask myself is who else might have passed an abstract thought or two in your general direction? I always find any suggestion of original thinking in a report from a field operative as highly suspicious, and I'm sure D.I. Ho would concur with that assessment? No matter. I can consider the topic a little later when I am in more convivial surroundings.'

Whitcott's eyes ran slowly round the bottom floor of the house with a look of undiluted horror.

'If I may cut through your psychobabble and get back to the facts, Mr Whitcott, I entered the café and met a waitress named Sharon, and an aged regular customer called John, both of whom confirmed that men from the site visited the Ridgeway Rendezvous some lunchtimes; and the said John, because of a shared sporting interest with the customers, was able to confirm that they were almost certainly of Albanian extraction. Plain unassailable, verifiable fact, Mr

Whitcott, so what exactly is the problem.......because I'm sure if there is one you are just the man to point it out?'

'My problem, Litmus? Minor I suppose in the big scheme of things but, nevertheless, slightly nagging when applied to your garbled version of events. Investigation revealed that the illustrious Ridgeway Rendezvous cafeteria was not in fact open for business on the twenty fourth of September; or at least it wasn't at the time you were supposed to have undertaken your unsolicited visit. The premises were closed for trading to the public that day as a company called Jardine Catering were in the process of preparing the revolting style of food required to fuel a children's fancy dress party that was to be held later on the same day.......themed, I am led to believe, on the well known kindergarten masterpiece, Wind in the Willows. Private hire, Litmus. An enterprising side-line introduced by the current manager, a Mr.....Mr.....I've got it here somewhere........Mr A.D. Claydon, to help balance the books in these rather difficult times.'

Whitcott peered again at the papers in his hand, licked his index finger and flipped over a page, before furrowing his brow and returning to where he had started.

'Children of breeding would doubtless have been those in attendance that day, Litmus. A lot more water voles and badgers than weasels would have been on view that Autumn afternoon one would suspect. However, there is always the odd renegade spirit who fancies their chances at pushing back the boundaries, even at that tender age. What would you have gone as, Litmus, given the opportunity? I think, having examined your character closely, I would perhaps detect a smattering of Mole. Passionate and willing to help others was Moley, but dangerous if allowed to follow his own inclinations. Better kept underground and out of the way for safety's sake; a bit short sighted, and not just in the literal term, and more than a smidgin naïve.'

Whitcott looked quite pleased with the analogy and pressed on with renewed vigour.

'Oh, and I almost hesitate to mention it, what with you being so certain of your facts on the subject, but despite the most exhaustive of investigations conducted in person by D.I. Ho.......give us a wave from your darkened corner Inspector Ho, so Litmus can see you haven't yet nodded off.......no trace whatever could be found of the elusive football loving, Albanian expert John, or even so much as one of his hand rolled, boot lace diameter cigarettes; and much though it pains me to relate, the good Mr Claydon, the manager of the café as you will doubtless recall, was able to confirm that there had been no Sharons employed at his establishment for as far as his records went back.'

'Well, I can assure you they weren't figments of my imagination. I met them both. I was as close to the pair of them as I am to you now. If I was going to fabricate characters, I think you might at least credit me with being a little more inventive.'

Whitcott turned in his chair and looked in the direction of D.I. Ho.

'Probably the only point in his favour, wouldn't you think, Ho? Doesn't seem to be much else. Right, let's park the bus on that for the present as well, and move on to the twenty fifth.'

Litmus rose and flicked on the central light which, because of the refurbishment work, lacked any form of lightshade. It had barely reached early autumn but already the darkness of winter was beginning to descend. The unshaded illumination revealed D.I. Ho scraping zealously at her notepad, displaying the type of malicious glee you would associate with a gnome that had abandoned its gardening duties and gone over to the dark side. On balance, Litmus wished that he had stuck with the gloom.

'On the twenty fifth,' Whitcott continued, 'you decided to put your assignment to one side, so you could join D.I. Mortley, our resident expert on inter-gang violence, for some well-earned rest and relaxation. Experiencing your work ethic first-hand, Litmus, has fostered in me a far greater understanding of why the Northern Powerhouse has yet to fire up the economic recovery we were all anticipating with such relish, and for that broadening of my education, I suppose I should be at least a little grateful.'

Whitcott withdrew a pristine handkerchief from his trouser pocket and noisily blew his nose.

'Ms Ho, who you observe currently wielding her pen with such dexterity over in the far corner took time out from other pressing duties to interview Mr Mortley before we ventured north, and it was drawn to her attention that when you weren't busy swilling ale together, you found a little time to discuss some aspects of the case; something for which the tax paying British public will be forever in your debt. Ho was made aware that Mortley had a theory he was anxious to impart; was that not the case, Litmus? Something that he considered of the highest importance that he thought had possibly been overlooked by the original enquiry. However, zealously though I have searched through your words of wisdom, I have as yet been unable to locate any reference to that viewpoint in the papers that you have submitted for my appraisal.'

Litmus remained calm. He had suffered interviews with Whitcott on numerous occasions and was aware of the tone in which they were invariably conducted.

'My brief was to evaluate if in my opinion the enquiry was heading in the right direction, but as I had been unable to gain an interview with either D.C.I. Sangster or D.I. Ho I had no real idea exactly which direction that was. In consequence, I thought it wise to speak to the heads of the Gang Related and Organised Crime units and compare their thoughts on the matter with what little I had been able to glean from my own investigations; and much though I was impressed with Mortley as a conscientious serving officer, when I got back up here and came to write up my thoughts on the subject, I was forced to conclude that Leeming's reading of what might have occurred was probably nearer to the truth.'

'So, you think the mysterious Jeremiah, to whom Mortley returns time and time again is a figment of his imagination?'

'No, quite probably he does exist. I'm just not entirely sure whether it's in reality or in Mortley's fertile imagination. Even if we take it on face value that there is a Jeremiah Jones out there lurking in the undergrowth, there is still no tangible evidence that he had any bearing on proceedings as we understand they transpired; and even if we accept D.I. Mortley's theory as correct, there's absolutely nothing that has yet come to light that says the man wasn't working under the direction of the Albanian faction or anybody else for that matter.'

Whitcott raised his eyebrows. 'Perhaps we could develop the second of those two points a little. Are you proposing that a West Indian fixer could have been working for the Albanians or that there was some degree of tribal cooperation between all parties? Have you any evidence to support either assumption?'

'No, none whatsoever, which is why I left any reference to it out of my report.'

'I might be able to shine a little light on what you have just said.' Whitcott fiddled in his case and withdrew a further sheet of paper.

'Although our friend Leeming states he had no knowledge of any collaboration between the gangs and the Albanian contingent, M.I.5. was also keeping an eye on comings and goings at the group's headquarters for entirely different reasons and they reported that there was a degree of traffic in and out of the building from what they eloquently describe as, *black faces that clearly weren't Albanian*. Sadly, however, there is nothing in their field reports that shines further light on the subject because for Five it wasn't an area of specific interest. Right, interesting it might be, but it doesn't appear to have taken us a lot further forward, does it? OK, let's forget tribal cooperation for the time being and move on.'

Whitcott suppressed a yawn and looked across at Ho who was still writing feverishly.

'Nearly finished the material I wanted to get through in today's session, Ho. Buck up, girl. Only a little longer.'

Christ, thought Litmus, it looks like the pair of them are coming back tomorrow for another crack. I hope this doesn't mean I'll be expected to entertain them tonight.

The horror in prospect was nipped in the bud as Whitcott resumed.

'On the twenty sixth, you stirred yourself from your lethargy and hit the streets with newfound zeal and ambition. However, you describe the day as totally unproductive other than a couple of vague references to local residents having viewed builders /people with East European accents out and about on the streets. Nice to see we were getting our money's worth out of you, Litmus. All that extensive training you had undergone in your formative years finally reaping dividends it would appear. Bravo! It does my heart good to see the level of enterprise you have bought to the table. Well done, indeed.'

Ho shuffled in her seat. Litmus remembered her saying she had no sense of humour, but he bet she was enjoying every minute of this performance. Whitcott chose this point to resume.

'On the twenty seventh you paid a call on D.I. Leeming of Organised Crime, who I understand was in the process of preparing a raid on an Albanian safehouse in a north London location.'

'Yes, but I only decided to meet up with Leeming as a fall-back option after having my appointment with D.C.I. Sangster at New Scotland Yard cancelled without any meaningful explanation. As soon as I'd received the brush off from Sangster, I made contact with D.I. Leeming by phone and arranged to meet him at Stoke Newington Police Station in North London where he had assembled a task force that he was planning to use on the Albanian raid later in the day.'

'And?'

'And that's what happened. I got to Stoke Newington, met Sangster, and was appraised by him of his proposed plan of action; and as I had nothing specifically against it, I signed it off.'

'*As I had nothing specifically against it.* A rather blasé approach to commending a course of action that resulted in four men losing their lives, and several more their liberty, if you don't mind me saying so.'

Litmus leaned forward on the desk.

'You told me quite specifically that unless I was two hundred percent sure that a case officer was taking an incorrect course of action, I was to be sure not to get in his way. Those are near as damn it your exact words. I committed them to memory.'

'I have no recollection of saying any such thing, Litmus. What I indicated, was that you should use your discretion ....which was precisely why I gave you the right of a veto on the raid in the first place. Not that I'm saying that in this instance you were entirely wrong. More, that you might have given the matter a little more consideration before proffering your signature with such gay abandon. As you may have gathered from your interview with the man, D.I. Leeming can on occasions be somewhat impulsive.'

'So, you are now holding me responsible for the mental stability of the head of Organised Crime?'

'You are being unnecessarily obtuse, Litmus. It should be quite obvious to you that I am obliged to examine every grain of sand. This report might in due course find its way onto the desks of some of the best minds in this country and the slightest error or contradiction will be seized upon with delight. Get a grip of yourself, man. Try a small glass of brandy and a soak in hot bath for an hour and I'm sure you will regain control of your senses. You do have baths up here, I presume? Ones for bathing, not for storing the coal?'

Whitcott refastened his coat closed his case.

'Right, ten o'clock sharp tomorrow morning; and Litmus, do try to pick up some decent coffee in the meantime. That last cup was nearly as bad as the one that woman tried to poison me with the last time I was up here.'

Whitcott hesitated on the way out.

'Just one more thing. D.I. Ho and I are stopping in the city centre and will probably end up eating at the hotel. Any local delicacy you could recommend? I have a delicate digestive system as I think you are aware but am always open to new experiences if they come recommended.'

'The black pudding is pretty much guaranteed to be good as a starter, and this part of the country prides itself on the quality of its fish, chips and mushy peas. It's very much a local delicacy, especially if you can get the chips cooked in beef dripping.'

'With this area's close proximity to the mighty ocean, who would ever have doubted that would be the case,' said Whitcott with heavy sarcasm. 'I'm positively salivating at the very thought.'

He and Ho pushed through the outer door and quickly boarded his car.

Well, that could have gone worse, Litmus concluded. I wonder what delights tomorrow will bring.

CHAPTER SIXTEEN

Sheffield, Wednesday October 15th 2025

Litmus rose early in order to fully embrace the full wonder of the October drizzle that hung in the air like a giant spider's web. He needed fresh air even if there was little doubt a good deal of cold water would feature as a backing accompaniment. Dressed in a manner suitable to combat the elements, he crossed the road and arrived at the entrance to the park. For this early in autumn, it was absolutely bloody freezing; though bracing might be the term better employed if you benefited from true Yorkshire blood or were of a naturally masochistic disposition.

He battled on, as the light rain realised its true potential and turned to hail, before settling in as waves of icy sleet. Past the boarded-up café, closed and battened down for the long winter months that lay ahead, past the children's adventure playground that in this weather presented a challenge too far for any but the most intrepid, past the joy rides and bouncy castle conceived to provide entertainment in different climatic conditions altogether.

Pulling his coat tighter, he climbed a small rise and heard the distant tinkling of running water as the small river that ran in from the moors fed into a muddy lake. It wasn't hard to see that even the ducks on the murky pond were mildly pissed off with the season's current offerings, and they were the creatures that were meant to enjoy weather of this sort. He pressed on, making a wide circuit of the adjacent woodland before collecting a few items of shopping and reaching the conclusion it was wise to cut his losses and head back home. It had been a damp and miserable start to a day that he didn't expect to significantly improve until he could usher Jerome Whitcott out of the front door and watch the boot of his car disappear over the horizon as he thankfully made his way home.

Litmus unpacked his purchases, made himself a coffee, moved a hard backed chair to where he had a clear view of the road outside, and cast his mind back over the events of the previous twenty-four hours. Not a great outcome, he was forced to admit, but it could have gone decidedly worse. Any interview with Whitcott was more about survival than coming out on top, and in that respect, he had achieved as much as could have been hoped for. Whitcott would ultimately reveal an agenda because Whitcott always had an agenda to reveal; you could pretty much take that as read. What the man wanted to achieve would at some stage become apparent, and it was only then he could decide on how best to react. It was a pity that at this moment in time he was totally in the dark, but he had expected nothing different. Whitcott's left hand was rarely acquainted with what his right hand was doing, but if it guessed at something unspeakable, it probably wouldn't have been too far out.

He had flirted with the idea of introducing the finding from his meeting with the sisters into the report he had submitted, but on consideration there had been too many pitfalls for that to be a sensible option. Firstly, the difficulty of keeping the girl's contribution completely anonymous might have proved difficult, and secondly, it didn't require a genius to see that the information their contact had provided in no way substantiated the course of action D.I. Leeming had actively pursued. A course of action that had at best benefitted from his tacit approval and at worst made him a willing accessory to the carnage that ensued.

It was important that he didn't let Sam down. Litmus had been entranced by her from the moment he had first set eyes on her at the other side of the bar. He would have pursued matters further if it wasn't for the obvious conflict of interests. What did they say about mixing business with pleasure? Why she had chosen to help him he still had no clear idea, but his gratitude genuinely knew no bounds. He almost wished that she hadn't offered her assistance, then there would have been the possibility that their relationship might have taken a different direction altogether. In retrospect, he should have explained the situation while the opportunity had presented itself, except, in his view, it would have sounded vaguely pathetic. Still, Sam was a lovely person with a gentle nature. There was always a possibility that if he told her about Beth and the intricacies of his current assignment she may have understood. Too late now, Litmus old son. The chance was there but you resoundingly blew it as per usual. Dithered fatally when decisive action was called for. Bloody idiot. Nobody's fault but your own. Perhaps you'll learn from this and make a better job of it next time around......if for you there ever is a next time, Litmus you mug.

He was stirred from his session of self-castigation by the sound of Whitcott's car arriving at the kerb outside. They crossed the threshold immediately, catching him almost unawares, with Ho looking more than a little off colour, he was delighted to note.

'I warned her to avoid the crab, but she wouldn't listen', said Whitcott without sympathy. 'Next time I travel north of St Albans I intend to bring sandwiches. As I've long suspected, it's positively primeval in this part of the world'.

Whitcott accepted the mug of coffee Litmus thrust into his hand with his usual ill grace and looked at it doubtfully.

'Where's lightning fingers got to?' he said, indicating Beth's vacant desk.

'I had to let her go', Litmus replied.

'Fingers in the till?' Whitcott questioned speculatively. 'Didn't like the look of the woman from the start. I can always tell.'

'Couldn't believe a word she said', Litmus countered. 'Reminded me of someone, but I can't think who. Don't know why you didn't sign her up for a job down at your place. She would have slotted right in. Would have been running her own section by this time next year.'

Whitcott chose to ignore the slur and move things along.

'D.I. Ho tells me your fortunes have taken a turn for the better, Litmus. A hefty deposit made to your current account a couple of weeks back, if Ho's findings are to be believed. Another relative die? You are exceedingly unlucky with both colleagues and relatives, aren't you Litmus?'

'You are a lot more successful at getting employees at my bank to pick up the phone and answer your enquiries than I am. Any chance you could give me a lesson on how you do it? Not that it's any of your business but to stop you worrying unnecessarily, I sold the house'.

Whitcott sat back in his chair and looked totally aghast.

'You mean somebody would actually want to possess this assault on the visual senses? Did you get it featured as eyesore of the month or put it in a raffle?'

Litmus decided it would be easier to play along. With any luck Whitcott would soon be running short of time and feel obliged to bugger off back to where he came from.

'This property has a lot of advantages that someone with limited imagination would probably fail to take into account. It's situated on a main road with easy access to the city centre, has a stunning view across open parkland, it has been totally reroofed and every window is double glazed; not to mention the instillation of a stylish new bathroom and kitchen. It's also had a lot of work done that isn't immediately apparent to the untrained eye. The new woodwork was purposely distressed to blend with the existing ambience which I am reliably informed, is a look that is much sought after by buyers with a discerning eye.'

'God, Litmus, I have to agree. The word distressed has rarely been used in more apt a context. I'm only surprised they didn't offer you a council grant to tear the wretched place down. Tell me, where do you intend to live when the new owner puts you out on the street? Surely, you'll find it impossible to move further down market than this. Are you considering getting a tent?'

'There's no hurry in that regard. The new owners are happy for me to stay on for the next six months and oversee the completion of the redevelopment project before I hand it over.'

'They really said that! God, the drugs must be strong in this part of the world.' Whitcott pondered for a couple of seconds.

'Do you consider yourself equipped to take on a renovation project like this, Litmus? I don't recollect you ever boasting of your prowess with a mallet or a chisel.'

'It's just bits and pieces that need finishing off. All the heavy lifting has already been done. A bit of rubbing down and repainting. A dab of varnish here, a floorboard replacing there. I can do the straightforward stuff. Especially if it earns me a roof over my head for the immediate future while I assess my options.'

Whitcott seemed partially satisfied. A one-off occurrence deserving of recording on a celestial calendar, in Litmus' opinion. He glanced across at Ho and despite all gentlemanly instincts to the contrary, took great pleasure in failing to offer her a cup of camomile tea. They settled down for another session that he sincerely hoped wasn't going to last for very long.

Whitcott commenced without further delay.

'Any problem with me asking you a few personal questions, Litmus?'

'Why?'

'As I have already explained, there is a reasonable chance that at some stage I will be obliged to provide your tawdry speculations to some of the sharpest minds in the country. In consequence, I need to be able to represent you as something other than a total cretin, if that potential catastrophe should ever come to pass. It is merely the preparation of a worst-case scenario. I freely admit that if those circumstances should ever arise, I would view suicide as a more appealing option.'

This was going in a direction Litmus had not anticipated. Probably best to stall and give himself more time to think.

'Well, what sort of stuff do you want to know?'

'General, Litmus, very general. It's merely that, if your personal credentials are in anyway questioned, I would like to be in a position to know what I can safely reveal.......and what I most certainly would be better advised to keep to myself. Two rules of thumb that this great nation is founded upon, my friend. Firstly, to never ask a question in a court of law to which you don't already know the answer; and secondly, and in my opinion far more importantly, to only answer a question with the complete truth if you are absolutely certain a constructive embellishment would not be to your greater advantage. The important point being, quite naturally, to know in advance which alternative to apply.'

'But I worked under your personal supervision for the best part of four years. You must already have a file on me several inches thick.'

'I do indeed, and unhappy reading it makes. Please don't think I take any great pleasure in this situation. If it were my decision, the less I was forced to know about your tawdry past the better I would like it. It's a standard format works, Litmus. If you need some sort of justification, put it down as a bureaucratic necessity rather than any form of personal slight. It's just the way that these things are done, I'm afraid.'

'Alright, if you put it that way', Litmus conceded.

'Well, if you are happy to go ahead then perhaps, we should start at the very beginning. You were born in Sheffield, the only son of Wilfred and Emily Litmus. Happy childhood?'

'Very,' said Litmus.

'Your teachers spoke quite well of you, you'll be pleased to learn. Cheery little brown faced boy who was always smiling, one said. Dressed as a super-hero whenever the uniform dress code was dropped for a day.'

Whitcott paused to frown at the paper in his hand.

'Weird that a teacher would remember something like that. You would have thought they'd have better things to occupy their minds. Little wonder the standard of education is plummeting year upon year. Still, it takes all sort, I suppose.'

Still looking vaguely perplexed, he immediately continued.

'Bright as a button and popular with classmates and teachers alike, was the general impression. The only thing I heard against you, Litmus, was that you were inclined to get upset when you considered evil was being perpetrated that was likely to go unpunished; and in instances of the sort, it was reported you had a tendency to take matters into your own hands. The Terry Willcox incident we touched upon at my last visit, you remember? How old would you have been at the time, seven possibly eight? Young Terry's fall from the apple tree followed a rather nasty incident when he was alleged to have held a small girls' head in a bowl of water and displayed a marked reluctant to release her even when it became obvious that she was in serious distress. She needn't have worried though because you had the situation in hand, didn't you, Litmus? Granted, clubbing Willcox minor over the head with a wooden chair might have been judged by some to be a little drastic, but it certainly resolved the situation, I'm led to believe. Young Terry's subsequent fall from the tree and his resultant incapacitation rendered any in depth enquiry into the matter of the previous incident completely redundant; but there was talk he had climbed the tree so as to avoid your further attentions, and I think it is fair to say that served to pose questions in a couple of your teachers' minds.'

Litmus laughed. 'You have got to be joking bringing that up after all these years. The kid, Willcox, was a psychopath in the making but I didn't push him. When he fell out of the tree, I wasn't anywhere near him. Murderous little git that he was.'

'Really? It must be that a number of witnesses misremembered the circumstances. Easy to happen with the passing of the years, I suppose. You can't claim he clubbed himself over the head with the chair though, can you Harry?'

Whitcott gave a satisfied grin.

'Anyway, I suggest we brush that aside. We have bigger fish to fry. I'm just pleased that we've been able to identify your motivation. I always think it's fascinating to understand why we do things like that, Litmus, don't you?'

Litmus shrugged. Whitcott straightened his papers and instantly looked business-like.

'Right, let us immediately return to the hallowed halls of chez Litmus for further enlightenment.'

He turned and looked at Ho who was starting to look like she might be staging something of a recovery.

'Feeling a little better, my dear? Perhaps a bacon sandwich mid-morning might settle you down? It always does it for me.' Ho immediately resumed her previous tinge of bilious green.

'Your father the builder, Litmus. Did you ever work for him?'

'No, I most certainly didn't.'

'He was originally a joiner working for a large local company, I understand, but later started up his own business which involved buying up dilapidated houses, gutting and refurbishing the premises and selling them on at a not inconsiderable profit. Are you sure you were never involved?'

'Don't be ridiculous. I was far too young. Well, I did a bit of labouring for him in the school holidays on the odd occasion, but that was about it. Mainly clearing stuff out of the houses and barrowing it into skips. It was filthy work. I had to go in the bath every night before I was allowed to sit at the table and eat. That's my clearest recollection from the time.'

'You must have learned a bit watching your father work though. To take on projects like that he must have been a jack of all trades. A bit of it must have rubbed off.'

'I was too busy to pay much attention. The old man was a hard task master. It was just his way. He thought it important that I learned the value of money right from the word go. So, if I wasn't working full tilt from the time I arrived 'til the time I went home, he deducted money from my wages. I resented it at the time but later I appreciated the lesson he was trying to teach. The old man was hard but on the other hand he was always scrupulously fair.'

'People of the church, your parents. Baptists I think?' said Whitcott, swiftly changing tack.

'Yes, they were both devout Christians.'

Whitcott appeared to consider.

'Baptists. More of an 'eye for an eye' philosophy than the 'turn the other cheek' brigade, if I remember correctly. I presume you got dragged along to the services?'

'As a child, yes. In fact, I didn't lose all faith in God until much later in life when I started working for you.'

Whitcott paid no attention to the reply.

'Tell me about your friend Arthur Rochester; at the time nobody was ever really clear about the circumstances of his demise.'

Litmus scowled.

'You really can't leave that one alone, can you? To repeat myself, Arthur fell down a flight of stairs when we were working a case together. I was in a totally different part of the house when it happened. I was only alerted to what had taken place when he cried out as he fell.'

'You were very close to Rochester, weren't you? Went through some of your basic training together and even shared a flat with him before he settled down and got married.'

Whitcott looked up and stared absently out of the front window.

'There were rumours it wasn't made in heaven; Rochester's marriage, that is. Ever see any evidence to support that? There was talk of raised voices, even the odd meting out of blows.'

'Arthur Rochester and his wife were a perfectly happy couple to the best of my knowledge. The only cause of friction was the long hours he had to work. Linda did encourage him to find something that would enable them to have more of a social life but, despite everything you put us through, Arthur was still in love with the job. It was the attack that changed everything.'

Whitcott said nothing but sat a little straighter in his chair.

'He got the hell beaten out of him when he was out buying a newspaper one Friday evening. Instead of steering clear and phoning the Police, he did his best to stop a bunch of thugs from robbing a corner shop and took a grade A kicking for his trouble. Several broken ribs, cuts and bruises all over his body; he ended up with more stitching than a piece of embroidery. I hardly recognised the man when I called in to visit him at the hospital. He came back to work after about six weeks' convalescence but to be honest he was never the same man. It wasn't the physical damage, it was the fact he lost the ability to concentrate. Although it was never diagnosed, I got the impression he had suffered brain damage. Probably akin to post-traumatic shock. After the beating he became what they would now term mentally fragile. I think that was when he started drinking.'

'What happened to the wife......Linda?'

'She emigrated. New start I think, and who could blame her? Canada, New Zealand, somewhere New World; I really can't remember the country she chose. After she got on the plane, we totally lost touch. Not even Christmas cards. She was a lovely lady and I hope things worked out for her because she deserved better than she got.'

Whitcott looked extremely serious for a moment.

'Sad story that, Litmus. I honestly had no idea.'

Litmus stared pointedly across the table.

'That was probably because you never bothered to find out. Like the rest of them, you just jumped to conclusions. While we're at it, let me tell you about Harold Bonnet, because I'll lay money his death is going to come up sometime in the next half hour.'

'By all means, Litmus. It helps to talk about these things even when it is somewhat belated,' said Whitcott in a patronising voice.

Litmus jumped to his feet and just as quickly sat down again.

'After I left M.I.5. and joined the Police Force, Harold Bonnet was the D.S. who took me under his wing when I first went into plain clothes. He was an old-fashioned no-nonsense copper but dedicated to the job and straight as a die. He had a wife who he adored and a daughter that he thought the world revolved around, and one day both of them were killed in a head on collision on the South Circular. A couple of months later, Harold Bonnet walked under a taxi while we were out working together. They recorded it as accidental death, but I have never seen an act that was undertaken with more deliberation. Manslaughter would have been the only sensible verdict, because from the time that car crash occurred, D.S. Bonnet was effectively a dead man walking. The other car involved in the collision was driven by a drug dealer who had sampled a bit too much of his own stash. He got eight years, and presuming he kept his nose clean and earned full remission, he'll be out walking the streets right now, and I'm buggered if I can see the justice in that.'

'You were standing right behind Sergeant Bonnet when it happened, I understand?'

'Within touching distance and I still couldn't do a damned thing about it. I get nightmares to this day.'

Whitcott wriggled uncomfortably in his chair.

'So, there was no truth whatever in the rumours that were circulating at the time?'

'Rumours about what? I never heard any rumours.'

'Well, there was talk that he had a mistress, and that his home life was not quite as convivial as you so eloquently describe. That he ran the house like he ran his job. That the wife and daughter were terrified of him; even that there were packed suitcases found in the wreckage of the car which made some people speculate that the wife and daughter had eventually plucked up the courage to pack their bags and walk out of the door. Nothing in any of that?'

'Malicious gossip. Bonnet was as loved in his home as he was down at the station. In all the time I knew him I never saw him look at another woman and he adored his little girl.'

'To change the subject a little, you came into a very nice little inheritance a year or so back.'

'I did. I got it from an Uncle who, if I am being perfectly honest, I could easily have passed in the street without recognising; but with my parents gone and no other relatives on the horizon the whole of his estate came down to me. Not a fortune but it was very much appreciated. This building probably most of all.'

'Really,' said Whitcott looking around with apparent disbelief. 'I thought you might have been paid the annuity as compensation for getting stuck with the property portfolio.'

Whitcott hesitated for a full ten seconds awaiting a response, but when none came, he continued at the same measured pace.

'The legacy really wasn't all that little, was it? Quite considerable, would perhaps describe it better. And yet your bank account was pretty much empty until the recent sale of this property. This house, Litmus. The place you claim to love so much, flogged off without a second thought to the highest bidder. The place nearest to your heart, I think you were telling me one minute ago, in case it has slipped your memory.'

'I have to admit what you say is true. It's embarrassing to admit but I've always been completely useless with money. It just runs through my fingers like water. My complete life has been one long financial balancing act. My father would have disowned me by now if he were still alive.'

'But the amount of water that ran through your fingers in this instance would have served to fill an average sized swimming pool. Where did it go if I might make to bold? You obviously didn't spend much of it refurbishing this dump.'

'Actually, the renovation work cost plenty..........but I must admit the bulk of my inheritance was spent on a holiday.'

'A holiday, Litmus! Where did you go? A space rocket to the moon? A world cruise on a twenty-berth yacht with Brad and Angelina?'

'It's simple. I had never taken a proper holiday in my entire life. School to University, University to M.I.5, Five to the Police Force and from the Police straight to working as an Enquiry Agent while renovating this place on the side. I somehow managed to get myself caught up on the escalator of life without ever having taken time out to see what else the world might have to offer; and as the money had come as a totally unexpected gift from the gods, I thought I would take the opportunity to redress the balance........and believe me, I did it in spades. I went totally mad and took the sort of holiday I had always been denied; and you know what? I don't regret one penny of the cash I frittered away because, for me, it served as a complete eye opener.'

'That's interesting, Litmus. Actually, I think we've got one or two bits of your holiday experiences on record, haven't we D.I. Ho? Ho, while you're on your feet would you be an absolute dear and fetch the other files from the car? It will give you a nice opportunity to be sick in the gutter, if you feel so inclined. Talking of which, Litmus, what have you planned for our lunch? I noticed an outlet advertising roast pork sandwiches down at the corner. No need to rush Ho, we won't need the files until after our lunch.'

CHAPTER SEVENTEEN

Sheffield, Wednesday October 15th 2025

Sandwiches. A selection of ham, cheese and tuna sandwiches on rye bread with vine ripened tomatoes on the side, which Whitcott complained bitterly about and Ho totally ignored. What were they expecting? He hadn't been to the supermarket this week and was pretty sure they wouldn't have had fatted calf on special offer even if the opportunity to shop had presented itself.

The coffee was judged to be too weak or was it too strong. The tap water too soft. (How could tap water possibly be too soft? There was no necessity to bounce on it. It wasn't like a bed!) The room temperature too cold, or possibly too warm. Everything was always *too* something or other, and when it wasn't, it was *not enough*. So, without further preamble the interrogation was once more kicked into life, more as a distraction from Litmus' catering deficiencies, than anything else.

'Tell us a bit about your holiday, Litmus. Somewhat extended, wouldn't you say?'

'I had the money and for once I had a pretty much unlimited window of opportunity at my disposal. Cut me a bit of slack. It was my first real break after God knows how many years of keeping my head down. It was my money to do with as I saw fit. It wasn't as if I was asking the Government to pay for anything.'

'I believe you started in Ireland. Ireland of all places. God forsaken country in my experience!'

'I went to Belfast first, took in Derry, still a divided city but gradually coming to terms with twenty first century realities; then headed down to Galway and Limerick, before finishing up in Shannon where I boarded a flight to America.'

'Did you meet anyone interesting. Dinner with Gerry Adams at Stormont or maybe the Taoiseach popped over for a breakfast meeting or something like that?'

'Pure leisure. Stopped at small hotels, caught up on sleep, walked the country lanes and drank too much Guinness. I loved Ireland and I loved the Irish. Such warm and charming people. It bought home to me that maybe somewhere along the line we have allowed ourselves to get our priorities skewed; started to overlook the very things that we should regard as most important in our lives; ignored the need that is in all of us, to occasionally let our hair down and totally cut loose. The Irish still seem to be able to get through a day at a time with a smile on their faces in a way that we have completely forgotten. It opened my eyes to a lot of things that I had previously been missing, I can tell you.'

'Yes, great fun the Irish when they aren't planning to blow you to kingdom come or shoot you in the back,' said Whitcott looking vaguely horrified.

'I flew direct into New York on one of those massive planes that are the size of a block of flats, and a bit later I travelled up the coast to Boston. Great scenery and, despite a bad press, I found the American people really hospitable. It's impossible to imagine spaces so vast unless you actually get to travel through them and view the distant horizon with your very own eyes. The total opposite of England. There is very little feeling of any form of constriction once you are out of the cities and onto the open road. It bought Jack Kerouac very much to mind.'

'Really, Litmus. You can get quite lyrical when the mood takes you. A crying shame that you didn't extend that talent a little more when you were writing the report, or was that a little mundane to fulfil your literary aspirations? If I am ever in a position where I am forced to present a copy to the Home Secretary, I think I'll die of shame. However, tearing ourselves away from your literary romanticising for one minute, and getting back to the more banal stuff, it was in New York where you were first bought to our attention.

149

Mixing in dubious company according to the initial F.B.I. field report, based on a sighting in a New York bar that is regularly kept under surveillance. Mingling with men and women of a Fenian persuasion; polite shorthand used by the Cousins when referring to supporters of the I.R.A. as I'm sure you are fully aware.'

'Put plainly, I didn't discriminate. I mixed with anybody who fancied a good night out and a few beers. I never asked questions about anybody's politics, though you know yourself that large swathes of the east coast of America have Irish blood dating back to the times of the famines, and it isn't really surprising where their sympathies continue to lie.'

Whitcott looked as if a bad smell had suddenly become apparent in the space directly below his nose.

'Boston and New York were prime funding grounds for the I.R.A.'s campaign of butchery and barbarism, and you found enjoyment swilling ale with people who were doing their level best to fund anarchy in our very own back yard.......if, in fact, that was all you were doing while you were there.'

'I've no idea what you mean. I was just on holiday. You talk as if I was committing some sort of crime.'

'Well, you'll be interested to know that the American Secret Service were less than impressed by your apparent closeness to your new-found set of buddies and tracked you for the rest of the time you were in their country. Extremely embarrassing for Five needless to say; you can imagine the tone of the communications that burned up the airways in an easterly direction. Anyway, after Boston you returned to New York and then took an internal flight down to Florida.'

'Yes, I saw no reason to deny myself some sunshine while the opportunity presented itself. I even travelled over to Cuba for a few days.'

'More than a few days, Litmus. Ten to be precise. The F.B.I. were so concerned at your apparent mateyness with your new set of chums that they passed you on to the C.I.A. for monitoring when you vacated their shores. You might take sole responsibility for having re-cemented a rupture in the United States security services that dates back to the days of Jack Kennedy. The two services hate each other's guts and yet were fully prepared to temporarily put their differences to one side in order to deal with what they obviously regarded as a far bigger hazard to their country's security. You, Litmus, you!'

Litmus shrugged. 'I can only think they are suffering from some sort of advanced form of paranoia. I was doing no more than enjoying myself on a well-earned holiday, for God's sake.'

'And from Florida you caught a plane to Jamaica. Was the sun in America and Cuba not hot enough for you, or was the motivation for this visit something entirely different?'

'Odd you should ask that, because the weather was decidedly ordinary for my entire stay in the southern states of America. A cyclone or an anticyclone; one of them. I never can remember which one is which. Jamaica was very much more pleasant though. Beautiful beaches. I stopped at a hotel on Montego Bay for part of the time. The colour of the sand and the warmth of the water is something that.......'

'Yes, yes, spare me the idyllic holiday reminiscences, Litmus. Why did you choose Jamaica?'

'It was the part of the West Indies my parents originated from. I guess you could say I was tapping into my roots. Fascinating place, interesting people. Riches and poverty rubbing shoulders with one another under a blanket of the warm Caribbean sun.'

Whitcott sighed. 'Kunta Kinte unleashed on the twenty first century; one dreads to think of the possible repercussions for the civilised world.'

Litmus looked out of the window awaiting his next prompt. Whitcott consulted his papers.

'I assume you found the experience very rewarding because you stayed in Jamaica for nearly two months, and when you eventually returned home it was via Ireland again. Quite the international jetsetter, aren't you Litmus? Under the circumstances I'm surprised you bothered coming back at all.'

Litmus smiled.

'England might be a bitch, Mr Whitcott, but I look on her as my bitch. Deep down I'm solid Yorkshire through to my very core. Cut me and I bleed the petals of the white rose.'

Whitcott smiled coldly as if he wouldn't be entirely averse to locating a sharp implement and giving that a try. Then he appeared to remember something that had previously slipped his mind. He hurriedly gathered his possessions and looked meaningfully at D.I. Ho.

'Look, the way things are going I think it will be better if I leave my final questions and summing up until tomorrow. D.I. Ho is still looking decidedly peaky, and I think I can suffer another night of the excruciating food at that hotel if I pick up some bicarbonate of soda on the journey back. Ten sharp again Litmus and hopefully we will be able to quickly wrap things up.'

Odd, that, thought Litmus, as Whitcott struggled to raise his umbrella as a shield against the light rain that had been coming down steadily all day. Even Ho looked vaguely bemused as they trotted side by side towards the car. It was apparent she was as much in the dark about what was going on as he was. Had the afternoon session gone too fast or too slowly for his inquisitor's liking? Whatever the reason, Whitcott obviously had no intentions of getting back on the road quite yet.

CHAPTER EIGHTEEN

Sheffield, Thursday October 16th 2025

The town hall clock chimed the ten o'clock hour as Litmus strode through the centre of the city. He glanced to left and right despite his heart telling him it would be far wiser to keep his gaze fixed firmly to the front. There had been unsubstantiated rumours that the Luftwaffe had been given relatively free access to the Sheffield city centre in World War Two, in an effort to draw German planes away from the steel making plants to the north of the city that were key to the war effort. Whether or not that claim bore any relation to the truth, it was blatantly obvious that at the cessation of hostilities the central precincts of the town had been left with very few fine buildings to bequeath the next generation.

A series of construction projects had ensued, each one delivering fewer prepossessing results that its predecessor, and none of them providing anything that offered the slightest degree of spectacle or splendour to admire. The current up-grade, at least the third or fourth and possibly the fifth, was once again concentrating its efforts on forcing vast quantities of characterless brick, toughened glass and soulless concrete into structures that would doubtless be torn down again in twenty or thirty-years' time to be superseded by a new generation of architectural carbuncles. Sheffield had quality stone quarried right on its doorstep, but for some unknown reason chose to ignore this in favour of materials that did nothing for the eye and a good deal less for the spirit. He suspected that even the beggars and buskers that currently plied their trade at the roadside precincts would feel vaguely uncomfortable that a better backdrop for their activities had once again failed to be commissioned by those in whom the inhabitants of the vicinity had elected to place their electoral trust.

Litmus' morning had started early with a blunt summons. Whitcott desired his presence at the hotel about which he had been assiduously complaining from the moment of his arrival. This was presumably so he could complete the debriefing that Litmus was totally convinced could have been comfortably wrapped up in the time already allocated if Whitcott had chosen to get his arse in gear. In light of this directive, he had chosen to set off early and walk the pleasant suburban thoroughfare that led down to the town centre in order to get some much-needed exercise. The weather had changed for the better again and weak sunshine periodically forced its way through the scant remains of yesterday's blanket of cloud. He had to admit he felt in relatively good spirits even if he could think of no reason why that should be the case.

Whitcott met him in the bustling reception area and straightway directed him to a private room that looked like it was ordinarily used for low volume business meetings or the high volume dumping of coats and hats. He was mildly surprised to see their party was boasting two additions to the taciturn D.I. Ho. Whitcott's driver, who was introduced as Terry, and a gorilla of a man somewhat withdrawn from the main ensemble, who Whitcott chose not to identify at all.

'Some developments since yesterday, Litmus,' Whitcott announced. 'Sangster's team have at last managed to track down the caterers.'

Litmus turned in the direction of Ho, who was immediately subordinate to Sangster and had presumably been the recipient of these glad tidings. His unspoken enquiry was met with an equally eloquent unspoken reply.

Litmus looked hard at Ho. When he considered the matter, he was pretty sure the Detective Inspector hadn't spoken a solitary word to him in the last two days and that situation didn't look like it was about to change any time soon. Ho had obviously taken a severe dislike to him but what specifically he had done to earn that accolade remained largely unclear. At the very least it seemed a little unfair, and on that basis perhaps he should remonstrate. On the other hand, it might be better just to accept that it wasn't possible to be loved by everybody, and mark Ho's case down as an object lesson in the need to try harder if the circumstances should ever arise by which he actually gave a toss. Mollified by this thought, Litmus shelved his feeling of grievance and refocussed on the subject in hand.

'What caterers?' he enquired, directing the question to the wide-eyed subject depicted in a reproduction of Vermeer's 'Girl with a Pearl Earring' that was hanging on a blank section of wall midway between where Whitcott and Ho had chosen to position themselves.

'The people who cooked and served the breakfast prior to the explosion, Litmus,' Whitcott replied testily. 'You have a recollection of the explosion, Litmus? The event you were commissioned to look into and write a report about? Is it coming back to you at all? Look, we've got a lot to get through this morning. Do make a supreme effort to keep up.'

Whitcott moved swiftly to settle himself in what was clearly the most comfortable chair in the room. He sat back and crossed his legs. Litmus took the seat opposite with only a coffee table loaded with tourist brochures acting as a grand divide. The other members took seats against the far wall, looking like three wise monkeys awaiting eleventh hour confirmation of their designated roles.

'The main thrust of Sangster's enquiry has always been to track down either the builders or the catering team', Whitcott continued in statesmanlike fashion; 'and after all these months at last there is a faint glimmer on the horizon.'.

'Well, I'm reassured to know Sangster's enquiry did have a thrust of some sort, even if it was one he never chose to share with me.'

Litmus stared meaningfully at Ho who was once again scribbling on a notepad and in consequence had the perfect excuse to completely ignore him.

'Three dinner ladies from Luton,' said Whitcott, as if he was pronouncing an incantation to ward off evil spirits, rather than choosing to update the chorus from the Mikado.

'Driven in on the morning by someone they referred to as Mr Bob and conveyed back home immediately after they had cooked breakfast and taken care of the washing up by the very same person. Paid two hundred and fifty quid a piece, about which they were highly delighted; especially as they were back home in time to shove a casserole in the oven, so the old man would be none the wiser if they took it upon themselves not to share.'

Whitcott quickly surveyed the room to be certain everybody was paying attention.

'Sadly, none of the women were a great deal of help with a description of Mr Bob except to say he was youngish with long fair hair, above average height, posh bordering on effeminate, and didn't like to talk when he was driving. A description that seems unlikely to take us a lot further on our travels but at least keeps the bus steering in the right direction. The driver seemed to have gone out of his way not to communicate any more than was strictly necessary. On the other hand, it appears the ladies had a lot to tell each other having been totally out of contact since the previous day, so there wasn't a lot of focus on a reticent driver who quite obviously preferred to keep himself to himself. They didn't come up with much on their clients either, because they had been forbidden to fraternise. However, loosely speaking, the customer base was reckoned to be young, well dressed, mainly afro-Caribbean and decidedly surly. The ladies speculated amongst themselves that they might be professional footballers or high-level athletes because most of them looked extremely fit and what one described as, *sort of competitive.* There was even some conjecture that they could possibly be missionaries newly returned from Africa because there was something vaguely other-worldly about them and the way they seemed to almost look through each other. No, the dinner ladies didn't see anyone they recognised that day, and no, they certainly didn't hear anything that in anyway resembled an explosion. The car they were transported in was either black, dark green or blue and not unlike the carpet in one of their front rooms, and it was either middle sized or big with brown or black upholstery. None of them noticed the make, let alone the number plate.'

'Presumably, they were questioned on how they came to be selected for the job?' Litmus interjected.

'Indeed, they were', Whitcott replied. 'It appears Mr Bob waylaid one of them at the school gates and asked if she would be interested in earning a few quid on the side and, if so, would she be able to put together a team of three. Once she was satisfied that she wasn't being propositioned she jumped at the chance and had no trouble pulling in two of her mates to make up the required number. Cooking a breakfast for fifty odd strangers was falling off a log for these three old girls and they were impressed by the fact the kitchen equipment was all new, and seemingly unused. In fact, they said if they got an offer like that again, they would jump at the chance because it had been the easiest two hundred and fifty pounds they had ever earned. The only reason they even came to the attention of Sangster's team was that one of the ladies told the story to her son, and he got suspicious and contacted the local nick. As far as Sangster has been able to gather, the ladies had remained completely oblivious to anything that happened following their departure, because none of them read the front end of a newspaper and they didn't pay any attention to television news programmes because they found them depressing. The interview is on-going, but the general feeling is that it would be unwise for anybody to get excited at the prospect of further developments. None the less, it does represent progress of a sort; just not a great deal of it.'

Whitcott unscrewed the top of a bottle of effervescent water which overflowed alarmingly. Litmus was sad to see none of the escaped fluid landed on Whitcott's pristine suit.

'Have you ever been to Luton?' Whitcott asked.

'No,' said Litmus, though he thought perhaps he might have many years ago, if he wasn't perhaps getting it confused with Watford or St Albans.

'Alright, would you mind if we now turned to the death of your father,' said Whitcott as if that was the logical follow on from the previous question.

Litmus levered himself forward and stood up.

'Right. Look, that's it. I've been pretty patient up to now but that was the final straw. I am now going to put on my coat and walk through that door and out of this building, and if my fee hasn't been paid into my bank account along with the relevant expenses when I check my bank balance at midday tomorrow then I'm placing the matter in the hands of my Solicitor. Goodbye Mr Whitcott, and please don't take that as meaning au revoir.'

Whitcott stirred, but only slightly.

'Alright, Litmus, perhaps you are right and it's now time we put an end to this charade. I've certainly had more than enough of it, and we can't keep going round in circles indefinitely. Take a seat and let me tell you how things stand. Malcolm,' he nodded towards the gorilla who was still propping up the far wall, 'will make sure we aren't interrupted, won't you Malcolm?' Malcolm duly picked up his chair and slowly moved it half a yard, so it was now in front of the door instead of by the side of it. A readjustment to the furniture that was totally unnecessary if you discounted the aura of menace it bought to the room.

'It's all comes down to too many coincidences,' said Whitcott. 'A few you can always expect but the number that have occurred during this examination is some way beyond ridiculous. And the sheer volume has forced me to re-examine something that initially would have seemed utterly preposterous and concede that it could be vaguely credible.... or in my very worst bloody nightmare, even distinctly possible.'

Litmus smiled at Whitcott. Whitcott failed to smile back.

'I have never met a man with the ability to use so many words to say so little. Mr Whitcott, I honestly haven't got a clue what you are talking about, but if you've got some sort of contrived accusation to make then don't mince your words, just spit it out. I've really got better things to do with my time than sit in here listening to this sort of garbage for the rest of the day.'

CHAPTER NINETEEN

Sheffield, Thursday October 16th 2025

Whitcott's voice graduated from harsh to gentle, until he sounded genuinely solicitous.

'Look, Litmus, I can make this easy for you if you just choose to cooperate. There's no reason in the world why this mess would ever need to get near a courtroom. It clearly reflects well on nobody involved.'

'Obviously, there would need to be some form of incarceration, but there are special places we could get you into where the accommodation is more like a luxury rest home than a detention centre. You are still a relatively young man. There's no reason this has to be the end of everything; look on it more as the opportunity for you to carve out a new beginning. No man could possibly carry this sort of weight on his conscience for the rest of his days. It would play on his mind; fester until it slowly drove him insane. The Shrinks can achieve wonders these days. They have limitless resources at their disposal and their understanding of how motivation is influenced by childhood trauma has risen to a whole new level. Developments in the criminal justice system mean that punishment is no longer the main issue, in a situation like this. Healing through atonement is what they are looking to achieve these days. You will be aware from your own experiences that retribution doesn't figure as a priority anymore. I would be delighted to testify as a character witness on your behalf. You gave years of honest and loyal service to your country, and I can guarantee that I won't allow that fact to be overlooked when the time comes for you to be judged. You worked under my personal direction, so I have a personal stake in you getting the best treatment possible and you have my word as a gentleman that a first-class rehabilitation program would be put in place to aid your recovery. Even if the hierarchical system under which people from our vocation were obliged to operate precluded us from ever becoming close friends, there are still some bonds that time can never sever. Put your trust in me and I can assure you I will not let you down. I'll be in your corner from day one, and I won't desert you in your hour of need. Trust me Litmus, I beseech you. The alternative really doesn't bear thinking about.'

Litmus nodded appreciatively looking a little unsure. 'Any chance you could dispense with the waffle and just tell me what the hell it is you're talking about?'

'Listen, Litmus, are you really sure you want to go through with this? I would have thought it would be in your best interests to save yourself the misery, but of course, that is a decision only you can make. The outcome can only go one way so what is the point in drawing out the agony? Listen, I'll run through the salient points if that will help you make up your mind. In the current circumstances, there's not much else I can do for you, I'm afraid.'

Litmus said nothing. Whitcott adjusted the knot in his tie and took the opportunity to ease himself further forward in his seat so he could easily spring to his feet if the need should arise. He addressed Litmus, maintaining the sorrowful expression of a headmaster placed in the awkward position of having to mete out punishment to a much-favoured pupil.

'As this is a somewhat unorthodox procedure, D.I. Ho will log nothing of what I am about to say. This is merely an opportunity for you to appreciate the mountain of evidence that has already been compiled, and the fact that absolutely none of it is in your favour. In the unlikely event that you can supply a rational explanation for any of your actions I for one would be extremely interested to hear it. You will of course be given plenty of opportunity to furnish your own version of events once I've completed my summing up, but at that stage I would encourage you to save us from wasting further time for no good purpose. In short, Litmus, I am hoping you will choose to face up to your responsibilities and save your friends, family and ex-colleagues from any unnecessary embarrassment by standing up to be counted and doing the right thing.'

Whitcott cleared his throat and adopted a look of concentration. The same one that would have been put into practise when selecting a lobster from the tank to be boiled alive. Litmus felt confident that a lobster placed in that position would not have harboured a grudge. It would have appreciated that being good to eat and easy to catch was a suffering that crustaceans had bestowed upon them from on high; and that with celestial misfortune came a certain inherent responsibility to get on with dying while not making an unnecessary fuss about something that was beyond its powers to control. Litmus felt vaguely sad that he had been blessed with no such degree of pragmatism.

Whitcott levered himself into an upright position and addressed the non-existent courtroom with a flourish worthy of a man who had waited some considerable time for this moment to arrive. Litmus was effectively in the dock, or possibly still occupying the holding cell in the bowels of the Assizes having refused to appear in the hope that this action might in some way irritate the presiding Judge. In either instance, he was to all intents and purposes completely invisible as Jerome Whitcott straightened the cuffs of his shirt and prepared to speak.

'Let me first assure you; nobody working in the Security Services had the slightest interest in Harry Litmus until the subject pitched up in America and set alarm bells ringing with our American Cousins across the water. As far as the authorities in Great Britain were concerned, Litmus would have been viewed as an unfortunate who had been unable to hack it in the Security Service, before demonstrating he was no better equipped to handle the pressures of working in the Metropolitan Police Force. If anyone had taken the trouble to consider Litmus at all, he would have been graded as a nonentity who had failed to make it in the big time or even the minor leagues and had now sunk so low he was scraping a meagre living by trailing after errant husbands and hunting down stray dogs in an unfortunate suburban backwater attached to a city that nobody had paid the slightest attention to since it stopped producing good quality knives and forks.'

Don't hold back in order to spare my feelings, Litmus felt tempted to interpose. Just give it to me straight. I can take it.

'However, as I'm sure we are all painfully aware, when the F.B.I. shouts jump, M.I.5. immediately leap in the air with their hands above their heads. Not because the domestic Security Services have any great interest in what the F.B.I. think about anything or anybody, but because the spooks across the water have resources that they are less reluctant to share if we convey the impression that we prepared to strike a match when they are blundering about in the dark. Besides, having a small rummage in the archives for somebody as easy to trace as Harold Sebastian Litmus, would give the desk jockeys something to do when they had finished reindexing their filing cabinets; and, all things considered equal, it would prove a small price to pay for oiling the wheels of international cooperation while at the same time earning a small quantity of brownie points which would come in useful some way down the line.'

Whitcott looked over at Ho who smiled appreciatively in his direction. Either that, or the crab was still having an adverse effect.

'So, on the basis that our American allies weren't overly enamoured with Mr Litmus cosying up to the boys who drink green beer on St Patrick's day, Five clenched their teeth and poked around a bit in their files, and to their horror they discovered that the good Mr Litmus was not only matey with the Fenians on the U.S. east coast but, worse, had recently spent over a month breaking bread and supping Guinness with their counterparts in our very own back yard. Well, as I'm sure you can well imagine, this shone a different light on matters altogether. Litmus was free to do pretty much what he pleased while he was on the other side of the ocean, out of sight being very much out of mind as far as the Foreign Office is concerned, but Ireland qualified as a more sensitive area altogether. And, as it seemed increasingly likely this country would be stuck with responsibility for the bickering factions at the top right-hand corner of the adjacent island for the conceivable future, ears that had previously been alert only to the commentary on Test Match Special were observed to be devoid of ear buds and bending in all directions like directional antennae in a force nine gale. And this attention was given not least because Dublin had recently made it clear through unofficial channels that it would be delighted to take the six counties back under its wing the day after it was positively confirmed that hell had frozen over. So, it seemed highly probable that we would be stuck with the squabbling juveniles and their unique set of contrived grievances for some years to come whether we liked it or not.'

Whitcott paused to draw breath, but for no apparent reason reconsidered the decision, and immediately pressed on. You could almost sense him trying not to lose his place as he listed out each point in his mind.

'Instead of proving a routine task, investigations of Litmus' past proved something of a revelation, and ultimately cast extreme doubts on whether the background checks conducted by M.I.5. are worth the paper they are written on. Even a scant delve into the murky pond that comprised Litmus' back catalogue cast him as the misbegotten prodigy of a coming together between Dirty Harry and the Angel of Death. How the hell he had ever got within fifty miles of being offered a job in the Police Force, let alone the home branch of the Security Services, is a question that will be subsequently addressed at the highest level if I have anything to say about the matter. The findings will then be followed by a full review. Something which in my humble opinion appears to be long overdue. Apologies, it's a matter close to my heart; I digress.'

Whitcott paused for a second to gather himself, while at the same time signalling his regrets to the twelve non-existent jurors that he had broken off from addressing. Litmus noticed he had gone quite red in the face.

'From an early age, the subject seemed to have adopted a warped belief that it was incumbent upon him to administer justice whenever he considered it had not been meted out to his personal satisfaction. This pattern was particularly prevalent where Litmus encountered a female victim, casting herself as the proverbial damsel in distress. It appears the motivation for Litmus' actions can be traced back to the misconduct of his father towards his mother...........a mother whom Litmus completely adored. As you will have observed, Litmus has proved reluctant to discuss this situation, but witnesses were tracked down who supported the fact, and were prepared to recount their memories. Perhaps a classic illustration of the adage '*Give me the child, I will give you the man';* though not in any way how the orator meant his words to be applied.'

'Litmus senior should perhaps have observed his son more closely and learned lessons from what he saw, because his death came about when he plummeted three floors from the roof of a building after an unexplained collapse of the scaffolding on which he was standing. Records indicate that young Litmus was assisting on site that day. Doubtless you still recall the incident, Harry; feel free to tell me if I am wrong.'

Litmus declined to reply and Whitcott quickly resumed speaking.

'Please don't allow me to give the impression that the subject's intervention would necessarily require female involvement as a precursor, but it was a common theme in any number of the cases that were re-evaluated by a cold case team that Inspector Ho pulled together for the purpose of sifting through Litmus' past. As time went on there were any number of instances where Litmus assumed the mantle of the righteous hero, and with the hand of God resting firmly on his shoulder set out to correct matters that had not been resolved to his satisfaction. Terry Willcox, Arthur Rochester and Harold Bonnet are, I fear, very much the tip of the iceberg. How many others passed under the radar due to the lack of judicial vigilance is anyone's guess, but investigations are still very much ongoing and there is little doubt further revelations will be forthcoming in the fullness of time. One might certainly question how carefully the death of Litmus' father was investigated, for starters. It's doubtful that patricide was even considered at the time. In short, the man you now see standing before you was prepared to act as a self-appointed righter of wrongs, and saw it within his powers to preside as judge, jury.........and as will shortly be revealed in the context of the current murder enquiry, mass executioner, as well.'

D.I. Ho sneezed very loudly, which broke everybody's concentration and caused them to jump. The room went completely quiet in case it was a prelude to her making some sort of contribution to the proceedings; but as it turned out she remained quiet.

Whitcott, straightened himself and flexed his arms, seemingly to indicate the preamble was over and we were now getting down to the serious stuff.

'OK, so it looked like the Security Services had failed abysmally in their efforts to conduct satisfactory due diligence on their intake of new recruits; and in the case of Litmus, it seemed they had further compounded their error by welcoming into their ranks a fully functioning homicidal maniac. However, it could be reasoned that at least these errors of judgement had taken place in the dim and distant past and, in mitigation, the foul criminal in question wasn't working for any branch of the Government at this point in time........and neither was there the remotest possibility that he would be involved with any branch of law enforcement at any time in the future.'

'It was admittedly an extremely poor show by people who should have taken their responsibilities a good deal more seriously, but not by any means a total disaster. If a benevolent perspective was adopted, the situation could now be evaluated as a recoverable halftime deficit, providing it never came under scrutiny by some bright young irk on a select committee who was seeking to get his name up in lights the easy way, and by so doing avoid the necessity of grinding out the hard yards; and not forgetting that it would of course be necessary that data relating to the subject having been provided with high level training in state-of-the-art weaponry while being employed at the taxpayers' expense was suitably suppressed. In short, it would not be inconceivable to imagine that the matter could be addressed behind closed doors and encouraged to quietly go away, if the right men were given the correct incentives to see that a satisfactory conclusion came about.'

Talk of weaponry and collusion in the same sentence as taxpayer's money caused Whitcott to feel in his pocket and retrieve a lozenge. The rest of the room looked on enviously as he slowly unwrapped it and popped it into his mouth.

'While Security was obliged to don a hair shirt for having let a fully functioning psychopath into their midst, there still didn't appear to be any logical explanation as to why the man you now see before you had taken it upon himself to cosy up to the I.R.A. Was he perhaps planning to make a belated attempt to redress unspecified ills carried forward from the period of the troubles? Somehow that didn't sound likely. Litmus took motivation from things that had affected him or those close to him directly; retrospective adjustments weren't at all his style unless he had at some stage become personally involved. Records were checked and rechecked but there was no sign of a crossover that would offer a satisfactory explanation. The enquiry was now pretty much back to square one.'

'In the meantime, Litmus had made his way home following his extended vacation, having taken in along the way visits to New York, Boston, Florida, in addition to the islands of Cuba and Jamaica, before sliding back into this country after a second stop-off in Ireland. But as security had been completely unable to identify any subversive intent that served to connect the dots, the file labelled H.S. Litmus was slowly working its way towards the bottom of a rather thick pile; and it's fair to say it would most probably have stayed there had it not been for the events of June 29th this year, which caused everything to be re-evaluated, and much to be viewed in an entirely different light.'

Whitcott paused to sip from his water bottle. Litmus smiled pleasantly as if the subject under discussion was nothing to do with him, but moderately entertaining, nevertheless.

'After June twenty ninth a great number of profiles were re-examined, and the first question asked on each occasion related to the possibility of the subject accessing volume quantities of Semtex high explosives. Semtex is of course an automatic pointer to Eastern Europe, but in the case of this country's unfortunate recent history, Northern Ireland also has a marked tendency to loom large.'

'Over the next days and weeks, vast numbers of files were carefully examined, before they returned to gathering dust.......but the one marked H.S. Litmus was not amongst their number.'

'No misunderstanding here. This was primarily due to his recent excursions abroad, rather than anything to do with his murky past history; but slowly, very slowly evidence started to mount, and the possibility of Litmus' involvement started to be taken rather more seriously than initially anyone might have guessed.'

'Did the subject's recent movements fit into the necessary time frame? After careful back checking this one was granted a small red tick. Did he have knowledge of explosives? Thanks to his extensive security training, again a tick. Did he have the required motivation? Well, possibly, though at the time we were still thinking of Harry Litmus as a person bent on some obscure form of personal revenge, having displayed a long history as a ruthless murderer. The thought that he might have become psychologically damaged by his upbringing would have been brushed aside as an irrelevance, and the thought that he might have been in any way affected by the deaths of his brothers in arms would, quite frankly, never have entered anybody's mind. At this stage, Litmus' true motivation was yet to become apparent, and I honestly wonder how much progress we have made in that area even now.'

Whitcott looked across at Litmus in the way you might view a specimen in a laboratory. He sadly shook his head and returned to his theme.

'Could Litmus have procured Semtex and smuggled it into the country? Well, once again, this was a possibility, but it certainly required a bit of a stretch of the imagination. How tight was security on ferries across the Irish sea now that fallout from The Troubles were largely a thing of the past? *Not very*, was the findings of an independent evaluation commissioned by the relevant branch of the Security Services, providing the perpetrators knew what they were doing, and the action took place at the right time of the day. Did Litmus have the necessary planning capability? We thought we could give a tick to that one as well. Had the suspect sufficient knowledge to oversee the renovation programme to the north London property? Yes, he could easily have picked up enough knowledge from his father to handle the building work. Did he know London well enough to find his way around comfortably? A yes to that one also, as he had been in the capital while operating for both the security agency and the Police Service. Had he the necessary wherewithal to finance the operation? A big tick in that column because he had recently received a large legacy, the majority of which was no longer in evidence. And another big one; could he handle the level of interface that would have been required to get forty or fifty hardened leaders of London gangs to congregate in one place when there was very little love lost between the rival factions? Half a tick on that one, maybe three quarters at a pinch. The colour of his skin would of course have worked in his favour when pitching the deal, and he had experience of acting from his student days and was certainly articulate enough......but even taking that into account it would still have been a monumental task.'

'It must be admitted, the argument in favour of Litmus being the much-sought after instigator of the deadly deed prospered as much from other candidates' perceived inadequacies, as from any significant additions to the evidence that had been assembled against him. The investigation had now reached a stage where days went by with nothing of significance being added to the file. In short, the case against Litmus was slowly beginning to stall. Yet despite everything, he was still the one person who was seen to offer real possibilities.'

'In consequence, lacking any other particularly attractive alternative, a low-grade covert operation was devised that might serve to flush the subject into the open. Litmus was offered a lucrative commission to look into the very Police investigation of which he was unknowingly already an integral part. He was tasked with investigating all aspects of the mass assassination and producing a brief report that would guide the enquiry in its future direction. No one could fail to be aware that he was ludicrously underqualified for the task, but it was hoped that the financial inducement would prove sufficiently attractive for him to put to one side the fact that he would be wasting his time.'

'Initially the approach proved totally unsuccessful. Litmus made it quite clear he was reluctant to become involved in the enquiry no matter what incentives were placed on offer. However, as previously stated, saving damsels in distress had proved a major feature in Harry Litmus' sordid past and the problem of a blank refusal had already been anticipated. So, with a degree of coercion involving both the carrot and the stick, the required objective was achieved. A case in point not of a beautiful princess being rescued after pricking her finger but, rather, of a calculating woman of the world being employed to finger someone acting like a prick.'

Whitcott beamed at the cleverness of this contrived allegory, looking distinctly reminiscent of Paul Merton, the quiz show panellist, on one of his more tiresome days.

'The plan was to give Litmus a free rein with his inquiry, while keeping tabs on any progress made from a discrete distance. To deny the man access to all but the barest of bones of the findings of the police investigation, in the hope that in attempting to plough his own furrow he would succeed only in digging his own grave. How that might come about, it must be confessed, initially, we had little idea.'

'However, we were surprised and not a little encouraged to see this strategy achieve an almost instant success. Shortly after arriving in the south, Litmus contrived to invent a meeting with two fictitious characters at a café adjacent to the site of the carnage; and it soon became blatantly apparent from the report of that meeting that the characters had been specifically contrived for the purpose of pointing the investigation in the direction he wanted it to take. Result, we thought; or at least slightly better than half of one.'

'The following day Litmus compounded this error still further. At a meeting with D.I. Calvin Mortley, who currently heads up the Gang Related Crime unit in London, he completely rejected any suggestions put forward by the officer that in any way contradicted the course of action he already appeared set upon. In a subsequent interview with the Detective Inspector, conducted by D.I. Christine Ho of the Metropolitan Police, Mortley stated that he had gone to some lengths to make Litmus aware that he had received information from a reliable source that a Jamaican facilitator named Jeremiah Jones was directly involved in summoning the victims to meet at the location where they were later executed; but Litmus had completely dismissed that prognosis out of hand. Mortley further pointed out to Litmus that whilst he was not at the time directly involved in the Police investigation it was very much his area of expertise, and in consequence he felt his findings should be given some degree of credence. That entreaty also fell on deaf ears.'

'It should at this juncture be pointed out that subsequent enquiries with the Jamaican Police Force established that a person by the name of Jeremiah Jones did or does exist, and that in the past he had proved what they ubiquitously termed, *a person of interest*. However, as Jones had never been charged with any specific crime and in consequence did not have a criminal record, details of his past history could at best be described as sketchy, to the point that the Jamaican authorities were unable to even provide a photograph of the man. A fact that seems beyond belief in a day and age when people seem incapable of going more than five minutes at a time without taking a photograph of themselves. This deficit in helpful information was further compounded by the fact that Mr Jones whereabouts at the time the enquiry was completely unknown.'

'On a broader front, Mortley stated that he gained the impression that Litmus had already made up his mind as to the identity of the individuals he wished to be held responsible for the bombing and had no interest in considering any initiatives that might contradict this fixed point of view. The Detective Inspector concluded his interview by saying he had no objection to his opinions being used in evidence in any subsequent proceedings that might in due course be considered necessary.'

Whitcott again paused and reached for his water bottle. He gave Litmus a look that appeared to say, *well you can't say I didn't warn you*. He then wasted no time in resuming his monologue.

'Subsequently, Litmus met with D.I. James Leeming who currently heads up the Organised Crime Squad in the capital. Leeming was, and is, a firm believer that an Albanian faction were responsible for the north London bombing, but like Calvin Mortley he was also not directly involved in the ongoing investigation.'

'By chance, Leeming was at that time pursuing a suspect Albanian group on an unrelated matter and had been intending to launch an imminent raid on their headquarters. Before proceeding, however, he was obliged to obey a protocol that I had purposely instituted and enquire if Litmus had any problem with the course of action he was about to undertake. Bear in mind Litmus had been granted the power to veto Leeming's proposed actions if he considered them to be incorrect or if there was any possibility they could interfere with his current line of enquiry. Leeming recorded in his log of the day's events that Litmus not only supported his proposed action, but willingly withdrew his power of veto and signed a document to demonstrate the fact. Leeming subsequently provided D.I. Ho with written evidence to corroborate this version of events.'

Whitcott turned a page and gave a meaningful look at a rather nice statue of Buddha, seated in a lotus positioned, which was resting on a side table. The Buddha appeared unmoved by the intrusion and stared unseeingly back.

'In due course Litmus returned north and wrote up a report as he had been formally commissioned to do. The document was scant in the extreme but contained the essence of what has been detailed above. It described his meagre investigative efforts in little more than a couple of pages and concluded that the only possible perpetrators of the outrage appeared to be the Albanian faction which by this time, thanks largely to the efforts of D.I. Leeming, had already been bought to book.'

'My concluding submission will take the form of a couple of short questions which will give us the opportunity to speculate. To give us all an opportunity to construct a picture in our mind's eye depicting what must have happened by utilising the canvas of circumstance and the colours provided on the pallet by expert witness testimony. Such a picture must surely be an accurate depiction, because it is fashioned only from the truth we have seen laid before us in a totally ungarnished form.'

'We do not have to stretch our imaginations too far to see that Mr Litmus had the finance, the motivation and the skill to cause this carnage; but in addition, he had the freedom of movement and the warped mindset that would have been necessary for his evil machinations to become a success. My first question would be, and bear in mind Litmus' contacts during his vacation when considering this point, who else could have sourced an explosive as deadly as Semtex and bought it into this country undetected? My second question would be, why attempt to direct the Police investigation away from one legitimate avenue of enquiry in favour of another? Could it be that Jeremiah Jones, or at least his impersonator, is even now present in this very room? Thirdly, who in their right minds would think that this degree of loss of life was appropriate when balanced against even the most heinous of crimes? I think there is only one answer to those questions and that the name of the perpetrator of this great evil is now clear for all to see.'

Whitcott, sat back in his seat obviously pleased with his efforts.

Litmus, seeing no more attractive option, applauded enthusiastically.

As they left the room Whitcott pulled Litmus to one side.

'Perhaps you can now see the attraction of confessing to your involvement and avoiding a good deal of unnecessary embarrassment. It can be a pretty humiliating experience, standing in the dock with all eyes pointing in your direction. I wouldn't imagine it likely that the general public would have a lot of sympathy for your predicament either; as for the members of the families attending the courtroom, one shudders to think. I can assure you, making a clean breast of things would be far and away your wisest course of action.'

Litmus seemed surprisingly untroubled.

'Nice try, Jerome, but I haven't yet heard anything it would be difficult to refute in a Court of Law. After all the huffing and puffing, is that really all you've got?

Whitcott smiled sympathetically.

'Have it your own way, Litmus. I suppose it would have been wiser to have just saved my breath. You appear incapable of making rational decisions these days, and I think that character flaw might be starting to put you in a lot of danger. You can get away with being a fool, Litmus, plenty have done it; but carrying off being a big fool over a protracted period is a good deal more difficult.'

Litmus looked slightly perplexed but couldn't resist another taunt.

'I have to confess I've been more than a little disappointed in what I've heard so far, Mr Whitcott. Surely there has to be more.'

Whitcott smiled coldly.

'A wise adversary never reveals all the weaponry at his disposal before the battle has even started, Litmus. Certainly, I've got more, but I think I'll keep you in the dark about the prosecution's star witness until it comes a little nearer to the date of your trial. I've got a person of unimpeachable character who will testify to your involvement.........'

Whitcott cut himself off midsentence and seemed to ponder a difficult decision. For a full minute he balanced desire against expediency, before reaching a conclusion that seemed to bring him little joy.

'Let's leave it like that for the time being. With all the aces on my side of the table I think at this stage of proceedings I would be ill advised to say any more.'

CHAPTER TWENTY

Sheffield, Friday October 17th 2025

The day had been bad enough, but the night had proved considerably worse. After being sparingly fed, Litmus had been confined to the precincts of the hotel accommodation and obliged to share his limited sleeping space with Terry the driver and Malcolm the gorilla. He had given his word that he would make no attempt to escape but, despite these assurances, his two roommates had chosen to split the night shift so that one of them was always awake, in case he might at some stage experience a change of heart.

Malcolm had proved a peaceful sleeper but disposed to muttering and occasionally grinding his teeth. Terry, however, was a restless sort, prone to articulating past grievances and generally thrashing about in the bed. On the brief periods when he was fully comatose, he snored loudly, his snuffles having a high-pitched whistle at the end which terminated with a decisive snort. Just occasionally the snort didn't happen, and that was the worse outcome of all. It was bad when the snort was there but far crueller when it failed to materialise because you found yourself listening intently in case it put in a late appearance and caught you unawares.

When covering the watching brief Malcolm listened to music and although he wore headphones and had the volume turned down to its lowest setting, a ticking sound managed to escape which set you off trying to identify the track he was listening to and, if you were successful in cracking that one, the artist performing, as well. On the other hand, Terry was a reader of low brow literature and evidently found his current epistle entirely to his taste, because he would chuckle softly to himself whenever he stumbled across anything that he found in any way amusing.

Litmus had nothing against either of these men. They were clearly the salt of the earth type of stand-up guys that a complete creep like Whitcott would choose to surround himself with in the hope of disguising his myriad deficiencies and attempting to appear halfway normal. Terry and Malcolm were men who were used to a bit of hardship and would buckle down and fulfil their individually defined employment roles to the best of their ability, no matter how difficult the situation in which they found themselves. You couldn't help but be impressed by their complete professionalism. They were thoughtful, polite and solicitous at all times. They had even afforded him a certain degree of respect, because in their line of business it was evident that it wasn't every week of the year that you got to watch over a potential mass murderer whose face might very soon be plastered across the front pages of every newspaper in the land. Yet, despite their countless unquestionable virtues, by the time the first rays of sunlight had penetrated the hotel's somewhat inadequate window blinds, he would have cheerfully battered both of them to death with a crowbar, laughing hysterically while doing so.

At seven thirty precisely Detective Christine Ho rapped on the door and advised the three men that breakfast would be bought to the room in fifteen minutes. Litmus showered, ate heartily in accordance with long established precedent, and prepared himself for the rigours of a new day at the mill. At eight thirty the party met in the corridor and walked crocodile file back to the room which they had occupied on the previous day. Annoyingly, both Whitcott and Ho looked to have slept well and to be in the best of spirits.

'Well, Litmus, now you have had a chance to sleep on it and before we get involved in the final detail, is there anything you would like to tell us?'

'Mr Whitcott, any chance you could ask Terry, Malcolm and D.I. Ho to get another cup of coffee or stand outside the door or something? There are one or two things that I would like to speak to you about and as they are of a somewhat delicate nature, I think it would be better if they were for your ears only. I'm willing to wear handcuffs, stay at the other side of the room or be lashed to the curtain rail with that effigy of Buddha balanced on my head if you are in fear of an attack.'

Whitcott's face immediately lit up.

'Sensible man, Litmus. A confession was always in your best interests as well as being good for the soul. Malcolm, position yourself directly outside the door. I'll shout if I want you in here,' said Whitcott cheerily, 'and if I do shout come immediately. Ho, Terry, amuse yourselves in the cafeteria for fifteen or twenty minutes. Will that be sufficient time for you to fully unburden yourself, Litmus?'

'Yes, that would be perfect, thank you.'

Ho, Terry and Malcolm returned the way they had come only moments before. Ho slammed the door as a gesture of defiance, obviously feeling she was missing out on a spectacle she would have very much enjoyed. The scrape of a chair leg on a hard surface could be heard as Malcolm settled at his post in the corridor outside the only available exit.

'Right, Litmus, fire away. I want to get off by lunchtime at the latest and obviously you will be accompanying me. Quick as you like, man. I'm all ears.'

'I would like to confess. You've built a cast iron case and there's no point in me pretending any different. Just clap me in irons and lead me away.'

Whitcott breathed out noisily through his nose and appeared genuinely stunned.

'I must admit this is an avenue I didn't anticipating us travelling down until somewhat later in the day. No protestations? Mitigating circumstances? Am I really hearing right?'

'Entirely, Mr Whitcott. I'm guilty as charged. I made contacts in Ireland, flew to the States and obtained a sign off from the East Coast Finian Mafia. I then secured the explosive on my way back, smuggled it into the country, organised the building work, set up the meeting and blew the whole bunch of those nefarious bastards to kingdom come. All in all, a wonderful piece of work that I thoroughly enjoyed from start to finish. I'm aware you might not want me to play it as straight as that, Mr Whitcott, but I thought I'd just give you a measure of my true range of versatility if circumstances should require.'

If it was possible Whitcott looked even more perturbed but continued his pursuit of the main theme.

'And you do realise that having confessed to committing mass murder in the first degree you could now spend the rest of your life behind bars.'

Change of tune there, Litmus observed. *Healing being the goal and penance coming out a poor second,* very soon went out of the window once a confession had been obtained.

'I very much doubt it. The prison's not been built that can hold Harry Litmus, the man of a thousand faces. I'd be over the wall in no time at all. Superheroes don't react well to being incarcerated as I'm sure you are aware. I can visualise knotted sheets hanging from the cell window, prison bars mangled and bent, guards laid out all across the prison yard. An audience would lap up that sort of thing, don't you think? Sorry, I'll try to control my creative juices and take things a bit more steadily from now on.'

'Litmus, are you totally deranged or is this some eleventh-hour attempt to be diagnosed as schizophrenic? If that is the case, I suspect the best you could hope for is Broadmoor, and I've heard that place is a good deal less pleasant than a conventional lock-up in every respect.'

'Come on, Mr Whitcott, try to enter into the spirit of things. There's only the two of us in the room so no witnesses are present to come back and haunt you in the days to come. Come on, I'm bursting to know. How did you intend the whole charade to play out?'

Whitcott's mouth opened to speak but nothing came out. He searched carefully in his jacket pocket for a stress ball that he had left in his suitcase in the hotel bedroom. As a consolation he located a lozenge which he unwrapped and slipped into his mouth. Suitably refreshed, he returned his attention to the present. Was there perhaps a chance that

Litmus had seized the opportunity to slip him a dose of hallucinogenic drugs? If that was the case, he realised it was important that he acted totally normally and remained outwardly calm.

'Play what out, Litmus?'

'Don't spoil it now, Mr Whitcott. You came very close to fooling me at one point but don't push it too far now I've figured it out. To your credit I've really enjoyed my part in proceedings up to now. I think it takes someone like you to bring out the best in me. I had absolutely no idea you had leanings in this direction, but then again, I suppose you do have a good deal of experience at calling the shots. Anyway, just tell me how you want me to play it from here and I'm sure I'll prove capable of coming up with the goods. My Macbeth got rave reviews in the student magazine back in the day, despite the fact I struggled with the accent having never been north of Pontefract. Did I ever mention that before?'

Whitcott shuffled uncomfortably. 'I think it's time I called Malcolm, Litmus. I'm sure he'll have something in his bag of tricks that will make you feel better.'

Litmus jumped from his seat.

'No, don't do that. I beg you not to do that. Malcolm might be dumb, but he not too stupid to take note of what is going on and he would be extremely credible as a witness. Talk in front of Malcolm and you could be leaving yourself wide open. A small slip like that and you could easily spend the rest of your life regretting it.'

Whitcott looked at his watch and was pleased to see it was still reading today's date and registering that he and Litmus had been alone for barely twelve and a half minutes. It seemed so much longer.

'Right, Litmus, let's play a little game. You tell me what you're talking about, and I'll make a big effort not to hook my tie round your neck and strangle you to death.'

'Tell me, Mr Whitcott, just tell me. How is it going to play out? Do you want me to guess? You do, don't you?

That will be half the fun of it for you, to see if I've worked it out correctly.'

'Yes, Litmus, that's it. That's what I want you to do', said Whitcott glancing nervously at the door.

'Well, it isn't easy, and I have to admit you've been very clever so far. Perhaps I could hedge my bets. Can I have two guesses?'

'Yes, Litmus, two guesses will be fine. In fact, you take as many guesses as you want.'

Whitcott scoured the room for something heavy that was within easy reach, but nothing remotely suitable caught his eye.

'Guess number one, you let it slip out to the press that you have a strong suspect but that the investigation is currently ongoing. You then arrange that word mysteriously slips out on social media that I'm the bloke in the frame. At that point all you have to do is sit back and wait for one of the bands of deranged nutters from the capital who are now lacking any form of leadership to catch the fast train north, track down where I live and put me in the morgue. Once I am safely out of the way, you finesse with a profound but sorrowful speech to the media, indicating that whilst it appears some sort of rough justice has been meted out, it was not an outcome that personally gave you any sense of satisfaction because every man, no matter how villainous he may be, is deserving of his day in court.'

Whitcott sought another cough sweet without success. So far this morning they were the only things that offered a small oasis of reassurance in a vast desert of uncertainty.

'Litmus, I'm not sure you have entirely grasped the implications of........'

'Hang on a second. Don't interrupt my flow. You said I had two guesses, remember.'

'Yes, but you don't seem to have fully understood the consequences of what you...........'

'Secondly, you take me back to London in handcuffs and parade me about a bit, so the world and its wife gets a really good look at my face. You then allow me to hire a decent beak and we go through the whole rigmarole of a court case, which duly collapses when my man in the silk robes points out that all the evidence presented by the prosecution is either circumstantial or just plain ludicrous; and that I can provide a cast iron alibi for all the key dates when I was meant to be committing the range of nefarious acts of which I am being accused. You then huff and puff to the press about being sorry you hadn't been able to make the prosecution stick, with a strong hint that the judge was either demented or partisan to the defence. You then conclude by announcing that you are not seeking anyone else in connection with the crime, thereby cementing the fact that I was one hundred percent guilty and just extremely fortunate to be the benefactor of judicial ineptitude. Once again matters are resolved to everyone's satisfaction when my corpse is recovered from a back alley a week or so later with a knife in its back. Come on, Whitcott, spit it out. Which one is it? I'm busting to know.'

'Litmus, is this your rather obscure method of confirming you are totally deranged; an attempt perhaps to demonstrate you aren't responsible for your actions. Surely, you are not now going to claim that you didn't do it?'

'Of course I didn't do it, but please don't pretend you weren't fully aware of that fact already.'

'But ten minutes ago, you said that you did. Let me guess. It was the bad half of Harry Litmus who committed the crime and at the present time you are under the control of the good half who was a mere bystander and is completely innocent on any wrongdoing?'

'Look, Mr Whitcott, I've got no problem with acting out some sort of charade for the benefit of your pals in high office if the money is right, but it has to be a performance where I don't end up dying in the final act. If I play along with this lunacy, can you explain to me how I'm ever going to survive, because unless you can give me a firm assurance in that respect, I'm afraid we are going to have to abandon the pretence and fall back on the truth.'

Before Whitcott could further respond raised voices could be heard coming from the hallway, quickly followed by a loud banging at the door. At this point Malcolm appeared from around the door jamb, with a head wrapped securely in the crook of his right arm.

'I told him he couldn't come in, but he wouldn't listen.'

Whitcott grimaced but quickly recovered.

'It's alright, Malcolm. Let the man go before you break his neck. I'll deal with the matter from here.'

CHAPTER TWENTY-ONE

Sheffield, Friday October 17th 2025

The journey from the hotel to Litmus' residence proved slow, and if he were being perfectly honest, somewhat laborious. The bus lane that should have accommodated at least some of the traffic was clogged with numerous parked vehicles so everything on two wheels or four was shoehorned into a single lane. Litmus acted as a tour guide for the party, drawing attention to a pub that had once been famous throughout the city for the quality of its hot roast pork sandwiches and a refurbished industrial building that had long ago been used in the opening credits of a long defunct television comedy programme. Nobody paid any attention to a word that he said, which Litmus considered rather rude.

Their departure from the hotel had been as sudden as it was unexpected. The Hotel Manager said he would be filing charges of assault against Malcolm. That Ho had wrongly and very loudly accused a member of his canteen staff of being overtly racist for referring to her as *that Chinese woman* instead of *that lady of oriental lineage.* That the party had booked two single rooms and one double with two single beds, but clearly five people had slept overnight as was confirmed by the fact that five breakfasts had been delivered by room service that very morning. That access to the private meeting room had been abused, in that it had been booked for a single day but was clearly in the process of being used for a second; and that wholly unfounded criticisms by Whitcott about the quality of the food in the hotel restaurant had caused the Head Chef to take to his bed with nervous exhaustion.

After a good deal of shouting the matter was resolved by Whitcott authorising a significant payment on his credit card, which was later joined by an even more significant backhander, paid in cash. However, despite these not inconsiderable demonstrations of contrition, the party were directed to book out without delay, and to their obvious chagrin immediately found themselves closeted in a doorway adjacent to the main pedestrian thoroughfare just as a force six gale announced its arrival from the north.

Litmus was by now thoroughly bored with the entire proceedings and announced that unless they were prepared to arrest him on the spot he was going home. So, it came as something of a surprise to find that Terry was promptly instructed to fetch the car, and that within minutes the full party of five people were cramped uncomfortably together in that self-same vehicle heading in a south-westerly direction away from the city.

As the day progressed, Litmus was no more delighted with the way things continued to unfold. Unsurprisingly, the downstairs office was exactly as he had left it the previous morning, only a good deal colder. However, for no accountable reason a set of ornamental bull's horns mounted over the door which had previously led to what was laughingly referred to as the vestibule, had detached from their mounting and now lay shattered on the floor.

Litmus turned on the central heating and grudgingly agreed to make drinks for the party. Whitcott refrained from criticising the beverages as he seemed anxious to pick up on their previous discussion without undue delay. Before doing so, however, he sent Terry and Ho out to purchase something to eat and banished Malcolm the gorilla to the kitchen area, where much to his delight he was permitted to put on his headphones and listen to music. In consequence, Malcolm could see what was going on without being able to hear a thing, while the other two, whether by accident or design, were effectively removed from the picture altogether.

'Litmus, you were saying'.

Litmus frowned. 'I sure you're right, but I can't for the life of me remember where I had got up to.'

'Some garbled nonsense about me knowing you were an innocent party all along.'

'Yes, that. Oh God, surely you aren't going to deny it. Please don't make me go through it all over again.'

Whitcott said nothing.

Litmus sighed.

'You must have been considering setting me up long before you took your first car ride north. That twisted little mind of yours had already seized on it as the perfect way to solve all your problems in one go. But the beauty of it was, you didn't need to make an early decision because I could still prove useful whichever way things panned out. I was perfect for the role. Just bright enough to stir the waters a little so you could get a better sight of the fish that were swimming near the bottom of the pond but dim enough not to realise that if they were disturbed then some of them would be likely to bite. The decision on how to play your hand didn't have to be rushed. It was better just to sit back and see how things developed, knowing that either way you couldn't really lose.'

'The crux of the problem is knowing how deeply you are personally involved, but as a demonstration of supreme gullibility, I'll temporarily give you the benefit of the doubt and assume you weren't the person who orchestrated the whole damn thing right from the start; and from where I'm currently sitting, I can assure you, that in itself takes a very big stretch of the imagination to believe. However, in a spirit of benevolence and generosity this is the point from which we will now proceed, so make yourself comfortable and prepare for a bumpy ride.'

Litmus seemed totally engaged. After a good deal of waiting, at long last his turn had come around.

'You aren't one to rush into things, are you, Mr Whitcott? Before you committed yourself to any course of action you would have made sure you had a pretty firm grasp of what exactly was going on and an even better handle on who was likely to be directly involved; and having completed your initial appraisal, your political nose would have warned you to be careful, because there was a distinct possibility that at some stage in proceedings there would need to be someone convenient to be held to account..........and that once the shit started flying it would stick to whatever it hit first so it would be a good idea to get them involved in the action at the earliest opportunity. Did you suspect that it would be you who would be tasked with organising the clean-up squad? You're the man they would look to if my reading of the situation is correct. I appreciate it is unlikely that you would answer that question with the truth on a point of principle, so let's just say we have now identified your two major requirements. Firstly, someone to poke around on your behalf and by doing so implicate themselves as much as humanly possible.........God, now I think about it you even provided me with all the right tools. Secondly someone who would be eminently suitable to take the rap. In light of my recent holiday and the slant you could put on past events, I must have seemed like a gift that had been sent down from heaven.'

Whitcott chuckled. 'Utter rubbish of course but don't let me interrupt your flow. This storyline is already sufficiently imaginative that it could prove the highlight of my visit to this misbegotten corner of the universe.'

Litmus accepted the invitation to continue.

'What initially raised your suspicions that all was not well with the investigation? The fact Sangster had been appointed to lead the team, when Christine Ho for all her faults, would have done a better job with a sack tied over her head? The fact that nobody from above was shouting and bawling that results needed to be achieved no matter what it cost in terms of manpower or money? Sangster had been put in to lead the enquiry with Ho as his backup, but Sangster was yet to break sweat and Ho appeared to have been delegated to making the break-time cuppa.'

'We also need to take into account that everyone with more than six functioning brain cells couldn't understand why Mortley hadn't been heading up the investigation from the start. And it would be about this time, I reckon, you sat down, locked your office door, put a towel over your head and quietly figured it all out. The answer being, this was essentially a victimless crime. A mass murder where virtually nobody gave two figs about the dead because it was reckoned that they had ended up getting exactly what they deserved. They were scum floating on the top of a murky pond. The specific element of society that we could most definitely manage without. They lived by the sword so why should anyone give a toss if they died by the sword? Tough luck on them, but there would be no tears from society at large. What else did low life like that really expect?'

'OK, there might be the odd family member, friend or loved one mourning their passing, but the gangs had already made sure nobody was making too much noise on that count in case it was interpreted as a sign of weakness; and nothing unnerves the gangs more than the thought that anyone could consider them weak, because weak and vulnerable are qualities that go hand in hand. The media hadn't quite dropped the story altogether, but you sensed a marked lack of enthusiasm for portraying the dead as anything other than a bunch of losers who had bitten off more than they could chew and ended up paying the price. The only people craving answers were your friends in Government, and that was not because they shed any tears for the victims. It was so they could never be accused of being uncaring, or worse still incompetent. All that was required to tuck this away in a bottom drawer to which someone had conveniently lost the key was a suitable scapegoat, and ideally one who was very much dead and therefore not inclined to shoot his mouth off at an inopportune moment. Get a wooden box stashed safely six feet underground, a press report speedily compiled using a bit of imaginative thinking, and the investigation could be neatly filed away. At which point, the country could get back to arguing about greenhouse gas emissions, who should have triumphed in the final of X Factor and the route to be taken by HS2, safe in the knowledge that all the bad stuff had finally gone away. But that still didn't answer the big question; why the investigation had been approached with such a lack of enthusiasm from the outset. It was almost as if the authorities didn't want the investigators to come up with any answers; and could that be because possibly they might not like what was found?'

'I thought, initially, you had roped me in and sent me on my merry way just to ruffle a few feathers, but over the course of the last few days, I've become a lot less convinced that that was the case. Your directive could not have been clearer though I notice you were careful never to put anything in writing. A sly reference to the difficulty in getting the guilty put behind bars for a suitable duration due to lenient sentencing by the judiciary. A mention of the importance that the report was compiled by an outsider *as a man from the inside would be compromised before he set foot outside the door.* I thought initially my Afro-Caribbean heritage was getting a smiley face emoji because it would appeal to that left-wing shower of bureaucrats you are obliged to report back to; if not, then maybe it was seen as an advantage if it came down to interviewing people with a skin tone similar to my own. But when you think about it, neither is an overly convincing explanation. Nobody is playing the race card much these days since the BLM mob started taking the piss. And any gangland interviewees of West Indian heritage would write me off as a grade A Uncle Tom before I'd even got my foot inside the door.'

'However, if you took a couple of paces back and viewed the situation from a different angle, the colour of my skin could come in very handy if you needed a stitch up putting in place somewhere down the line. What were your words, Mr Whitcott? *Could it be that the impersonator of Jeremiah Jones is even now present in this very room?* '

Whitcott seemed to be thoroughly enjoying himself.

'Wonderful, Litmus. Absolutely, wonderful. Your imagination truly knows no bounds.'

'I must admit I'm still at a bit of a loss as to the significance of Sharon and John. Whose camp were they in? Yours maybe, but it's hard to be certain of that. It's very confusing this enquiry, don't you think? Difficult to figure out exactly who is batting for which side. Everybody disguising their true intentions. Were they supposed to guide me in the required direction in case I was too dim to work it out for myself? Quite possibly, that could be the case. There was no need to take any chances. A bit of underlining wouldn't do any great deal of harm in case I was in any doubt about which direction was required.'

'I reckon the manager of the café would have said whatever was required if the money was right. Jobs like his aren't falling off the trees these days, and it never hurts to be friends with the boys in blue when at any moment a drunk could trip over the wrong flowerpot and a licencing renewal be put in question. Always good to have a well-positioned friend waiting in the wings when something like that might come to bite you on the bum.'

'Which brings me rather neatly to D.I. Mortley; one minute my brown skinned brother in arms, and the next pushing to the front of the queue of those waiting to put a knife between my shoulder blades. He became a mate a little too quickly, did Mortley. Didn't know me from Adam and yet he was pouring out his innermost angst inside the first hour that we met. That was a clever move when you consider it objectively. You always look more carefully at someone who is willing to tow the party line, than someone with a chip on their shoulder because they reckon they've been given a raw deal. You secretly empathise with a person who thinks their pet theory isn't being taken seriously, because, let's face it, we've all been there at one time or another, and there's a fair chance we could end up there again. As it was, I learned more from D.I. Mortley once he had drunk a few beers and was happy to have got across his side of the story. He is genuinely on excellent terms with the gangland mafia, and he does get to hear things that someone less well connected certainly wouldn't get to know. Hard to believe, but he wasn't bull shitting when he said he was looked on by the street tribes as one of their own. I checked in case he had been writing his own press release and had got a bit carried away, but as it turned out his story stacked up one hundred percent; and for that reason alone, if not for any other, Mortley must have proved a major asset when leading the Gang Crime Division. He lives the job twenty-four seven, keeps his ear to the ground, and you can tell he's right on top of his brief. In those circumstances, you might question how the whole gangland meeting was put together without him ever getting a sniff of what was happening out on the street. Ok, it was only the top dogs who were going to be in attendance, but they would have needed to be briefed at some stage, and are you telling me nobody further down the food chain noticed a subtle change in the direction of the breeze? Difficult to believe that anything this big could have been put together without Mortley hearing a whisper, don't you think? There were just too many people involved to keep the whole thing totally under wraps for any length of time. It must have occurred that somebody, somewhere would have taken a snort too many when in the company of an audience they wanted to impress.'

'Let's change the subject before it gets tiresome. Who, I wonder, gives orders to D.C.I. Sangster? Or is the better question, who is the person who whispers in his ear? Ho might know but Ho doesn't like me very much so she would never tell me even if she knew the answer to that question. Mind you, Ho is very quiet with everybody these days, have you noticed that at all? A bit like she's waiting for something to happen and wants to be the first one out of the door the moment that it actually occurs. A bit of a mystery woman, D.I. Ho. Was she seconded as your stenographer so you could keep her away from the action in case she picked up on too much and started to interfere? Seems like a waste of her talent to be fetching take-out meals and scribbling notes on a pad of paper that nobody will ever bother to read. Mind you, Sangster will be hanging up his bicycle clips in a matter of months and someone will be needed to take his place. The way this investigation has proceeded to date he's hardly likely to go out in a blaze of glory, but I don't think that will bother him very much. Always presuming you don't manage to pin it on me, of course. But let's be honest, that doesn't look very likely unless there's something devastating that you're keeping up your sleeve. The appointment of a Chinese D.C.I. to replace Sangster would be popular with your political friends, wouldn't it? The Metropolitan Police Force seen to fully embrace ethnic diversity at long last would have mandarins from the Home Office beaming from ear to ear. If it was you who orchestrated the move then I reckon it would be worth looking out for your name in the New Year's Honours list, don't you think?'

'And Leeming; good old Leeming with his single burning obsession. At least Leeming is the sort of policeman we can really relate to. Bugger sophistication and niceties, the ferrets are shoved straight down the rabbit hole when Leeming's involved. Leeming goes straight for the jugular, and we quietly applaud him for doing so, even if our clapping is done under the table, so we won't get grassed up to the thought police for displaying insensitivity. Most people would probably think that the balance has tilted a little too far in the direction of the wet and windy in the last thirty years and to have a Leeming amongst the current flock of sheep must be vaguely reassuring. We can't let the snowflakes have it all their own way, after all.'

'He would have his uses as well. I reckon there's a fair chance that if someone told Leeming to get one of the Albanians to testify that he had personally witnessed a couple of his bosses working on a plan for the North London bombing, then a suitable confession would be in your hands in a matter of hours. And I'm pretty sure that in this specific instance the men involved would turn out to be the two high ranking officials that were shot and killed in the raid on their premises, don't you? Pure coincidence, naturally. And oddly, that in itself would also be vaguely comforting, because nobody likes a case filed away while the villains of the piece could still be out there walking the street. If luck were against us, it could be our turn next. So could it possibly be the case that.........'

Whitcott raised his hand like a traffic policeman confronting a negligent motorist. 'Litmus, Litmus, please stop before I burst my sides. Nothing you have so far advanced is anything other than pure speculation. Surely it has occurred to you that there's only so much of a conspiracy theory that even the most gullible would be prepared to swallow.'

'I'm assuming you won't be interested in my theory of how it happened then, Mr Whitcott? No problem, I'm happy to put it on the back burner until we get the opportunity to meet up in court.'

CHAPTER TWENTY-TWO

Sheffield, Friday October 17th 2025

One thing was quickly established. Jerome Whitcott wasn't partial to pizza, fish coated in batter, or chips that were thicker than a woman's index finger. He also didn't like kebabs, burgers, sausages or fried chicken, and he particularly despised pulled pork because he said it was disrespectful to the dead animal, and more importantly got stuck between his teeth. In case there was any chance of a mistake when Terry was despatched back out to scour the high street for more suitable cuisine, he listed another dozen or so items of food which he found repellent, amongst which pride of place was given to what he euphemistically termed, *greasy foreign muck.*

Terry departed clasping a double portion of cod and chips firmly to his bosom, Malcolm and Ho sat down to eat, and Whitcott took out his phone and retreated to the farthest corner of the room. Litmus paced the bare boards armed only with firm resolution, two battered sausages and an unprepossessing pickled egg.

Ten minutes elapsed before Whitcott re-joined the main party, and to Litmus' eye he looked distinctly crestfallen. He ordered Malcom back to the kitchen, sent Ho out in search of Terry, thereby effectively re-establishing the status quo that had been in existence before their belated lunch.

'Do I assume it didn't go as well as you might have hoped when you reported in?' enquired Litmus, somewhat less than tactfully.

'Litmus, your company is becoming more repellent by the minute. Can you do us both a great favour and spill out the lurid hypothesis that has now seized control of your addled brain so we can draw this matter to a speedy conclusion, and I can get on my way.'

'No,' said Litmus. 'That doesn't work for me. Let's consider an alternative option.'

Whitcott put his hand to his temples in a gesture of exasperation but said nothing.

'It occurs to me that D.I. Ho hasn't been doing a lot of writing lately. Which in turn leads me to think there are probably a lot of things you don't want on the record; and as I'm afraid there is no great likelihood of that situation changing anytime in the immediate future, might it not be a good idea for you to despatch her and Malcolm back to London as it's one hundred percent obvious that they aren't going to fulfil any useful purpose hanging around up here counting their thumbs.'

'Don't concern yourself with the welfare of my staff, Litmus. We can drive back as a party as soon as you have astounded me with the latest instalment of your imaginative fairy tale.'

'But that's the problem, Jerome. I can't....or at least I'm not going to. First we have a few things to sort out.'

Whitcott cast an eye to the section of half emulsioned ceiling directly above his head and exhaled loudly. 'Lord, give me strength.'

'The fact is, the story I propose to tell you may or may not be totally true. Parts of it, I must admit, are pure conjecture.......... but at least it is conjecture based on solid fact which is more than can be said for the rubbish you've been peddling for the last two days. What I propose might not give all the answers, but it makes a lot more sense than any other scenario I have considered.......and believe me I've thought through every contingency on offer. On the plus side, I think you will be forced to concede my explanation makes better sense than anything you've managed to come up with so far, but the reasoning also carries a pretty heavy minus because, even if you believe every word that I say, you are going to absolutely hate the conclusion it will force you to draw.'

Whitcott looked suitably unimpressed.

'From your viewpoint, I would have thought that fact alone would make the telling all the more enjoyable. You make no secret of the fact that you despise me and all I stand for.'

'That's true, but if you decide my version of events is not what you want to hear, that still leaves you with the fallback option of reverting to plan A and trying to pin everything on me; and whilst I'm confident I could handle anything that you can throw at me in a Court of Law, why would I need to take the chance?'

'You could always change the habit of a lifetime and trust me.'

'Mr Whitcott, one of the biggest difficulties I have had over the last few weeks is trying to identify just how involved in this thing you actually are. I still can't figure out if you were the man who came up with the big plan in the first place or were merely the not very humble Joe who got saddled with washing up the glasses and emptying the ashtrays once the party was over and the guests had gone home. You understand my dilemma?'

Whitcott showed no flicker of emotion. 'And your proposal is?'

'Like I say, stick Ho and Malcolm on the train home and then devote the rest of the day to getting the payment you owe me into my bank account. I'll run a check at close of play this afternoon and if I can see the transaction has taken place then we can meet up tomorrow morning and finalise business. Oh, and don't forget the expenses. It's all or nothing with this one, I'm afraid.'

'Litmus, as you are well aware these things have to go through certain accounting procedures before they are cleared, and that sort of thing takes time. And if you think I'm spending another night in this God forsaken hole then forget it!'

'Last time we had a similar discussion you suggested that I gave negotiating terms another try when I had a better hand of cards. Well, this time round I think I've got enough in my hand to make that a worthwhile option. So, that's it.

That's my proposal, and if you like you can call it an ultimatum. As far as I'm concerned, this time round it's my way or not at all.'

'I know we don't much like each other but let's try to be civilised while we sort this out. A little give and take from both of us at this point would perhaps be no bad thing.'

'As far as I'm concerned what I'm offering is reasonable. First off you owe me the payment and secondly, once the money is safely in my bank account you have limited your ability to screw up my life. I don't think even you would have the brass neck to put a man on trial whose bank balance you had just increased by several thousand pounds. And with the cash end sorted and the hangman's noose no longer swaying in the breeze I can tell you my story without fear or favour, because it won't bother me one little bit whether you like it or not.'

CHAPTER TWENTY-THREE

Sheffield, Saturday October 18th 2025

Litmus rose early and went to view the kingfishers that lived in the park directly opposite his place of residence. There were a mating pair on the top pond that had been settled in the locality for some years and now seemed oblivious to the intrusions bought about by the wide-angled lens and the sudden grab for the leather strap fastening on a binocular case. Their calmness belied their skittish reputation. They had seen it all before and long ago acquired the t-shirt. *Bring it on mate, we can cope. How exactly would you like me? I'm ready for my close-up, Mr De Mille.*

Providing the water didn't ice over the birds seemed happy enough. No shortage of small fish in the murky depths beneath their favoured perch but a lot of mallards, mandarins, coots and moorhens competing for space on the bustling waterways. No shortage of enterprising seagulls either. Muggers dressed in church surplices that declined a trip to the seaside now the fishing industry was firmly in decline. Better rewards for skulking around town, waiting for the far richer pickings that would inevitably come their way if they remained vigilant and didn't allow themselves to become affected by issues of pride.

There was a heron as well, that stared sharp-eyed down at the water with the sort of concentration you would associate with a gambler assessing his options before confidently placing a bet. Resolute, beady eyed and slightly prehistoric in looks. A gangster on stilts that would snaffle a chick the moment a mother became unwary. An unwelcome visitor treated with suspicion and distaste by all of the local residents, but considerably too large to be run out of town.

Litmus sighed. It was all too lovely, and as he was totally innocent of all the charges levelled against him, he was damned if he would lose any of it without putting up a fight. The view of a brick wall and a couple of inches of sky through prison bars would never do it for him. Today was a day that was going to lay the foundations for a lot of his tomorrows, and he was painfully aware there would be no room for mistakes.

He ran through what he needed to say and the manner in which he needed to say it. It was a bit of a balancing act, but at least he knew Whitcott's weaknesses. The trouble was, Whitcott knew his just as well. He had placed a revolver in the top drawer of his desk as a precaution. The weapon was old but still serviceable. He had no intention of using it, but you rarely got penalised for being over prepared. The bright morning clouded over and the first drops of rain began to fall. Litmus took one last look at the jewel on the lake, then turned up his collar and trudged across the parkland, heading for home.

Whitcott and Terry, had been fortunate enough to find local accommodation. Terry said the hotel was nice if a little bit refined for his taste. He had noticed a lot of the people had been eating fruit and toast for their breakfast and it had been something of a weight off his mind to see that bacon and eggs were also on offer, to demonstrate that life in the north wasn't entirely at odds with the way he had imagined. Whitcott looked in the direction of the sky and muttered under his breath before directing the driver to the kitchen. Almost immediately the strains of pop music could be heard from behind the closed door.

'Thanks for the payment.' No point in not rubbing it in while the opportunity presented itself.

Whitcott answered with a scowl.

'Coffee before we start?' Might as well temper the rapier's thrust with a dash of civility.

'Litmus, I currently have one desire and one desire only. To briefly examine the heap of bullshit you are about to set before me, before having the pleasing task of rejecting it out of hand. At which point I will get into my shiny new car and drive away from this mausoleum with all possible speed and spend the journey home planning the nature of your demise. You might think you have had the last laugh here, Litmus, but be assured, my memory is long, and I take great pride in forgiving absolutely nothing. My revenge will be as swift as it is merciless, rest assured of that. The only question you should now be asking yourself, is how long have you got before it is meted out.'

'Pity, you are taking that attitude, Mr Whitcott, because for the right price I could see you coming out of this very well indeed. A gong in the offing and a lot of tricky questions to which only you would know the answers. Possession of the sort of information that would guarantee that certain people in important job placements would have no choice but to bend to your will. I don't know how you can turn your nose up at it, but that's your choice, I suppose.'

'Here we go again, round and round in ever decreasing circles. The time to put up or shut up has now arrived and surprise, surprise, Harold Sebastian Litmus has nothing to offer. Go on, stun me, Litmus. Tell me what it is you think you know that I don't?'

Litmus smiled. 'Who did it......and more specifically how they did it.'

'Well, come on then. Spill the beans so I can look on in awe. Demonstrate how you outsmarted the entire Metropolitan Police Force in the space of less than a couple of weeks.'

Litmus shrugged. 'What's in it for me?'

'Satisfaction, Litmus, and that's all you really need, isn't it? If I offered you more money you would only squander it as fast as you did the last lot. Admit it, Litmus, all you need to be happy in your strange little world is the satisfaction of knowing that you were right, and in consequence the rest of the world was wrong. That you are the hero of the hour and can look down on the rest of us mere mortals with utter disdain.'

'Bit deep for me, that, Mr Whitcott. Bit cheap as well. How about ten thousand? Just a little something to round things off nicely before we wave a fond farewell and go our separate ways. I can assure you it will be the best money you have ever spent.'

'My God you really are pathetic, Litmus, but never let it be said I was a man who quibbled over coppers. Alright, ten it is.'

'And this time you pay up on the nose?'

'Your vernacular on occasions leaves me speechless. To think the taxpayer spent good money on that education. Listen, I'll pay you what I owe before I leave this room. Want me to get Terry in to act as a witness?'

'Yes, I can just see Terry testifying on my behalf in a Court of Law. Highly likely, that would be. You'd have him out on his ear in thirty second's flat. Alright, mug that I am, I'll take you at your word.'

'Now that you've eulogised the rights of the humble working man versus the mighty juggernaut of the state to your complete satisfaction, is there a possibility that we could just get on with it? Another night up here and I'll be making the return journey in a wooden box.'

Litmus steadied himself.

'There are two coherent versions of what might have happened in London in June this year and from the choices on offer the one you need to throw your weight behind is the one you already have stashed in your briefcase. The second version, the story that I'm going to tell you now, should be kept in a locked safe and shared with no one. The better bet might be to record nothing at all and commit what I say to memory........and then develop amnesia before you get home. Also, don't lose sight of the fact it will only be useful if you are nursing an exclusive. I hesitate to use the word blackmail, but I can guarantee that whoever is in possession of these facts will have access to an awful lot of leverage in the years to come.'

Litmus stood up and peered towards the kitchen, but it was apparent the music from the radio was still playing at sufficient volume that nothing could be heard over the strains of raucous singing and twanging of guitars.

'I don't want to be accused of operating under false pretences, so let me make one thing clear before I start. What I tell you will only act as a door opener. I'll lay out the numbers, but you will need to do the adding up. I've been out of the loop for several years now. I don't know who reports to whom these days. I'm not even sure that I ever did. And I certainly don't know who looks out for friends and kindred spirits because their fathers went to school together or belonged to same Masonic lodge. In simple terms, I'll tell you who in my opinion committed the dastardly deed and you'll have to work out who stood on high and issued the orders for it to be carried out. I'll provide a motive for the perpetrator, but you'll have figure out how this comes together into the bigger picture. Deal?'

Whitcott smirked and pinched his nose theatrically.

'Yes, Litmus, very good; so far you have done your usual act of talking a lot whilst providing me with no information that's of the slightest use.'

Litmus responded immediately.

'Of course, it would make this job a lot easier if you clarified whose interests you're representing, but even if you told me I probably wouldn't be hearing the truth.'

'Just get on with it, Litmus, will you. Leave the analysis to people who are considerably better qualified to handle it. Just blurt out the facts. Always presuming you've got any to blurt.'

'You denied me access to Sangster, Mr Whitcott; either that or Sangster made the decision off his own back. It left me with the impression there was something I wasn't meant to know. So, I used that as a starting point.'

'Beth: you remember Beth the hacker? My receptionist come lodger. The woman you were so successful in easing in through my front door. Smart as they come was Beth, you admitted it yourself. I phoned her from London where you had left me intentionally isolated. I explained my problem and asked her how difficult it would be to get access to everything that had so far been put online by Sangster's investigating team. She thought for no more than a couple of seconds before replying that it probably wouldn't be very difficult at all. It appears that if you make a career out of breaching the firewalls of multinational companies, then hacking into the computer system of the Metropolitan Police doesn't hold out much of a challenge. Inside an hour she had fixed me up with a link that gave me the authority to look at anything I liked pertaining to the investigation, and just for good measure she provided me with a read facility on the Met's personnel files as well.

Fascinating stuff you can pick up from personnel files if you have the leisure time to browse through them, and being stuck down there with no one to talk to, let alone interrogate, gave me all the time in the world. For instance, did you know that D.I. Leeming's grandmother was Serbian? Surname of Stojanovic if I copied it down right. It was she who raised him. It will be from her that be got his initial tutoring about the ways of the world. No wonder our Mr Leeming isn't overly keen on Albanians. The two countries have been kicking the shit out of each other since God was in short trousers.'

'Sadly, the rest of the officers who I had encountered on my rummage in the files proved a lot less interesting, though Ho's Grandfather had at one time been a member of the Chinese hierarchy a long time back, and I noticed Mortley's father came over on the Windrush, which I suppose makes him some sort of a minor celebrity to people who take notice of that sort of thing.'

'I checked through report after report. God, it was laborious. They provided useful background, but none of it took me very far forward. The Albanian line of enquiry still looked the most promising by far, but John and Sharon's arrival on the scene had been a bit too convenient so I took it for granted that that was the wrong trail to follow. In the end I got bored with reading statements and went back to staring blankly at the register of the deceased. I was sure it ought to tell me something, but unfortunately I couldn't for the life of me figure out exactly what that was.'

'Frustrated, I decided to focus my attention on Jeremiah Jones. If you discounted the Albanians, then Jones was a sort of catalyst for what had gone on, and yet he had successfully remained invisible throughout the entire investigation. I was informed by a contact in the security services that nobody could find a date when the man had entered the country, and there was certainly no record of him having headed back in the opposite direction. I backtracked through the interviews that Sangster's investigating team had conducted concentrating exclusively on references to Jeremiah Jones. Ninety-five percent of the interviewer's questions had been met with a decisive, *No Comment,* but the odd person who had condescended to mumble a few words for the record had invariably stated that they had never seen Jones in the flesh and were not aware of anyone who had.......and yet somebody must have, or how did the Jamaican manage to get his party invitations distributed. It was all very strange.'

'I was still pondering this when I got something of a break. It came from one of the file updates covering an interview with someone with the street name Goose who had connections to a middle-ranking outfit operating in Woolwich. Goose had been pulled over in a routine stop and search operation on his home turf, which had turned up a bag full of narcotics and a meat cleaver in the boot of his car. Goose, being not entirely stupid, had offered to break silence to detectives working on the North London investigation if the local Police dropped the offensive weapon from the charge sheet and it was never recorded that he had opened his mouth.'

'Presumably, a bit of bartering went on before Goose let rip with all he knew, which as it transpired wasn't a lot. The one bit of salient information that made me prick up my ears, was that Goose swore he had heard that someone called Booky, or Brooky (he couldn't remember which) was the person putting out the word on the street on Jeremiah

Jones' behalf. He remembered hearing this being said by somebody higher up the food chain in the Woolwich network, because they had qualified it by adding, *and who in their right mind would trust anything they heard from a gobshite like that.*'

'When advised this piece of information didn't cut it as useful enough to buy himself out of a charge of carrying a deadly weapon, Goose added that he was pretty sure the man in question was top dog in one of the penny-ha'penny outfits north of the river. Needless to say, Goose didn't have any idea which gang that was, but at least it gave me a starting point.'

'So, I went back through all the files yet again and the nearest I could find to the name was a *Brooksy* who was detailed as the leader of a small firm operating out of Holborn; but if the records were right, and I had no reason to doubt them, Brooksy was one the fatalities of the explosion that had already been confirmed. Bugger! One step forward, one step back; but at least it was something, even if at that point in time I couldn't figure out exactly what that might be.'

'A new strategy was called for. I pinned a map of the London boroughs to the wall and marked out rough territories and related them to the listing of the deceased. The fatality list had increased a little since the original had been distributed but nobody pretended that, even now, it was one hundred percent complete. The first thing that struck me was that there were no deaths attributed to the City of London, but that made some degree of sense because it was virtually all office blocks and commercial premises, and the drug supply was catered for exclusively by the Albanian consortium. However, there was also no record of any fatalities in the Borough of Hackney, which was more surprising because at least three large gangs were known to operate in the area and logically they would have all had representatives in attendance at the meeting for fear of missing out on what was being sold on the street as a Willy Wonker ticket for entry to a potential goldmine. That apart, the spread was much as would have been expected between areas with high crime rates and those that were somewhat better blessed.'

'I put that to one side for a minute because a couple of things were tinkling at the back of my brain. One I managed to confirm from the personnel files but the second took a good deal longer to figure out, but when I finally made sense of what it might mean I was at last able to stop flailing around like a blind man and begin to get my brain into gear.'

'I went back to the original fatality register; the one that had been couriered up to Sheffield the night before I caught the train south. There was a name on that listing that for some reason was bugging me and had been for several days, but for the life of me, I couldn't think why. Shaun Simons, street name Squid. Mr Squid being Brooksy's number two in the Holborn gang. It was the *Squid* reference. It leapt out from the page and immediately caught my eye. I don't think Shaun Simons as a name would have made any impression on me one way or the other. I thought about it for days on end until it drove me nearly way insane.'

'Eventually I remembered, and it doesn't say much for my powers of recall that it took so long for me to eventually bring it into focus. As a sundry note on one of Sangster's computer files there had been a reference to Squid Simons, but I'd read several hundred of those throw away notes over the preceding days and couldn't recollect the specific context. In the end I Googled the name and got a full picture provided, courtesy of the London press. Simons was dead. Very dead indeed. He had been brutally murdered about a week after the explosion had taken place. Someone had rammed a broken beer bottle into his throat. No CCTV, no fingerprints, no traceable DNA and hence no arrest had been forthcoming; and going by the flavour of what I was reading, not much chance of a breakthrough anytime soon. The enquiry was ongoing, but don't hold your breath while waiting for a result or you'll probably finish up in the morgue, was the general flavour of the by-line. So, there you had it. Mr Simons appeared to have died twice. If there was something to learn from this it appeared to be that there was no point in arguing with the Grim Reaper once he had your name on his list, because by hook or by crook he'd catch up with you in the end.'

'So back to the digging, which revealed that Squid should never have been on the original listing provided by Calvin Mortley, because he hadn't attended the Enfield meeting, let alone died in the explosion. On the morning 29th June Squid had been picked up for a motoring offence and due to a lack of cooperation with the officer who flagged him down had ended up in a cell in Camden Police Station where he had spent most of the rest of the day. No discredit to D.I. Mortley; anyone can make a mistake.'

'Now that was cleared up, there appeared to be two distinct possibilities as to how the deceased could have been persuaded to meet his maker. Either Squid had been butchered by a member of a rival gang in retaliation for a perceived involvement in the Enfield carnage, or for some reason the unfortunate Mr Simons had needed to be put out of commission for an entirely different reason altogether.'

'The first seemed more likely so I trawled through all reports relating to his death and eventually located a report from an informer embedded in a gang located in Finsbury Park. At the time when the murder was still hot news, this individual had been asked exactly the sort of question that was now on the tip of my tongue; and his reply had been to forget the idea because it would never have happened. The possibility of Simons having been killed as a result of inter-gang retaliation was pretty much zero because there was no kudos in it for anyone concerned. Broadly speaking, Squid wasn't regarded as being worth the bother. Sure, he would qualify as a worthy target for insults, or even threats, if you met him in the street but he was recognised as a bit of a joke and putting him out of action would only have earned contempt, not approval, for anyone carrying out such an action. Squid was looked on as a fat, stupid has-been who should have got out of the game years ago. He wasn't even in the best of health. At the time of his death the Holborn gang had been in the process of replacing him themselves. He had only been allowed to retain his rank in the first place because Brooksy was a colleague of many years' standing and felt sorry for him. Killing him would have been akin to mugging a blind match seller. Even the gangs had standards, though not admittedly very high ones, but this would be viewed as crossing the line.'

'So, if the gangs considered it beneath their dignity to snuff out Squid Simons' life, then who might the people be who didn't hold such high moral standards?'

'I thought I had most of the pieces to the jigsaw, but I was still struggling to put them together. So, I sat back for several hours and pondered the question until I eventually came up with an idea of what exactly might have transpired. You are very quiet, Mr Whitcott, do you want to hear what that is, or are you still anxious to get started your journey home?'

CHAPTER TWENTY-FOUR

Sheffield, Saturday October 18th 2025

Terry made tea and brought it in on a wooden tray with handles made from twisted lengths of raffia that were starting to unravel. Litmus had never possessed such an item to the best of his knowledge and yet it had clearly come out of his kitchen. This seemed to offer up a whole new avenue of possibilities. Could it be possible that there was an ancient trove of Viking gold buried underneath the fridge-freezer? If that was the case, he was more than ready to start digging for it now as long as it got him out of another session with Jerome bloody Whitcott. He could clearly picture a deep black hole in his mind's eye, and every time it reappeared, he was one step nearer the edge.

Whitcott retreated to his special space at the far side of the room and made a couple of phone calls while Litmus and Terry filled in time by discussing the Friday evening football game that neither of them had seen, but about which they both had opinions. A dog approached the front window and looked in expectantly, before cocking its leg against the lower brickwork and departing in the same direction from which it had come. Litmus opened the drawer of his desk and checked that the pistol hadn't disappeared before closing it and returning to finish his tea. The wall clock would have ticked ominously in the background, like the one in the film High Noon, if it were not for the fact Litmus had failed to wind it up. Whitcott finished his calls and returned to his seat. Terry took this as his cue to return to the kitchen. The final lap of the marathon had almost begun, and it looked like it couldn't be finished quickly enough for either of the competitors involved. Winning or losing had little interest for them now. It was more about staggering over the line.

In a voice that sounded almost apologetic and certainly resigned, Litmus plodded on.

'In order to understand what was going on, it was necessary to appreciate who was calling the shots, and you seem to have had that figured out from very early on, Mr Whitcott; though how you arrived at the conclusion, only you will know. In simple terms, it came down to the classic goodies versus baddies scenario with any unnecessary niceties being brushed discretely to one side. Even without the cheerleaders kicking their legs and banging their tambourines it would not have been difficult for an audience to know which side they were meant to be rooting for. It was so blatantly obvious; the bad guy might even have been excused from having a pencil thin moustache and wearing a black hat.'

'Why had that moment been selected as the appropriate juncture for battle to commence? After some consideration, I think I figured that out. Rising crime figures fuelled by Magistrates and Judges handing down inappropriate sentences and excusing their action by referencing the lack of suitably secure accommodation in our crumbling prisons? Nah, don't think so. Barely worth mentioning, as we've had that same situation for year upon year. Far more likely that it was Whitehall getting the first bleep on its radar that insurrection was ready to break out on the streets. A tipping point had eventually been reached, as more and more of the general public felt less and less confident for the safety of their families and loved ones. Banner headlines in the press, incessant in-depth investigations and always the same conclusion. That, slowly but surely, we were losing the battle for the mastery of the very roads on which we lived, with the distinct likelihood that in years to come things would only get worse. So, under those circumstances, I guess it was thought drastic action was the appropriate solution and, credit to the planners, when the time came for them to stand up and be counted there was certainly no evidence that they chose to hold back.'

'It must have been planned for some time because Leeming had records showing he had been chasing the Albanian faction for a clear three months before Enfield went up in flames. Good forward thinking. No reason that particular bit of the operation should be jeopardised if the other part failed to make the necessary progress. When you are passing round the collection bag and the congregation is small, every little helps.'

'I presume the drug consignment that the Albanians received the night before Leeming's raid was a set-up. A bit too convenient for it all to have come together quite that neatly, don't you think? I initially thought Leeming's team must have carried the narcotics in with them and distributed them around the building as they went from room to room, but silly me, that was of course completely unnecessary. I had forgotten that Leeming already had a man working on the inside. That would also have better explained the tone of the subsequent interview I had with Leeming's mole, because he clearly didn't trust the Detective Inspector to whom he was reporting one little bit. But, thinking about it, why would he? Belushi had seen him in action and knew precisely what to expect. To D.I. Leeming the ends would always justify the means, and an operative of Albanian heritage would be sacrificed without a second thought as soon as his usefulness had come to an end. Are you finding this believable, Mr Whitcott? I can stop now if it's not entirely to your taste.'

Whitcott sat stony faced, as if his thoughts had escaped elsewhere. He and Litmus both looked completely drained.

'Can you just get on with it, Litmus, and preferably without indulging your penchant for theatrics. I'd like to get out of this place before I lose the will to live.'

'The other part of the jigsaw was of course a good deal more complex, but it was also the part that could play out in spades if it worked out correctly. The only problem was it was also the part that was dangerous in the extreme.'

'I got the fact that Jeremiah Jones was the key to solving the problem but struggled to see how he fitted into the bigger picture. The few facts that had been established weren't any great degree of help and the man himself had disappeared, leaving only a trail of smoke and mirrors. It was a while before the only feasible explanation came to me. A bit speculative I must admit, but I think you'll find it works on all the right levels if you give it time.'

'The key is to take on board from the onset that Calvin Mortley had to be Jeremiah Jones. He was the only person who had the feel for the streets, the necessary understanding of how life worked on the other side of the fence and the natural charisma to carry the thing through. He was also the only one of the big players who had the right colour skin. But how could he act the part of the Jamaican messiah when his face was well known to the very people he would be attempting to lead to their deaths? The answer was in his knowledge of the makeup of each individual street gang. It was his prime area of expertise, a fact he was rarely reluctant to emphasise as soon as he had gained an appreciative audience; even when it consisted only of me.'

'Mortley possessed everything that was necessary as a skill set and could identify the most effective point of contact, because he knew precisely which seniors from gangland had never crossed his path. A tin pot outfit operating out of Holborn with a small amount of street credibility, led by a gullible loudmouth who would readily buy into his story without asking too many awkward questions would fit the bill very nicely, thank you very much. I bet Mortley spent an age weighing and sifting before he settled on Holborn as the best available option; and you would have to commend his choice because ultimately his selection proved pretty much ideal. The only minor downside to the way things panned out was that he had ended up talking to both leader and vice president of the Holborn gang at the same time when selling his story; but that was a small problem because there would be no difficulty in persuading Brooksy and Squid that the attendance of both of them at the grand conference was critical in order to ensure a good outcome ....and of course he knew for certain that anybody who turned up at the grand jamboree would not be using the return half of their golden ticket after the event. It was going to be the last waltz for all concerned, regardless of whether they had come with a partner or not.'

'It appeared to have worked out amazingly well. Brooksy might not have been the sharpest chisel in the toolbox, but he spread the gospel according to Jeremiah Jones with total belief. He even wrote himself into the script to nourish his ego, and, vitally, he reported back details of who had bought in to the scheme so Mortley could keep his tally of attendees updated for future reference. This information would help with the fatality listing, which would inevitably be delegated in his direction. It would also come in useful in any mopping up operation that might be put into practise after the event.'

'As for other aspects of the setup, we're unfortunately obliged to rely on conjecture. Somebody conducted the negotiations covering the rental agreement for the hotel, but I would be a liar if I claimed to know who that was. Mortley could have done that as well, as long as he was provided with cue cards, but then again, so could anyone else. Somebody also procured the team of East European builders to carry out the work on the hotel. I know how that was done, but again I can only speculate as to who it was who oversaw the project. A small amount of general supervision would have been necessary, but not very much. The quality of the work was not critical as the building would be demolished in a matter of weeks by the bomb, and the hired workers were experienced enough to get on without the need for anyone to hold their hands. As long as the work looked alright superficially that was the only thing that mattered and if you employed experienced builders then they would pretty much take care of themselves.'

'Somebody placed the explosive under the floorboards, and by necessity that would have needed to have taken place at the very last minute; one would presume once the builders were safely off site. A bit of explosives knowledge required here, but not hard to come across if you put your mind to it. No big deal in the big scheme of things. Loads of ex-servicemen with the necessary experience swelling the dole queues after Libya, Iraq and Afghanistan.'

'It was critical that there was a cut out working the front office. A person who fronted-up the operational interests without necessarily knowing a great deal of the detail. Someone who liaised between the organisers of the operation and the employed workers.......the builders, the suppliers, the catering staff and anybody else who might get indirectly involved. A sort of master of ceremonies, smoothing the waters between the performers and the audience; someone capable of singing the song perfectly in tune without knowing the meaning of the words. This person would have been extremely vulnerable. They were identifiable, and if ever apprehended could have given descriptions even if they didn't necessarily know names. I would be surprised if this person is still breathing. He would have been an Achilles heel to the whole procedure if ever detected. Mind you, the way things have progressed under D.I. Sangster's direct supervision, there probably wasn't any great danger of that.'

'I'm still at a loss as to whether John and Sharon were genuine or hired to act out a part. If we give them the benefit of the doubt, then the two Albanian football fans would also have actually existed, and the only thing we can be reasonably sure about on that count, is that they wouldn't have been Albanian and had probably never set foot on a building site in their lives. They would have had no need to; they had an entirely different role to play in the subterfuge. They were a conduit linking fact with supposition. Their purpose was to point an arrow at a conclusion that would be convenient for all concerned. Somebody had to be guilty and with the number of fatalities involved it was essential that those identified as guilty were also those who would prove most conveniently culpable.'

'The explosive? Absolutely no idea. Best guess is that it was seized in the troubles and stored somewhere safe for use at an opportune moment; and from an authoritarian perspective, this was about as opportune a moment as was ever likely to arise.'

'Leeming and Sangster were presumably involved, but Mortley had the critical role to play. To his great credit he only made two errors; well, if we are being pedantic, one significant mistake and one misjudgement that if it stood alone would probably not even have been noticed. In the ordinary course of events Squid Simons escaping the explosion would not have registered as a seismic event. However, being the only person walking the planet who could identify Mortley and Jeremiah Jones as one and the same person made him a major problem that needed to be speedily resolved. Squid was small fry, but there was a very real chance that at some point in the future he might stumble across Mortley's image and add up the numbers. There was an even greater likelihood that with Squid's limited brain capacity a situation might arise where he would be arrested and need to trade in what had now become extremely sensitive information in order to secure some sort of break. Squid had to go, and you can be pretty sure that Mortley would have chosen to take care of that part of the operation himself. It isn't really the sort of thing that somebody like Mortley would feel comfortable delegating and, in the circumstances, who could blame him.'

'You might remember that earlier I mentioned the access to personal records. D.I. Mortley was off work with a cold the day Squid Simons was murdered. He returned to work the next day fully recovered, citing *one of those twenty-four-hour bugs*. Draw your own conclusion. I know that I did.'

Whitcott bristled. 'You are seriously suggesting that the Detective Inspector who heads up the Gang Related Crime Unit is a cold-blooded murderer? Litmus, are you totally out of your mind?'

'What other explanation fits the established facts? The mistakes made were comparatively minor, and in an operation of this size it was only surprising that there hadn't been more. Mortley, in order to be prepared for the big day, and knowing he would be put under immediate pressure to provide a lot of the background data, started to prepare a list of the deceased prior to the actual event having taken place. There was no way he could afford for it to be totally accurate because that would have looked too obvious, but pride in the quality of his work would have dictated that he made a good job so as to demonstrate that he was earning his corn. Naturally, he included Squid's name because he knew for certain Squid Simons would be in attendance, and that would have been the case if it were not for the mischance of him getting pulled over by the traffic cop. It was his first slip, and in the big scheme of things a very minor one.'

'There would have been a lot of confusion in the ranks of the Police Force following the explosion and Mortley would inevitably be leant upon to come up with an initial listing of the deceased as quickly as possible. No problem. He had anticipated this eventuality. He had a list already prepared that was ready for release. Pats on the back for D.I. Mortley. A smart piece of work by anyone's standards. But when it later transpired that Squid had ducked his celestial calling, Mortley had no alternative other than to correct that oversight because someone was walking the planet who could recognise him as Jeremiah Jones. I probably wouldn't have given the matter a second thought if Holborn hadn't been highlighted when the man Goose was picked up by the stop and search team in Woolwich. Suddenly there were questions to be answered and a strange coincidence to investigate. It wasn't anywhere near conclusive but at least it opened the door.'

'Mortley's second error might have been instigated by either sentimentality, self-preservation or possibly a mixture of the two. Shoreditch, Bethnal Green, Poplar and Stepney had all been well represented at the grand get together, but Hackney, probably larger in area than any of them, and rarely referenced as a byword in the annals of card-carrying pacifism, was a borough seen to have provided no delegates at all. It couldn't be that word had failed to reach the humble burghers of that section of the inner city when all the surrounding districts had put in a show. It was a plain case that the Hackney gangs had chosen not to attend, but why would that be the case when word on the street indicated that big things could be on offer to those who demonstrated an interest in lining their pockets? Could it be that the gang leaders had been warned by someone from their home turf that nothing good was likely to come out of the meeting? I'm not suggesting any detail would have been given out directly, but maybe a suggestion was allowed to filter through that Jeremiah Jones was a fantasist and only fools would invest time and petrol on what would turn out to be a total waste of time.'

'Calvin Mortley was born and raised in London Fields and I suspect a lot of the feedback he received came from the locals that he grew up with in that area. Perhaps a subtle word in the ear of a few of the right people was made, so well worked channels of communication were not put in danger of becoming impaired. Mortley's major strength was that he got to hear things early on. There could possibly have been a degree of self-preservation in an action of that sort. On the other hand, it might have been motivated by pure nostalgia. It would be a lot easier to butcher people you didn't know particularly well than those you might have shared an ice cream cone with twenty years before.'

Whitcott sighed loudly.

'Is that it, Litmus? Totally fatuous, completely misguided and certainly not worth the time I have been obliged to spend listening to it. Utter piffle. Pure speculation from beginning to end.'

'Hangs together though, doesn't it, Mr Whitcott; and for my crashing finale I would suggest that unless a better suspect materialises in the next five minutes, then the favourite for the role of organisational supremo and structural mastermind would have to be you. It was you who prodded me along in the direction you wanted me to go, and it was you who decreed what information I was given and what I didn't get to know. You provided me with a burner phone for communication purposes, and it didn't escape my notice that Leeming, Mortley, probably Sangster, and possibly even D.I. Ho all mysteriously acquired that number. I can't think of anyone who the cap fits better. If I were placing a bet, it would be that you orchestrated the entire operation, right from the word go.'

'Utter tripe Litmus, and if you ever repeat a word of your suspicions to anyone outside this room you will find yourself in a Court of Law.'

'Please, Mr Whitcott, can you just go. I am so sick of this business. I'm past caring who did what to whom and why. I don't care who did the organising, who did the killing and who just went along for the ride. Just clear out and close the door behind you. As far as I'm concerned everyone involved in this whole sordid business can go to hell.

CHAPTER TWENTY-FIVE

Northamptonshire, Sunday October 19th 2025

Watford Gap Services has rarely been looked upon as a thing of beauty, but it fulfils a necessary function and over the years has probably experienced as much footfall as any of the picturesque abbeys and grand stately homes in the land. Litmus had once witnessed a football coach arrive there late at night and its passengers denude the self-service bar of all but the stainless-steel fittings, before reluctantly shelling out for a cup of tea at the checkout. It had been like watching locusts strip an African plantation of all visible vegetation and had taken considerably less time.

He had been considering telling the story to Nigel Woodberry but had decided against it. Woodberry wasn't the sort of person who could listen to a tale of this sort without interrupting to enquire how they had managed to shovel the fried eggs into their mouths without breaking the yolk. Woodberry was a man who resided in the world of minutiae and specifics. He could never be a broad-brush stroke sort of person even if he tried.

'Well, Litmus, like the buses nothing for an age, then two encounters come along in quick succession. It took me two hours to get here even with the roads being almost entirely devoid of traffic. I hope you are the bearer of glad tidings.'

'Yes, apologies for disturbing you on a Sunday, Nigel, day of rest and all that.'

'No matter, the zoo doesn't have the same magic now they've stopped you from feeding buns to the elephants. Unreasonable course of action on first sight. A diabetes threat, would you think?'

Litmus yawned.

'You remember our last discussion, Nigel? I thought it would be wise if I fleshed things out a little. First a small confession. The big beast I mentioned when last we were together was Jerome Whitcott; couldn't say much at the time what with one thing and another, sure, you understand.'

'Whitcott? Well, I'll be damned. Are you telling me that you are working for Whitcott again? Didn't see that one coming.'

'*Was* rather than *am*, Nigel, and that's what I thought it would be wise for us to talk about. To put no finer point on it, Whitcott appears to have suffered some sort of mental breakdown.'

Woodberry looked startled.

'Really? Are you sure? No word of this had reached the south side of the river I can assure you.'

Litmus held his hands in front of him palm up and pursed his lips, as if to indicate that what Woodberry had told him came as no great surprise.

'It's a bit of a long story so I'll give you the potted version. Whitcott commissioned me to provide a brief report on how I thought the Police were coping with the gangland murders in London. I duly did what he commanded but he was unhappy with the results. He appears to be under the impression the whole thing was a giant conspiracy cooked up from on high. A grand liaison of The Met, Gang Related and Organised Crime supplemented by anyone with the odd half hour to spare doing a bit on the side, and, put your fingers in your ears if you are of a nervous disposition, orchestrated from Westminster. Well, you can understand anyone giving the notion a salute as it sailed by up the river. I'm sure that, considering the facts, we would have done just the same. But to actually take it seriously? And I can tell you with my hand on my heart he most certainly does believe in every single word. Anyway, it was something I couldn't in all conscience go along with and in consequence I am once again in his bad books, and I feel that on this particular occasion that sorry result has come about through no fault of my own.'

Woodberry closed his eyes as he considered the implications.

'Well, as long as he keeps his thoughts to himself, I don't think there's very much harm done. Let him think what he likes. Despite all evidence pointing to them being totally barmy, the flat earthers still appear to be doing alright.'

'That's the problem, Nigel. I don't think he's going to........keep it to himself that is. The way I read his body language I think he intends to find some way to use it, but I must confess I don't know how.'

'Don't worry, Litmus. He'd be laughed out of court.'

'Maybe; but take into account the job Whitcott's currently holding down and the fact the Police have made no significant progress with the investigation. Then layer over the nature of the way the operation was put together and bear in mind that the press hasn't had much to write about since we got a handle on Covid and the turmoil over the Brexit trade deals eventually died down. In my opinion, the conspiracy theorists could have a field day. They would jump at the chance to get their teeth into something a bit different. The moon landings and JFK's assassination are probably getting a bit tedious for them by now.'

Woodberry looked pensive.

'I don't quite understand why you are telling me all this. There's not much I can do about it.'

'Don't you consider, in the circumstances, it might be a smart move to shut Whitcott up?'

'Litmus, this is Whitcott we are talking about. Whitcott shuts people up, it doesn't work the other way round. Trust me on this. I've had first-hand experience.'

'He couldn't say much if it was announced from on high that the Albanians had accepted responsibility for the bombing. Even Whitcott isn't going to contradict Whitehall if they announce that the culprits have been positively identified and the investigation satisfactorily put to bed. And, of course, it could easily come into the public domain via a leak on social media that the Albanian responsibility was exactly in line with an independent report that the

Government had previously commissioned. Whitcott would be in no position to deny that either because it's perfectly true.'

'But how would we get a copy of the report for verification? Nobody in their right mind would fly blind on a thing like that.'

'I reckon that if you went to the counter and ordered two teas and a couple of bacon sandwiches, by the time you got back a copy would have mysteriously appeared on the very table on which you are now resting your elbows.'

Woodberry looked aghast. 'I don't think I could Litmus. It would be my career at stake if anything went wrong.'

'I suspect the report would have been found on a tube train in London and handed in by a member of the public. I think that by pure chance an agent from Five would be travelling on that same train and having noticed that the front of the file was endorsed *Top Secret*, they would have been alerted to a potential security breach. I think they would have shown their credentials to the authorities and taken charge of the paperwork, which they would then have passed to someone on the top floor for safe keeping as soon as they arrived at work. Somebody on the top floor who was perhaps no great friend of Whitcott's; such people are not yet an endangered species I'm led to believe. A person with a high degree of authority who had already been briefed about the details of our current discussion and would be extremely keen to support any course of action that might avoid H.M.G. getting egg on its face.'

Woodberry looked vaguely disgusted. 'Talking to you, Litmus, is little different from supping with the devil.'

'I think you are overestimating my powers of authority, Nigel. I also think that a person who was alert to the dangers of how this situation might unfold, and who took the necessary decisive action to prevent any embarrassment to H.M.G, would be much smiled upon by those in positions of power. National heroes have been a little thin on the ground since the old boy with the Zimmer frame was so sadly plucked from our midst.'

'Let me think for a minute. I was intending to visit the zoo. I didn't come mentally prepared for this sort of discussion.'

'While you are cogitating, two further things to consider. I would suggest that an eye is kept on D.I. Christine Ho from the Met. She was working as Whitcott's stenographer for most of the time he was in the north, and they appeared to be very much singing from the same hymn sheet in relation to their expectations from the report I compiled. The woman is murderously ambitious and for reasons I would rather not go into, I don't trust her one little bit. I get a distinct feeling that she could become very dangerous if she were promoted beyond her level of competence, and it appears to me that situation might well have already been reached.'

Woodbury was still deep in thought and said nothing.

'And secondly, when you are looking for written verification that the Albanian brotherhood were the perpetrators of the foul act, look to D.I. Leeming for guidance. He's a natural at that sort of thing. His force of personality alone, I feel, would serve to carry the day.'

'I hope you realise there is every chance you will be put out of commission when the details of this become known, Litmus. I've heard of people have been put up against a wall and shot for a good deal less.'

'I don't see why that should be the case. It won't be my copy of the report that will mysteriously turn up on the Piccadilly line and I've got no intention of going anywhere near London in the foreseeable future, so how could the situation have anything to do with me? We understand each other on this, don't we Nigel? It is vital that my name is never mentioned.'

Woodberry frowned, then pushed down on the tabletop and rose to his feet.

'I hope your luck holds, Litmus, because if not I've got a strong suspicion you are going to take me down with you. The bacon sandwich, do you require red or brown sauce?'

After they had eaten and Litmus had departed for all points north, Woodberry sat back to leaf through the file that had appeared on the tabletop much as predicted. The first thing he noticed was that the inside leaf of the folder had been subjected to scribbled writing that was all but indecipherable. He dug out his glasses in an effort to better understand the scrawl and could just make out the notation. *Index copy two, Detective Inspector Christine Ho (Met).*

Woodberry gathered together his possessions and immediately headed towards the door. Litmus had always been a bad person to get on the wrong side of, and the passing of the years didn't seem to have changed that situation to any significant degree.

CHAPTER TWENTY-SIX

Sheffield, Saturday November 1st 2025

Litmus had experienced a busy couple of weeks. Barge lifting and bale toting didn't come into it. Blow torch burning and the rubbing down of a variety of wooden protuberances had proved the order of the day. The application of filler to dark caverns that had never previously been apparent, the slapping on of emulsion with a roller and the more precise varnishing with the aid of a hog's bristle brush. A variety of tradesmen in and out of the front door doing the bits and pieces that required a degree of sophistication that was beyond his compass. The kettle permanently on the go. The house was at last starting to look something like the way he had envisaged it, not that his imagination had ever been vivid enough to imagine an awful lot.

He had pretty much finished refitting the floorboards. He had hired a weird sort of scraping machine that had scoured the varnish off the areas that were still in good condition, but there had still been several sections that had needed to be replaced. Under one of the damaged boards, he had found a hammer, ancient, but still in first rate condition and quite as good as anything that could be purchased today. He had turned it in his hands and tried to imagine the frustration of the workman who had lost it a couple of centuries previously. As he noted the minor damage inflicted to the tool all those years previously by an unknown artisan, it felt like he was balancing a small slice of history in the palm of his hand.

The hammer incident caused Litmus to dredge something back from the depths of the distant past. Years ago, when he was in his teens, he had been told a story by an old bloke in a pub about a builder named Mortimer Yarker who had been working on a renovation project at the other side of town. When he had pulled down a large section of the original plasterwork from an aged ceiling, he had discovered his name carved into one of the joists above his head. His exact names, both of them, letter for letter. He had apparently been so shocked by the revelation that he had fallen off his ladder and broken his leg in two places. The property he was working on had been an old coaching inn which had been standing since time immemorial, so the etching of the name of his presumed ancestor would have occurred three, possibly even four hundred years previously; and to make matters additionally interesting, the premises were reputed to be haunted. A story like that, you couldn't make it up........or as the old bloke telling it often claimed to have been employed on a contract basis by the Belgium secret service, possibly you could.

It was nearly seven o'clock and Litmus had just decided to pack up for the night when he heard a loud rap at the front door. He didn't lock up when the builders were in and out all the time and wasn't sure why he bothered to drop the catch after they departed for the night. There wasn't a lot to steal, and he was working close at hand so would be sure to hear anybody who entered the premises uninvited.

A tall rangy figure was silhouetted on the doorstep in the fading light.

'Bob Travis, the last person I expected to see. What the hell are you doing here. Has the run of the play come to an end?'

'It has for me, Litmus. I told them precisely what they could do with their half-baked production and walked out of the door. In my heart I always knew it was a mistake. I never liked Kes. Appalling play for an audience to suffer through; not a single moment's mitigation from undiluted, abject misery; positively morbid and as depressing as hell. Put it on in the south and you either enunciate the dialogue in character, fully conscious that nobody in the audience will understand a word that you're saying or deliver the lines in the Queen's English and be aware you are underselling your talent and coming across as a fraud. The

Director had the effrontery to accuse me of being wooden, can you believe that? Me! Wooden! The man didn't have the first idea he was witnessing a master class in holding it in. The play is set in Yorkshire, isn't it, a location where the residents are hardly famous for wearing their heart on their sleeve. It's Barnsley, not Beirut bloody high street, I told him; not that he took the slightest bit of notice. They don't go for wailing to the heavens and rubbing ashes in their hair up that way, I can tell you. You'd be lucky to see a handkerchief out in church if a jumbo jet had experienced engine trouble and come down on the orphanage. Complete waste of time of course. I might as well have saved my breath.'

Travis paused for effect, but quickly regained his stride.

'It was a travesty from start to finish. A total shambles. The bloody kestrel had moulted so much by the third week that we might just as well have had an oven ready chicken dangling off the fishing line over our heads. They were far too mean to replace it though, so we were obliged to soldier on with a featherless lump of bird flesh right in our eyeline for a major part of the second act. I ask you, how can you give of your best in circumstances like that? We were hired to light up the stage with our oratory and tease at the audience's emotions, but as long as there were bums on seats nobody gave a fig about the quality of the production. Backstage we were treated worse than the director's dog. As I was preparing for my final exit, I told the understudy I'd light a candle for him next time I passed a church. If that play is still running in two weeks' time, I'll stand hanging.'

'Sorry to hear that, Travis, but good to see you, even if your arrival is a little unexpected. Do you want to pop up to your room and freshen up? Excuse the mess. As you can see, the renovation project is still ongoing. The attic's not been touched so far so your stuff should be exactly as you left it........not that you left an awful lot if I remember correctly.'

'I could use a drink, Litmus. Whiskey if you've got it but anything will do. Just a little something to keep out the cold. Listen, there's something I need to talk to you about and I suspect I'll get my point across better if I've got a glass in my hand.'

Litmus located a bottle of brandy covered in plaster dust that was left over from the Christmas festivities; now that he thought about it, it was those that had taken place the year before last. The benefit of brandy was that it didn't go off, and its recipient didn't look overly discriminatory. Travis drank from a toothbrush beaker that had mysteriously found its way downstairs from the storey above. He cradled his drink to his breast like a favourite child from which he couldn't bear to be parted.

'It's money, Litmus, I've run a little short.'

'What happened to the salary you've been earning at the theatre?'

'Gone, Litmus, all gone. The ponies haven't been kind of late and I've needed a generous supply of coke to keep my spirits up while performing in that god awful play. One minute the cash had looked abundant, but in a trice it had dwindled to a state of insignificance and in the blink of an eye it was completely gone.'

Travis adopted a look of introspection and rubbed gently at his chin.

'It wasn't such a small favour that you got your friend to ask me to undertake now I consider the matter in retrospect, and the consequences of my actions was something not touched upon at all. It was more of a starring role than that of a bit part player, now I've had time to consider it further. And I did carry it off to absolute perfection, as I'm sure you have already been made aware. Those builders were an absolute nightmare that I was obliged to confront on a daily basis, and the dinner ladies were complete hell when you had to endure all three of them in a confined space. The smell of moth balls and camphorated oil made my eyes water, and I swear they never stopped talking from the time they got into the car until the moment they got out at the other end. What with that and the play, have you got any idea how many hours I was obliged to work on any given day?'

Litmus pursed his lips.

'Sorry, Travis, I'm at a bit of a loss. Everyone seems obsessed with builders and dinner ladies these days. I wish someone would let me in on the joke. The last time we spoke you said you expected to be away for at least six months and possibly as long as a year, so quite naturally your arrival has come as a bit of a surprise. How did you get up from the station? Did you get a taxi or walk?'

'I'm not a fool, Litmus. I got dropped off down at the roundabout and walked up the rest of the way. Your secret remains safely intact.'

'Secret? You're losing me, Travis. What secret? Anyway, how much would you be looking for to.........to tide you over until you can get another job.'

'A couple of grand would be useful for starters. Cash disappears so quickly these days as I've discovered to my cost. I'll need to get my stuff shipped back up as well because I think I'll need a complete rest before I can face another round of auditions. They can prove to be terribly draining if you aren't in the right frame of mind to give of your best. My old room would suffice if you've got nothing better on offer, but to be honest I always found it rather gloomy. I would prefer the one at the front if that wouldn't be too much of an inconvenience. I don't mind giving you a hand with moving my possessions across, if you think you will find it difficult managing. I don't go out much so there would be no great danger that I would be spotted, not that anyone would be likely to recognise me even if I did. I've dropped half a stone and my hair is far shorter than it was in the summer.'

Travis hesitated and took the opportunity to top up his drink. A third of the bottle had disappeared in a matter of minutes. He looked like he was preparing his words prudently, but once he started speaking they still came out in a jumble.

'It was you who made the recommendation, wasn't it Litmus? You were responsible for the way the introduction came about. That friend of yours made no secret of the fact............and now I consider it carefully, I'm the one that everybody will remember. The only face that could easily be recognised, and if recognised could lead a trail back to........not that it's likely of course, but in my book you could most definitely justify a significant further payment based on that fact alone. A bonus as a salve to your conscience, having belatedly recognised my not inconsiderable contribution to the success of your venture. Royalties? Bloody royalties. Your friends kept talking about royalties but how the hell do I get paid? They didn't even take my bank account details and they told me to keep my Agent completely out of the picture because he might present a future complication. So how was that supposed to work? What were you doing getting mixed up with a thing like that, Litmus? To be honest, you never struck me as the type. You really are a very naughty boy. Nobody gave me any idea what I was getting myself into, and as you might guess I wouldn't have touched it with a bargepole if I had been conversant with the true facts.'

'You've lost me again, Travis. I suspect you've been overworking because I'm struggling to make sense of anything that you're saying. Look, maybe a good night's sleep would be the best thing. We can sort this out in the morning when you've had a good rest and are feeling a bit more like your old self.'

'Sorry, that won't wash, Litmus. Memory loss isn't going to cut it with me. We both know what happened.......and more importantly, exactly what I did and the chances I took........and I want paying for it, and paying properly this time.'

'Travis.......Bob, you seem to be labouring under some delusion concerning who you're talking to, and most certainly your current standing in relation to living under this roof. You knock on my door with no pre-warning and ask to borrow two grand, *for starters.* You say you intend resuming your tenancy for an indefinite period and even request an upgrade in accommodation when you haven't paid me a penny in rent for the last four months. Added to which you seem to think I owe you something for some favour you did me. What fucking favour, Travis? You've never done me any favour. If you cast your mind back, I think you might remember that I did the favour for you. Perhaps I can jog your memory. I offered to put you up at a very low rent when you were out of work and down on your luck....and I offered to store your gear for an even smaller recompense when after two months of mooching about you landed that role in the south. Now will you explain what the hell you're talking about or I'm going to put you and that ragbag of junk you've got littering my attic out onto the street, and if I have to get physical in order to do it then that will only add to my pleasure when fulfilling the task.'

'Now don't get hasty, Litmus. You will be making a very big mistake if you choose to take me on. I was used and all I'm requesting is fair compensation for the services I rendered. Ok, look, perhaps you're right. Possibly the matter is best discussed in the cold light of day, but don't for one minute think that is going cause me to lessen my quite reasonable demands. You've got a lot more to lose than I have on this one, Litmus. I can legitimately claim to be a victim of circumstance because I was lied to from the very start.'

'You're babbling again, Travis. Stop talking and just take yourself off to bed. How much of that stuff have you been shoving up your nose in the last few weeks?'

'I can't. It isn't possible. I need to go out. I met a Casting Director on the train on the way up and he thinks he might have something for me in a Christmas pantomime at the Lyceum. Not my natural cultural medium you will understand, but the money is excellent, and you'd be surprised how that sort of thing can widen your appeal and draw your name to the attention of the people who matter.'

Litmus glance at the brandy bottle that had only a couple of inches nestling in the bottom.

'Are you sure you are in a fit state to attend a business meeting? Listen, do you want me to come down with you?'

'I'm perfectly lucid, Litmus, thank you very much. I'll have no difficulty in taking care of myself. I've always been able to hold my drink.'

'Alright, if that's the case I'll leave the back door on the latch for when you get back. Make sure you don't fall over the bowl of food I leave out for the fox.'

'Thank you. I always knew we could resolve this matter civilly. I'm only looking for a just settlement. I'm not a greedy man. Perhaps it would be wise if we don't meet up too early in the morning though. I probably won't be late getting back, but just in case.'

'Where are you and this casting bloke meeting up?'

'That little cellar bar on the corner West Street. The one with the bullfighting posters on the wall and rickety stools at the bar. It will be busy being Saturday; probably packed full of students and lecturers from the University, but what can you do? I should be back early, like I say.........but if things go well, it is just possible we might go on somewhere. Anyway, see you in the morning. Don't wait up.'

Travis paused on the way to the door and spun on his heels.

'Nearly forgot; can you sub me a hundred as an advance against us resolving that issue? Bloody expensive that place if I remember rightly, and I can't have him thinking I am down to my uppers or my negotiating power will have gone out of the window before we've even got started.'

'Fifty, Travis, and that's your lot. God, I must be stark raving mad. Tomorrow I want to know exactly what you're implying, after which we'll be having a meaningful discussion about how you're going to sort out the back rent, understand?'

It was a waste of words; with a speed that belied the amount of alcohol that he'd already poured down his throat, Travis had disappeared into the night.

CHAPTER TWENTY-SEVEN

Sheffield, Sunday November 9th 2025

November was always an unpredictable month in the County of South Yorkshire. It could herald the onset of winter with snow tipping in from the Peak District, causing cars to skid out of control on the steep and treacherous hills; or courtesy of one of easterly beasts that had been referenced as cold snaps by citizens of a previous generation, it could freeze the marrow in your bones to such an extent that the less hardy residents of Hallamshire might consider it prudent to dig out a second t-shirt from the laundry basket and, on the odd rare occasion, even give thought to putting it on.

Alternatively, there were days when it could be mild and balmy enough to lull you into a false sense of security for what to expect from the long winter months ahead. Days when there was sunshine in sufficient quantity that ice cream vendors could be heard cursing their luck for having locked away their vans prematurely when there was still trade in the offing and money to be made.

Today was very much on the better side of fine and Harry Litmus was seated on a park bench not four hundred yards from the door to his home, taking advantage of the exceptionally clement weather. Litmus had things to consider and for that specific purpose he considered the location he had chosen was almost ideal. The only sadness was that his current disposition failed to match the climatic conditions, or even get close.

The practise of reading newsprint rather than scratching away on the internet was undoubtedly regarded as old fashioned in this day and age, but it was still Litmus' medium of choice for keeping abreast of events. He felt saddened that within the space of his lifetime it was quite conceivable that reading matter of the sort he now clutched in his hand would cease to exist. Then again, perhaps he was worrying unnecessarily as he had recently been informed that the practise of downloading books from the internet was heavily in decline........and if that were the case, who was to say there wouldn't be a similar upturn in fortunes for the venerable scribes of Wapping, and even those from yet further afield?

The starting point in his speculation was provided by an article in the local newspaper that appeared to confirm beyond any shadow of a doubt that Bob Travis was dead. This news had come as little surprise to Litmus, as he had seen not hide nor hair of the actor since their brief meeting which had taken place more than a week previously. He had duly retreated to the park and adopted his current position so he could study the details of Travis' demise without interruption. Sadly, the time when he could have taken any direct action to benefit Travis' wellbeing appeared to have long since passed.

There was little doubt that the actor's death had the potential to cause severe ramifications. There were only two clear beneficiaries from Travis' death. The first was whoever had managed to entice the bit part actor into playing the lead role in the saga of the North London bombing, and the second was himself.

As it seemed clear, Travis had met his maker shortly after attempting to pull off his cack-handed blackmail attempt. Out of the entries in the two-horse race, it seemed pretty obvious which horse the smart money would be on.

In a rare moment of clarity, Travis had pointed out that his was the only face that could be easily recognised. What he appeared not to have taken into account was that acting as liaison meant he was also the only person who could recognise any members of the bombing team. This would have increased his vulnerability exponentially and presumably had led to his rapid demise.

Litmus was conscious that it had been sheer stupidity on his part not to have anticipated trouble. What chance was there that Travis would have met up with somebody who would offer him a job on his train journey north? As near to zero as made no difference. If he hadn't allowed himself to become agitated by the actor's pathetic attempts to put together that ludicrous blackmail attempt, then he would have thought to issue a warning or at least to insist on accompanying him on his trip into town.

Litmus was forced to admit that a lot of his outrage had come about because Travis' outpourings had forced him to reflect on his own vulnerability. Travis had been his lodger. There was little doubt he was in the frame for having provided the introduction that enabled Travis to be recruited, and presumably the actor would have been prepared to testify to the fact. Ergo, he had all the motivation required to stop that happening. It was as simple as that. He might as well acknowledge the fact and move on.

To make matters worse it was blatantly obvious that Travis had been recruited for that precise purpose. The plan was brilliant in its conception, and it clearly had Jerome Whitcott's fingerprints all over it. Bastard of the first order Whitcott undoubtedly was, but it was difficult not to admire the sheer deviousness of the scheming old sod. The question was, given the current circumstances what could he do about it? That conundrum would require a lot of consideration, so for the moment at least it was probably best if he put it to one side.

The thinking part of the exercise over for the time being at least, and recognition of his personal exposure to harm having been duly noted, Litmus reached for the local paper to acquaint himself with the sordid details leading up to Travis' demise.

The weekly publication usually focused its attention on roadside tree felling (too much of) cycle lanes (not enough of) and decisions by the grandees of the local council (incorrect and displaying thorough incompetence). However, it was not averse to dipping its toes into the murkier waters of death by misadventure when an opportunity afforded itself, and the article Litmus now confronted appeared to have been compiled with a certain degree of relish.

Bold on finite detail and no less courageous on implication, the article described the horror of motorist Kyle Broadbent (28) who found the bonnet of his aged VW Passat under assault by what he took to be an overstuffed bin bag when he was driving along the dual carriageway close to the town centre in the early hours of Sunday 2nd November. Mr Broadbent was quite naturally taken aback by the unexpected confrontation. He slammed on his brakes and stepped from his car to investigate what was afoot; at which point, to his utter dismay, he discovered that the binbag was not a binbag at all. It was in fact the body of a man of considerable bulk who was now lying prone in the centre of the road some ten yards behind his vehicle's rear wheels.

It later became evident that there was a slight factual error when the newspaper article referred to *the body* as lying behind the back wheels of Mr Broadbent's vehicle. The implication that it was *the whole body* that was positioned in this manner proved somewhat misleading. In the pursuit of journalistic accuracy, it would have been better termed *the majority of the body* because due to the violence of the impact a level of separation had come about, and as a result the head of the unfortunate victim was found to have lodged in Mr Broadbent's Volkswagen's front grill. As a responsible family publication viewed by readers of all ages, the local newspaper had felt it unbecoming to dwell on the more macabre details of the accident and had quickly moved on.

There had been a variety of witnesses to the incident, but due to the rather late hour at which the collision had occurred many were heavily intoxicated. This fact alone may have contributed greatly to the considerable variation in the content of statements taken at the scene.

The deceased had either walked out, run out or appeared to fly out of a narrow alleyway which linked the carriageway to a pedestrian precinct that led directly to the town centre. Depending on which version of events you chose to believe, Broadbent had been doing about 30mph and accelerating, was cruising at about 40mph, or was speeding at more than 50mph and weaving all over the road at the time of the collision.

(Broadbent strenuously maintained he had been driving at precisely 28mph in the inside lane with both hands on the steering wheel, positioned in the prescribed manner at two and ten of the clock.)

In one version of events, a witness testified that she definitely saw a girl with long blonde hair and wearing a light-coloured sparkling dress jump out of Broadbent's car and run off into the night immediately following the collision. In another sighting, a girl wearing a dark coat was seen to serenely exit the car and examine the body in the road before walking slowly away while reapplying her lipstick. In a third, a hooded man had emerged from the alleyway and examined the body before quickly turning about face and returning the way he had come. In yet another, a large man had got out of Broadbent's car, walked calmly across to the other side of the road and attempted to flag down a taxi.

(Broadbent protested vehemently that he was a happily married man and there had been no passengers in his car, and most definitely not a girl with or without a sparkling dress.)

Broadbent was breathalysed at the scene and found to be significantly over the drink drive limit, but he explained that he had imbibed heavily from a hip flask provided by a bystander while they were waiting for the Police and Ambulance Services to arrive because he was suffering from shock.

(This was later substantiated by an independent witness, the owner of the flask in question, who gave every appearance of having imbibed quite heavily from the same source himself.)

An autopsy performed on the cadaver in the days following the accident estimated the man's age to be round about middle thirties, his weight at approximately twelve and a half stone and his height at six feet four inches. There was evidence of large quantities of both alcohol and cocaine in his bloodstream.

The victim was described as clean shaven, a non-smoker, and his hands showed no evidence that he had ever undertaken any form of hard physical labour. He was missing two wisdom teeth, had a small scar on his temple and had a full head of hair. He was well dressed but carried no identification documents of any description. In his inside jacket pocket was a photograph of himself standing in front of a nondescript brick wall dressed in a kilt and sporran and carrying underneath his arm a set of bagpipes. Distributed about his person were three five-pound notes and a small amount of loose change. The body remained unidentified at the time the paper went to press, and a Police spokesman said they were most anxious to speak to any witnesses from whom they had not already taken a statement. Especially a girl with long blonde hair and wearing a light-coloured sparkling dress who had been seen attempting to hail a taxi at the nearby St Mary's Gate roundabout shortly after the accident had occurred.

In an attempt to assist the identification a photofit likeness of the deceased had been appended to the bottom of the article, with copies having been forwarded to The Edinburgh Evening News and the Glasgow Herald .

Litmus closed and refolded the paper. It must have been a difficult job for the Police Artists to get a good likeness considering the condition of the face they were attempting to replicate so presumably they had leant heavily on the photograph in Travis' pocket. Either way, to his eye, the results were remarkably accurate. The question was, were they good enough for anybody who knew Travis less well than he did to positively identify this likeness. More than a week had already elapsed since his lodger had gone under the car and nobody had yet come knocking on his door. In his favour was also the fact that Travis wasn't a local man by birth and in consequence wasn't well known in the area.

As a less reassuring counterbalance to that line of reasoning, the local paper had only been carrying the image for a matter of days, so it was far too early for him to get complacent yet.

The one thing that was crystal clear to Litmus was that Travis' death had been no accident, and following that assertion to its logical conclusion, it seemed highly likely that Whitcott had been the person pulling the strings. However, proof rather than supposition was what was now required and, in that respect, he didn't have anything in the way of evidence that he could use to his advantage.

The sun continued to shine brightly, and Litmus replaced the local paper with a far weightier tome that until now had been nestling at his side. He tried to make every movement in a totally unhurried and casual manner. It was important that he remained organised and calm. In the days to come his very life might depend on it. He flipped to the political section where the name Jerome Whitcott leapt from the page with the athleticism of a tiger that had just spotted its lunch.

In a statement to the press that appeared to have attracted no great degree of interest outside the Westminster bubble, Jerome Whitcott had formally announced that by mutual consent he was stepping down as chairperson of the Pre-emptive Logistical Augmentation Directorate with immediate effect. He stated, that while he had greatly enjoyed directing the course steered by PLAD over recent months (and felt that he had considerably enhanced the stature of the organisation by so doing) it was now an opportune moment for a younger person to take up the reins; most particularly as he now wished to devote more time to leisure activities, his close friends and family.

Whitcott strongly denied that there had been any friction between him and the serving Home Secretary and issued an outright and quite vigorous denial that he had ever referred to her as *a bloody stupid cow*. He substantiated this repudiation of the rumours that had been freely circulating in the corridors of power for some days by pointing out that he had nothing at stake, as his was only an advisory role.

He also took the opportunity to put on the record that he had at no time tried to direct any section of the Police Force to carry out his personal bidding, in contradiction of the statute of limitations covering his former post. In closing, Whitcott vehemently condemned a small band of malcontents who he claimed were peddling inaccurate versions of the true facts and described them as a posse of misguided agitators with little interest in anything other than tarnishing his legacy. He signed off by pointing out that it was only too easy to mistake robust debate for acrimony if your intentions were to subvert the smooth running of the well-oiled wheels of Government, and confirmed that the current incumbents of high office would continue to enjoy his full support and approbation. He further stated that if, at some point in the future he could prove of further service to this great nation, be it in a less time-consuming role, he would be delighted to take up the challenge.

On the facing page a statement by the Home Secretary covering the North London explosion of June this year stated that an in-depth Independent Enquiry had concluded that the perpetrators of the massacre had now been positively identified as the two suspects gunned down in the Police raid on an Albanian safe house earlier this year. She passed on the Nation's thanks to the Metropolitan Police Service for its energy and diligence in bringing the investigation to a speedy conclusion and singled out D.I. James Leeming and D.C.I. Edward Sangster for a special mention, as two exemplary Officers always prepared to go to any length to root out evil so that we could all sleep soundly in our beds.

Litmus noted the Government official had chosen to make no mention of Whitcott's impending retirement while handing out the accolades, which if they had parted on such amiable terms seemed more than a little strange. The weird machinations of people holding the reins of power never ceased to amaze him.

Litmus binned both publications in a nearby receptacle and went to feed the ducks.

CHAPTER TWENTY-EIGHT

Sheffield, Thursday November 23rd 2025

Today was that day, and in order to honour it in an appropriately prestigious manner bunting and flags should be hung from the rafters and beacons lit on every hilltop throughout the kingdom. After interminable hours of arduous labour, the project was finally completed, and Litmus felt reasonably confident he had inhaled vast quantities of cement powder and brick dust for the very last time.

Oh Joy! Praise to the mighty gods of renovation work, wherever on their celestial mountain tops they might at this time be. As they looked down with a calculating eye upon chez Litmus, they would pull up dead in their tracks and with open mouths observe that everything that needed attention had now been attended to, and anything that needed fixing had been most thoroughly fixed.

Even while their attention had been diverted elsewhere, swathes of new material of every quality, denomination and class had been nailed, screwed, bolted, filled, glued, cemented or plastered into place. Now at last the work was done with, completed, finished, finalised and decidedly bought to a close. Now he could proudly announce to those deities on high that the whole project had most definitely been put to bed, and that the decor was superior to anything that had been witnessed in the immediate proximity for touching on one hundred and fifty years.

The stairs had been the biggest problem, but replacement spindles that matched the originals had eventually been sourced and he had fastened them snugly into the crevices that he had chiselled out to accommodate them. Even the pock-marked banister rail now looked stunning, having survived hours of mortal combat with a variety of abrasive materials that had blistered his thumb, chipped his fingernails and all but broken his weary heart.

On the wall he had hung period prints which worked sympathetically with the muted colour of the glutinous matt emulsion. The original fireplace had been refitted as a period feature, although the grate was now loaded with artificial coal. It was a job well done. It was far from flawless, but he could say with some degree of confidence that he'd seen a good deal worse.

Now it was completely behind him, he could admit that he had enjoyed the project. Hated it as well, especially when things had stubbornly refused to go to plan. Now it was finally finished he felt oddly satisfied and strangely sad, both at the same time.

Unwittingly, perhaps, Beth had inspired him to complete a mission that he was proud to have accomplished to the best of his ability. Now it was over though, what exactly came next? This was the point at which he needed some well-earned acclaim. Beth to materialise out of the ether and admire his handywork. To smile warmly, pat him on the head and tell him that he was the cleverest of boys.

At that thought his mood swung unfalteringly in the direction of an unwanted counterpoint. He might as well face up to it, Beth wasn't likely to be putting in an appearance anytime soon; not anytime soon and quite probably never. It was a fact he had been reluctant to acknowledge, but now that the work was completed and he had nothing else to occupy his thoughts, it seemed he had little choice.

He had reread Beth's letter any number of times, and with each fresh revisit the door that had once seemed slightly ajar was increasingly recognisable as being resolutely shut. She had sensed the ferocity of the forces mounted against him, and they had scared her enough to put her to flight. They had scared him as well, there could be no denying. The difference between them being, he had no alternative but to stand up and fight, because there had been nowhere else for him to go.

He was also forced to admit that his motivation had undergone a major change over recent months. Once he had been fuelled by adrenalin and conviction and prepared to take up any challenge that had come his way. He had been effectively anaesthetised to any sense of danger by his strength of purpose; his firm conviction being that what he was doing was right.

Now it was very different. Experience had taught him that guilty or innocent, if it isn't your day, you still stand to lose the same amount of blood. Now he no longer had the burning conviction that he must win at any cost, because it would have been unthinkable to lose. You can only give everything when you are totally convinced in the justice of your cause. That day had come and gone. Now his motivation was purely to survive. Self-preservation was a quality that was much belittled, but it was the only thing that counted when you balanced it against the alternative.

Where had all the righteous indignation of yesteryear come from? God alone knew the answer to that one. It appeared to have been in his DNA from birth. The superhero with a mission to gain some form of redress for the man and woman in the street that they would never be able to obtain for themselves. It sounded ridiculous but that was the truth of it. The thought that he was helping good overcome evil offered him comfort, but when push came to shove, the recompense had been entirely for himself. He had taken justice entirely into his own hands. Weighed, balanced and delivered a verdict against which there could be no appeal. Worn the black cap without the slightest sense of guilt. Turned from a man who had rarely thought rationally into one that was possibly borderline insane.

It might have proved easier to seek out forgiveness if he were able to summon up some form of regret, but even that was beyond his capabilities. He could see now why Batman was depicted as stern and unsmiling when he surveyed what remained after his enemies were vanquished. Hollow and unsmiling, because every victory came at a price; when you had given out everything, nothing remained to provide solace for yourself.

Whitcott had been so astute in the construction of his case that he could offer nothing but admiration. Once he had calculated where he could best place the blame, he had pursued his quarry in a way that only Whitcott was capable of. For a time all had seemed lost, but then he had considered the Whitcott he had worked with for all those years. The man who gave cunning and avarice its true incarnation. The man who always demanded more than anybody was capable of giving and remaining sane.

So, there was the problem but what was the answer? What would Whitcott find more appetising than a sacrificial lamb served spit roasted and seasoned for his delectation? What was a more succulent morsel to tempt Whitcott's delicate palate? When he thought it through, the answer had always been staring him in the face.

No need for an outline, the story was already written and blanked in on the page. All he had to do was weave the separate chapters together into a believable narrative and surely that wasn't beyond the realms of his imagination. He could do inventiveness with his eyes closed, literally, figuratively, subliminally; whatever worked best could be instantly delivered on request.

Selling his version of events was always going to be something of a challenge, and selling it to Whitcott, the man who doubted everything, would represent the ultimate test. That had left him with plenty to think about, but it was amazing how things could be nudged into place if your very survival was at stake.

He had to be selling from a position of confidence. His version of events must be obvious to anyone with a brain in their head. How had nobody else worked it out before now? Wasn't the answer plain to see, staring you back in the face? Lying was what he did best so he didn't doubt his ability to sound plausible; but the bait that he dangled had to be tailored specifically to his chosen prey. Whitcott had to allow greed to override intuition. It was the only way this plan could possibly work. Otherwise, he was too convenient a scapegoat to be untethered and allowed to wander off unscathed.

Casualties would be unavoidable. Calvin Mortley would need to be offered up as the prime sacrifice, but he most certainly wasn't shedding any tears about that. Mortley had been the first person to knife him in the back when it suited his purpose, and the Detective Inspector was too perfect for the role for there to be any temptation to cast his eyes elsewhere. Mortley had a suitable background, could be credited with the appropriate motivation and even had the right colour skin. Besides, Mortley's discomfort would possibly only be temporary. If he managed to sound plausible, ultimately it would be the accursed Whitcott who would suffer the tortures of hell.

And all praise to providence, Whitcott had signed up and become a believer. Grudgingly, of course, because Whitcott had the word *grudgingly* etched on his soul. It had been a hard-fought battle but ultimately Whitcott's lust for power had triumphed over good common sense.

So now at long last Litmus could breathe a little more easily. He had money in the bank and if his luck held good for just a little longer, a clean bill of health. His efforts to distance himself from the very plan he had been advocating appeared to have been successful. No witnesses were available to offer testimony one way or the other. Whitcott had to become the author of his own demise; to have dug the pit in which he would hopefully be buried for all time.

Litmus sat back and contemplated his next move. Everything he could think of seemed to be in order. Nothing but bad luck could bring him down now. All he needed to do was to leave things alone and let time take its course. Not to chase the small boy up the tree like he had in days of old. Deep breaths, Harry. Let the waters find their own level. No need to overplay your hand. There was a sensible course of action and for once he intended to take it. He had his whole life in front of him. Perhaps there was a small possibility he was learning at long last.

Litmus rose from the chair he had been occupying for such a long period of time that his legs had stiffened up from lack of use. Get a grip, Harry. Start looking forward and prepare to dump the past. Some food was the first item on the agenda and maybe a glass of something to accompany it wouldn't go amiss. The hours of daylight had slipped by largely unnoticed, but they hadn't been entirely wasted. He had thought through the current situation to the best of his ability and at least he now had a clear idea of exactly where he stood.

He angled his body to pass through the doorway to the kitchen, before collecting a mug and plate from the rack on the draining board and opening the fridge door. He selected eggs, bacon and mushrooms before reaching for the box of tomatoes, and cooking utensils. He moved to pull down the blinds that rested over the large window overlooking the back garden. Then he froze as something out of the ordinary caught his eye. What the hell it was exactly, it was difficult to be sure of in the fading light. It looked like.........but that was ridiculous, quite obviously it couldn't be............but it looked like a body.

Litmus dropped the saucepan that he had only seconds earlier retrieved from the cupboard. He yanked on a pair of old trainers that he wore when he ventured outdoors regardless of the weather. He threw open the back door which flew back with remarkable velocity now that he had oiled the hinges and sanded down the areas that had always caused it to stick. He vaulted down the garden at pace. Surely it couldn't be........ and as he arrived, to his consummate relief it became immediately clear that it most certainly wasn't, even if the very sight of it still made the hairs stand up on the back of his neck.

It wasn't a body, thank Christ, of that at least he was now completely sure; but if it wasn't a body, it was quite certainly a replica that was intended to substitute as the next best thing.

Litmus dropped to his knees to examine his find. A dummy. What do they call them........mannequins? The synthetic models you see in dress shop windows, displaying the finery the store has on sale. This one wasn't made of hard shiny plastic though. It had been fashioned from some form of robust material that was more lifelike than anything he had ever seen before. It had properly formed facial features and a delicately curved body. You could have propped it up in a corner seat in a restaurant and received nothing but admiring glances from your fellow diners. The features were beautifully formed. It was little short of a work of art.

The figure was dressed as well; dressed in clothes that were decidedly modern and dare he say, more than a little stylish; something he would have been far better qualified to comment on if he had any real idea what fashionable female attire comprised. The wig was dark, lustrous, slightly askew as if it had been viciously tugged but had resisted the onslaught, and when you looked at it with care it was reminiscent of......of.......God almighty it was meant to be Beth.

Beth in caricature. Looking like Beth. Dressed exactly like Beth. There was no doubt about it, a perfect reproduction. Much too good a likeness to be anyone else.

And as he looked closer, he could detect more and more detail. The model was lying flat on its back in a puddle with its dress hiked up to the waist and its throat ripped out. A fact whoever had left it had been so keen to emphasise that a red liquid, consisting of something that Litmus didn't even want to think about, had been daubed on the area of the trauma and across the front of the chest. Jesus H Christ, what sort of warped mind could think to construct a vision like that?

Now his eyes were better adjusted to the fading light he could also see a note pinned to the mannequin's chest. Small in size and written in a freehand scrawl, it had already become smudged by the rain, but he could still read the top section quite clearly. *Anyone you recognise, Mr Litmus? Look carefully. You'll be seeing me very soon.*

A warning quite clearly, but a warning against what? The answer to that seemed patently obvious but he wasn't ready to go there quite yet. His mind spun but failed to arrive at a logical alternative; either he played along with the way Whitcott wanted things to go or he suffered the consequences, and they amounted to...........

In an instance everything changed. Every thought for the future was instantly banished. He was again his old self. He could tolerate threats against himself; he had even been prepared to ignore the death of Travis, but Whitcott had chosen to take it still further. He had put up with quite a lot in the preceding weeks and tried to shrug it off, but there was a certain point at which you were obliged to draw a line in the sand and that time had now been reached. Whitcott obviously wasn't going to let things rest and if that were the case there was only one course of action that was open to him. Alright, Mr Whitcott if you want to play hardball, I'll show you what hardball is all about. Litmus gripped the figurine around the waist and carried it into the house. He walked to the front of the house and withdrew the pistol from the drawer of his desk. He then started to prepare for the long journey south.

CHAPTER TWENTY-NINE

London, Tuesday November 25th 2025

The room could hardly have been described as vibrant or elegant. Certainly not plush, and nowhere approaching luxurious. Areas of the walls and ceiling had originally been overlaid with top quality white oak, but the woodwork had over the years been blackened by cigar smoke and gnawed by the ravages of time, so it now gave the impression that it had only recently been extracted from a barrel of pitch. The plaster would once have been painted in buttermilk cream or gleaming white, but which specifically, the passing of the years made it impossible to determine. These days the dominant tone leant towards urine yellow, but there was little evidence the current clientele paid this fact any great heed.

It was easy to see that the curtains had been tailored from sumptuous velvet; but velvet that didn't give the impression it had embarked on a journey to the dry cleaners anytime within living memory. The furniture was upholstered in a mixture of quality brocade and opulent leather, but the odd sag would soon become apparent if a meticulous inspection was conducted, indicating that the seats had been subject to a good deal of wear. The doorknobs had been fashioned from the finest brass, but rather than beaming out assertively at their subdued surroundings they were dull and compliant, offering the feeling they spent their days untroubled by the ministrations of unctions, polishes, or sprays. The rugs, and there weren't so many that they could ever be accused of encouraging a fellow in his cups to be wary of his footing, showed every sign of having been woven from wools and silks of the highest quality, but nobody would claim that the colours were sufficiently vibrant to brighten the room. There was a little dust, but without that added enhancement you got the impression the place just wouldn't have felt right, and with a room like this the feel was the most important factor by far.

The room had a distinct ambience, but to notice this, let alone remark on its existence, would be to entirely miss the point. The intention of the chamber was to be understated to the degree that even its lack of pretention was unobtrusive. Each vestige of the whole being restrained to the point of mute silence, but a silence not bought about by embarrassment, but rather one that conveyed supreme confidence in itself. Blather and bluster had no place in these surroundings. They could not and would not be tolerated for even a single night for the fear they might breed.

This was a self-confident room that was at ease with the terms of its existence. It didn't desire to be anything more than it already was, and it would have been supremely ungrateful for any form of enhancement as it was firmly of the conviction that it could not be improved upon. Less was more in this vicinity, and more was undesired only marginally less than a torturous death.

Although it was vast in proportions the room was surprisingly quiet; separate dining areas having been discretely fenced into booths to ensure social distancing was maintained as a regular observance, not merely when a plague of massive proportions was seen to ravage the lands. It was a room where service was sought by the flicker of an eye, or a discreet cough. Where the flourish of a finger in the air felt like an overstatement of intent, and the use of speech an outright affront to the form of nicety that must always be seen to prevail. It was a room that had seen the high and the mighty rise and fall and, on the odd very rare occasion, rise again for a second time. It was a room that you never entered uninvited, and rarely as a guest, but where a table and the warmest of welcomes always greeted your arrival if you were deemed to belong.

It was impossible to buy access to this room, be you sheik, oligarch, potentate, emperor, sultan, or prince. Money had little meaning in this cloistered chamber, unless

251

you were known not to have any, and renown and reputation counted for considerably less. Admission for entry was conferred like a knighthood or an award for gallantry. An invitation for membership, if such an iniquitous demonstration of unthinkable vulgarity had ever been permitted to exist, might conceivably have read:

*We confer on you permission to enter our noble precincts and for that right we permit you to pay an annual fee that is little short of extortionate. (*The specific level of exorbitance had until recently been expressed in guineas, but pounds were now reluctantly accepted as the management wished to demonstrate they were not averse to moving with the times.) *For our part, we will offer an unparalleled service, ultimate discretion and guarantee the availability of wholesome food and the finest wines and spirits for which we will charge you an outrageous price about which you will not choose to quibble. For your part, you can revel in the knowledge that you are no longer upwardly mobile but have been seen to arrive.*

Jerome Whitcott and his guest were comfortably seated at a somewhat battered oak table and appeared in relaxed mood. They were halfway down a bottle of vintage red which sprouted dregs that clung to the side of their glasses like lichen to a rock face. It was their first bottle, but unless an untold misery beset them during the next thirty minutes it was unlikely to be their last. They gave the impression of being perfectly at ease, which was just as well because they had much to discuss.

Whitcott lifted his glass in a toast. 'To failure.'

Edward Sangster looked momentarily perplexed.

'To our success in appearing to have failed ignominiously, sounds better.' He smiled, 'but of course you are right. Despite the gentle words from the Home Secretary's shell-like mouth, they won't be handing out any medals for this one.'

Whitcott looked vaguely amused. 'I think that would be ear, Sangster. Though now that you've planted the allusion, I have to admit it does have a certain merit.'

Sangster glanced at his watch. 'Shall we get started? Do you want me to go first?'

Whitcott said nothing, but with a barely perceptible shrug of his shoulders indicated his indifference. Sangster was always going to go first, but it was nice of him to volunteer.

Sangster ran his eyes around the room and quickly came to the conclusion Whitcott had been right in this choice of venue. Nobody minded each other's business in a place like this. It would have been bad form, and bad form was the one sin for which there could be no forgiveness. He glanced across to the corner of the room where waiters in pristine uniforms were gathered, waiting to be summoned. Undeniably, he was experiencing an altogether different world.

'Leeming's conscript apart, I only used a couple of middlemen,' he began, with such suddenness that it appeared to catch Whitcott momentarily unawares. 'Both long serving. People I knew I could trust. The one that played the major support role was in ill health and has since died. He wanted to leave his widow well catered for and he achieved his objective and passed on content. Take the right course of action and you write your own epitaph. I don't think there's a lot more you can ask.'

'The second man was also some way past retirement age and is spending his remaining years at the other side of the world soaking up the sun. We won't be hearing from him again, you have my word on that. The best course of action for all concerned, I'm sure you would agree.'

Sangster gave his colleague a questioning look, as if requiring some word of support for his judgement. This was totally ignored. Whitcott was busily assessing the possibilities. Sangster was an accomplished liar but there seemed no good reason for him not to be telling the truth on this occasion. Anyway, as long as his two henchmen were out of the way on a permanent basis, it didn't really matter what had happened to them. Whitcott gave a belated nod accompanied by the smallest of shrugs and Sangster quickly resumed.

'Most of what I'm about to say you know already, so I'll do my best to keep it brief. The builders were recruited from street corners and paid in cash. East Europeans to a man as that worked best for our requirement. Men with visa issues or just men who were desperate not to return home. You'd be surprised how many of those are still over here eking out a living, despite the stuff you read in the press.'

Sangster paused again, as if to gather his thoughts.

'The first of the middlemen I mentioned had some building experience and was also conversant with explosives. This was the reason I selected him; well, not the only reason, but perhaps the most important. In his formative years this chap had undertaken freelance work in different parts of Africa and the Middle East, not all of it legal if my understanding of the situation is correct. As it turned out he was a bit out of practise and got somewhat overenthusiastic when it came to deploying the explosive; but as that ultimately worked significantly to our advantage, I saw no reason to complain. He oversaw the project from beginning to end, and along with his colleague took turns to brief the idiot actor on requirements for each of the following days.'

Sangster drew a deep breath conveying displeasure.

'He proved very difficult to work with, that Mr Bob, which is what the thespian clown chose to call himself; but I can fully understand why you decided to involve him. A lovely tie-in to your man Litmus which I have to applaud. One it will be all but impossible for him to refute when the time comes for you to turn the screw. The one bit of fortune we experienced was that the theatre where Travis was performing proved to be close at hand. In consequence, the ferrying back and forth between the building site and his day job didn't provide him with a major headache......not that you would have known it from the man's incessant whining. To put no finer point on it, Mr Travis proved a total pain in the arse from beginning to end.'

Sangster broke into a small anticipatory laugh as he prepared for the next part of his narrative.

'With a minor degree of difficulty, we managed to convince the gullible actor that he was appearing in a pilot for a reality TV show and all the action on set was being picked up by well-hidden long-range motion sensitive cameras. He was advised that the completed film would be edited down and released on cable in America and that over the course of time the royalties that would be coming his way would be lucrative in the extreme. My people emphasised that it would doubtless prove a breakthrough role for him and that nothing but good could come of it. Bloody idiot! He bought into it totally. Strutted around like a peacock. Said he couldn't understand how this sort of opportunity had been so long in coming and he would need to check out the air quality in L.A. so he was completely prepared. Total fantasist. Out of his head most of the time and out of his depth for the rest of it. Just a pity we couldn't have left him in the building with the rest of those morons when the explosion took place.......but I realise that would have somewhat defeated the purpose of the exercise. Damned pity, anyway. It would have cheered me up no end if he had been blown through the roof with the rest of the inadequates. He was a complete menace right from the start.'

Sangster stopped talking as two men walked by, deeply engrossed in their own conversation. He started again as soon as he judged them to be out of earshot.

'The money the man got through; it literally ran through his fingers like water. No matter what we paid him, it was never enough. His dope bill must have been astronomical. I trust he was taken care of once his usefulness was over. I could have had people queuing up for that job who would have been happy to do it for free.'

'I'll cover that a little later', Whitcott replied, as if it were a subject on which he had no desire to dwell at the present time.

Sangster appeared to be checking off items against a mental inventory and saw no reason to waste words.

'You know how we went about recruiting the dinner ladies already, so I'll give that a miss unless you want me to go over it again.'

Whitcott smiled, but only slightly. He nodded his head at the first question and shook it at the second but spoke not a single word.

Sangster took a large swig from his wine glass.

'A word of praise for Leeming's man Belushi. The man was a star performer throughout. We planted him in with the site workers, so we had a handle on what they were thinking, just in case......well, you know how it is.......just in case any of them got unhelpful ideas about what we were trying to accomplish. Belushi knew where the builders from that part of the world congregated when they were looking for work, which made recruitment a lot easier than it might have been. He had the ability to turn his hand to pretty much anything, so he blended in seamlessly with the new intake. Because of his heritage they accepted him as one of their own and from what I can gather he was one of the most popular men on site. He even helped out by driving the van when that blasted actor was out of his skull. I was really sorry when we had to withdraw him from frontline service, but a couple of the builders saw him talking with the two men I had running the show. There might have been awkward questions and by that stage we were far enough advanced that it seemed wise not to take any chances. I sent him back to Leeming with a heavy heart and, strange though it seems, I could tell he didn't really want to go. I think if I had offered him a permanent position he would have snatched my hand off, but that would have been pretty much unforgivable after Leeming had lent him to us without complaint. To this day I don't know what the man's real name is, which is a sad indictment of the planet that we are obliged to inhabit.'

Whitcott suspected Sangster might not have been so accommodating if his retirement date hadn't been quite so imminent. He said nothing, and in a second Sangster was off again.

'I didn't let either of the men I recruited into any more detail than I considered absolutely necessary. Mortley, Leeming and of course Belushi know bits of it, but there's only you and me who know what exactly went down..........unless you were tempted to talk out of school, that is. There's four of us with blood on our hands and one more with an insight if you count in Belushi, but we all know the consequences if word should ever leak out and we all have experience at keeping our mouths shut so there shouldn't be a problem. In my opinion, information's been contained as tightly as could have been hoped for, considering the circumstances. As far as I can see there are no obvious loose ends.'

Whitcott, obviously wasn't so confident. 'No loose ends? You wouldn't say that if you knew the people that I'm dealing with.'

Sangster looked hard across the table.

'Nothing will leak from the people sat at my side of the table. I'd stake my life on it. In fact, I think you'll find I already did just that. It's your problem to apply the gags to the men in grey suits up the road from here, and I wish you the very best of luck with achieving that my friend.'

Whitcott laughed sardonically and topped up both glasses.

Sangster also saw the humour in the situation. It was common knowledge that Whitehall leaked like a sieve, but it was equally apparent that the rumour mill had already been overloaded to breaking point on this particular subject. It had got to the stage where conspiracy theories were now like pebbles on a beach where the bombing was concerned. He continued as if there had been no interruption from the man sitting across the table.

'And apart from that it was just a question of keeping my head down and getting away with dragging my feet.'

'And that I presume was the hardest part,' said Whitcott, displaying as much irony as he thought he could safely get away with.

Sangster wasn't entirely sure whether he detected a note of sarcasm in that remark, but Whitcott's face betrayed no hint of emotion, so he decided it would be wise to give him the benefit of the doubt.

'Well, it was certainly an interesting exercise in reverse logic, and if you don't mind, I'll just leave it at that. It certainly wasn't my finest hour.' Sangster chuckled softly, in remembrance of the events.

And yet it probably was, Whitcott mused, making a supreme effort not to let any trace of a sentiment become evident. Taking into account the desired overall requirement, you were right on the money with your contribution, my friend. Sangster had always been recognised as a class act when it came to achieving very little. As long as you didn't need him to accomplish anything specific, or better still, anything at all, Sangster was recognised to be sound as a pound.

Nearing completion, Sangster seemed to loosen up. Perhaps the wine was helping in that regard.

'It might surprise you to know that the first time we discussed this matter I walked out of your office thinking you were completely mad,' he confided cheerily. 'I could never in a thousand years have imagined we would finish up in a place like this, calmly reviewing how we butchered ninety percent of London's Street mafia in a single morning on a sunny day in June.'

'Don't exaggerate, Edward, it was only the band leaders that ended up dead. The members of the orchestra are still out there committing unspeakable acts, though I have to admit the figures detailing the mopping up rate are improving all the time. It has worked out very much as we said at our initial discussion. Take off the head and the body will wither. It was only ever likely to be a question of time before the odds turned in our favour.'

Sangster clutched at a new thought.

'Tell me, how did you ever get me appointed to head up the investigation? I wasn't exactly best qualified for that job.'

Whitcott only just managed to stop himself from laughing out loud. You, the best qualified? That's a classic understatement if ever I heard one. Sangster wasn't the best qualified at anything other than achieving nothing that was good........but he was always kept close and held in the highest regard because his contact list was the envy of everyone in the trade.

'Race prejudice, Edward', said Whitcott, picking the first thing that came into his head that someone like Sangster would probably accept without question, 'as simple as that.'

His lunchtime guest might be retired from front line service, but he doubted if he was yet ready to hear the unvarnished truth; not that he intended that a small obstacle like that would stop him having a bit of fun. He could get away with it as long as he chose his words carefully and applied a degree of delicacy.

'It should have gone to Mortley as I'm sure we are both aware, but that appointment would have presented certain disadvantages in that he would have felt obliged to bring the investigation to a conclusion that might not have been in total accord with our preferences. The Met is gradually coming to terms with a multicultural Britain, but things were never going to change overnight. I knew from the start if I blew your trumpet loudly enough, we wouldn't be short of cavalry lining up for the charge. Once you were in total control of the investigation, we knew it would be certain to grind to a halt sooner or later. You did a great job. I was never concerned in the least.'

Sangster nodded his appreciation but didn't smile; was he supposed to take that a plaudit or an insult? He wasn't entirely sure one way or the other........ but as he considered the barbed inference, he realised that neither did he really care. This was a farewell to arms not a team briefing where he would have felt morally obliged to take offence. As things stood, he saw no good reason why he should give a damn. Whitcott had always possessed a perverse sense of humour, so probably best to ignore the old bugger. He remained utterly serene and calmly moved on to the next item on his check list.

'Thanks for getting Christine Ho off my back, incidentally. Every time I ducked another decision, I could feel her eyes aiming daggers at my back. Will she move up now that I'm out of the door?'

Whitcott pondered for a second.

'No, Edward, sadly that won't be the case. It appears young Christine has somehow blotted her copy book, which in many ways works to my advantage because it avoids any unpleasantness resulting from a difficult decision it will soon be necessary to take. Not exactly sure how her transgression came to pass, but I'll have the opportunity to look into it in detail in the fullness of time.'

Whitcott mused the vagaries of life; how was it possible that transgressions took place and were noted without him being fully aware of how they came about? He had better find the answer to that question before it became habit forming. Taking that into account he chose his next words carefully.

'If I am ever going to use Litmus again it is pretty much essential that D.I. Ho stays exactly where she is, and I am very keen that we do everything in our powers to keep Litmus onside because he's already displayed amazing potential. There was no love lost between him and Ho, as I explained a little earlier.'

'Use Litmus again? You surely aren't serious.'

'Let me come back to that, Edward. I think you'll understand the reasoning a little better once you've heard my side of the story. I've had my eye out for an apprentice to supplement our ranks, and I've reached the conclusion that Mr Litmus has a great deal to offer. Although I'm almost frightened to speculate on what front his contribution would be most effective. As for your old job, I think we have little choice but to ensure it falls into the lap of D.I. Mortley. He made one small miscalculation but, by and large, I'm forced to concede, he did very well. Very cooperative was Mortley, once he realised the course of action that would be in his best interest, and a West Indian heritage will probably trump one from China until Huawei, Hong Kong and the Uighur Muslims find their way out of the news headlines.'

Sangster changed course at what he seemed to feel was an entirely opportune moment.

'How about we take the opportunity to eat? With one thing and the other I didn't get time for breakfast before I set off this morning.'

Sangster eased back into his seat and let his eyes rove around the room, and the ambience waft over him. Other worldly didn't begin to cover the feeling you got in this place; it was more like he had been transported back a century in time. Was the man at the far side of the room wearing spats? Nothing would surprise him.

He felt like he should make the effort to engage more with Whitcott. Despite working closely together they had made it a policy to never meet socially. Now the opportunity had finally arisen it occurred to Sangster that putting their current project to one side he didn't have very much to say. He made an effort anyway, for the sake of at least having put in the effort.

'To the best of your knowledge, are they still using cauldrons in the kitchen, Whitcott? It's hard to imagine them ever letting a microwave or an infrared grill through the door. Those two fellows with top hats. In species definition, would we be leaning towards Maître D or bouncer?'

Whitcott frowned and looked slightly uncomfortable.

'Don't tell me the answer to that, Whitcott. It was idle curiosity. I can tell by your face it's the sort of subject about which it's better not to enquire.'

CHAPTER THIRTY

London, Tuesday November 25th 2025

To Sangster's total surprise, the menu proved to be all about pies and puddings rather than the expected elegant dining. Public schoolboys harking back to their Alma Mater, he speculated, without being entirely sure what having an Alma Mater involved. In his school you had taken spam sandwiches in the hope that they would prove too boring to get nicked by the micro-thugs that ruled the playground area, so matters of that sort fell some way outside his comfort zone. Whitcott looked happy enough which was something. The man was reputed to have a delicate digestive system, but the way Sangster had witnessed him shovelling down spotted dick appeared to belie the fact. He still felt that the pair of them sitting in this place for a debriefing session was somewhat bizarre. Murderers conducted this sort of discussion in darkened back alleys, not in surroundings of this sort. No point in pretending anything different. Murderers were precisely what they were.

He remembered reading a good quotation, but he couldn't remember where it had come from. Someone French, was it? It usually turned out to be someone from that part of Europe when you eventually got round to checking it out. *Kill one man and you are a murderer. Kill a million and you are a conqueror. Kill them all and you are a god.* He wondered what fifty odd qualified you as. Ineffectual, in all probability. Not really one thing or the other. In the counting of corpses, it looked like Team Whitcott might have somehow contrived to fall somewhere between the stalls.

The table service had proved remarkably efficient, Sangster was unsurprised to notice. The plates had been whipped away the minute they had concluded their meal and another bottle of wine had appeared without Whitcott appearing to have done anything more meaningful than raise an eyebrow. It was expertly opened by their dedicated waiter and left to breathe on the side.

The new bottle had a different label Sangster noticed, but what that indicated he had no clear idea. He would have been the first to admit that his knowledge of wine bordered on the non-existent. The annoying thing was, that as Whitcott appeared to converse with the sommelier subliminally, it was highly likely he would leave this illustrious gathering of the chosen few as ignorant as when he had first walked in the door.

Whitcott cleared his throat and under other circumstances Sangster would have been inspecting the point of his pencil in readiness to take notes, as the great man prepared to resume. He had a lot of questions but maybe answers would be provided in the minutes to come without any need for him to open his mouth. He leaned a little forward, partly to encourage Whitcott to speak softly and partly to make sure he didn't miss anything important that was said. Despite feeling confident that they could not be overheard, old habits die hard for members of the school of hard knocks, which was where he had gained his mortarboard and gown.

Whitcott stirred. 'A glass of port, Sangster? It's something of a tradition in this place.'

Sangster hated port. A drink for tarts and posh boys, and he took great pride in being neither. How anyone could stomach the stuff after the glutinous pudding they had just spooned down their throats was beyond him. The waiter arrived almost before Whitcott had finished speaking so it would have seemed churlish to refuse. The bottle had dust on it, but then again everything in this place seemed to have dust on it, including, he suspected, a good deal of the clientele.

'Litmus,' Whitcott said, immediately returning to the subject that he obviously wished to develop as his central theme. 'An interesting character. He was picked up straight from university and worked under my direction for four years when I was stationed on the south bank. I took a personal interest in him and, I have to confess, felt more than a little let down when he chose to jump ship. Bright enough; best I ever had if the truth were known, but his heart was never quite in it. Got distracted by irrelevant issues and didn't cope too well with the mundane.'

Whitcott issued a sigh, which appeared to be directed at days gone by and opportunities missed.

'He went on to spend several years working as a Policeman. No idea what gave him the idea that employment in that branch of the Service would be any more interesting than life on the river. He then moved north and worked as an enquiry agent...... well, an enquiry agent of sorts.'

Sangster stifled a yawn by pretending to cough. He hoped this wasn't going to drag out for the complete afternoon. He found the subject of Litmus something of a bore.

'To be frank, Litmus went completely off the radar after he headed north, so it was something of a surprise when the Cousins reported that he had been spotted in New York fraternising with men of a Fenian persuasion. Nothing in it of course. You know what the Yanks are like. Panic had always been their default setting and they've got considerably worse since nine eleven made the hairs stand up on the back of their necks. But, regardless of that, it served to get me thinking. It was pretty obvious that once we had committed the foul deed, it would be necessary to muddy the waters as comprehensively as possible, even allowing that we had already identified suitable miscreants to take the blame; and in that respect could it perhaps be that young Litmus might offer a helping hand?'

'Anyway, I decided there was no harm in having a background check undertaken, working on the principle there was little to lose, and to my great surprise it threw up all manners of interesting bits and pieces. To put no finer point on it people working closely with Litmus had a habit of coming to a sticky end. Nothing he found difficult to explain away, you understand, but I'm not a great believer in coincidences, as I think you are already well aware. He also appeared to have a unique ability to disassociate himself from anything that was out of character with how he perceived his calling in life. As an illustration, I sincerely believe that Litmus could have been arrested standing over a bloodied corpse with a dagger in his hand and still have found no difficulty in pleading his innocence with the utmost conviction; and to compound the situation still further a polygraph test would doubtless have substantiated that he was telling the complete truth. There would be no necessity to erase a murder or any similar crime from Litmus' mind because that process was undertaken automatically. On planet Litmus, people like him weren't capable of committing transgressions of that sort and in consequence he was innocent, and no amount of evidence to the contrary would convince him of anything different.'

'When the Litmus blip showed up on the radar, it seemed to me like fate had provided us with the ideal victim because as long as we could fix it for a psychiatrist to substantiate the existence of this rather unusual mental capability, and label it as some sort of fancy syndrome, then our man could plead his innocence until the cows came home, without much fear that a jury would give credence to a single word he said.'

Whitcott hesitated as if undecided on how best to proceed from here. When he had eventually reached a decision, he issued forth on an entirely different tack.

'Excuse me changing the subject completely, Edward, but now that you've handed in your warrant card and truncheon what exactly do you propose to do to occupy your time? Only I've been made an interesting offer and there's an opening for a man with experience of Police procedures and a suitable array of contacts in the trade. Obviously, I thought of you straight away when they ran it past me. We're very different people, but putting that to one side, I feel we bring out the best in each other.'

Whitcott stopped again and his brow furrowed. He seemed to want to make an additional point without knowing exactly how best to put it into words.

'That was the reason the Home Secretary asked me to step down from the Directorate, you understand. A fact that was made entirely clear to me with no ambiguity whatever. The discussions did get somewhat heated I must confess. It took me a little time to realise that what they were offering me was in fact a promotion. The new operation will be strictly under-cover of course; cloak and dagger to the ultimate degree. It's the perfect front for a clandestine venture because officially I will be drawing my pension. They'll pass it off as a little part time consultancy work in the unlikely event that anyone should take an unwelcomed interest.'

Sangster shifted uncomfortably in his seat. As the word *promotion* trickled from Whitcott's mouth, he got the strange impression the man was trying to convince himself as much as anybody else in his audience of one. That was good. It helped him to reach an immediate decision. The proposition didn't feel right, and he certainly hadn't received a warning that a job offer was anywhere on the horizon. Today was meant to be a debrief and summing up session on what had gone before, not some sort of perverse interview about future employment. Sangster felt surprisingly comfortable easing into his reply.

'Putting my feet up came very much at the top of my list, Jerome. I had a bit of a scare a couple of years back and it bought home to me that I needed to start looking after myself a little bit better. To be honest, the offer to get out a little bit early on a full pension came at exactly the right moment.'

Whitcott considered this information carefully. As far as he had been able to establish, Sangster hadn't broken sweat in the last decade and the only scare he had ever experienced was when required to put in a full day's work. However, for all his faults he did know the sort of people who would doubtless prove useful in the months to come, and if he needed to set up a new team that knowledge alone would count for a lot.

'A little premature don't you think, Edward. You've still got years in front of you, old boy. Just think about it for a minute. Your wife's left you and clearly doesn't entertain thoughts of coming back, you haven't got children to worry about, you never take holidays, you don't play golf, you hate gardening, and you haven't got the patience to play bridge. Sitting at home watching snooker on the telly and wallpapering the spare bedroom? Don't make me laugh, with that sort of regime you'd be bored ridged inside a month.'

Sangster's reply was instantaneous.

'I'm not driven like you are, Jerome. Never was, never wanted to be. I'll be content enough pottering around in my dressing gown, getting out of bed when I like and eating a fry-up without anyone nagging me about my cholesterol levels. A few pints at the local and a trip to the bookies. Might even get a computer. There are all sorts of stuff to amuse you on-line if you believe what the blokes down at the station have been telling me. I might join a club. I might even meet someone, you never know, stranger things have happened. A social partner with privileges would suit me admirably the way things are placed at the moment, providing there were no strings attached.'

'But look what we've achieved together, Edward. Didn't it stir your blood? We took out more of the scum polluting our streets with a couple of months of dedicated work, than you probably managed in the rest of your entire career put together. What I'm offering is the opportunity to do more of the same. This time we were flying by the seat of our pants and haunted by the knowledge that if everything went horribly wrong, we would be out on our own. Alright, I'm not pretending we wouldn't still be deniable this time around if we made a mess of things, but that wouldn't happen because the resources at our disposal would be limitless, now that they've seen what were able to achieve. I can't tell you how impressed the faceless wonders were with what we delivered, and they are positively gagging for more of the same. More to the point they are prepared to pay for it, and they don't give a damn how much it costs. In short, they are offering us carte blanche if we are prepared to give it another go. We can pretty much write our own ticket. Come on man, what do you say to that?'

Sangster considered, but only for a moment.

'No, Jerome, I'm afraid it's not for me. I was fully in support of a one off hit to balance out some of the old scores that had been backing up over the years, and I can't pretend the extra money won't come in useful to supplement the pension, but that's as far as I want to go. If you're thinking about setting up Murder Incorporated second time around, you would do better to look elsewhere.'

Whitcott frowned but appeared to quickly recover.

'No problem. Just thought I would run it past you, and let me assure you the offer will still be on the table if you change your mind once you've had time to think it over. Now, where was I? Yes, Litmus.'

Whitcott, broke off to pour two large glasses of port. To Sangster the drink tasted like cough medicine and had the consistency of warm blood. Whitcott talked more slowly now. It was as if he'd got the main item on the agenda out of the way and could now address *matters arising* at his own steady pace.

'I changed tack. I admit it, I had a complete rethink. It suddenly occurred to me that with Litmus' background and, how shall I put it, his unusual proclivities, he was the sort of man it would be useful for us to take on board. I wasn't entirely sure of him though. Did he really have what it took to deliver results or was it a better bet to stick with my original thinking and fit him up as I had previously intended? In the end, I decided to give him a trial run. Nothing to lose. No need to make an instant decision. Put the fellow under pressure and see what he was made of. At which point I allowed myself to indulge in a wonderful irony. How would it be if I persuaded him to compile that meaningless bloody report. A report on the investigation of the crime I might in due course accuse him of perpetrating. Over-elaborate you think? Probably. But I've got as much right as the next man to have a little bit of fun once in a while, when it comes to evening up the scores. Owed the fellow for the way he had walked out on me after I had invested so much in his tuition when I was working at Five. Ingratitude of the first order. Walked out of the door without so much as a backward glance. The thought of seeing the rivulets of sweat soak into his shirt collar as he came to the realisation that he had been comprehensively out-thought appealed no end. The fear he would feel of being stranded in the wilderness as the light began to fade, and the big beasts readied themselves to hunt.'

Sangster shrugged. It all seemed ridiculous to him, but Whitcott usually knew what he was doing. The port was very sweet and cloying but he'd be able to get through it if he chugged it back, so it didn't spend too much time on the tongue. He nodded at Whitcott as if he were engrossed in his tale. His host misinterpreted his response and took it as an invitation to refill his glass. Sangster moved to cover the lip with his hand, but he reacted too slowly. God, was there no end to the torture of having to knock back this glutinous muck?

'I got Ho in on the act as well,' Whitcott resumed. 'Told her Litmus' back story with suitable embellishments. Added a bit of colour for entertainment value. I think she quite enjoyed herself, scribbling her notes and waiting for Litmus to break down and plead his innocence; anticipating that the man to which she had taken such a fervent dislike would perhaps finish up crawling across the floor begging for mercy. Ho appeared to want to see him broken considerably more than I did. She never took to Litmus, right from the very start. Said she had the ability to sense latent evil, and that he emitted it like beads of sweat, from every pore of his skin. It looks like you can take the girl out of China but not China out of the girl. Perhaps that's the basis on which they conduct prosecutions in that part of the world.'

Whitcott suddenly looked very sober. As if he was castigating himself for an unwarranted error.

'Thoroughly underestimated the man though, might as well admit it. He came back with a wonderful story. One that I'm forced to admit was entertaining in the extreme. It would have been utterly believable, as well, if I hadn't known the truth of the matter. Put his fabrication and my notional version of events together, and you would have gone with his account every day of the week.'

Whitcott looked at Sangster to check that the ex-Chief Inspector was still paying attention.

'Most worryingly, Litmus' account was horribly near the truth. Certainly, far too close for me to consider allowing his speculations to ever see the light of day. He placed Mortley correctly as Jeremiah Jones and seemed to have you pretty much worked out as well. Sangster was clearly on his radar and by the end of our interview I could almost feel the rope tightening around my neck as well. Frightening what can happen when you invite a well-ordered mind to run riot having provided the enticement of self-preservation as an incentive. That's a mistake I don't intend to make again, I can tell you. Proved one thing conclusively, though. Corner Litmus and he would fight like a tiger. Impressed me no end, I had to admit it. I was forced to the conclusion that he was definitely equipped for the job.'

Sangster began to feel horribly sleepy. That would be down to the port. He had never got on with the stuff and usually avoided it like the plague. His eyes wanted to close, and he was struggling to keep Whitcott in focus.

'Very resilient, Litmus, but I won't pretend he isn't bloody annoying into the bargain. He always had the ability to get under my skin. The constant need to be the person who squares up every issue by striking the final blow. He always demanded to come out on top, no matter who he was up against. To prove that he was right, and that in consequence everybody else was wrong. It was exactly the same when he worked for me back in the old days. He never had the ability to take a step back and leave well enough alone. A deeply Irritating person: but strangely admirable, I have to admit.'

Sangster was now sweating profusely. He was starting to lose track of what Whitcott was talking about. Why was he so obsessed with this fellow Litmus? What was the matter with the man? Litmus had been bad news from day one in Sangster's estimation. Why Whitcott had felt the need to introduce him into what was already a complex mix was totally beyond him. In many respects they were just as bad as each other. Consign the bastard to history and move on was the sensible option, but for some reason Whitcott didn't seem capable of viewing it that way.

'Ran Litmus' profile past the in-house Shrinks, to see what they made of him. They seemed fascinated, but again I suppose they are the sort of people who would be interested in something a bit out of the ordinary after dealing with run of the mill nutters all day. The general consensus was that Litmus is a manic depressive, schizophrenic, with strong delusional tendencies as defined by confabulation and dereistic thinking. That his mindset is deeply influenced by an overriding desire to protect women, something that they suspected could be traced back to his childhood. In summary, they said Litmus would be fine right up until the point where he wasn't, whatever the hell that was meant to mean. They seemed to think that behind a bluff exterior he was deeply vulnerable, and it wouldn't take too much to push him over the edge. They were really keen to have him in for a session, which of course is completely out of the question. I love these people who plod around in white coats with the time on their hands to overthink every case that is placed before them. I wish I had that sort of time on my hands.'

Sangster wished with every ounce of energy that he still possessed that Whitcott would shut the fuck up about bloody Litmus. He now had double vision, and wanted

271

nothing more than to excuse himself, so he could go to the toilet, throw water on his face, and be violently sick. Whitcott, on the other hand, looked like he was a man who had just been given a new lease of life.

'Bob Travis was the tie in as you correctly observed, Sangster, and nuisance though he undoubtedly was, he was more use to us alive than dead. I had him watched twenty-four seven and even put an operative on the train with him when he inexplicably decided to pack up his job and travel north to meet up with Litmus. That, it appears, was Mr Travis' fatal mistake. No idea what went on at their cosy little get together, but Travis didn't show for a prearranged meeting with the man I had sent north to keep an eye on him, and the next thing we knew his body was being hauled out from under a car. Needless to say, it will have been nothing to do with Litmus. Just another unfortunate accident to add to the long list of pure coincidences that continue to dog him, and always result in someone ending up in the morgue.'

Whitcott momentarily look nonplussed, but swiftly rallied.

'Not that it will make any great difference. There are good images of Travis in a local rag distributed in the godforsaken backwater that Litmus inhabits, so he will have very little wriggle room if he tries to get bolshie when I lay his new contract of employment on the table. Dead or alive, Travis was undeniably Litmus' lodger and we've got a small pack of dinner ladies who can't fail to recognise him at the other end. Mr Bob remains my main bargaining chip if Litmus rails against the option to join my new team, and I certainly don't intend to give him the chance to say no.'

Whitcott suddenly stopped talking and leaned solicitously across the table.

'You feeling alright, old chap? Want a refill? You've got quite a colour all of a sudden.'

'I think I had better get some air, Jerome. Feeling quite peculiar. Don't get up, I'll ring you later this evening in case there's anything more we need to discuss. I'll be as right as rain once I'm out in the open.'

Whitcott held out a hand which Sangster barely touched as he headed for the door.

'Well take it easy, Edward. Speak to you later. Good to catch up.'

With Sangster safely out of the way Whitcott pushed the port to one side and poured himself a glass of wine. He'd had this one on a previous occasion. Far too good to share with Sangster, of course. Wonderful stuff even if it did cost a small fortune. Just a pity he wouldn't be able to drink the whole bottle. Well, not if he intended to get any work done for the rest of the day. But then again, didn't he perhaps deserve a small treat after all the hard work he had put in over the course of the preceding months?

CHAPTER THIRTY-ONE

London, Tuesday November 25th 2025

Whitcott was completely content with his own company. Following his guest's rather rapid departure he settled down to tie up the last of the loose ends. Poor old Sangster. Not really up to it these days, but his experience would definitely have come in handy. He had suspected the fortified wine would do for his ex-partner in crime. No stomach for port, the likes of Sangster. He had always been able to identify a beer swiller on sight. Served him right for throwing the job offer back in his face. He'd come crawling back in due course. He felt fully confident it would only be a matter of time.

Whitcott poured himself another glass. He had been useful, Sangster, he had to admit, useful and useless in equal proportions. Wasn't that so often the way? When you wanted somebody to sit on a case, Sangster was your man. An innate ability to look busy while achieving absolutely nothing. A wonderful talent if utilised correctly. They really ought to teach it in schools. Come to think of it, with the job applicants he'd come across recently, quite possibly they did.

He wondered if Sangster's decision to bail out could prove to be messy. Sangster didn't know all of the details, of course, but he was certainly in possession of more knowledge than was good for him if he was serious about taking retirement. Whitcott was forced to admit that perhaps he had said a bit more than he had intended when recapping on the course of events, but after all the months of keeping everything buttoned up inside him it had been a relief to unburden himself to someone who was equally involved and could be relied upon to remain as quiet as the grave.

There could be no denying everyone liked neat endings, and the people who currently called the shots were no exception in that respect. Sangster would be wise to keep a weather eye out just in case. With the knowledge that he possessed it was undeniable that there would be certain advantages in shutting him down.

For his own part, Whitcott fully intended to be the last man standing because they were the ones who got to write the history books. His version of events should be the authorative version when he got round to composing his memoirs. He would have the ultimate artistic license because he would see to it there was no one around to disagree.

Before meeting up with Sangster, Whitcott had taken the opportunity to speak to D.I. Mortley by phone. He concluded that it would be necessary to keep a very close eye on that young man, because there was every chance we would need him again in the future. As a detective Mortley was second to none but he was very ambitious and, as a consequence, might be tempted to offer his allegiance to whoever he surmised would offer him the best route to the top. In the recent past they hadn't always seen eye to eye, but if he championed Mortley for Sangster's old job the Detective Inspector would be in his debt. Even if they weren't kindred spirits, it was better if Mortley was in his tent pissing out, rather than the other way around.

On the subject of Mortley, Whitcott had taken the opportunity to question him over the death of Squid Simons, but the results had been inconclusive to say the very least. According to Mortley, Litmus' version of events was totally ridiculous.

Yes, he had entered Simons' name on the original list but that had been because at the time he had put pen to paper nobody had seen hide nor hair of Squid at Holborn's gang headquarters. Brooksy had also been missing, and as the pair were virtually inseparable the money bet was that they had both been blown up. Given the circumstances, what other logical conclusion could he have drawn?

No, he hadn't had any proof at the time that Simons was dead, but neither did he have any firm evidence about any of the others that he had put on the list. You had to take a minor leap of faith on the information you had managed to gather somewhere down the line or it would have been a case of waiting to see if half a fingernail was located by the pathology team and matched up by DNA.

No, of course he hadn't murdered Squid. Why would he do that? He had only met with Squid and Brooksy face to face on a single occasion, and he had of course taken the precaution of disguising his appearance. Did Whitcott think he was totally stupid? This was the sort of thing he did for a living.

Word on the wire had it that Simons had been taken out as retribution for the Holborn gang's involvement in what had turned out to be a complete disaster, but at this point he had no firm proof whether that was true.

Yes, he had re-entered Squid's name on the list even though he hadn't been killed by the original explosion. His brief had been to provide names of deceased gang members whose deaths could be *attributed* to the bombing, and although Squid hadn't actually been murdered at the building site, in Mortley's opinion his death had occurred as a direct result of the bombing having taken place. In consequence he had felt obliged to put Squid's name on the list.

Yes, he had re-entered the man's name on the same line after having previously crossed it out, but that was after he had first tried to erase the original crossing out, and before he had discovered an error in the original recording. He noticed when he referred back to the original entry that he had mistakenly entered Sean 'Squid' Simons instead of Shaun 'Squid' Simons. In consequence he reemphasised the crossing out and rewrote the name again, alongside the original, with the corrected spelled.

No, he had no idea why leaders of the Hackney gangs had chosen not to attend the north London meeting. He wasn't bloody psychic. Whatever the reason, one thing was for certain, they hadn't heard anything from him.

No, he hadn't suffered from twenty-four-hour flu or a cold or anything else on Monday 8th July. He didn't get flu or colds or shit like that, but if he was working undercover then he often booked himself out that way because he wanted to be totally off the radar.

No, he didn't know where he had been working on 8th of July, and NO he most certainly wasn't going to drop everything and go and check it out with his diary........ and if Mr Whitcott had any more questions on the subject, he could shove them where the sun didn't shine.

Fascinating. Whitcott now didn't have a clue whether Litmus was lying, Mortley was lying, or they both were lying. Had Litmus even had a computer link that got him into the Metropolitan Police files, or had he made the whole thing up? He wasn't sure about the answer to that question either. The only thing that was clear, once you could see through the fog of deception, was that regardless of whether or not Litmus had entered the numbers correctly on the page, he had still somehow managed to come up with the right answer. In Whitcott's book that counted for a lot. He had no great interest in how his ex-employee had arrived at the correct conclusion. Perhaps he had a Ouija board or was related to one of Napoleon's lucky generals.

It occurred to Whitcott that he had wasted the best part of an entire afternoon searching out answers, and all he had ended up with was a further list of questions, some of which were more complex than the originals. He giggled at the ridiculousness of the situation, then forced himself to cease his merriment and sit up straight and pull himself together. Drunkenness was deeply frowned upon in these hallowed surroundings. The last person to be banned from this place was the Duke of Tullibardine, who, towards the end of the eighteenth century, had ridden his charger through the portals and into the dining hall with a naked lady tied horizontally across the neck of his mount. The duke had been fully aware of the rules regarding female admittance, so he hadn't a leg to stand on when the matter went up before the committee. On hearing the verdict that he had received a life ban the Duke had done the honourable thing and shot himself, his mistress and his horse. He was a strong believer that through good times and bad, collective responsibility was key to a well-ordered society, and he saw no reason to believe these principles would not be equally salient in the afterlife that imminently beckoned. A painting depicting the sorry affair hung at the head of the main flight of stairs, as a salutary warning to potential transgressors that actions of that sort were not without consequences. Why that story had sprung into his mind, Whitcott had no idea. He was, however, aware that the wine he was drinking was one of the finest he had ever tasted, so he decided to finish the bottle and wave a cheery two fingers at the outside world.

CHAPTER THIRTY-TWO

London, Wednesday November 26th 2025

Whitehall was bustling. Whitehall was always bustling, which was not to say that the energy expended always equated in equal proportions to the productivity desired. The offices were like a giant humanoid beehive, but one where the honeycomb was safely stashed behind locked doors, and it was considerably more difficult to identify the workers from the drones. It was a place where you needed to keep your wits about you at all times of the day and night. To have been seen to offer active support from the very start if the cause resulted in an euphoric triumph, and to have resisted with every fibre in your body if it languished in turbulent waters before sinking without trace. To have been seen standing as close as possible to a person when their career was on an upward trajectory, and to have been notable only by your absence on the day that they crashed and burned, having flown a little too close to the sun.

In Whitehall you were hot, or you were not. There was no middle ground. So, it was necessary to always know in advance of any unscheduled stops or detours the train might have cause to make before you decided whether or not it was wise to purchase a return ticket. This required a degree of telepathy and nous that could not be taught. It was pure instinct. The ability to know which walnut shell covered the dried pea, where the lucky lady was hiding herself and what the rabbit had been up to the night before it had found its way into the conjurer's top hat; and having acquired this valuable piece of information it was most important that you shared it with no one but yourself.

It is said that any individual who is made privy to an important secret would feel an irresistible urge to relay it on to at least one other person, on the basis that a secret is only a secret if at least one other person can testify to the fact that you were reliable enough not to share it. In Whitehall, this only worked if you could verify first-hand that your confidant had been certified as dead, had a stake through the centre of their heart and had never displayed any desire to experience reincarnation. Second chances were a rarity in the seething metropolis; even first ones weren't easy to come by. The only edict that had any true meaning was, never get caught screwing up.

Susan Smallstone, the Home Secretary, made no secret of the fact she had come up the hard way. She was a person who feared no evil when she walked through the valley of death, because compared with the malice she experienced on a daily basis, it could legitimately have been viewed as a walk in the park. Besides, if the prospect of that sort of foot-slog had ever presented itself, she would have had every inch of the terrain scouted out by heavily armed troops carrying mobile missile launchers before she even considered spraying expensive perfume behind her ears, let alone donning her Christian Louboutin ankle boots and Hermes silk scarf.

The Minister stood out from her contemporaries in Government as a blood-soaked cannibal in the company of ethical vegans. In consequence she was awarded all the jobs where it might prove necessary to get your hands dirty, as well as those where there was a small possibility of getting a splattering of mud on your shoes. Jobs where her colleagues would loudly applaud each success once it had been safely achieved, while silently praying that her luck would run out and she would fail ignominiously the next time around.

More out of enjoyment, than because of any need for an infallible twenty-four-hour defence mechanism, the Home Secretary chose to rule by tyranny. She supplemented this protocol by being loyal only to herself and putting the fear of God into everybody who worked for her, as well as the vast swathes of people who would sell their souls to the devil in order not to. She adhered strongly to the adage that you should speak softly but carry a big stick, except for the bit about keeping your voice well-modulated. This lady was going places and God have mercy on the soul of anyone who was unfortunate enough to be using the pedestrian crossing when the time arrived for her to slip behind the wheel, turn up the burners and put her foot to the floor.

Barrymore was already sweating, and he hadn't yet put his well-polished size nine and a half across the threshold of her office. What he had been summoned to report was at worst a partial success so God alone knew how he would be feeling if it had turned out to be a total failure. He sprayed with a breath freshener, took two of the pills that he had been warned by his doctor could become addictive if he didn't take immediate steps to reduce his daily intake, and rapped on the door in a manner that he hoped conveyed an air of confidence that he most certainly didn't feel.

As he pulled up a chair, the Home Secretary was observed to be enthusiastically polishing what looked like a long, metal disembowelling tool. Barrymore craned forward suspiciously but could see no obvious signs of blood on the yellow duster she was employing for the task. She smiled balefully in his direction as she glanced up, and immediately his blood ran cold. Things rarely went well when she greeted anyone with a smile.

'So, Mr Barrymore, what news from the land of the Fold-Back Paper clip?'

'On the whole, it worked out extremely well, Home Secretary. Went pretty much according to plan. For clarification, that is the plan we didn't discuss in the meeting we didn't have on Monday of this week.'

'Just for additional clarification, Mr Barrymore, we aren't having this one either. You might want to make a note of some of what we discuss but if you so choose, please be certain to memorise it and dispose of the paper before you leave this room. We wouldn't want things getting into the public domain that could serve to confuse a story we might decide to leak later in the week........once we've settled upon the version of the truth that would be most appropriate for public consumption, that is. Right, to business. When you use terms like *on the whole* and *pretty much* it always makes me nervous. Is one man dead and the other enjoying dreams of an illustrious career that will sadly be put beyond his reach by a cruel twist of fate early next week; or is the former only *pretty much* dead which, loosely translated, could equate to him being also *pretty much* alive?'

Barrymore felt momentarily relieved. Not only was he on fairly safe ground with this one but he was further reassured to see it wasn't a disembowelling tool the Home Secretary had been polishing with such relish, but a metal rod with a hook at the top that she used to raise and lower the office blinds.

'Oh, they are dead Home Secretary. They couldn't be more dead I can assure you. I even saw one of the lifeless bodies with my very own eyes.'

'I notice you were speaking in the plural before reverting to the singular, Mr Barrymore. Would that perhaps explain why you are squatting down in that obsequious manner, looking like a rabbit frozen in the headlights of a very fast car?'

Barrymore hesitated, and too late realised that by doing so he had just made a grievous error. The first rule of survival was never to hesitate when addressing a cabinet minister, and that rule applied even in the rare cases when you intended telling them the truth. That was it, he was roundly buggered. There would be no mercy for him now. Why hadn't he tried for diplomatic immunity somewhere in South America while he still had the opportunity? The Ecuadorians must be a push over if they put up with that tosser Assange for all those months. Oh well, it was only a minor mistake. She couldn't shoot him for it. He raised his head and looked deep into those clear grey eyes that held not the slightest hint of pity and realised that it was blatantly obvious that she not only could but would in all probability take enormous pleasure in doing so. No point in procrastinating. He might as well jump in with both feet and get it over.

'In accordance with the Monday morning discussion which as you previously observed didn't take place, I met up with Whitcott and gave him verbal confirmation of the job offer you outlined. He had cooled down considerably since our previous conversations and received the news with a degree of equanimity that I found extremely encouraging. He promised he would relay the news to his man Sangster without undue delay and contact me at my office for further discussions. At this point I retraced my tracks, scooted across the river, and collected the three officers from the Security Services, as per your instructions. *Those three officers*, Home Secretary. The ones we don't talk about except in the special meetings on Mondays that don't take place. We retraced my previous route and located both targets lunching at Whitcott's club. We then stationed ourselves out of sight, so we had a clear view of both the front and rear exits.'

Barrymore mopped his brow and kept the handkerchief in his hand as he had a horrible feeling its work for the day was not yet complete.

'There was no activity for nearly two hours and then Sangster emerged from the front of the club looking a little the worse for wear. He was duly tailed to his home address by one of the men you had put at my disposal, entry was gained by the pass key provided, and he err......... Mr Sangster died peacefully in his sleep. A heart attack, I suspect, will most certainly appear on the relevant certification as the cause of death.'

'Don't *suspect* anything, Barrymore, I've warned you about *suspecting* on several previous occasions. Just see that it is taken care of without any undue faffing around. OK, that sounds pretty much tickety-boo so far, so would I be right in thinking that you've saved the introduction of Mr Cockup at our meeting until the very last? Spit it out, Barrymore. What happened to Whitcott?'

Barrymore squirmed.

'Whitcott didn't emerge from the club for nearly an hour. He also gave the impression that he had imbibed a little more than was good for him. To put no finer point on it, Home Secretary, he seemed quite drunk. A fact, that I think that is fully substantiated by what happened next.'

'You aren't going to disappoint me are you, Barrymore. You know how I hate to be disappointed. Come on man, spit it out.'

Barrymore looked for inspiration. What would be the most delicate way for him to convey information of this sort? Then he began to relax. It didn't really matter; she would rub his nose in it whatever he chose to say. Right, there was no point in delaying. The best option would be to quickly lay it on the line, then feign a heart attack while she was distracted, thinking of the best way to kill him while inflicting the maximum amount of suffering.

'He walked across the pavement as if he were going to flag down a taxi but........'

'But, Barrymore?'

'..........but instead of doing so he abruptly changed direction, squeezed between two parked cars, and threw himself under the wheels of a bus.'

The room remained in complete silence for a full thirty seconds.

'How many of you were there outside Whitcott's club, Mr Barrymore?'

'Including me there were three. One man was not yet returned from.......from......'

'From ensuring Mr Sangster passed away peacefully in his sleep, Mr Barrymore?'

'Indeed, Home Secretary.'

'Yet despite there being three men, *including you*, loafing outside the club on expenses and at time and a half, it was still possible for the second target to position himself beneath the wheels of a vehicle the size of a London Transport omnibus without any one of you finding it within your powers to do anything about it? Did we not discuss in some detail the need to make sure that the two deaths occurred some days apart and in totally different parts of the country? Was it not the case that Whitcott was due to collide with a fence post while striving to avoid a coming-together with a stray sheep in a rural locality no sooner than seven days hence? These men were associated, Mr Barrymore. Don't you think that two people who had just dined at the same table, taking it upon themselves to drop dead within minutes of one another might look vaguely suspicious? Is this your idea of tidying things up? If the press picks up on this then heaven alone knows what we can expect.'

'I did have a thought, Home Secretary', said Barrymore straining desperately to make up lost ground.'

'God, Barrymore, don't you think we are in enough trouble already without making matters worse?'

'What about if we return Whitcott's body to his home address and arrange the circumstances so that the cadaver isn't discovered for a few more days? I don't think it's badly damaged. The bus didn't actually run over it. It was more of a decisive but unforgiving nudge.'

'Where exactly is the body now?'

'In the morgue. I don't know which one specifically, but I could very soon find out.'

'So, you are proposing we kidnap a body that might already be stuffed full of formaldehyde or is at best in the process of happily decomposing of its own volition and smuggle it back to.......

'His London flat is in a high-rise in Wapping, overlooking the river.'

'........back to Wapping and tuck it up in bed so it can be rediscovered in a week's time? Do you not think we might just be leaving ourselves a teensy-weensy bit open to being accused of tampering with evidence if that course of events ever found its way into the public domain? Something which, in my opinion, it most certainly would. Presumably, there were witnesses to the coming together between Mr Whitcott and the omnibus; and in those circumstances, do you not consider there might be a remote possibility one of those witnesses might have taken a photograph on their phone? If that didn't happen, then it is possibly the only noteworthy event that has taken place in the last ten years that wasn't digitally recorded and posted online within minutes of it having taken place. Even by your abysmal standards Barrymore, that suggestion is truly pathetic. That having been said, I suppose there's always the chance that I'm worrying unnecessarily, because thanks to your incompetence we could very soon be arrested on a charge of murder, in which case any evasive action, pitiful or not, will become totally irrelevant.........and while we are on the subject, if that sad state of affairs does come about, remember, you cough for the lot or I'll pull a few strings and see to it that you're sharing a cell with a couple of twenty stone men with proclivities that I can guarantee you won't very much enjoy. Can you still touch your toes, Barrymore? If so, it might be wise to do so now and get it out of your system while you've still got the chance.'

The room went silent again. The Home Secretary leaned back in her swivel chair, kicked off her shoes and rested her bare feet of the corner of the desk.

'Tell me about Whitcott. In detail this time.'

'Well, it all happened so quickly. One minute he was walking along the pavement in the direction of where I was standing, and then for no apparent reason his demeanour completely changed and he veered off, lurched between two parked cars, and before we could stop him leaped under the wheels of the bus. We were all too far away to intervene. There were only a couple of people in a close proximity, the nearest being a young black man walking in the opposite direction who seemed to anticipate what Whitcott was going to do and lunged to stop him. He was almost successful as well. I thought for a moment he had managed to get a grip on Whitcott but that proved not to be the case. Sadly, it appears, he was fractionally too late.'

'What happened to this man? Was he able to offer any clarification?'

'He disappeared, Home Secretary. Almost immediately, a crowd gathered. You know what it's like when there's an accident; scores of people appear from out of nowhere when a few seconds before there was nobody in sight. One minute the man was there right in front of me and the next minute the crowd had swallowed him up and he had disappeared from sight. Shall I put out an appeal?'

'Barrymore, you seem to be struggling to grasp the fact that we aren't actually trying to promote this incident. We are in fact endeavouring to give the publicity machine as little oxygen as is humanly possible. Bearing that in mind, how do you think an appeal for witnesses to come forward would further our aims? Kill any reference to Whitcott's death in the papers but adopt a degree of subtlety while doing so. Not a D notice, that would only serve to draw more attention. *A word in the ear of*, sort of approach. Go big on *being in the national interest* and *saving his family from unnecessary distress* by drawing unnecessary attention to his early-stage senile dementia. Get a backdated report from a reputable Doctor on that count; you know the drill. Do you think you can handle this without it becoming front page news or should we perhaps be discussing your transfer to a less arduous tour of duty? Anything more to add?'

'No, Home Secretary. That is, yes Home Secretary. There was a witness. One of the passers-by who was nearer to Whitcott than we were said she heard him shout something out as he took his final leap. She said she had a clear view of his face and he looked absolutely terrified. She said it sounded like he was yelling, *Christmas, don't do it. I'm on your side. It's all a mistake.*'

'Well, we were prewarned the man was away with the fairies, so, I suppose this should come as no surprise. Perhaps in his fragile condition the drink had served to push him over the edge.'

The Home Secretary paused in order to consider her options.

'It's only a month until Christmas, so perhaps we can look on this charitably. We'll treat Whitcott's demise a bit like they did the majority of the Covid deaths from a couple of years back. Something that was going to happen anyway by an entirely different means, but which got bought forward slightly due to unforeseen circumstances. At least we can take solace from the fact that Whitcott's death is unlikely to lead to the country becoming destabilised for the foreseeable future.'

She broke off to frown at a bird that was hopping about on the windowsill searching for something to eat. It noticed her, squawked, and immediately flew away. Barrymore followed its retreat with a feeling of unparalleled envy.

'Let's stay calm. There's no point in over-reacting at this early stage. It isn't like Whitcott would have had any use for green bananas. You only pre-empted his sad departure by a matter of days. Let's look on the bright side. Providing the press don't get wind of what has happened it will serve to cut down on the overheads, and if they do.......well, let's not worry about that now, but lay in a good stock of antidepressants just in case.'

She paused again, taking the opportunity to scratch the calf of one leg with the toe of the other. Her dress had now ridden up over her thigh, an occurrence Barrymore was trying desperately not to notice.

'Right my man, three things and three things only. Firstly, find out who leaked the information that Whitcott was losing his marbles. Not who reported it, because that will inevitably be a top floor paper shuffler eager to take the credit. I want the person who actually gleaned the information and bought it in-house. We need some new blood in this department and if I've got to start setting on staff, I would prefer it if they could count above ten without taking off their shoes. Secondly, check out who Whitcott engaged to compile that accursed report that everyone is getting so excited about since that Chinese broad with the personality defect left her copy on the tube. Thirdly, figure out who the person is that Whitcott wanted to bring in as a new member of his team. Now the house cleaning has been completed on phase one, we need to give a thought to setting up phase two with minimal delay, and it occurs to me that if the late lamented Mr Whitcott wanted this person to join his merry little band of murderous thugs, then inviting him in for a quiet, little tete-a-tete might not be a bad place to start.'

Barrymore felt morally obliged to register an objection, even if he were certain that it would prove a complete waste of time.

'Don't you think that course of action might be a little premature, Home Secretary? Might it not be a better idea to let things die down a little first?'

'If your efficiency on the last job can be taken as a measure of things to come, then by the time you get back to me with answers on the three questions I've just asked, things will have died down by a little bit, Barrymore. Now get your arse in gear and find me some answers.'

As the door of her office clicked sharply into place, confirming Barrymore had successfully negotiated his exit strategy unscathed, the Home Secretary moved to the window, picked up a cactus plant from the inside sill, and upended it into her metal wastepaper basket. She then pulverised every vestige of the unfortunate flora out of existence with the metal rod she used to adjust the window blinds. The bloody thing had pricked her this morning and having let Barrymore off with a reprimand she couldn't allow herself to be seen to be going soft.

CHAPTER THIRTY-THREE

Sheffield, Monday December 1st 2025

Having returned from a brisk walk over open countryside, Litmus now felt able to confront the forces of the world on an equal footing. The forces he anticipated encountering did not, however, have Beth recumbent in their midst. Something which his garden chair most certainly did. Litmus found this spectacle extremely unsettling. He wasn't a man who coped well with surprises, even if this specific offering was the single thing that he desired most in the whole wide world.

'So, Litmus, you are still alive and looking comparatively well, which I must confess comes as something of a surprise given the circumstances in which we parted company. What exactly happened? How is it that you are still breathing?'

Well, she said she'd come back and here she was. So, now he needed to tell his tale and before he had opened his mouth, he was conscious the words in his head just wouldn't sound right. He didn't like the way it would sound, and neither would she. There were certain aspects of the story that were open to misinterpretation when viewed from a certain perspective. In fact, when regarded from a variety of angles he was forced to admit it didn't always show him up in a particularly good light. Perhaps, rather than burden Beth with what had actually taken place, wouldn't it be wiser to search out something a little more reassuring? A tale where accuracy encroached when it aided the narrative but was never permitted to hog the limelight when it seemed intent on subverting the plot. Where truth put in a cameo appearance when it didn't interfere with the storyline but stood nobly aside when its merits became a hindrance to clarity and lucidity. The start and the finish need only be a stone's throw from reality, but in between a delicate wash of rose-coloured invention should be inserted in order to keep focus on what was important, which would in turn permit him to discard that which was not. It was his story after all, even if it did constitute little more than a pack of lies. It wasn't Le Carré at his finest but, taking into account the time constraints that had been forced upon him, he thought that it hung together rather neatly. He saved Whitcott's encounter with the bus for the crashing finale and was disappointed when his audience reacted in an entirely unexpected manner.

'Thank you for breaking the news so gently. What a terribly tragic way for poor Mr Whitcott to die. He was such an unusual character but the colossal effort he put into funding that orphanage showed the man in his true colours, don't you think? How will they ever manage now that he's gone? If my understanding is right, he was pretty much their sole benefactor. It's heart-breaking to imagine all those young lives being affected by such a random act of ill fortune. Sometimes life seems so brutal and callous. With so much evil in the world it makes no sense that such a good man should have been chosen to lose his life in such an arbitrary fashion. It just doesn't seem fair.'

Litmus sat with his mouth open for several seconds before he could fashion a reply. 'Whitcott......Jerome Whitcott funded an orphanage? I had no idea that he..........'

'Dedicated every spare moment to the project, by all accounts. Regarded the venture as his life's work. Every penny he earned went into the upkeep and development of the buildings. He confided in me that he hated his job but felt he was tied to it for the duration because he wouldn't have been able to face himself in the mirror if he let those poor homeless children down. It's a tragedy. What ever will they do now?'

'But that doesn't make......'

'By the way, I'm off to America', Beth said, as if the previous subject had been so distasteful that she couldn't bear to dwell on it for any longer than was absolutely necessary. 'I picked up a job for a big outfit in Southern

California doing the same sort of stuff, only coming at it from a totally different angle. More on the inside looking out than the way things have worked for me in the past. Market competition to be targeted mercilessly with no quarter given. Well, that's the way it was explained in the job interview. Fantastic money by anyone's standards and it is west coast beach territory, so it looks like I've finally landed my place in the sun.'

Litmus was horrified but tried to respond with a smile.

'I was hoping you'd come back to claim your old room. Well, the whole house if you want it. I mean, you paid for it. It's yours, in everything but name. I'll hand over the deeds right this minute if I can find where I've put them. You liked it here, didn't you? You said looking out at the view across the park made you feel happy.'

'Litmus, I don't want your bloody house. Though I must admit it looks a good deal better than the first time I walked in the door. It's yours. You earned every penny I paid you. We're quits. I only came back to pick up the rest of my stuff. This was only a stopping off place on the road to somewhere completely different for me, but you could turn it into a proper home if you put your mind to it.'

Litmus struggled to find a meaningful response and knew before he started that he would fail miserably.

'I didn't realise you saw it that way. I was hoping that you intended to move back in. That we might get to spend some time together and get to know each other a little bit better. If I'd known you were coming, I would have laid something on. We could have gone out for a.....'

Beth looked puzzled. 'Sorry, you weren't expecting me? Are you saying you didn't get my message?'

'Message? No, I never received a message.'

Beth checked her watch distractedly, which only served to emphasise to Litmus that this conversation was a minor priority in her newly constructed world, and she had far bigger things on her mind. She responded in sharp little soundbites, jumping from topic to topic as she did her best to cover a lot of ground in the least possible time.

'I called in last week........well maybe ten days back. It's hard to remember exactly when because it's all been a bit hectic. I thought I was bound to be back before now, but I've been chasing around gathering up my stuff from all over the place. They've sorted out the visas and they pay the shipping costs, you see. The company I'll be working for will stand the bill for everything, but it's strictly a one-off opportunity; and as I've got no intention of coming back unless something terrible happens it seemed dumb not to take advantage. But when I called round the first time the house was empty, none of the neighbours knew where you'd gone, and obviously I couldn't get in. Why did you change the front door when you redecorated the house? I had a key to the old one, but it didn't fit into the new-fangled lock. I could have just grabbed my stuff and been gone if you had left things the way that they were.'

Litmus struggled to settle on specifics from the jumble of words but got the broad outline. He was clearly in the wrong, even if he wasn't entirely sure why.

'I left Rosanna at the bottom of the garden. The little girl that looks like me; or it did before I grew six inches and put on a stone and a half in weight. My mum got it for me when I was a kid. She worked as a tailor. You must remember, I told you at least half a dozen times. The other kids only had dolls, but I had a proper twin sister with a cool sounding name. She was better than a real sister because she never argued back, and we never had a cross word over who got to wear the new dress to the party. I told you this already. Why do men never remember anything that's really important?'

'Hang on. That model thing at the bottom of the garden; that was you?!'

'Who the hell did you think it was? Didn't you read the note? I said I'd be back to see you as soon as I could. I dressed Rosanna in some of my clothes and pinned the note on her front with one of my hair grips, so you'd know it was me who had written it. After all the weird stuff that had gone on in the last couple of months, I thought I had better

293

make it crystal clear it was me that had been visiting. If you had a letter box in your new front door like normal people none of this would have been necessary. I stood Rosanna up on the patio at the bottom of the garden to be sure you couldn't miss her. Litmus, please tell me she isn't still out there. That girl is like the little sister I never had.'

Beth had at last run out of steam, or at least Litmus hoped that was the case. He quickly fashioned a stumbling reply.

'Yes. That is no. I saw the figure in the garden, but it was lying on its back in a puddle and the note was really hard to understand because the words had got smeared in the rain. The figure, the mannequin, your sister, Rosanna, that thing, whatever you call it. She...it...she had her throat ripped out and there was blood where she'd been mutilated. I thought it was you for a minute. It was one of the scariest moments in my entire life. Where did the blood come from? I assumed it had been left as some sort of threat.'

They looked at each other for ten seconds in complete silence. Then spoke simultaneously.

'That bloody fox!'

Five minutes later a taxi pulled up outside. Beth refused any help as she dragged her suitcase across the pavement area for the driver to manhandle into the boot of his cab. Litmus watched from the front window as she gave instructions for her destination and waved him a final goodbye. He was just about to walk out onto the pavement to see her off in a civilised manner when Jilly, the new hairdresser with the American accent who worked at the salon next door, scampered along the footpath hauling an oversize trunk. The two girls threw their arms around each other and kissed on the lips. Then hauled the new item of luggage into the passenger area they were now sharing, slammed the door, and immediately were gone. Litmus waved from the doorway, but nobody appeared to be looking back in his direction. He headed to the kitchen and made a fresh mug of tea, aware that his lack of perception had just broken new ground.

CHAPTER THIRTY-FOUR

Mid Atlantic to New York, December 3rd 2025

Beth Newall couldn't sleep despite the pampering that had been lavished on the passengers enjoying the opulence of first-class accommodation. She had never been great at relaxing on long distance flights, and it was nobody's fault but her own that she was still staring up at the ceiling four hours after getting tucked in for the night. She had been provided with enough blankets and soft pillows to equip a small army, but the extra glass of champagne and the brandy and coffee after the meal had brought her insomniac tendencies to the fore. She really should have had more sense, but it was too late to worry about that now.

Jilly was snuggled comfortably in the seat next to hers and appeared to be dead to the world. This was always a good time in a relationship. The part that Beth enjoyed the most. She hoped this one was a keeper because she had been here so many times before and the situation was beginning to get a little bit too repetitive for comfort. Three months of fun whilst exploring new territory, three months of stability when the period of adjustment had been completed and you didn't need to work at it quite so hard, then three months of hideous rows and recriminations as the rapport disintegrated and the relationship ground to a shuddering halt. It was invariably her fault she had to admit. Her boredom threshold bordered on the non-existent. After it was over, she would tell herself that this was definitely the last time she was getting involved, because the breakups were just too damned painful; and at the time she would mean every word of it. Then five minutes later another fluffy little blonde would appear over the horizon and give her a come-hither smile, and the saga would start up all over again.

When she thought about it, this liaison was especially stupid even by her modest standards. Jilly was Canadian working in the UK on a visa and they had only been an item for about three weeks. Still nothing ventured, nothing gained. If you couldn't show a bit of optimism at this stage in proceedings, then there wouldn't be much hope for you further down the line when things would inevitably get more complicated. Maybe this would be the exception that proved the rule and Jilly would turn out to be the love of her life. She really hoped that would be the case because it seemed that this time around the timing was right and, so far, the omens had proved promising.

She cast a thought back to Litmus and felt thoroughly ashamed. He had waved them off from the front of his house looking two steps past melancholy and one short of suicidal, but she had pretended not to notice. She knew she had treated him abysmally from the minute they met, but the man did have a tendency to bring out the worst in her.

Whitcott meant absolutely nothing to her, so what had caused her to do it? Was it out of guilt for him having died in such appalling circumstances that she had conjured up that elaborate story about him funding an orphanage? Sometimes weird stuff like that just came into her head and her mouth started moving before her brain was properly in gear. That wasn't it though, if she was being perfectly honest. She had done it from devilment as much as anything else. Litmus had looked like he was enjoying himself a little bit too much, telling his contrived story of Whitcott's demise. A tale that he was obviously making up as he went along in order to impress her. He was looking horribly self-satisfied, which had caused a vision of her father to form in her head. Her father, the man above all men that she most deeply despised. Poor Litmus, it wasn't his fault that in that moment he brought back long buried memories of parental confrontations; but it somehow served to make the temptation to prick his bubble totally irresistible. Once she had associated Litmus with her father, nothing in the world could have stopped her trying to wipe the stupid smile off his face.

She was fully aware that if she had later confessed to inventing the whole thing, he would immediately have forgiven her without a second thought, but she hadn't wanted to let him off the hook quite that easily. It had been far too entertaining to watch him wriggle and squirm. She was an evil cow, she had to admit it. Sometimes she felt scared by the stuff that went on inside her head.

That ridiculous thing with the mannequin, was another perfect example. She had seen it in a skip, hauled it out and dusted it down. Spruced it up to look as much like her as was possible with the cosmetics at her disposal and dressed it a selection of her old clothes. She had done it specifically so it would scare the life out of him. She had known very well the effect it would have.

Then, on her latest visit, indicating that the lump of window dressing was a much-adored pretend sister was something else that had just flashed into her mind out of the blue. Anyone else would have laughed in her face, but Litmus being Litmus had chosen to accept her lurid tale as if it were the most natural thing in the world. What was the matter with the man? He had an extremely good analytical brain and was enormously astute around other people, but from the very start she had always had the ability to twist him round her little finger. It was almost like he relished being mistreated. No matter how long she lived, she would never understand men.

A warning was given by the stewardess in the very smart dark blue uniform with matching scarf that the descent to JFK had begun and seat belts were required to be fastened, and almost immediately the full landing palaver kicked into gear. A lot of the passengers were still half asleep and looked like they had been dragged through a hedge backwards, but she knew that even at her most dishevelled she would still look gorgeous. She had been born beautiful and by some perverse miracle had remained beautiful ever since. It wasn't as if she worked at it; it was just the way it was. She could eat what she liked without putting on weight, her skin was always radiant, her hair glossy, and she could go without sleep without there ever being the slightest trace of a dark circle underneath her eyes. At thirty-three she could pass for ten years younger if there was any advantage in doing so. She was a freak, she readily admitted it; but a freak who was blessed with all the advantages and none of the drawbacks. It was as if the stunning outwards shell had been given to compensate for the maelstrom in her head. She took all the advantages that it offered and thoroughly enjoyed that it just wasn't fair.

The queues at the airport stretched out as far as the eye could see. The plan they had devised, after much consultation, was to stay in New York for three nights. Do some shopping and take in the sights, before catching a flight that would take them to their eventual destination on America's west coast. However, the way things were currently shaping up, it looked like there was every chance they would still be stuck in this same line of passengers in three days' time. Progress was interminably slow and when they eventually did get near to passport control Jilly was ushered into a separate queue, possibly because she was a Canadian national. Time trudged on, and finally she was waved through by the man in the booth. Did they really ask all those questions to everybody entering the country? It was hardly the welcome she had expected to the land of the free and the home of the brave. She walked slowly forward looking for Jilly but there wasn't a sign. However, there were three large men right in her path wearing the traditional fedora hats so beloved by FBI agents in television crime dramas, and she couldn't help being aware that their eyes hadn't left her from the moment her foot cleared the threshold of emigration control.

Suddenly questions were buzzing in her head, with answers being provided all too readily by a brain that had just started to operate rationally. Jilly, a three-week relationship. Her willingness to pack her bags at a moment's notice and take a chance on love. Canadian citizen? Americans sounded exactly the same as Canadians as far as she was concerned. She had never seen Jilly's passport, after all. She could be from anywhere. The stern warning from Whitcott that she had chosen to ignore, advising her that she would become liable to prosecution in America if one of her trading partners chose to turn nasty. The last interview with Cleveland Shultz International, when they had transferred the final instalment of cash, hadn't gone as smoothly as she might have hoped. The west coast employment offer coming as a total surprise, right when it was least expected. Who had provided the recommendation and the contact details? It had never occurred to her that it might be wise to enquire. The job entailing the sort of work that was bound to be of interest to someone like her, and the company being located in a place she had always wanted to visit. Too many coincidences, surely; and why was she only starting to notice them now? The answer to that one was easy. Because her brain had been befuddled by a cute little blonde.

There was no place to go so she might as well grit her teeth and tackle the problem head on. She walked brazenly up to the three men and smiled her very best smile. The one that made hulking men with tattoos on their necks go weak at the knees.

'Is it me you're waiting for? Elizabeth Louise Newall, UK citizen.'

The eldest of the three men looked her straight in the eye, smiled in a sardonic way and appeared to consider the possibility. Then, in a flash it was as if she didn't exist as all three men became totally absorbed in something that was happening over her shoulder. She spun round and followed their gaze which appeared to be centred on a small middle-aged man with a bald head and remarkably unkempt toothbrush moustache.

'Wish it were, honey, but life ain't that good', said the largest of the three as they immediately abandoned her and galloped off in the direction of their quarry.

A moment later Jilly appeared at her side.

'Bloody customs officers. Hands everywhere. Do I look like a drug smuggler? And even if I were, do they seriously think I'd be likely to have shoved it up there?'

Beth smiled as she felt the tension leave her body. Suddenly life was wonderful all over again. Men stared at you if you were beautiful. She should be accustomed to it by now. Usually it was complimentary and welcome, but sometimes it could scare you out of your wits.

'Come on, lets grab the bags and find a hotel. We've got too much to cram in to hang around here for the rest of the day. We're going to have a great time Jilly, and we're not going to miss a single damned thing.'

CHAPTER THIRTY-FIVE

Sheffield, Thursday December 4th 2025

Litmus had spent large parts of the previous day industriously employed. The house wasn't exactly spotless, but it was a good deal cleaner than he would have considered possible when the building work had been in progress. Things that had needed sorting were now taken care of, things that had the potential to be deferred were postponed indefinitely, bills that usually lodged behind the old clock on the mantlepiece until the very last moment had now been paid and the invoices neatly filed in datal order. The entire framework of his life had been spat on and wiped clean with the corner of a mother's white lace handkerchief and, as long as nobody took the trouble to examine it under a microscope, it would most definitely pass scrutiny and project wholesomeness to any onlooker from the outside world.

After careful thought he had taken a number of momentous decisions. Judgements that he was painfully aware would affect not only his life, but the future of others as well. As a salute to his much-troubled past, he had endeavoured to do the right thing, or at least get as close to that illusive aspiration as was possible in the time he had at his disposal. He appreciated this time limit was self-imposed but that made it no less rigid. He was not prepared to cut himself any slack. The body was weak, and he was determined to allow no opportunity for a deferment, and certainly not a change of mind.

He had written to Sam in London. Sam, another missed chance to add to the catalogue of names that seemed to stretch back almost forever. Sam, who had touched his heart, but whom his fabled relationship incompetence had permitted to disappear off into the night. Sam, the person who had trusted him so completely that, despite hardly knowing him, she had done the unthinkable and taken him at his word.

Into a large reinforced manilla envelope he had deposited the letter, his two sets of house keys, and all the bumph he had been able to locate that related to the building he had been proud to call home. He had kept the correspondence brief. Told Sam and her sister that due to business commitments he would be going away for a long period of time and, as they were nice people and he felt somewhat in their debt for their kindness and good cheer, he was bequeathing them this property to do with exactly as they chose. That it was a gift that he hoped they would very much enjoy. No need to acknowledge the correspondence because due to time constraints he would be setting off immediately. Sadly, he would not be contactable for a very long time.

For once he needed to face up to his responsibilities. He couldn't ignore that he had betrayed everything he had stood for by causing Whitcott's death. A classic misjudgement on his part. A bad man who to his surprise had turned out to be good; had been revealed by Beth to be a good man who had died due to his unforgivable mistake. His impetuosity in jumping to totally the wrong conclusion had led to the error of judgement which had resulted in the loss of Whitcott's life. His screw up, hence his responsibility. His fault in every respect.

The only correct course of action was to own up and suffer the consequences. To do the right thing so he could look himself in the eye. A prison cell would be hard to take but at least it would represent some form of justice and, as it was justice that he had sought all his life, he could have no cause for complaint.

He would hand himself in at the Police Station in town. Make a full confession of what had happened. Maybe even tell them a little of what had occurred in the past. Enjoy the long walk that would take him there, along the streets and past the shops that he knew so well; enjoy it more in the knowledge that it was a stroll he would be making for the very last time. The weak winter sunshine had thrown off its seasonal cloak of gloom and was caressing the tarmac as he stepped outside the house. It felt like the right sort of weather for waving a final goodbye.

As he headed down the roadway towards town, he paused to take a final look across the parkland to his left-hand side. Despite the time of the year, to his eye it had never been more beautiful to behold. He walked on in no particular hurry, hands in pockets, savouring the moment, relishing every split second as they quickly ticked away. He paused in front of the old roundabout that had once acted as boundary marker for the city. It was currently entwined with mangled shrubbery and matted grass but in a couple of short months he knew it would be ablaze with snowdrop, crocus and daffodil. Even now, he could see them plainly in his imagination. Perhaps only now he was seeing things clearly for the very first time. On again, past side roads and buildings each as familiar as the back of his hand. No hurry. Drink it all in. Savour the memories, because each recollection would need to sustain him for a very long time.

It was late morning already and he had walked barely a mile. Dawdling on purpose; difficult to deny. Looking at the shoppers, the joggers, the beggars in the street; those meandering along, swept by an uneasy current; people with no burning purpose to get anyplace fast. While he was ruminating, a gaggle of students pushed past. Oriental, probably Chinese. Sheffield had the biggest population of Chinese students outside of the capital and had benefitted greatly from heavy Chinese investment in recent years. Good on anyone putting money into this part of the country because it needed every penny it could get after the demise of heavy industry and the cutlery trade, which had been the mainstays of commerce once upon a time.

He forced himself to refocus. Pull yourself together, fella. Stop fooling around. Let's get this thing done. He tugged his cap lower until it rested just above his eyeline and pulled the zipper of his hoody as high as it would go. There might be sunshine beaming down, but the month was

December, so it did little to counter the bite of a northerly wind that had cut its teeth on chilling bones.

He was still adjusting his clothing when it happened. It felt like some sort of shift in atmospheric pressure that sucked every bit of air from his lungs. One minute he was on his feet and the next he was flat on his face in the middle of the pavement with everything out of focus and swirling in circles. He could feel blood running down his face from a cut on his forehead. It felt bad but had no idea how it could be because as far as he could tell there was nobody anywhere near him to have inflicted the injury, and he sure as hell hadn't done it himself. He looked up, and there was a sort of bright white light in the sky and for a moment he could feel the muscles in his body stiffen in a most unnatural way. Jesus what the hell was happening to him? He struggled to pull himself to his feet because he knew he needed to take some form of positive action, but his head was buzzing, his joints ached like they were falling apart, and his legs felt like lead.

CHAPTER THIRTY-SIX

Penistone, Friday December 12th 2025

Marion Lambert was peeling potatoes. She was lost in thought because she had spent so much of her life peeling potatoes that she could fulfil the task without the need for even the most minor degree of concentration. It was nice to be up here for a change of scenery, but she wasn't sure Penistone would suit her on a permanent basis. It just wasn't what she was used to. A market town two spits from Barnsley that seemed like it was positioned right on top of the world.

The people up this way communicated in what her neighbours in the south would have considered a completely different language. Just going to the shops was a mind-boggling experience. Marion was the first to admit her hearing wasn't what it used to be in her younger days, so she struggled to pick up a lot of what they were saying first time around, and she didn't like to keep asking them to repeat themselves in case it seemed a bit rude. Like they weren't speaking proper English, which was of course precisely the problem in the first place; but she didn't want anyone to get the impression she was drawing attention to their shortcomings in case they thought she was lording it over them because she could pronounce her words properly. The last thing she wanted was for anyone to think she was stuck up. That wouldn't do at all. In order not to give offence she found herself forced into taking calculated guesses at what people were saying, and that was what had got her in trouble with that woman serving in the baker's shop the day before yesterday, and all through no fault of her own.

It was better with Kyle and Darren because the boys had grown up in a household where one parent spoke broad Yorkshire and one had the more flattened southern vowels.

In consequence they had developed a sort of hybrid way of talking that stood somewhere in the middle. Not that there was any point in kidding herself that it would remain like that for very much longer. Now they were both of school age they would soon adopt the same words and sounds that they heard from their mates in the playground. It was just what you did to fit in, and she had every sympathy, because she and Ernie had done their share of fitting in over the years, and that hadn't always been easy.

Allison had been up here for nearly fifteen years now. It was amazing how the time had flown by. She had met Derrick at a concert in Leicester and from that moment on it had been plain to see the writing on the wall. They had been seeing each other for barely three months, and what meetings they had managed in the meantime had been very hit and miss due to the distance involved, when Allison had packed her bags and bid her family home a final farewell. Marion could see no good coming of it, and she had told Allison straight out what she thought would become of her.............but as it turned out she had been proved very wrong. A year later and the pair of them had tripping up the aisle looking as if they didn't have a care in the world; be it the aisle at the local Registry Office, but kids didn't seem to mind much about where they said their marriage vows these days, and that was when they bothered at all. Pity it had been up here, though, and not in the south where she could have invited a few friends along, but the pair of them seemed happy enough, so who was she to complain.

It hadn't been all plain sailing, mind. Derrick had lost his job in the steel works a few years back, but he had very quickly picked up work doing something or other with the council that appeared to suit him just as well, so that had turned out alright in the end. Allison had told her she was over the moon that Derrick had managed to land another job so quickly because positions like that didn't grow on trees in this part of the world. Plenty of his mates who had been made redundant at the same time had been stuck on Job Seekers Allowance for months on end, and it was inevitable that would put pressure on a marriage, no matter how secure. Allison had also whispered quietly in her ear (because you weren't supposed to say, it even if it was true) that she was relieved there were no mining jobs around here anymore. If push came to shove that would have been the fall-back option, and if Derrick had gone down the pit Alison said she would never have slept easy for a single night while he was working underground.

Marion had always made a point of travelling north to see her daughter twice a year, regardless of whether or not Allison and Derrick managed to bring the kids down to her place in the south. She could get a bus that ran straight up the motorway and one or other of them would always be on hand to collect her at the other end, so she didn't need to worry about getting a taxi. Ernie had been buried for twelve years come April so she could please herself what she did with her time, and her job offered good holidays even if the pay wasn't much to write home about, so it was always possible to work something out.

She really had no good reason to go out to work at all, because Ernie's pension covered her needs now the mortgage was finally paid off, but she wouldn't have missed it for the world. Seeing the girls she worked with behind the counter was something that never failed to bring a smile to her face and brighten her day. The current team had worked together for what seemed like two lifetimes and they knew each other inside out and back to front so you could talk about virtually anything without getting embarrassed. In fact, they got on so well together that they socialised outside work as well as managing to have a few laughs when they were cooking in the kitchen at the school. The bingo was always a laugh, and they visited the cinema on the odd week when they were showing a film that they had any chance of understanding; something that year on year became increasingly rare. They even went to a pub for a meal if it were a birthday or some other cause for celebration; as long as they could find one that had a special offer on, something which wasn't difficult since all the pubs down her way were looking out for an extra bit of trade. Yes, all in all she had little to complain about. There were worse places than Luton to live and working as a dinner lady at a local school suited her down to the ground.

Marion pressed on with her labours. She always used a sharp knife when she was peeling potatoes. She had a magnet on her fridge at home that read, *potato peelers are for wimps*, which always made her smile as well as pretty much summing up her views on the matter. It was when she stood up from retrieving the washing up liquid bottle that she had caught with her elbow, and which had unaccountably managed to wedge itself underneath the cooker that she noticed it. A sort of scribbly drawing on the newspaper that she had put on the draining board to catch the peel from the potatoes and avoid getting muck on the aluminium surface that she was doing her best to keep clean. She knew that face. Yes, she was sure that she'd seen it quite recently but for the life of her she couldn't recall where that might have been. She racked her brain, but no matter how hard she thought it wouldn't come back, so in the end she gave up and got on with her work; and that was the point that it came back to her.

'What are you doing now, Mum?' Allison had that tone in her voice. She seemed to spend half her life trying to get her mother out of the kitchen.

Marion made one of those faces that mothers have been making at their daughters since the beginning of time.

'Just peeling a few potatoes to have with that pie you got from the butchers. Don't get your knickers in a twist. Come here a minute. Take a look at this bloke in your local. I know him. Remember me telling you about that man who picked us up at the school and took us down to London for the day? The coppers were looking for him, weren't they. We ought to tell someone. Do you think........'

'Mum, please, not that again. Remember we agreed, we weren't going to talk about that anymore. From what that Sergeant down at the station said, you were lucky you didn't end up in jail.'

'But that's him, Allison. I'd swear on a stack of bibles. I was sat in the back of the car on the left, and I had half his face in front of me for nearly an hour. He was distinctive, girl, I'm telling you. I could pick him out of an identity parade with my eyes shut.'

'Come on, Mum. Think about it. What are the chances. That isn't even our local paper. It's something Derrick used to wrap the leeks in when he bought them home from the allotment, and while we're on the subject I don't want you putting it on my draining board either, because it's probably full of germs.'

'But Allison, he's the dead spit. His hair's shorter but apart from that he's exactly the same. There couldn't be two faces that looked like that. His was distinctive, I'm telling you. That's Mr Bob for sure.'

'Mum, it isn't. It just looks a bit like him. The man who runs the bicycle repair shop at the top of the road looks like that drawing as well. There are probably hundreds of people out there who look nearly the same.'

'Well, I suppose you're right, but I would still put my week's wages on it. I might not be as sharp as I used to be but my eyesight's as keen as it ever was. I can still read the number on the thirty-one bus when it's two hundred yards down the road. I've got better eyes than people half my age. The optician said..........'

'Here, give it a rest for a minute and pass me those peelings so I can put them on the compost. Don't you say anything to Derrick about what you just told me when he comes in. He's only just got over the last lot. We'll just chuck the paper in the bin and forget all about it, alright? Now come in the front room and put your feet up for a bit before the kids get back from school. It'll be your last chance; they'll be here in a minute. Then you can forget about getting any peace.'

Marion trudged into the front room and took the seat that she always used by the window. There was no point in arguing with Allison. She had always known how to get the last word, even when she was knee eye to a grasshopper.

Her teachers had always said she had a mind of her own and didn't mind sharing it with anyone who would listen, and that hadn't changed with the years. Perhaps that was why she had settled in so well up this way. No shrinking violet was Allison, never had been, never would be. God knows where she got it from. She had always minded her P's and Q's and Ernie had never been the sort to say boo to a goose. Praise the Lord they weren't forced to share a kitchen, because that would have been a recipe for disaster. She had always known what was best for everybody had that one, and she had never needed any encouragement to tell them what she thought, whether they wanted to hear it or not.

Marion shuffled to get comfortable in the chair still feeling resentful. It was the absolute spitting image of Mr Bob, that picture in the paper, no matter what her daughter said. Then again, she had to admit she had never been very good with faces. She had always got Dean Martin mixed up with Robert Mitcham which Ernie had thought was hysterical; though why he found it so funny she had never been clear because when they were dressed up in their posh suits, they did look very much the same. Alright, perhaps it might be best to let it go. Perhaps it was better for all concerned, especially if she wanted a quiet life. Anyway, the kids would be back in a minute, and they were more than enough to be going on with without having anything extra to think about. She would grit her teeth and bear it; but she was sure that she was right, just the same.

CHAPTER THIRTY-SEVEN

Sheffield, Thursday December 18th 2025

Litmus was standing in the wings of the stage, a position from which he could clearly see all that was going on without being noticed by the audience. How he had got here wasn't entirely clear, but he had managed it somehow, and that was all that mattered. The midwife who had completed over fifty years' service, the parking warden who had performed CPR on the woman who had collapsed in the road, and the man who had rowed across the channel using only one arm in aid of a charity that had supported his wife in her dying days had already collected their awards. The Policeman who had dived into the frozen river to save a drowning dog was currently being interviewed by Magnificent Max. He was the first Policeman to receive an award of this sort for very many years, which perhaps indicated that the resentment directed at the South Yorkshire Police Force in the wake of the Rotherham Child Abuse Scandal was finally being put to one side, even if it would never be completely forgotten. There was not an empty seat in the entire auditorium which in itself was surprising as the weather was inclement, and Christmas was barely one short week away.

Magnificent Max told a ribald story about Jimmy Savile, Rolf Harris and Gary Glitter, men who you weren't really meant to mention anymore. The audience howled with laughter. This was Magnificent Max, he set his own rules and got away with things that would have seen other men hung, drawn and quartered.

Max, Max Higginbottom to give him his full title was that rarity in life, a retired sportsman who was warm, funny, articulate, and painfully polite. This was all the more surprising because Magnificent Max was a retired superheavyweight boxing champion who had gone toe to toe with some of the best pugilists of his generation. Coming from a sport not renowned for producing men who combined a high degree of eloquence with a genial disposition, Max was something of a rarity; or to put it more bluntly, he was totally unique. The man was on nodding terms with the inner circle of the Royal Family, and a first call whenever they organised a charity gala or wanted a man of the people to take tea on the lawn with specially invited guests. Providing a good cause benefitted from the proceedings, Max was guaranteed to be up for pretty much anything. He opened fetes, performed feats of strength, ran, cycled, planted commemorative trees, jumped out of aeroplanes, dedicated new buildings, the list was truly endless. Comperes fought to get him to appear on their talk shows. Television panel games never seemed quite complete unless he put in a guest appearance somewhere down the line. He even held babies at the font providing the well-heeled father was prepared to stick his hand in his pocket and donate generously to the cause for which Max was currently raising funds. He was the son that every mother dreamed of bringing into the world, though doubtless the woman in question would have rather taken him under her wing a little later in life when she didn't have to clothe and feed him, because Max stood only three inches short of seven feet in height and weighed in at more than nineteen stone.

All that besides, the cherry on the top of the cake from a local perspective was that Max Higginbottom was Sheffield born and bred. In consequence, if there was ever a clash of appointments bought about by his busy itinerary, his hometown would invariably come out on top. Litmus greatly admired the man. He was truly inspirational. Pity he was wearing a bright red suit that glowed on and off like a Belisha beacon and hurt Litmus' eyes, but what the hell. You had to make allowances. This was Magnificent Max after all.

Litmus changed his posture and distributed his weight a little differently. It had been a very long time since he had been on his feet for so long without a break. Bright lights still persisted in his vision but at least the ache from his body had numbed to a minor extent. If anything, he felt a little lightheaded which was strange because he had no recollection of having been given anything that would make him feel that way.

As far as he could remember, this was his first excursion into the outside world since his accident so it was only natural that he should feel a little weird. He was only grateful that he was no longer suffering the spells of excruciating pain.

The Doctor, who had a parrot on his shoulder and left a trail of blue smoke when he walked past Litmus' bed, had warned him that it was probably too soon for a venture of this kind, but he had chosen not to listen to the advice. This was the only chance he would get to put matters straight and there was no way he was going to pass up on the opportunity. This was an obligation to himself as much as anybody else and just for once he didn't intend to let anyone down.

There was loud applause as the dog rescuing policeman left the stage wearing his *Extra Mile* medal on a ribbon round his neck. The man had extremely long legs in relation to the rest of his body which Litmus found strangely comforting. That probably gave him a significant advantage when he was chasing down wrongdoers and miscreants in the course of his work.

Magnificent Max wasted no time in re-engaging with the audience. He quickly repeated the terms and conditions under which the local radio poll had been conducted. Then reminded the audience that this was the final presentation of the night and that before inviting the recipient onto the stage to collect his award he felt obliged to reiterate the circumstances under which the rescue had taken place.

The audience went completely silent. Max removed the microphone from its stand, straightened his tie, moved his legs slightly apart and stared out unseeingly into the void.

It was clear to see, he had the entire auditorium nestling in the palm of his hand.

Without further ado he immediately painted the scene using bold strokes of vivid colours for his purpose. He referenced the loud blast of the exploding gas main and the details of everything that followed, leaving nothing to the imagination. The licking tongues of the merciless flames. The acrid stench of the billowing smoke. The climb up the unstable drainpipe, which had very nearly parted company with the wall. The smashing of the window using a rag of torn coat for meagre protection against the biting shards of glass. The painful injuries sustained in gaining entry, forgotten in the thrill of rescuing the three little girls with matching polka dot bows in their hair, and their shellshocked mother, unaccountably attired in a black lace negligee and fishnet stockings at that hour of the day.

The four journeys up and down until the entire family were delivered to the safety of the pavement below, to be comforted by the fast-expanding crowd of awestruck onlookers. The final return to search for other survivors in case anyone had been missed in the panic to get free. The second explosion which had thrown the rescuer into the air, only for his plummet to certain death to be arrested by the branches of a tree. The cries from the crowd as that fickle branch broke under the unaccustomed weight, causing its undesired burden to tumble earthbound once more. The inglorious finale as the mangled body of the rescuer was deposited on the roof of a van parked out on the open road. The belated sound of sirens in the air. The broken ribs, the dislocated shoulder, the burns, the cuts, the abrasions and the bruises that had been manfully sustained. The audience was spared no harrowing detail, nor did it appear to desire any avenue of escape from the lucid cataloguing of carnage and gore.

Finally, Max's tale drew to a conclusion. He turned in Litmus' direction, smiled warmly and beckoned with an outstretched arm.

314

'And now let me introduce you to the man of the hour. Here, against medical advice and looking like he has just stepped out of the ring having completed eight rounds with me in my heyday, allow me to introduce the one and only, Mr Harold Sebastian Litmus.........plain Litmus to his friends, of which I count myself in that number.'

Deafening applause. Cheers. Photographs by the score. Litmus quickly abandoned his sanctuary in the wings and staggered across the stage to reach the microphone. Even louder applause. He tapped the top of the microphone in what he hoped was a competent manner and cleared his throat ready to begin.

'My thanks to Magnificent Max and to you kind people for your very warm welcome. This is the proudest moment of my life and there is nothing I would like more than accept this award............but I'm not going to because I am not the right person to be presented with such a prestigious honour. To accept it, would be a discredit to you, to the other people who have been honoured tonight, and to the veracity of the medal itself. I am not worthy of this award because I am not a good person. The reason I am here is because I thought I should at the very least explain that I take this action not out of disrespect, but in an attempt to show some belated honesty. I apologise to all the people who voted for me. I apologise to you in the audience. I assure you in all sincerity, I am the last person who should be given any sort of honour. This is no false modesty. I am truly not worthy of any form of acclaim.'

Total silence. Litmus backed from the microphone and prepared to drag himself towards the darkened corner of the stage from which he had emerged to such a tumultuous welcome only moments before. A hand the size of a pressure cooker lid gently restrained him.

'I think my friend Mr Litmus is operating under a misapprehension. He appears to think he knows better than we do, ladies and gentlemen. Might I remind him that these awards are not won or lost on the opinions of Mr Harry Litmus, they are voted on by us, the general public, and I take that qualifying factor particularly seriously because one of them is me.'

Max paused for effect and found it necessary to raise his hands in the air to quell the roars of support which were still circulating long after he was ready to resume.

'Allow me to assure Mr Litmus that nobody who ever collected one of these gongs is a thoroughly good person. I doubt if some of the recipients are good even half of the time, but the fact remains each one of them undertook a singular act of bravery or fortitude when there was an alternative, and for that show of courage, we choose to honour them. If I might take the opportunity to offer a salient word of advice Mr Litmus, it is this. You might not be good enough to receive this medal in your opinion, but you're chuffing well good enough to walk out of here with it hanging round your neck in ours, and according to the voting system that's currently in operation, that's the criteria that counts. Now get yourself over here and let me tie it round your neck because there is no way you'll outrun me in your current condition, old son.'

Tumultuous applause. Litmus shook hands with Magnificent Max, received the award, offered his thanks and was cheered to the rafters. Stars appeared to drift around inside the hall and a number took the opportunity to explode. Litmus looked out into the great void with tears running down his cheeks as dizzying fireworks exploded against the ceiling beams and rivers of colour ran down the walls.

God, he felt tired, but it was undoubtedly the happiest moment of his entire life. A buzzing sound started up, and somebody with a plaintive voice was talking incessantly, but it was only a background distraction to the standing ovation that progressively got louder and louder. He waved one last time, steadied himself, and flew backwards into the air. As he ascended higher and higher the world turned upside down and began to explode, right in front of his eyes.

CHAPTER THIRTY-EIGHT

Sheffield, Thursday December 18th 2025

'Staff......Emma, quick as you can. Litmus, bed four. I think I've lost him.'

'No, you haven't. That machine has always been iffy. When they die it's a different sound altogether. Not a shriek like that. More of an annoying whine. Try giving the plug a hard kick or turning the bloody thing off and on a couple of times. I don't think it can do much harm. Quick now, before everybody in the ward wakes up or we both go completely deaf. When did it start making that horrible whistling noise?'

'Right this second. Well, just now. Only a minute ago. I was standing right next to Mr Litmus' bed, when he began to twitch and mumble so I stayed by his side just in case he was coming out of the coma.'

'Well, you got that bit right anyway. At least I think so. There's something definitely going on inside his head, though I'm not going to guess what it is. What happened again?'

'Well, he's been moving about all evening. Thrashing around. Not at all like the way he's been since we first had him in here, when he just lay there like tripe at ninepence and didn't move at all. Tonight, it seemed like he was dreaming. First off, he seemed really subdued. He was mumbling to himself and making a sort of whimpering noise like a dog that was being beaten. Then all of a sudden everything changed, and he seemed really pleased, even you might say, happy. Then that bloody machine started making that terrible noise and I thought he'd died on me; and I can't tell you how much that really pissed me off because it's the first time he'd had anything like a smile on his face since they wheeled him in through the door.'

'OK Debbie, get hold of a sponge and wipe his forehead and clean up his face as best you can. Be careful round the cuts. He hasn't had the stitches out yet. Try talking to him or singing to him or something like that. Do you know any poems? That works sometimes, so I've been told, though I can't claim to have had any personal success with it over the years. See the way his eyelids are flickering. That's usually a good sign. I wouldn't be surprised if he comes out of it before the night's out, though what condition he will be in when that happens, I wouldn't like to guess. Second thoughts, perhaps we had better play it safe. We'll give it fifteen or twenty minutes and if he's still like this we'll get hold of the doctor on call, just in case......not that he'll be able to do anything useful. He only looks about fifteen and a half and I think it's his first week on nights, the poor little lad. Look, I'll just sort out Mr Johnson in the other ward and I'll be straight back. Keep him amused for ten minutes then we'll decide how best to play it from there.'

'What do I talk to him about, Staff? I've never done anything like this before.'

'Anything you like. Use your imagination. He'll probably not be able to hear what you're saying anyway, so it doesn't matter a lot. Tell him about what's been happening since he's been in here.......but don't mention about tripping over that bedpan on Tuesday and getting it all over his sheets in case he comes round in the middle of the story and decides to take us to court.'

'Right, right. Well, here goes, nothing................Hello, Mr Litmus...... Debbie calling, is there anybody there..........?'

'Well, Mr Litmus, my name is Debbie and I'm the nurse whose been looking after you. I'm going to talk to you, but feel free to interrupt anytime you want and, I can assure you, I definitely won't feel the least bit offended. You are in hospital, Mr Litmus. You came in on fourth December by ambulance in a semiconscious state, then you went into a coma, and you've been pretty much sound asleep ever since. I heard that you collapsed in the road and that the doctors don't know why that happened which is why they are still running tests.........but it might be best if you forget that bit because it's possible you aren't meant to know what's going on; what with you being the patient, that is.'

'You banged your head when you fell to the ground, but the cuts are only superficial and there won't be scarring........at least they don't think so. Well, not unless I opened up the wound again when I was cleaning up your face, but I was as careful as I could be, though I know I can sometimes be a bit cack-handed in stress situations because I'm always being told off..........but we won't worry about that for the time being, will we, Mr Litmus? When things like that need to be taken into consideration, we'll make sure that you're safely tucked up in your happy place.'

'You've been a very good patient, all in all. No trouble at all, relatively speaking. You have just laid quietly on your bed and been no bother to anybody. I wish they were all like you, only I suppose it's quite lucky that they aren't, or I'd probably be out of a job and with the way things are in this part of the world, that wouldn't do at all.'

'You've had a lot of visitors, Mr Litmus. We got your home address from a card in your wallet but first of all we couldn't make any contact because it looked like nobody was there to answer the phone. Then, after you had been in here for a few days, we got talking to Tomas and Pat and Sam who we understand are house sitting for you. Do you remember those names, Mr Litmus? They are your friends and they have been coming here to see you for the last few days but obviously you wouldn't know that because you've been stuck in a coma for all of that time. The lady called Sam has been reading you stories and it is a great shame that you missed them because the bits that I overheard have sounded really good. Better than a lot of the stuff they get on the radio in my opinion, not that I'm any judge.'

'There have also been two visits and a lot of telephone calls from a man called, Mr Barrymore. He sounds very important does Mr Barrymore, and we are under strict instructions to ring him up on a special number the minute that you regain consciousness, no matter what hour of the day or night that might be. Mr Barrymore says he needs to speak to you very urgently, but obviously I don't know what that is about, although whatever it is, it seems to make Mr Barrymore feel very nervous, because he starts twitching and has to swallow more of his pills.'

'The lady called Sam.........is she your girlfriend, Mr Litmus? I know she isn't your wife or your sister or anything like that because I asked her, but she does seem very fond of you. I'm not sure who she was talking about, but she also seemed anxious for you to know that Eric's settled in very well. Sam held your hand when she didn't think anyone was watching, and I quite got a lump in my throat for a minute or two even if that is a bit daft in my profession, where you are meant to be unaffected by that sort of thing because you see folks being carted off to the mortuary all hours of the day and night.'

'I'd be really grateful if you would wake up now, Mr Litmus, because I'm running out of things to talk to you about and there's no sign of Staff Nurse Beaton coming back, and I think she might have slipped out for a fag at the back of the canteen where the security cameras can't pick you up. I don't want to be sitting here not saying a word when she does eventually put in an appearance because I'm pretty sure she thinks I'm a bit soft in the head as it is, and that will only serve to confirm her thoughts on the matter.'

'If you don't wake up in a minute, Mr Litmus, I'm going to have to sing to you because I can't think of anything else to say; and I think that if those circumstances should arise, it's only fair to take this opportunity to warn you I've got a terrible voice and in my opinion it would be a very sad state of affairs if the first sound you heard after being unconscious for two weeks was my rendition of *I will Survive;* but I'm afraid it might come down to that because I can't think of any other songs where I know all the words except perhaps *Crackling Rosie,* and I'm not even sure about that one, to tell you the truth. If it comes down to the singing, Mr Litmus, I don't want you to think that living isn't really worth the trouble, or that living in a vegetative state is definitely preferable to being subjected to the sort of horror that is being forced upon you at a time when you aren't able to put up any sort of meaningful resistance.'

'Mr Litmus, is it possible........'

'Nurse, please stop talking. Please, I beg you. Who are you? Debbie. Debbie, don't worry I've got it now. Debbie, I'm awake now so you don't need to talk anymore......and you definitely don't need to sing. Am I back in hospital, Debbie? How did that happen? A minute ago I was up on the stage collecting my award? Could you get word to Magnificent Max that I'm really sorry for flying off like that, right in the middle of everything.......and Debbie, do you know where they might have put my *Extra Mile* award? Just point if your voice is feeling strained, Debbie. No need to talk.'

'Mr Litmus, welcome back to the world. It's really good to have you back in the land of the living but I think there's a very good chance that one of us is hallucinating and I'm not really sure which one of us that might be.'

CHAPTER THIRTY-NINE

London, Monday December 22nd 2025

The Home Secretary bustled through the outer office of the clerical department gnawing on the remains of a scotch egg. Everybody took this as a cue to look totally engrossed in their work. Barrymore was stationed some distance away, delving into the bottom drawer of a very large filing cabinet, but she successfully gained his attention by putting the fingers of her free hand between her lips and issuing a piercing whistle. Crumbs of mincemeat and egg flew in every direction, but nobody appeared to notice. The office staff were well practised in not noticing occurrences of the sort. The Home Secretary inclined her head toward her private office in a sidewards motion to indicate he was to join her straight away. Immediately, all traces of colour could be seen to drain from Barrymore's cheeks.

'Monday morning meeting, Mr B. Always the highlight of my week,' Susan Smallstone said mockingly, as they settled into seats either side of her oversized desk. 'Remind me, whose turn is it to go first? Shall we flip a coin? Spin a bottle? No, probably better if I decide. Let's pretend we did the bottle spinning and the neck finished up pointing at you.'

'I'll just fetch my notes', said Barrymore, immediately realising this was a cardinal error. The Home Secretary wasn't overly keen on people writing things down, especially with a pen.

'Ad lib, Barrymore. Live a little. Treat this like a walk on the wild side. Remember the exhilaration you felt that time you turned up on dress down Friday not wearing a tie? Play your cards right and you could experience that sense of raw elation all over again.'

'Do you want me to start with Litmus, Home Secretary?' said Barrymore, sounding as if that particular memory was one that he would feel far happier to leave buried in the past.

'Start where you like, Mr Barrymore. Just keep it short and entertaining. I've got the Police Commissioner and that mob from the other side of the river this afternoon, which is never a bundle of laughs at the best of times, so treat this as if you are the warm-up act, with the big hitter waiting in the wings.'

'I'm pleased to confirm that Harry Litmus is not dead, Home Secretary. He was hospitalised with a suspected heart attack coupled with possible brain damage, sustained when he banged his head on a stone wall after he collapsed. The heart attack proved to be a misdiagnosis, Ma'am. The hospital staff are currently investigating other possibilities. At this point in time Litmus remains under assessment and, for reasons I will later specify, I've ordered a twenty-four-hour watch.'

Barrymore considered it had been a shrewd ploy to get the most important piece of news out in the open as early as possible because Susan Smallstone lived very much in the present moment and if the meeting dragged on for more than an hour, she would probably lose concentration or be too drunk to remember. At least now he could legitimately claim to have told her, even if she would vehemently deny it if it later suited her purpose.

'Who were we talking about, again?' asked the Home Secretary struggling out of the legs of her tights and selecting a bottle of crimson nail varnish from the top drawer of her desk.

'Litmus', said Barrymore, going red in the face. 'Litmus, the man you told me to track down. The man we have been discussing at twice weekly meetings for the last three weeks.'

'Well, who's the sourpuss this morning, Mr Barrymore. Just trying to lighten up proceedings a tad. No need to go into a sulk. The festive season is very nearly upon us, and Human Resources are encouraging me to informally engage with my office staff as much as possible, so we can march into a glorious new year under the banner of peace and harmony. They are only referring to those who haven't already left the Service of their own volition and aren't detailed on the redundancy lists that will be released after the Christmas break, I presume. No real point in wasting goodwill on the other buggers, is there? Continue, Barrymore; smile for the benefit of anyone looking in from the outside office and fill me in on all you have learned in your travels to the far corners of our fair land.'

Barrymore wished with all his heart that the two houseboys the Home Secretary had taken under her roof on the pretext that they were refugees from Myanmar would bugger off back to the godforsaken country from which they had come. The Home Secretary was a lot easier to cope with when she was her usual bad tempered, foul mouthed self. The jolly facade she had been adopting since the start of the month had the whole department worrying that she had either found God or was back on the gear.

'Sheffield, Ma'am. In a geographical sense it's pretty much in the middle area rather than lurking in one of the corners. Right, allow me to recap.'

Barrymore, paused to gather his papers before realising that he didn't have any to gather.

'We established that the man Harry Litmus was the person Whitcott wanted to add to his team when he was under the mistaken impression that his work for the department was to be ongoing. We also discovered that Litmus was the source of the report relating to policing procedures concerning the north London..........'

'Yes, yes, Barrymore. I'm not senile quite yet. We already covered the dross. Leave that out and get straight to the nitty gritty. For Christ's sake, just get on with it.'

'The third thing you asked me to establish was the source of the report that indicated Whitcott was suffering from some form of mental disorder. That information, I can now confirm, was conveyed by a MI5 employee named Nigel Woodberry. I dug into Woodberry's past history, and it transpires his basic training was undertaken in the company of none other than our good friend Harold Litmus. It appears all roads lead to Litmus, Home Secretary, so we can safely forget about Rome, for the time being at least.'

Susan Smallstone frowned. Not, it transpired, at Barrymore's somewhat feeble jibe, but because a small blob of nail varnish had missed its target and adhered to her lower leg. She picked up a memo from the abeyance pile, spat on it and scrubbed enthusiastically at her shin. After a minute or so she seemed to notice Barrymore was still in the office and attempted to pick up the thread of the conversation.

'Yes, Barrymore, and you say that your enquiries have succeeded in confirming that the man Litmus remains alive?'

Barrymore tried to appear unperturbed. The Home Secretary was a woman and as such would doubtless be capable of multitasking in a delayed reaction scenario, as well as in normal time.

'Home Secretary, I'm afraid It now begins to get a little dark.'

Smallstone capped the varnish bottle, extended her legs across the desk and wiggled her toes in an attempt to speed the drying process. For the first time, she also looked more than a little interested. Dark was her favourite shade by far.

'In what respect, Barrymore?'

'Ma'am, I thought it a strange coincidence that a fit young man like Litmus should be struck down at the very moment he had his finger in such a variety of interesting pies. In consequence, I secured all possible CCTV footage from cameras in the vicinity of the bus shelter where he suffered his unfortunate accident.'

'And?'

'The camera directly opposite the fatal scene clearly showed that moments before Litmus collapsed a party of Chinese students pushed past him on the pavement. Facial recognition software indicated a ninety seven percent plus probability that the figure at the very back of the group was

D.I. Christine Ho, a Metropolitan Police employee who was until recently on secondment to Jerome Whitcott. The same person who operated as Whitcott's stenographer, and the same person who was accused of mislaying her copy of the Litmus report into police activity on the London tube.'

'So, you are saying Ho attempted to kill Litmus?'

'I can think of no other rational explanation, Home Secretary. As far as I can see, it's a cast iron certainty.'

Barrymore hesitated as if deciding whether to go further. He made a hurried and possibly rash decision, that it couldn't do much harm.

'There are whispers in the corridors that the finding on the train of D.I. Ho's copy of what we now know to be a report compiled by the man Litmus, might not be all it seems. That people with a vested interest in blackening Ho's name might have had cause to block her route to promotion. She was thought to be a shoo-in to replace D.C.I. Sangster at the Met, as I'm sure you will remember. Only office gossip, but I thought you would be interested.'

Susan Smallstone looked pensive. She removed her feet from the desk, swivelled in her large leather chair, and withdrew a litre bottle of vodka from the freezer compartment of the small office fridge that was positioned directly behind her desk, disguised as a bookcase. She took a dimpled tumbler from her lower desk drawer and filled it to the brim. She knocked back the measure in single gulp, before repeating the process twice more.

'And what conclusion did you draw from this, Mr Barrymore?'

This was the point at which to be careful, thought Barrymore. It was so difficult to know which way to jump. It was probably better to stall and then enthusiastically support whichever lunatic idea the crazy lady across the desk settled upon. It would certainly be better than putting forward a logical argument which invariably proved a complete waste of breath.

'Well, short of the fact that Ho quite obviously bore a grudge against Litmus, I wasn't sure what to think. In the circumstances I thought I was best advised to take no action. To bide my time until I had the opportunity to consult with you and obtain an updated directive. I passed instructions that Litmus was to be kept under observation at the hospital and if by chance he was released in the inevitable Christmas clear out that occurs in every hospital at this time of the year, that he be followed so we knew where to lay hands on him, if the need should arise.'

Barrymore would have been happy to rest on his laurels at this stage in proceedings but knew from the looks he was getting from across the office that he was obliged to say more.

'I understand that a puncture wound in Litmus neck has already been noted by the consultant overseeing his case, and I think it highly likely that in the fullness of time a more thorough understanding of the cause of the reason for the patient's incapacitation might find its way into the public arena.'

'Try that again, Barrington. In English this time.'

'I think it highly likely that in the next few days someone will work out that Litmus was stabbed in the neck with a syringe containing some sort of noxious potion that brings about a condition that might be mistaken for a heart attack; and if that proves to be the case it is highly likely the matter will be referred to the local Police, who if they are diligent in their enquiries will very soon be seeking to question Detective Ho.'

The Home Secretary reached for her handbag and withdrew a thin black cheroot from a crumpled yellow packet depicting a bumblebee in flight. She struck a match on the side of a staple gun that from previous markings was obviously employed exclusively for this purpose. Barrymore glanced anxiously at the smoke alarm above her desk, but it appeared to be malfunctioning again. In the centre of the Home Secretary's desk, he noticed a pair of wallpapering scissors with rubberised handles protruding from a Bavarian drinking tankard that held an array of different coloured pens. He thought he could take a pretty good guess as to why the sprinkler system was once again failing to operate satisfactorily.

After several minutes' complete silence, the Home Secretary rose to her feet in order to stub out her pungent cigar in an empty pot plant holder. It occurred to Litmus that there had been a bedraggled cactus on the windowsill in recent times, but it was now no longer in evidence. He envied the plant its release from the stresses of being under Susan Smallstone's direct control.

'Are you paying attention, Barrymore? You seem to be drifting off.'

Barrymore forced himself to sit straighter in the chair and adopt an alert and interested expression.

'Right, decision time, Mr B. The first thing to realise is that you can only play the cards that have been dealt into your hand, or to put it more succinctly, make the best out of the fuckups that haven't yet occurred and paper over the ones that have already happened. Let Litmus go his own sweet way for the time being but keep him under surveillance. We'll get back to him in due course but now clearly isn't that time. Track down the illustrious D.I. Ho and tell her we would like her to take over from Whitcott with immediate effect. Give her new job some sort of fancy title but don't go overboard with the wages. Ho will jump at the proposal because the way things stand, she won't have much else in the pipeline. There's no need to be overly generous with the taxpayer's money; this is the Home Office after all, not the bloody B.B.C. Make it clear to Ho from the start that it's an employment opportunity that is totally results driven, and that progress evaluations are conducted on a fortnightly basis by me personally. Don't mention the Litmus business. We'll hold that back in reserve.'

'Next, contact Calvin Mortley, and remind him I am looking forward to receiving the breakdown of the remaining gangland entities that we discussed last week. Emphasise that there is no need to rush with the report, and that as long as it's on my desk by first thing Wednesday morning all will be well. Also, enquire if he's made any progress with locating persons similarly placed to himself in other major cities. He won't have; but it will keep him aware that I haven't forgotten any of the stuff we were talking about.'

The Home Secretary looked thoughtful.

'That person you were just telling me about............... Gooseberry?'

'Woodberry, Home Secretary.'

'Woodberry, that's the fella. Arrange for his transfer from over the river. We'll put him together with Christine Ho and see how they get along; that way at least we've got all our damaged eggs in one basket.'

Barrymore wriggled uncomfortably in his chair.

'Home Secretary, in relation to D.I. Ho, I really don't think you can promote someone on the basis that they have proved unsuccessful in committing a brutal murder. It would set an unhealthy precedent at the very least.'

'That's more like it, Barrymore. If I didn't know you better, I could easily have mistaken that for a joke. Don't worry; I have every confidence. As far as I can see Ho is pretty much ideal. Reasonably intelligent, homicidal, ferocious and extremely devious. From where I'm sitting the lady is ticking all of the right boxes.'

Susan Smallstone paused, poured herself another drink and for a moment stared at it sadly.

'You have to make allowances, Mr Barrymore, it isn't easy being me. Everything I set out to accomplish carries an absurd level of expectation because I have to oversell it to get it past that set of numpties up the road. Westminster seems to have market exclusivity on paper shufflers who couldn't take a decision if their very lives depended on it, and they naturally resent anyone who isn't tarred with the same brush.'

She paused, and for one unbelievable second Barrymore thought he could detect a tear forming in the Home Secretary's eye. He quickly pulled himself together and dismissed the possibility as utterly ridiculous.

'They hate me, Barrymore. Hate me and everything I stand for. While at the same time realising that they can't manage without me, and in consequence are obliged to tolerate my faults, my little peccadillos. They desperately want the crime figures to go down and yet have no idea how that could be accomplished. They choose not to acknowledge that our forces are outgunned, out financed and a lot of the time out thought, and yet they still want me to make an omelette without breaking eggs. If I didn't sanction the cutting of corners, we would very soon be experiencing anarchy. Anarchy, Barrymore; anarchy allowed to flourish in what anybody with half a brain recognises as the true cradle of world civilisation. Unthinkable, don't you agree? Anarchy in the UK!'

'But if you promote Ho you are giving an attempted murderer free rein to wreak carnage. To assassinate British citizens with Government approval! Your approval, Home Secretary.'

'It isn't assassination when it's undertaken with Parliamentary authorisation, Barrymore. My latest directive will have it classified as *expeditious quota adjustment* until such a time as I can get a judicially enforced voluntary euthanasia programme up and running. From which point things will look different again, Barrymore, old bean, that I can one hundred percent guarantee.'

Susan Smallstone, looked out of the window, slightly misty eyed. The vodka was obviously starting to hit home.

'You have to deal with each situation as it stands, Barrymore. Currently, there are too many of them and not enough of us, so we are obliged to readjust levels to bring about a happy state of equilibrium. Look at it rationally. The country is all but bankrupt, the Government is running scared and large swathes of the younger population are wetter than a weekend in Wigan. In the circumstances, what else can we do?'

'I follow your reasoning, Home Secretary, but handing a promotion to a cold-blooded killer can't possibly be right; and a seemingly incompetent one at that.'

'Hot blooded, I would suspect, Barrymore, rather than cold; and it isn't actually a promotion. It is in effect a deferred death sentence. In order for D.I. Ho to carry out the job successfully she will need to accumulate specific areas of knowledge, and because in the fullness of time that knowledge could prove detrimental to certain people higher up the food chain, she will in effect be signing her own death warrant the minute she agrees to take on the job. Whitcott, Sangster, where are they now? Even Leeming and Mortley, effectively operating on borrowed time. Litmus might have ended up in hospital, but I suspect he doesn't know how lucky he is.'

'But........'

'But me no buts, Barrymore. Buts are for people with the time to be indulgent and that must not include either of us. If necessary, blindfold your conscience, but in any eventuality just get on with doing what needs to be done. Tell D.I. Ho I will be expecting her to be ready to rumble first week in the new year so she might think it is in her best interests to work through the holiday period. I'm only being kind, Barrymore. It will be better to keep her occupied. She'd probably fret if she were sitting around the home during a holiday period with nothing to do.'

Barrymore stalked down to the basement, put on his sports kit and spent fifteen minutes pummelling an oversized leather punch bag with a bamboo pole. He then returned to his desk and made a series of phone calls. He hated his job, but the way things stood at the moment there was no obvious means of escape. He hated the Home Secretary as well. Most especially when it was highly probable that she would end up being proved right.

CHAPTER FORTY

The evening was balmy and warm. Sounds drifted into the back garden of the large house opposite the park from people making their way home from the pub, possibly having utilised the services of the late-night fish and chip shop or pizzeria on the way. The van with *Tomas-Litmus, Building & Renovation* stencilled boldly on the side had been successfully immobilised and was now parked halfway up the kerb at the side of the house. All the tools including the cement mixer were safely locked away for the night. Tomorrow, being Saturday, would be an easy day with a late start and an early finish. On a scale of one to ten, life was closing in on a nine. All was right with the world, or as near as it was likely to get before the next disaster came along. There was even the possibility that Greta Thunberg might be wearing a smile.

The order book for the newly registered company boasting the accolade, *Big enough to cope, small enough to care*, was already full until early December and if the workload didn't decrease to more manageable proportions as autumn turned to winter it would be necessary to take on yet more extra labour as they were already struggling to keep their heads above water. That was tomorrow's worry. Today marked the completion of several weeks when they had worked every hour that God sent, and this night offered a brief opportunity for two extremely frazzled builders to relax, have a drink and generally regain their strength.

The patio at the bottom of the garden was far enough away from the house so the odd random sound would not disturb a light sleeper, and the beer from the fridge was cold and refreshing. Life was good, and there was every chance that it would remain that way as long as the beer swillers didn't disturb their respective mates when they crawled into bed after the final bottle had been appreciatively imbibed. It wasn't a night that cried out for words, but sometimes they turn up without an invite to the party, and nobody has the heart to tell them to go home.

'Litmus, we are partners, right?'

'That's what it says on the van, Tomas....and we agreed that Korczak & Litmus didn't sound right, if you remember. So, we are equal partners and split everything down the middle. You provide the know-how, the building skills, the experience and all the other day to day essentials that keep the business thriving. I drive the van, pass the screwdrivers, carry the heavy boxes and charm the customers by whistling tunefully and smiling a lot. It's the fairest of partnerships, from my perspective. If I learn how to wire a plug, you should probably consider promoting me and putting me in charge.'

'Mr Litmus, always the man with the jokes. I could carry my own boxes up the stairs but who would be there to make me laugh when we are sitting down, drinking our tea? Listen Mr Joke-teller, partners who work together every day.........they have no secrets, right?'

'Everybody has secrets, Tomas. Do you tell Pat everything? Do I tell Sam everything? Sometimes it is good to tell a white lie because it is a kinder version of the truth for the person listening. In certain instances, cowardice might also come into the equation, but I'll explain about that in greater depth next time we've got a couple of hours to kill.'

'It's not the sort of secret for a joke, my friend. It is the sort of secret that is better when it is split in half.'

'Shared, Tomas, not split in half. OK, then tell me. Is it something terrible? Have you got a wife and three children back in Poland?'

'Worse. Mr Litmus. I am a killer. I killed two men when I was working in London because...........because they were men who had no respect.'

'They were bad men?'

'Yes, I think they were very bad men, but I didn't get to know them very well.'

'Well, maybe it's better if you don't tell me anymore, Tomas. Believe me, I will have no trouble in forgetting the bit you told me already. I have a terrible memory for anything like that, especially when I am talking to a friend while drinking a beer on a pleasant evening without a worry in the world.'

'No, I think it is better if I tell you everything. We are together in work. We are together as a family in your house because of the sisters. We are like brothers, you and me, so I think you should know.'

'Yes, Tomas, we are exactly like brothers. Better than brothers, maybe, because brothers from the same family don't get the opportunity to choose. OK, if you want to tell me, I am ready to listen; and I am even more ready to forget.'

'When you first talked to the sisters in London, they asked me about the work on the building site and I told them what I knew; but about the explosives, I didn't tell the truth because I thought it would cause trouble. There were two men...........two men who put the explosives under the floorboards. I saw them. They came at night, but I was still at the building site because I didn't catch the van to go home. The driver is Mr Bob the idiot, so he never counts how many men get on board or where they get off. When I was meeting with Pat, I would wait behind in the hotel and read the newspaper to improve my English. I would walk down to the sisters' house later, when Pat is home from work. It is my business what I do, and the other men working with me were friends, so nobody talked.'

'Let me get this right. You saw two men putting explosives under the floor of the hotel building? When?'

'Two nights, three nights maybe, before the explosion. They put it under the floor very carefully. Then they glue down the floorboards to fix them in position. They don't hammer in nails in case it makes an explosion happen. The noise, the bang from hitting......you understand. I don't think they were clever, but not stupid either. It was an easy job so there is no problem. I worked in the mines in Poland when I was young. I work with explosives every day. I know explosives. These men, maybe good for easy job like this but they don't know a lot.'

'Jesus Christ, Tomas, what did you do?'

'They don't see me, so I keep quiet like a mouse and listened to what they say. They talk about someone called Zangker, no Zankser maybe, something like that. Zankser wants all of the building to be destroyed. Big explosion, big bang. Smash into tiny pieces so it is difficult to make a good investigation when they look later. They use too much explosive, so Zankser is happy. The hotel will be like matchsticks and Zangser will be pleased with what they had done. They said they would make the explosion start......how you say?'

'Detonate.'

'Detonate the explosive. Good word. I remember that one. Yes, they will detonate the explosive from the old store at the back of the building, then they will walk away over the fence, and whoosh they are gone. They laugh, like it is very funny to blow up a building I have been working on with men who have been my very good friends for many weeks. They laugh like idiots, but I don't think it is funny. It made me feel angry instead.'

'Bloody hell, Tomas, why didn't you tell me any of this before?'

'It has a bad ending. I only tell you now because we are like brothers in a family, and I trust you. I did a bad thing, and I don't want Pat to know anything about what happened. Maybe this is a sort of white lie, like you say?'

'OK. No problem, Tomas. Definitely a white lie. I fully understand.'

'So, I wait until they go, then I get my toolbox and gentle, gentle, gentle I take up one floorboard and pick up the explosive in my hand. Then I take it to the storeroom at the back where we keep the tools and the supplies that we need for working on the job. The building is full of sand

and cement bags and tools and tins of paint and lots of other stuff. It was where we made tea and ate our sandwiches if the weather is bad. It is a safe place to be when the building goes bang because the glass from the windows would break for sure and could be very dangerous. Glass like that can cut off your head, but you would be safe if you are hiding behind bags of sand or cement.'

Tomas paused to expertly remove the top from a new bottle of beer with the aid of a garden trowel that happened to be within easy reach. He took a long swig and nodded approvingly.

'I wrapped the explosive in paper, and I put it in an old plaster bag which I hide at the back of where they will sit. Not close in case they see it and move it away, but not very far. When they blow up the hotel building the noise would be very loud and would defecate......'

'Detonate, Tomas, detonate.'

'Yes, I remember.......would detonate the explosive in the plaster bag. So, if they blow up the hotel building, they will also be dead. They will kill themselves. Their choice. Their problem, I think. I just make sure I am not around when it happens.'

'You didn't know they were planning to blow up people in the explosion, Tomas? There was no way you could have known that would happen.'

'No. I know nothing about that until I saw it on the television the next day. I don't know why the men are blowing up the building, but I never thought that people would be inside when it happened.......but this is not the story.'

'Sorry? Not what story?'

'This is not the story of why I do what I do. There is another reason I put the explosive in the bag of plaster. It was because I had seen those two men before, one, maybe two weeks earlier. I have a friend who was working on the building site. Like me, he was working from the start. He is a good man. Always happy, always smiling. A good worker. Everybody likes him. He used to sometimes steer the van when the idiot driver Mr Bob is falling asleep. One day I see my friend talking with these two guys. Not smiling. Talking, like it is a serious conversation.......and the next day he is gone. No goodbyes. No nothing. Just gone. I think something bad happen to my friend and I think it because of these men. So that is why I do what I do.'

'If it were my friend, Tomas, I'm pretty certain that I would have done exactly the same thing. Your friend; was he Polish like you?'

'No, Albanian, I think because he could read the posters on the wall in the storeroom.......but he didn't like to talk about where he was from, so I respected his wishes.'

'Why were there Albanian posters on the wall of your storeroom?'

'I don't know. Maybe my friend put them up to remind him of home. We all get lonely for our homeland sometimes. It is natural.'

'What was your friends name, Tomas?'

'Belushi. He called himself Belushi. A nice man. I don't know if it was his real name.'

Litmus wanted to go to sleep but his brain refused to shut down. A small hangover was beginning to kick in, and it had nothing whatever to do with the alcohol that he had drunk. Perhaps it was the lateness of the hour, but all of a sudden everything made a lot more sense than it ever had previously. Each fact he had learned seemed to have forced open a door to a further supposition, and each subsequent hypothesis appeared to his befuddled brain to be irrefutably correct.

Zankser was obviously Sangster; so at least his involvement explained why the investigation had been effectively strangled at birth. Belushi was obviously his friend from the other side of the door at Stoke Newington Police Station. Leeming's undercover representative had plainly been spotted taking to the men who planted the explosive and had needed to be quickly withdrawn from front line service. Tomas had misinterpreted the reasoning for Belushi's disappearance and set a small snowball rolling down the hill, which had quickly turned into an avalanche.

Surely, his involvement in this whole bloody saga hadn't become necessary just because Tomas had unwittingly thwarted Whitcott's grand plan by causing the storeroom at the back of the building site to explode, and by doing so destroy all evidence of an Albanian involvement in the plot? It was beginning to look very much like that was precisely what had happened. It also explained why Leeming already had the Albanian gang under surveillance and was just waiting for Whitcott to drop the starter's flag so he could hunt them down. Without the direct link to Albanian involvement there would have been no immediate impetus to take the investigation in the desired direction. So, it was presumably at this juncture that it had occurred to Whitcott that he might do worse than to get dumb old Litmus involved as a readymade scapegoat. The cunning old bastard. There were truly no depths to which the man wouldn't sink.

For a moment he felt outraged. Then it occurred to him that with Whitcott and Sangster both dead and links to Leeming extremely tenuous, there was nothing much he could do about the situation; and it was at this point he experienced an even more frightening realisation ....that try though he might to summon up the necessary motivation, somehow, he just couldn't care. This was a ridiculous situation. He had spent his whole life demonstrating undue concern about every issue where an injustice had been perpetrated, and now that one involving himself directly had come to pass, it appeared he was incapable of reacting with anything other than full blown lethargy. Worse, it appeared that because of overuse of the emotion, he might be emotionally cared out. He chuckled softly as he savoured the realisation, before coming to the conclusion that indifference was actually something he could most definitely learn to live with; and he was just giving the matter a thorough examination and marvelling at its true splendour, when a sharp elbow dug him in the ribs.

'Stop giggling, Litmus, and go to sleep or I'll hit you with something really heavy.'

'Yes, dear, I was just thinking about........'

'Well don't! Think in the morning. That's what mornings were invented for.'

Litmus turned over, circled Sam with his arms and buried his face in her neck. At last, it was over and done. He even had a tenuous justification for having murdered Whitcott that his conscience might find vaguely acceptable if he caught it in a particularly forgiving mood. Goodnight, bloody Vienna. The whole sorry business was finally buried in the past, and with his newly acquired super-power that was the place it could happily remain. He cuddled closer to Sam and in a matter of seconds was soundly asleep.

Three minutes later a vicious fight between Rufus the fox and Eric the cat set off the intruder alarm in the garden. As he stumbled down the stairs to sort out the mayhem, Litmus was forced to concede that while superpowers were definitely useful, they only got you so far.

MORE FROM John Huggins:

Gabriel 'Angel' Smith is a gang leader returning to his old stamping ground after ten years pursuing his "career" in foreign parts. He comes back to a turf war between his old Eastgate gang and The Tyson Mob. The police's organised crime squad in disarray and D.I. Daniel Loache is shacked up with Smith's sister. Things can only get worse...

'A Dip in the Gene Pool' is a demonstration that you can attain anything you desire, so long as you crave it with sufficient avarice and are prepared to encourage other people to work hard enough to make it worth your while claiming the credit once your goal has been satisfactorily achieved.

A team of 'experts' is appointed to assist with the logistics of establishing a training facility for competitors in the 2012 Olympic Games. However, difficulties soon arise, stoked by a variety of vested interests and compounded by the existence of the elusive and highly endangered, Carriage Clock Moth.

MOTHBALLED

JOHN HUGGINS

Charlie Brinsworth is a career criminal who, on his release from a long stretch moves back to his old stomping ground and the pub bequeathed to him by his father, which was being managed for him in his absence. He hates the place, but he intends it to be temporary while he sorts himself out.

It doesn't quite go to plan – he attracts attention from the police and the local gang who are involved in a turf war; then all hell breaks loose as he gets drawn into a conflict he would have been very happy to avoid.

The country of Volgaria, controlled by its formidable First Minister Stanislav Brastic, had long been dung on the boots of progress. Aborted, then isolated by its mother country Aspadria in the mid seventeenth century, Volgaria had endured a precarious survival as an independent state.

A survey team from a large American conglomerate discovered that Volgaria, so long the ugly duckling, was instead a swan of unsuspected beauty. Overnight, the country's fortunes were transformed.

Volgaria, meanwhile, accelerated its evolution from a primitive backwater into a twenty-first century, techno-powered, macro- Klondike.

Into this scenario stumbled Thomas Farlowe, an unstable, newly qualified engineer with a desire to escape the mundane and a thirst for adventure. He clearly couldn't have chosen a better place to launch an illustrious career.